Laurence Sterne, James P. Browne

The Works of Laurence Sterne

Vol. I: With a life of the author

Laurence Sterne, James P. Browne

The Works of Laurence Sterne
Vol. I: With a life of the author

ISBN/EAN: 9783743373730

Manufactured in Europe, USA, Canada, Australia, Japa

Cover: Foto ©Andreas Hilbeck / pixelio.de

Manufactured and distributed by brebook publishing software (www.brebook.com)

Laurence Sterne, James P. Browne

The Works of Laurence Sterne

THE WORKS OF

LAURENCE STERNE.

𝔅𝔞𝔩𝔩𝔞𝔫𝔱𝔶𝔫𝔢 𝔓𝔯𝔢𝔰𝔰
BALLANTYNE, HANSON AND CO.
EDINBURGH AND LONDON

LAURENCE STERNE, A.M.
Prebendary of York &c. &c.

Sir J. Reynolds pinxit.   J. Nagle sculp.

PREFACE.

"To friendship and to feeling dear,
    Immortal Sterne should next appear,
    With Cupid gaily running after,
    Encircled with a myrtle crown,
    And clothed in a cleric gown,
        The jest of Jollity and laughter."

THUS did Charles Phillips portray the mental characteristics of the famous author of "Tristram Shandy,"—a man pronounced by Sir Walter Scott to be "one of the most original geniuses that England has produced;" and of whom Mr. Elwyn, author of an admirable essay upon Sterne in the *Quarterly Review* for March 1854, says, "No novelist has surpassed Sterne in the vividness of his descriptions, none have eclipsed him in the art of selecting and grouping the details of his finished scenes. And yet, next to Shakespeare, he is the author who leaves the most to the imagination of the reader."

These phases of Sterne's genius are so characteristic that a single rapid perusal of "Tristram Shandy" will hardly suffice to unravel the clue to the hidden meanings with which the spirit of his narrative is occasionally imbued. He adopted this style of composition, no doubt, because his intimate knowledge of the human mind taught him it was calculated to arrest the attention and call forth the discriminating powers of the reader, whose pleasure is enhanced by reperusal, bringing palpably to light that which before

was screened from his mental vision. It was owing, probably, to this peculiarity in style that passages in his writings were often misunderstood and misinterpreted, to the
detriment of his character: and this Sterne felt sorely, as
is shown by his letter to Doctor Eustace, in America, thanking that great admirer of "Tristram Shandy" for a curious
walking-stick which the doctor had sent to him: "Your
walking-stick is in no one sense more Shandaic than in its
having more handles than one: the parallel breaks only in
this, that, in using the stick, every one will take the handle
which suits his convenience. In 'Tristram Shandy' the
handle is taken which suits the passions, their ignorance, or
their sensibility." He bitterly continues—"There is so
little true feeling in the herd of the world, that I wish I
could have got an Act of Parliament, when the books first
appeared, that none but wise men should look into them.
It is too much to write books and find heads to understand
them." After consoling himself with the fact of "the
people of genius being to a man on its side," Sterne says,
somewhat spitefully,——"A few hypocrites and Tartuffes,
whose approbation could do it nothing but dishonour,
remain unconverted." He concludes by saying,—"I am
very proud, sir, to have had a man like you on my side
from the beginning: but it is not in the power of every one
to taste humour, however he may wish it; it is the gift of
God; and besides, a true feeler always brings half the
entertainment along with him; his own ideas are only
called forth by what he reads; and the vibrations within
him entirely correspond with those excited: 'tis like reading
himself, and not the book."

Such, no doubt, was his object in leaving so much to the
imagination of the reader. But was the adoption of that
artistic style of writing simply the result of a studied plan;
or did it take its rise in the instinctive tendency of Sterne's
intellect? To the latter source is its adoption in all likelihood to be attributed; for his attention to minuteness of
detail does not seem to arise so much from statistical tendencies, as from a conviction that the adoption of such a

style, in matters of trifling import, is likely to excite in his readers a keen sense of the ludicrous, as well as to ridicule a prolix mode of writing. Instances of his attention to minuteness of detail are shown in his account of Mr. and Mrs. Shandy's marriage settlements,, in the catalogue of travellers, and also in the "Curse of Ernulphus," where his care in dwelling on particulars is strikingly noticeable, in the latter case being carried to a length that is tiresome, disgusting, and repulsive. Yet it would be wrong to aver that the genius of Sterne was blemished by a tendency to prolixity, or that it was wanting in taste, notwithstanding the minuteness with which he describes that furious anathema in all its disgusting details, it being clear that he used it as a means of pointing his satire at the Catholic Church; and also because it enabled him to use it as an instrument in the hands of Dr. Slop himself, whereby he could the more effectually overwhelm that signal victim of his uncle Jaques Sterne's political animosity with the out-pourings of his sarcastic humour. But, on the other hand, Sterne enables one to discern the inmost thoughts of his characters, even when they utter not a word. "I have left Trim my bowling-green, cried my uncle Toby.—My father smiled.—I have left him, moreover, a pension, continued my uncle Toby.—My father looked grave."

Even his particular notice of the successive gestures of his personages, while moving from one position to another, is dramatic in a high degree; whilst he elsewhere displays the clearest knowledge of human nature in its loving and pathetic moods. Nowhere is this fact more charmingly and feelingly shown than in uncle Toby's humane visit to the bedside of the dying Le Fevre, which is a fine instance of Sterne's command of detail in the production of picturesque verisimilitude.

Here it may be inquired if the man, who was capable of conceiving such a story, and picturing in such pure and natural colours characters so interesting and attractive, was himself cold, heartless, and selfish, as he is represented to have been? Selfish, indeed, he might be, but hardly possible

for him to be utterly cold and heartless wh
delight in the glowing delineation of su
Uncle Toby and Corporal Trim; and one
give Sterne credit for really feeling those
human nature, which he has so vividly,
truthfully portrayed.

There can be no doubt that "Cupid, cl
gown," had a mighty influence over the in
feelings of the author of "Tristram Sh
evident that he was no less subject to
promptings of the careless and joyous
There is room also for the charitable co
indelicate passages of his writings, thoug
by the instinctive goadings of the mischiev
were nevertheless indebted, in consider
their presence to the suggestions of a jolly

Some have asserted that Sterne was, in te
those fine affections of the mind which he
described. Horace Walpole said that he w
though ready to shed tears over a dead ass,
less as to withhold relief from his own
utmost need. This poor lady, who was
great distress, strove to earn her bread by
in Ireland, in conjunction with her daught
her effort, owing, it is said, to the extravaga
and would have been consigned to gaol,
testimony of Walpole, had she not been sav
ing disgrace by the generosity of the paren

Surely such heartless neglect of so near a
is utterly inconsistent with the genuine
Sterne to have his wife and beloved d
supplied by his bankers in Paris with wh
required during their long stay in France.
of his letters, that "while he has a shillin
ninepence of it." And, as it is a fact t
means careful of money, it is not likely
relieve his mother when she was in w
his power to do so.

... has been adduced of Sterne's having
... his mother, yet it does not follow that
... may not have actually taken place: and
... Mr. Blake,* affords evidence of his hav-
... her comforts, and gladdened by the pro-
... her from her pecuniary embarrassments.
... care for the comfort of his wife and
... be most unjust to withhold from him
... promptitude in forestalling all their
... were sojourning on the Continent, and
... evidence in various letters, in which
... with the utmost minuteness, everything
... to be of use to them.
... heartless are not always thus provident
..., " says Mr. Percy Fitzgerald. To this
... —"It is something to find that Mr.
... not likely to judge too gently of a cha-
... was struck by these letters from abroad.
... the popular notion of neglect and

... then, with justice be denied that Sterne,
... and follies, was a man, as Charles Phillips
... to friendship and to feeling dear." That
... istically fond father is proved by his
... undeniable evidence, also, of his anxious
... luckless mother out of trouble; and his
... at Paris, and to herself, show his care
... fort. To be sure, there is no special merit
... for having acted thus to his wife—a lady
... of youth, had inspired him with love,
... for him was marked by an act of gene-
... no doubt of its sincerity.
... is thus feelingly narrated to his daughter,
... written by himself,—and which are
... dition of his works,—" I then came to
... and my uncle got me the living of Sutton:
... acquainted with your mother, and
... found in Mr. Percy Fitzgerald's "Life of Sterne."

courted her for two years. She owned she liked me, but
thought herself not rich enough, or me too poor, to be
joined together. She went to her sister's in S. (Stafford-
shire), and I wrote to her often.—I believe then she was
partly determined to have me, but would not say so.—At
her return, she fell into a consumption; and one evening
that I was sitting by her with an almost broken heart to see
her so ill, she said, 'My dear Laurey, I can never be yours,
for I verily believe I have not long to live: but I have left
you every shilling of my fortune!'—Upon that she showed
me her will.—This generosity overpowered me.—It pleased
God that she recovered, and I married her in the year 1741.'
But it was not a happy marriage, owing to incompatibility
of disposition. The sedateness of her nature ill accorded
with the frivolity of his; nor could his ill-concealed amatory
tendencies fail of causing, to some extent (if not entirely),
an estrangement of her affections.

Sterne on one occasion wrote to Hall Stevenson that he
was tired of his wife, and there is evidence that the estrangement was mutual. Nor was this dependent solely upon his
sentimental amours, but arose, likewise, from the marked
disparity in their dispositions. While in the south of
France, he writes to Mr. H. Stevenson—"My dear wife is
against all additional expenses; which propensity (though
not of despotic power) yet I cannot suffer—though, by-the-
by, laudable enough.—But she may talk, I will do my own
way; and she will acquiesce without a word of debate upon
the subject. Who can say so much in praise of his wife?
Few, I trow."

In allusion to a severe fever by which he was struck at
Montpellier, he writes to his banker, Mr. Foley, at Paris, in
January 1764:—" I have suffered in this scuffle with death
(a fever) terribly; but, unless the spirit of prophecy deceive
me, I shall not die, but live.—In the meantime, dear F., let
us live as merrily, but as *innocently,* as we can. It has ever
been as good as a bishopric to me, and I desire no other."

In a letter to Mrs. Foley, he says:—" After having discharged them (his physicians), I told Mrs. Sterne that I

hould set out for England very soon, but she chooses to
:main in France for two or three years. I have no objec-
ion, except that I wish my girl in England." And to show
ow tired he was of French society, he says:—"I believe I
hall step into my post-chaise with more alacrity to fly from
hose sights, than a Frenchman would fly to them; and,
xcept a tear at parting with my little slut, I shall be in
igh spirits; and every step that brings me nearer England,
ill, I think, help to set this poor frame to rights." Having
iven his consent, evidently with painful reluctance, that
is wife and beloved daughter were to remain in France for
.wo years, he writes:—"My wife goes to Bagnières, and I to
iy wife, the church in Yorkshire." And he thus strives
o console himself by this reflection:—"We all live—we all
ve the longer,—at least the happier, for having things our
wn way.—This is my conjugal maxim:—I own 'tis not the
est of maxims;—but I maintain 'tis not the worst."

Such was the unhappy ending of a tour through France,
hich was projected by Sterne for the purpose of sharing
is own enjoyments with those of his wife and daughter;—
nd the affectionate and unselfish spirit in which he induced
hem to join heartily in his proposal, affords strong evidence
o show that he was not careless or neglectful of their happi-
ess. Nor could he be indifferent to their long absence,
hen he wrote from Paris to Mrs. Sterne thus:—"I long
o see you both, you may be assured, my dear wife and
hild, after so long a separation. • • • • • Do
ll for the best, as He who guides all things will, I hope, do
or us! So Heaven preserve you both!

"Love to my Lydia.—I have bought her a gold watch,
o present to her when she comes."

Gratitude—that noble offspring of a generous and sym-
athising mind—cannot justly be withheld from the cate-
ory of Sterne's dispositions; for an ardent spirit of thank-
lness is shown in his intercourse with that unrivalled
ctor, Garrick, the man who at once appreciated the
riginality of his genius, the brilliancy of his wit, and the
atiric pungency of his eccentric humour. Though it might

seem impossible that such rare intellectual qualities as Sterne possessed could remain long unnoticed by the public on his first visit to London, yet the *éclat* by which the author of "Tristram Shandy" was then hailed with was, in the first instance, due to the penetration and kindness of David Garrick. To him he was indebted for an immediate introduction to the most distinguished men of the time, both for birth and superior talents; and as the introduction took place at the hospitable board of his friend, Sterne had an opportunity of displaying his social qualities, which, it may be presumed, were of an attractive kind, since from that moment he was so overwhelmed with invitations to dinner, that any one who wished his company was obliged to engage him a fortnight in advance.

Amongst those who then highly valued the genius and sprightly manners of Sterne were the accomplished Lord Chesterfield, the friend of Pope and Bolingbroke, the liberal and high-minded statesman, and friend of Edmund Burke; Lord Rockingham; the kind and enlightened Lord Bathurst, the friend of Swift and Pope; and the "prodigy," Charles Townsend, that man of "most refined and polished wit," whose great oratorical powers were such as enabled him "to hit the 'House' just between wind and water."

The convivial manners of Sterne must have been of a congenial kind to gain the admiration and friendly companionship of the wittiest man of his time. How idle, then, the criticism, and how warped the judgment, of Horace Walpole, when he pronounced the author of "Tristram Shandy" devoid of wit and humour! He could never be excited to laughter by anything that Sterne had written. But Walpole seems to have been biassed by animosity against Sterne; for, if such were not the case, he could not have been so ready to infer, from the fact of Sterne's mother becoming bankrupt in her attempt to keep a school in Ireland, that her son was consequently neglectful of her safety and comfort, and would have allowed her to "rot in gaol" if the compassion of her pupils' parents had not prevented it by raising a subscription for her relief. The letter to Mr.

John Blake, just alluded to, serves to blot out the stain which such unholy negligence, if true, would impress upon his reputation.

Amongst other admirers of Sterne's genius was Warburton, Bishop of Gloucester, who styled him the English Rabelais, and who presented him, moreover, with a purse of gold as a token of his admiration and goodwill. He even went so far as to hold up the genius of the author of "Tristram Shandy" in a company of bishops. But startled, perhaps, by the outcry raised by the literary reviews against the gross allusions which unfortunately tarnish, with an indelible stain, a fictitious history, that contains many pictures of moral excellence, which, for purity of colouring and harmony of proportion, have seldom been equalled,—startled by that outcry, and his own dislike of the offensive passages, he felt bound to offer to the author, in whose success he took so great an interest, friendly advice. This was given by letter in a tone of kindly remonstrance, and received by Sterne in a proper spirit. But, upon the appearance of two "Lyric Odes" regarding Sterne, written by Hall Stevenson, and denounced by Warburton as disgusting specimens of lewdness and impiety, the bishop addressed, still in the spirit of a sincere well-wisher, another admirable letter to his protégé, which must have made a deep and galling impression upon the sensitive nature of the latter. Sterne, however, while taking the wily satire of the remonstrance in good part, fails not to give a manly display of independence, with a promise that he would endeavour to avoid in future what the bishop found to be objectionable in Tristram, but yet, he says, "I will laugh as long as I live, my lord, and as loud as I can too." To this letter there is a short rejoinder from Warburton, which terminates the correspondence and all intercourse between these remarkable men. Sterne, however, did not alter the Shandean spirit of his book; and for this disregard of his wholesome admonitions, or perhaps from a purer motive, Warburton, according to Dr. Hurd, said that Sterne was an "irrevocable scoundrel." But the offensive and arrogant nature of the author of "The Divine Legation,"

was in the habit of giving hard names to those literary men
who disregarded his opinion.—(*See* Appendix.)

That Sterne was not entirely deaf to the remonstrances
of his critics, his letter (No. 131) shows, although he felt a
difficulty in meeting their views.   He there promises his
friendly critic that, in revising Tristram, he "will use all
reasonable caution," but that he must not spoil his book:
"that is, the air and originality of it, which must resemble
the author;" surely, when such was the case, it can hardly
be with reason denied that compassion, in its most tender
phases, found a congenial receptacle in the natural instincts
of the author of the story of "Le Fevre,"—one of the most
affecting and least affected pieces of writing to be found in
the whole range of literature.   Nor could any one delineate,
in forms so pathetic and with incidents so dramatic and
natural, the scene of Yorick's deathbed, unless he was
possessed of real tenderness of feeling.

Yet it might be thought that Sterne, in the guise of
Yorick, was not warmed by the glowing flame of genuine
benevolence, or he could not have acted as he did on his
first interview with the poor Franciscan friar whose form
and air and manner he has so inimitably portrayed.   Certainly, maxims of political economy and universal philanthropy, with perhaps a lurking leaven of religious bigotry,
did on that occasion cause him to repudiate, somewhat coldly
and hurtfully, an appeal to his charity, made with graceful
humility and pardonable obtrusiveness.   But reason, and
policy, and even religious bigotry, were not of force sufficient
to subdue the promptings of pity in the mind of Yorick, for
he says:—"My heart smote me the moment he shut the
door.—Psha! said I, with an air of carelessness, three several
times,—but it would not do; every ungracious syllable I
had uttered crowded back into my imagination: I reflected
I had no right over the poor Franciscan but to deny him;
and that the punishment of that was enough to the disappointed, without the addition of unkind language.—I
considered his gray hairs:—his courteous figure seemed to
re-enter, and gently ask me what injury he had done me?

and why I could use him thus? I would have given twenty livres for an advocate. I have behaved very ill, said I, within myself."

In this dramatic episode Sterne has bequeathed to posterity a moral lesson, which could not fail to make an indelible impression upon the heart and understanding. It shows the superior power which meekness, adorned with innocence, possesses over sudden resentment in disarming unmerited aggression, and in converting the adversary into the cordial advocate: for he tells that, notwithstanding his ungenerous and cutting refusal, "the poor monk made no reply: a hectic of a moment passed across his cheek, but could not tarry:—nature seemed to have done with her resentment in him; he showed none, but letting his staff fall within his arm, he pressed both his hands with resignation upon his breast and retired."

Its influence, moreover, in assuaging the pangs of self-accusing remorse, is admirably told, where he describes the subsequent meeting of Yorick with the patient and forgiving votary of St. Francis, at the "Remise;" and where the latter presents Yorick with his horn snuff-box as a token of reconciliation. The influence of so virtuous a man upon the feelings of Yorick is afterwards shown at the grave of Father Lorenzo (that being the monk's name), where he says,—"When, upon pulling out his little horn box, as I sat by his grave, and plucking up a nettle or two at the head of it, which had no business to grow there, they all struck together so forcibly upon my affections, that I burst into a flood of tears:—but I am as weak as a woman; and I beg the world not to smile, but pity me."

The above passage calls to mind a leading feature of Sterne's intellect, namely, the faculty of perceiving similitudes and of detecting incongruities with discriminating subtlety; and, as there is scarcely to be found in Nature an object less suited than the nettle to rest upon the grave of the patient and inoffensive monk, it is natural that Yorick should pluck it out of the soil which held the remains of a man, in whom "Nature seemed to have done with her resentments."

It is not reasonable to suppose that the man who could portray, in colours so truly captivating, the finest qualities of human nature, was himself devoid of those qualities, since to delineate them so naturally and render their less obvious beauties so palpable and fascinating, demanded the instinctive possession of them. If Sterne's opponents have refused to allow that he was possessed of genuine sympathy, and assert that his melting pathos is unreal and affected, they have not, on the other hand, failed to paint in most glaring colours the reckless pruriency which has left a stain upon his literary escutcheon that can never be effaced, and must for ever narrow the influence of those passages in his writings meant to promote the reign of harmony and goodwill among mankind.

Though these indelicate passages may render his works unfit for the perusal of modest females, to a young man who is a law unto himself there is little danger, however offended he might be, of having his moral sense contaminated by such passages. Still there is reason to infer, from a letter of his to the Earl of S——, that Sterne was not a gross sensualist in reality, while there is room for thinking that the ardent protestations of love contained in his letters to Eliza, and in those to Miss Fourmantelle (his dear, dear Kitty), were the expression of such a friendship and admiration as may coexist with purity of conduct. Out of many passages, of the same import, may be quoted the following to Eliza: —"Thou leavest me nothing to require,—nothing to ask,— but a continuation of that conduct which won my esteem, and has made me thy friend for ever." The same Platonic spirit pervades his letters to "dear Kitty," though these are expressed with even greater fervency of attachment and evince signs of a more intimate relationship. Yet, in one of them he complains that the world is so censorious that it will not admit the possibility of a man and woman being ardently attached to each other without its being accompanied by immoral conduct; and, if his assertion in the letter to the Earl of S——, before referred to, be true, he had grounds for being chagrined at the bitter assaults upon his reputation as a gross sensualist;—an odious imputation which he solemnly repudiates when writing to his lordship.|

By the kind permission of Mr. Murray, of Albemarle Street, I am enabled to lay before the reader a series of thirteen letters from Sterne to Miss Fourmantelle, which have never before found a place in any edition of the collected works of Sterne. These letters show that he had long been an ardent lover of the young Huguenot lady, but his neglect of her, when she came to London to join him in thanksgiving for the signal honours he was receiving from the most conspicuous men of the time, was such as showed him to have been, as a lover, selfish and unfaithful. Mr. Murray's father received those letters from a Mrs. Weston, who stated that Sterne had promised marriage to Miss Fourmantelle, but that he broke his promise by marrying Mrs. Sterne; that his desertion deprived the poor girl of her reason, and that she was the original of the hapless Maria of Moulines. As it will be found, however, that some of these letters were written so late as 1761, the loss of her reason could not have been caused by her faithless lover's marriage, which took place in 1741. Possibly, it may have been in allusion to that unhappy lady, whom he coldly neglected in the day of his brightest success, that he acknowledged to Hall Stevenson, not long before his death, that, if he lived but three or four years longer, he would rectify something that was causing him disquietude.

Subsequently Sterne became enamoured of Mrs. Draper, the wife of Daniel Draper, Esq., of Bombay. This lady he has immortalised in his letters to Eliza. But it were well for his reputation if those letters had never seen the light, for in one of them he confesses he did not tell truth when he asserted that their mutual friend, the good Mrs. James, had discontinued her acquaintance with some ladies in London, because of their ill-will to his adored Eliza, hypocritically veiled under the guise of friendship. The bitterness with which he assails the intentions of those ladies probably had its rise in the fact of their becoming alarmed for the honour of their friend and the purity of her cha-

racter, which were likely to suffer in the opinion of society if
she remained on intimate terms with the author of " Tristram
Shandy," and the bosom friend of John Hall Stevenson, of
Skelton Castle, the Prior of the Demoniacs who used to
assemble at that hospitable dwelling, where Sterne was known
as " the blackbird," owing to his skill in playing on the bass-
viol, and whom his friend celebrates under that name in one
of his macaronic poems.

Possibly Sterne had good reason for his bitter hatred of
those ladies, but there is no excuse for uttering a falsehood
to strengthen his admonition, even though the safety of the
dearest object of his heart depended on it. How humiliat-
ing the acknowledgment of such a transgression ! But this
he could not avoid doing, as it involved the name of his
honoured and most esteemed friend, Mrs. James, to whom
he wrote his last letter, a few days before he died, in a strain
so desponding, that, at last, the heart of poor Yorick seemed
really about to break.

The strain of Platonic affection which pervades his letters
to " Kitty " and " Eliza " tends to weaken the doubts that
naturally arise as to the purity of his intentions and acts ;
but if we are to credit his own solemn declaration, there is
room for questioning the existence of that sensuality which,
in the eyes of the world, has indelibly tarnished his fair
fame, and has rendered his writings a sealed book to the
female portion of society, who could not fail to be delighted
and improved by the practical lessons he has left us of
the benign effects of benevolence and brotherly love. In
a humorous tone he banters his friend Sir W., in a letter
(September 19, 1767), for having mistaken his meaning
when he alluded to Venus in regard to his bathing in the
sea. "The body," he says, "guides you—the mind me."—
And, after saying that coarse pruriency was disgusting to
him, he writes—" I had rather raise a gentle flame than have
a different one raised in me.—Now I take Heaven to
witness, after all this *badinage*, my heart is innocent—and
the sporting of my pen is equal, just equal to what I
did in my boyish days, when I got astride of a stick and

galloped away.—The truth is this—that my pen governs me—not me my pen." But this last assertion must be ill-founded; for, on the contrary, his pen was governed by the instinctive suggestions of dominant feelings, while the salutary promptings of reflection lay dormant. What else could have induced him to stain the page illumined by the chaste figure of charity in the person of the fair Beguine, by indelicate insinuations, while she was ministering to the wound from which Corporal Trim was suffering? But it might be doing Sterne an injustice to infer that he was insensible to the charm of unsuspicious chastity, while in the guise of that beauteous handmaid of benevolence and piety, and perhaps be more correct to assume that he could not resist his predominant sense of the ludicrous, which he was enabled to gratify by showing whimsically the cause of Trim's having fallen in love.

The intellect of Sterne was of a high order, but apparently limited in its sphere of action, especially when put in competition with the intellects of Smollett, of Fielding, and of Swift. It was characteristically metaphysical, but not mathematical, more contemplative and imaginative than practical, though some of his letters prove him to have been a man of practical good sense, when there was necessity for applying himself to the conducting of the ordinary business of life. To use the pen was the darling hobby of his soul, yet the tenor of its unpremeditated course did not lead him to the improvement of the sciences, or to their practical application, either in politics or mechanics. With all his genius he could never become a Newton or a Burke. But for knowledge of the faculties of the mind and their varied combinations, which go to constitute variety of character, few men have equalled him. Where, out of Shakespeare, or, may it be said, even there, can be met with anything to surpass the beautiful character of uncle Toby? whose "guileless disposition," says Sterne, whose "unparalleled modesty of nature I once told you of.—But where am I going?—These reflections crowd in upon me ten pages at least too soon, and take up that time which I ought to bestow upon facts."

Sterne's tendency to digress caused Walpole to say that he told his history of Tristram backwards. But he himself with truth says,—"Tristram is <u>digressive and progressive at the same time</u>." This style was adopted from the whimsical satisfaction he derived from disappointing his readers' expectation. For, he says, if he thought that any one could anticipate what he was about to write in the next chapter, he would tear it out of the book. Even his blank pages impart much meaning—more, perhaps, than words could express. An example of his skill in the portrayal of feeling by a gesture is shown where Mr. Shandy, while standing behind the chair of his brother Toby, said something gratifying to Uncle Toby's benevolent heart; the latter, without saying a word, passed his hand gently behind the chair and give Mr. Shandy's a squeeze.

The character of Trim is admirable. His desires are always in harmony with those of his master. He possesses almost as much kindness and warmth of heart, but knows the ways of the world better. He possesses some inventive power, which he often displays in a ludicrous light. For instance, in making the fortifications in his master's bowling-green, he does not hesitate to take the ropes from the window-sashes, the jack-boots that were a sort of heirloom in the family, and even his master's favourite tobacco-pipes, to complete the defences of his garrison. How good, too, is his notion of the fifth commandment! and his solution of the nature of radical heat and moisture is droll, while unfortunate Dr. Slop's scientific version is ridiculously incomprehensible. Sterne takes great delight in casting ridicule upon whatever is said or done by this luckless subject of his sarcastic drollery. The original of Slop was Dr. Burton, of York, an M.D. of Cambridge, a distinguished practitioner in midwifery, and the writer of a book on that subject, with plates, which was deemed worthy of being translated into French, receiving the approval of many Societies as a work of value. A demagogue and a Jacobite, as such he incurred the bitter hostility of Jaques Sterne, Prebend of York, a furious and bigoted partisan of the party then in power.

He was also a distinguished antiquary. His figure was short and thickset, his head large, and, mounted on his diminutive pony, afforded Sterne a fine subject for ridicule, which he took an unmerciful advantage of in his ludicrous description of Slop's encounter with Obadiah on the big coachhorse, as well as in other more serious matters. The character of Widow Wadman and her insidious assaults upon the innocence of Uncle Toby are admirably delineated. Indeed all the characters are portrayed with rare discrimination, from that of the generous, amiable Yorick, down to Mrs. Bridget and Susanna.

Having trespassed already too far upon the space allowed for this Preface, I am reluctantly constrained to forego my wish to notice many things relating to Sterne which would add to its interest. His lively disposition was strongly manifested at school, in Halifax, where he became a favourite of the master, who even then foresaw that he would be a remarkable man. But he was desultory as a student, reading hard for a short time, then ceasing to study the prescribed tasks for many days in succession. Such tasks must have been irksome to one of his mirthful and eccentric disposition, and even at that early day he made himself remarkable by sallies of wit and humour. Original in all things, he was not satisfied to follow the lead of other boys by cutting the initial letters of his name on the desk, but dared to adorn the newly-whitewashed ceiling of the schoolroom with his name in full. At Cambridge, where he entered as a sizar at the age of eighteen, he felt a dislike to the ordinary curriculum of study, which he ridiculed in "Tristram Shandy," where he levels his satiric humour, with wonderful effect, against speculative philosophers in the person of Mr. Shandy, whose natural sympathies were strangely subservient to the obstinate sustainment of his philosophical theories.

It was at Cambridge he formed an intimacy with Hall Stevenson, who was then a youth of engaging manners and of handsome face and figure. But his strong sensual tendencies rendered him a very unsuitable and dangerous friend to a young man about to enter the Church. This friendship was fostered by the nearness of the vicarage of Sutton, which Sterne soon acquired, to Skelton Castle, the residence of Hall Stevenson, whom Sterne has immortalised as Eugenius. It was here he had an opportunity of reading those strange and scarce books which seem to have biassed him as to the path his genius was specially to pursue in the wide domain of literature. Here he found Bruscamville, Bouchet, and others, old French humorists, remarkable for their talent, but which was tarnished by grossness and impurity. Rabelais, too, and Cervantes he delighted in—the latter he held in the highest estimation. But though Sterne was called the English Rabelais, and justly so for his indelicacies, for his pathos he was indebted to no man. And surely no writer ever delineated the charming influence of compassion, the tender glow of friendship, or the moral duties of mankind, with more truth and beauty. This is manifested not only in his two great works, but also in his sermons, as well as in his unpremeditated, graphic, and delightful letters.

Though the mind of Sterne was deeply imbued with a sense of the ludicrous, yet his versatile nature was so alive to the charms of what is beautiful in all things—whether of a material or spiritual nature—that it tinged his predominant jollity with that fine spirit of whim for which he was so remarkably distinguished. Few men were possessed of a finer perception of form, whether it be displayed in painting or in sculpture; and, had he given his mind to either, there is reason to think that he would have been successful as an artist. In this faculty he differed much from his contemporary, Smollett, who saw but little beauty, if any, in the Venus de Medici, for which want of taste he was laughed at by Sterne, who nicknamed him Smellfungus.

Sterne had much musical taste, and played well upon the viol. Love of the drama was also a marked feature of his mind; and from these sources he chose, for his faculty of comparison, materials which render his similes animated and pleasing. He was fonder of fame than of power. His ardour in pursuit of pleasure amounted to unrestrained selfishness; but his selfishness was not the result of self-love, engendered by self-esteem. It arose rather from the excessive fervour of his feelings, by which he allowed himself to be carried beyond the bounds of propriety, owing to want of firmness and due consideration for his own dignity. He was hurried on in these courses, so fatal to his good name, not so much by gross and vicious tendencies, as by a rare buoyancy of spirit proceeding from unflagging hope and unbounded mirthfulness; accompanied with a keen perception of graceful form, which enabled him to appreciate female beauty, and caused him to yield to those allurements which so often attend its presence, and which his instincts were too prone to sympathise with and admire.

To a man of such a turn of mind the unprecedented honours he met with in London, on the publication of the two first volumes of "Tristram Shandy," must have been hurtful; and that this was the case we have the authority of his warmly-attached friend, Garrick, who said, sorrowfully, "He degenerated in London, like an ill-transplanted shrub. The incense of the great spoiled his head, and their ragouts his stomach."

So great was the change in the author of "Tristram," a work which was written "in the corner of the kingdom, and in a retired thatched house, where I live," says the author, "in a constant endeavour to fence against the infirmities of ill health, and other evils of life, by Mirth; being firmly persuaded, that every time a man smiles,—but much more so when he laughs,—it adds something to this Fragment of Life." Sterne was, indeed, like his prototype, Yorick, "as mercurial and sublimated a composition, as heteroclite a creature in all his declensions; with as much life, and whim, and *gaité de cœur* about him, as the kindliest climate could have engendered and put together." But, "with all this sail, poor Yorick carried not one ounce of ballast." When this "Fragment of Life" was about to be closed, Sterne manifested feelings of the tenderest nature in a letter to his daughter, where he tells her Mrs. James will watch over her, when he himself is no more, and from whom she will learn to be "an affectionate wife, a tender mother, and a sincere friend."

By the kind permission of Mr. Percy Fitzgerald, I am enabled to close this Preface with the last letter ever written by Sterne. It is sorrowful, yet characteristically hopeful; and is as follows:—

"Mr. Sterne's kindest and most friendly compliments to Mrs. James, with his most sentimental thanks for her obliging inquiry after his health. He fell ill the moment he got to his lodgings, and has been attended by a physician ever since. He says 'tis owing to Mr. Sterne's taking James's powder, and venturing out on so cold a day; but Mr. Sterne could give a truer account. He is almost dead, yet still hopes to glide like a shadow to Gerrard Street in a few days, to thank his good friend for her goodwill. All compliments to Mr. James—and all comfort to his good lady."

It gives me pleasure to quote the following feeling remarks of Mr. Fitzgerald:—"What he took for a 'vile influenza' became a pleurisy; and on the Thursday following (March 10), he was bled three times, and on the next day blistered. He was prostrate and exhausted for several days after this violent treatment, but as he lay there, the thought of the child he loved so dearly came upon him, and with a feeble hand he was just able to write a few tottering characters to his friend, Mrs. James. So piteous and touching an appeal has rarely come from a deathbed. It was the poor, broken, gasping, dying Yorick's last letter" (but one). "In it we seem to hear an humble acknowledgment of errors, and a cry for pardon for follies which 'my heart, not my head, betrayed me into!'—a declaration which we may accept as genuine, and which is the true key to all his Shandean sins, errors, mistakes, and follies."

JAMES P. BROWNE, M.D.

P.S.—As this edition contains a memoir of Sterne, written by himself, it only remains for me to add to the foregoing brief estimate of the genius and disposition of the creator of such characters as Uncle Toby and Corporal Trim, and of

Yorick, whose character was evidently made up of the leading features of his own, that he died, without a friend at hand to comfort him, on the 13th of March 1768, at his lodgings in Old Bond Street, in the 55th year of his age, and was buried privately at Edgeware, in the new cemetery of St. George's, Hanover Square.

And now let me tender my gratitude to Mr. Fitzgerald for his valuable advice and assistance, which greatly facilitated my humble efforts in bringing out this edition of Sterne, and for his kindness in permitting me to publish several letters to Mr. Blake, of the York Cathedral, which have appeared only in his "Life of Sterne." And I beg to repeat my thanks to Mr. Murray, the Messrs. Longman and Green, and to Mr. W. Durrant Cooper, for their kindness in permitting me to make use of and publish many letters which have never before appeared in any collected edition of Sterne's works, and which must serve to enhance materially the value and intrinsic interest of this.

These letters will be found in an Appendix, together with the plagiarisms in Ferriar's "Illustrations of Sterne." The latter, when put together, would scarcely fill a dozen pages, and certainly add nothing to heighten the beauty and originality of Sterne's genius.

J. P. B., M.D.

ADVERTISEMENT.

THE works of Mr. Sterne, after contending with the prejudices of some, and the ignorance of others, have at
length obtained that general approbation which they
are entitled to, by their various, original, and intrinsic
merits. No writer of the present times can lay claim to so
many unborrowed excellences. In none have wit, humour,
fancy, pathos, an unbounded knowledge of mankind, and a
correct and elegant style, been so happily united. These properties, which render him the delight of every reader of taste,
have surmounted all opposition:—even Envy, Prudery, and
Hypocrisy are silent.

Time, which allots to each author his due portion of fame,
and admits a free discussion of his beauties and faults, without
favour and without partiality, hath done ample justice to the
superior genius of Mr. Sterne. It hath fixed his reputation, as
one of the first writers in the English language, on the firmest
basis, and advanced him to the rank of a classic. As such, it
becomes a debt of gratitude to collect his scattered performances into a complete edition, with those embellishments
usually bestowed on our most distinguished authors.

This hath been attempted in the present edition, which com-
prehends all the Works of Mr. Sterne, either made public in his
lifetime or since his death. They are printed from the best and
most correct copies, with no other alterations than what became
necessary from the correction of literal errors. The Letters are
arranged according to their several dates, as far as they can be
discovered; and a few illustrations added, to explain some tem-
porary circumstances mentioned or alluded to in them. Those

which are confessedly spurious, are rejected; and, that no credit may be given to such as are of doubtful authority, it will be proper to observe, that the Letters numbered 129, 130, 131, have not those proofs of authenticity which the others possess. They cannot, however, be pronounced forgeries with so much confidence as some * which are discarded from the present edition may be, and are therefore retained in it.

That no part of the genuine works of Mr. Sterne might be omitted, his own account of himself and his family is inserted without variation. But as this appears to have been a hasty composition, intended only for the information of his daughter, —a small number of facts and dates, by way of notes, are added to it. These, it is presumed, will not be considered as improper additions.

It would be trespassing on the reader's patience, to detain him any longer from the pleasure which these volumes will afford, by bespeaking his favour either for the author or his works :—the former is out of the reach of censure or praise; and the reputation of the latter is too well established to be either supported or shook by panegyric or criticism. To the taste, therefore, the feelings, the good sense, and the candour of the public, the present collection of Mr. Sterne's Works may be submitted, without the least apprehension that the perusal of any part of them will be followed by consequences unfavourable to the interests of society. The oftener they are read, the stronger will a sense of universal benevolence be impressed on the mind; and the attentive reader will subscribe to the character of the author given by a comic writer, who declares he held him to be a "moralist in the noblest sense: he plays, indeed, with the fancy, and sometimes, perhaps, too wantonly: but while he thus designedly masks his main attack, he comes at once upon the heart; refines, amends it, softens it; beats down each selfish barrier from about it, and opens every sluice of pity and benevolence."

* See the Preface to a Work published in 1779, entitled, "Letters supposed to have been written by YORICK to ELIZA."

MEMOIRS OF THE LIFE AND FAMILY

OF THE LATE

REV. MR. LAURENCE STERNE.

WRITTEN BY HIMSELF.

———◆———

ROGER STERNE* (Grandson to Archbishop Sterne), Lieutenant in Handaside's Regiment, was married to Agnes Hebert, widow of a Captain of a good family. Her family name was (I believe) Nuttle;—though, upon recollection, that was the name of her father-in-law, who

* Mr. Sterne was descended from a family of that name in Suffolk, one of which settled in Nottinghamshire. The following genealogy is extracted from Thoresby's Ducatus Leodinensis, p. 215.

SIMON STERNE of Mansfield.

Dr. Richard Sterne, Arch-=Elizabeth, daughter of
bishop of York, ob. June, | Mr. Dikinson, ob.
1683. | 1687.

1. | 2. | 3.
Richard Sterne, of | William Sterne, of | Simon Sterne, of=Mary, daughter and
York and Kil- | Mansfield. | Elvington and | heiress of Roger
vington, Esq., | | Halifax, ob. | Jaques, of Elving-
1700. | | 1703. | ton, near York.

1. | 2. | 3. | 4. | 5. | 6.
Richard. | ROGER. | Jaques, LL.D., | Mary. | Elizabeth. | Frances.
| | ob. 1759. | | |
Richard. |

LAURENCE STERNE.

The arms of the family, says Guillam, in his Book of Heraldry, p. 77, are, was a noted sutler in Fianders, in Queen Anne's wars, where my father married his wife's daughter (*N.B.* he was in debt to him) which was on September 25, 1711, old style.—This Nuttle had a son by my grandmother,—a fine person of a man, but a grace- less whelp!—what became of him I know not.—The family (if any left) live now at Clonmel, in the south of Ireland; at which town I was born, November 24, 1713, a few days after my mother arrived from Dunkirk.—My birthday was ominous to my poor father, who was, the day of our arrival, with many other brave officers, broke, and sent adrift into the wide world, with a wife and two children;—the elder of which was Mary. She was born at Lisle, in French Flanders, July 10, 1712, new style.— This child was the most unfortunate.—She married one Wee- mans, in Dublin,—who used her most unmercifully;—spent his substance, became a bankrupt, and left my poor sister to shift for herself; which she was able to do but for a few months, for she went to a friend's house in the country, and died of a broken heart. She was a most beautiful woman,—of a fine figure, and deserved a better fate.—The regiment in which my father served being broke, he left Ireland as soon as I was able to be carried, with the rest of his family, and came to the family seat at Elving- ton, near York, where his mother lived. She was daughter to Sir Roger Jaques, and an heiress. There we sojourned for about ten months, when the regiment was established, and our house- hold decamped with bag and baggage for Dublin.—Within a month of our arrival, my father left us, being ordered to Exeter; where, in a sad winter, my mother and her two children followed him, travelling from Liverpool, by land, to Plymouth.—(Melan- choly description of this journey, not necessary to be transmitted here.)—In twelve months, we were all sent back to Dublin.—My mother, with three of us (for she lay-in at Plymouth of a boy, Joram) took ship at Bristol, for Ireland, and had a narrow escape from being cast away, by a leak springing up in the vessel.—At length, after many perils and struggles, we got to Dublin.—There

---

Or, a chevron between three crosses flory, sable. The crest, on a wreath of his colours, *a starling proper.*

Trifling circumstances are worthy of notice, when connected with distin- guished characters. The arms of Mr. Sterne's family are no otherwise important than on account of the crest having afforded a hint for one of the finest stories in The Sentimental Journey. See Vol. II. of the present edition, p. 27.

my father took a large house, furnished it, and in a year and a half's time spent a great deal of money.—In the year one thousand seven hundred and nineteen, all unhinged again; the regiment was ordered, with many others, to the Isle of Wight, in order to embark for Spain in the Vigo Expedition. We accompanied the regiment, and were driven into Milford Haven, but landed at Bristol; from thence, by land, to Plymouth again, and to the Isle of Wight;—where, I remember, we stayed encamped some time before the embarkation of the troops—(in this expedition, from Bristol to Hampshire, we lost poor Joram,—a pretty boy, four years old, of the small-pox)—my mother, sister, and myself, remained at the Isle of Wight during the Vigo Expedition, and until the regiment had got back to Wicklow, in Ireland; from whence my father sent for us.—We had poor Joram's loss supplied, during our stay in the Isle of Wight, by the birth of a girl, Anne, born September the twenty-third, one thousand seven hundred and nineteen.—This pretty blossom fell at the age of three years, in the barracks of Dublin:—She was, as I well remember, of a fine delicate frame, not made to last long,—as were most of my father's babes.—We embarked for Dublin, and had all been cast away by a most violent storm; but through the intercession of my mother, the captain was prevailed upon to turn back into Wales, where we stayed a month, and at length got into Dublin, and travelled by land to Wicklow; where my father had for some weeks given us over for lost.—We lived in the barracks at Wicklow one year—(one thousand seven hundred and twenty) when Devijeher (so called after Colonel Devijeher) was born; from thence we decamped to stay half a year with Mr. Fetherston, a clergyman, about seven miles from Wicklow; who, being a relation of my mother's, invited us to his parsonage at Animo.—It was in this parish, during our stay, that I had that wonderful escape in falling through a mill-race whilst the mill was going, and of being taken up unhurt: the story is incredible, but known for truth in all that part of Ireland, where hundreds of the common people flocked to see me. From thence we followed the regiment to Dublin, where we lay in the barracks a year. In this year (one thousand seven hundred and twenty-one) I learnt to write, &c.—The regiment ordered in twenty-two, to Carrickfergus, in the north of Ireland. We all decamped; but got no further than Drogheda:—thence ordered to Mullingar, forty miles west,

where, by Providence, we stumbled upon a kind relation, a col-
lateral descendant from Archbishop Sterne, who took us all to
his castle, and kindly entertained us for a year, and sent us to
the regiment at Carrickfergus, loaded with kindnesses, &c. A
more rueful and tedious journey had we all (in March) to
Carrickfergus, where we arrived in six or seven days.—Little
Devijeher here died: he was three years old: he had been
left behind at nurse at a farm-house near Wicklow, but was
fetch'd to us by my father the summer after:—another child
sent to fill his place, Susan. This babe too left us behind in this
weary journey. The autumn of that year, or the spring afterwards (I forget which), my father got leave of his Colonel to fix
me at school,—which he did near Halifax, with an able master;
with whom I stayed some time, till, by God's care of me, my
cousin Sterne, of Elvington, became a father to me, and sent me
to the University, &c., &c.—To pursue the thread of our story,
my father's regiment was the year afterwards ordered to London-
derry, where another sister was brought forth, Catherine, still
living; but most unhappily estranged from me by my uncle's
wickedness and her own folly. From this station the regiment
was sent to defend Gibraltar, at the siege, where my father was
run through the body by Captain Phillips, in a duel (the quarrel
began about a goose!): with much difficulty he survived, though
with an impaired constitution, which was not able to withstand
the hardships it was put to; for he was sent to Jamaica, where
he soon fell by the country fever, which took away his senses
first, and made a child of him; and then, in a month or two,
walking about continually without complaining, till the moment
he sat down in an arm-chair, and breathed his last, which was at
Port Antonio, on the north of the island. My father was a little
smart man, active to the last degree in all exercises, most patient
of fatigue and disappointments, of which it pleased God to give
him full measure. He was, in his temper, somewhat rapid and
hasty, but of a kindly, sweet disposition, void of all design; and
so innocent in his own intentions, that he suspected no one; so
that you might have cheated him ten times in a day, if nine had
not been sufficient for your purpose. My poor father died in
March 1731. I remained at Halifax till about the latter end of
that year, and cannot omit mentioning this anecdote of myself
and schoolmaster:—He had had the ceiling of the school-room

new white-washed;—the ladder remained there: I one unlucky day mounted it, and wrote with a brush, in large capital letters, LAU. STERNE, for which the usher severely whipped me. My master was very much hurt at this, and said, before me, that never should that name be effaced, for I was a boy of genius, and he was sure I should come to preferment.—This expression made me forget the stripes I had received. In the year thirty-two,* my cousin sent me to the University, where I stayed some time. 'Twas there that I commenced a friendship with Mr. H——, which has been most lasting on both sides. I then came to York, and my uncle got me the living of Sutton: and at York I became acquainted with your mother, and courted her for two years:—she owned she liked me; but thought herself not rich enough, or me too poor, to be joined together.—She went to her sister's in S——; and I wrote to her often.—I believe then she was partly determined to have me, but would not say so.—At her return she fell into a consumption;—and one evening that I was sitting by her, with an almost broken heart to see her so ill, she said, "My dear Laurey, I can never be yours, for I verily believe I have not long to live: but I have left you every shilling of my fortune."—Upon that she showed me her will.—This generosity overpowered me.—It pleased God that she recovered, and I married her in the year 1741. My uncle † and myself were then put upon very good terms; for he soon got me the Prebendary of York: —but he quarrelled with me afterwards, because I would not write paragraphs in the newspapers:—though he was a party-man, I was not, and detested such dirty work; thinking it beneath me. From that period he became my bitterest enemy. ‡—By my wife's

---

* He was admitted of Jesus' College, in the University of Cambridge, 6th July 1733, under the tuition of Mr. Cannon.

Matriculated 29th March 1735.

Admitted to the degree of B.A. in January 1736.

Admitted M.A. at the commencement of 1740.

† Jaques Sterne, LL.D. He was Prebendary of Durham, Canon Residentiary, Precentor and Prebendary of York, Rector of Rice, and Rector of Hornsea cum Riston, both in the East Riding of the county of York. He died June 9th, 1759.

‡ It hath, however, been insinuated, that he for some time wrote a periodical electioneering Paper at York, in defence of the Whig interest.—*Monthly Review*, vol. 53, p. 344.

means I got the living of Stillington :—a friend of hers in the
South had promised her, that, if she married a clergyman in
Yorkshire,—when the living became vacant, he would make her
a compliment of it. I remained near twenty years at Sutton,
doing duty at both places. I had then very good health. Books, *
paintings, fiddling, and shooting were my amusements. As to
the Squire of the parish, I cannot say we were upon a very friendly
footing : but at Stillington, the family of the C——s showed us
every kindness : 'twas most truly agreeable to be within a mile
and a half of an amiable family, who were ever cordial friends
—In the year 1760, I took a house at York for your mother and
yourself, and went up to London to publish † my two first volumes
of Shandy.‡ In that year Lord Falconbridge presented me with
the curacy of Coxwold ;—a sweet retirement, in comparison to
Sutton. In sixty-two I went to France, before the peace was
concluded ; and you both followed me. I left you both in
France ; and in two years after, I went to Italy, for the recovery
of my health ; and, when I called upon you, I tried to engage
your mother to return to England with me : she § and yourself are
at length come, and I have had the inexpressible joy of seeing
my girl everything I wished her.

* A specimen of Mr. Sterne's abilities in the art of designing may be seen
in Mr. Wodhul's Poems, 8vo, 1772.

† First edition was printed in the preceding year, at York.

‡ The following is the order in which Mr. Sterne's publications appeared :—

1747. The Case of Elijah and the Widow of Zarephath considered : a Charity
Sermon preached on Good Friday, April 17, 1747, for the support of two
charity-schools in York.

1750. The Abuses of Conscience : set forth in a Sermon preached in the
Cathedral church of St. Peter, York, at the Summer Assizes, before the Hon.
Mr. Baron Clive and the Hon. Mr. Baron Smythe, on Sunday, July 29, 1750.

1759. Vol. 1. and 2. of Tristram Shandy.

1760. Vol. 1. and 2. of Sermons.

1761. Vol. 3. and 4. of Tristram Shandy.

1762. Vol. 5. and 6. of Tristram Shandy.

1765. Vol. 7. and 8. of Tristram Shandy.

1766. Vol. 3, 4, 5, and 6. of Sermons.

1767. Vol. 9. of Tristram Shandy.

1768. The Sentimental Journey.

The remainder of his works were published after his death.

§ From this passage it appears that the present account of Mr. Sterne's Life
and Family was written about six months only before his death.

I have set down these particulars relating to my family and self for my Lydia, in case hereafter she might have a curiosity, or a kinder motive, to know them.

As Mr. Sterne, in the foregoing narrative, hath brought down the account of himself until within a few months of his death, it remains only to mention that he left York about the end of the year 1767, and came to London, in order to publish *The Sentimental Journey*, which he had written during the preceding summer at his favourite living of Coxwold. His health had been for some time declining; but he continued to visit his friends, and retained his usual flow of spirits. In February 1768 he began to perceive the approaches of death; and with the concern of a good man and the solicitude of an affectionate parent, devoted his attention to the future welfare of his daughter. His Letters, at this period, reflect so much credit on his character, that it is to be lamented some others in the collection were permitted to see the light. After a short struggle with his disorder, his debilitated and worn-out frame submitted to fate on the 18th day of March 1768, at his lodgings in Bond Street. He was buried at the new burying-ground belonging to the parish of St. George, Hanover Square, on the 22nd of the same month, in the most private manner; and hath since been indebted to strangers for a monument very unworthy of his memory; on which the following lines are inscribed :—

" Near to this place
Lies the Body of
The Reverend LAURENCE STERNE, A.M.
Died September 13th, 1768,*
Aged 53 Years.

Ah ! molliter ossa quiescant !

" If a sound Head, warm Heart, and Breast humane,
Unsullied Worth, and Soul without a Stain,
If Mental Pow'rs, could ever justly claim
The well-won Tribute of immortal Fame,

* It is scarcely necessary to observe, that this date is erroneous.

Sterne was the *Man*, who, with gigantic Stride,
Mow'd down luxuriant Follies far and wide.
Yet what tho' keenest Knowledge of Mankind
Unseal'd to him the springs that moved the Mind,
What did it cost him ?—Ridicul'd, abus'd,
By Fools insulted, and by Prudes accus'd !—
In his, mild Reader, view thy future Fate ;
Like him, despise what 'twere a Sin to hate.

"This Monumental Stone was erected by two Brother Masons ; for, although he did not live to be a member of their society, yet as his all-incomparable performances evidently prove him to have acted by rule and square, they rejoice in this opportunity of perpetuating his high and irreproachable character to after-ages.

"W. & S."

IN MEMORY OF MR. STERNE,

AUTHOR OF THE

SENTIMENTAL JOURNEY.

—•—

With wit, and genuine humour, to dispel,
From the desponding bosom, gloomy care,—
And bid the gushing tear, at the sad tale
Of hapless love or filial grief, to flow
From the full sympathising heart,—were thine!
These powers, O Sterne! but now thy fate demands
(No plumage nodding o'er the emblazon'd hearse,
Proclaiming honour where no virtue shone)
But the sad tribute of a heartfelt sigh.
What tho' no taper cast its deadly ray,
Nor the full choir sing requiems o'er thy tomb,
The humbler grief of friendship is not mute;—
And poor Maria, with her faithful kid,
Her auburn tresses carelessly entwin'd
With olive foliage, at close of day
Shall chant her plaintive vespers at thy grave.
Thy shade too, gentle Monk, 'mid awful night,
Shall pour libations from its friendly eye;—
For erst his sweet benevolence bestow'd
Its generous pity, and bedew'd with tears
The sod which rested on thy aged breast.

A CHARACTER AND EULOGIUM OF STERNE, AND HIS WRITINGS:

IN A FAMILIAR EPISTLE FROM A GENTLEMAN IN IRELAND TO HIS FRIENDS.

[*Written in the Year* 1769.]

WHAT trifle comes next?—Spare the censure, my friend,
This Letter's no more from beginning to end:
Yet, when you consider (your laughter, pray stifle)
The advantage, the importance, the use of a trifle—
When you think too beside—and there's nothing more clear—
That pence compose millions, and moments the year;
You surely will grant me, nor think that I jest,
That life's but a series of trifles at best.
How widely digressive! Yet could I, O STERNE,*
Digress with thy skill, with thy freedom return !——
The vain wish I repress—poor YORICK! no more
Shall thy mirth and thy jests " set the table on a roar;"
No more thy sad tale, with simplicity told,
O'er each feeling breast its strong influence hold,

---

* The late Reverend *Laurence Sterne*, A.M., &c., author of that truly original,
humorous, heteroclite work, called, The Life and Opinions of *Tristram Shandy;*
of a Sentimental Journey through France and Italy (which, alas! he did not
live to finish); and of some volumes of Sermons. Of his skill in delineating
and supporting his characters, those of the father of his hero, of his Uncle
Toby, and of Corporal *Trim* (out of numberless others), afford ample proof.
To his power in the pathetic, whoever shall read the stories of *Le Fevre, Maria,
The Monk,* and *The Dead Ass,* must, if he has feelings, bear sufficient testi-

From the wise and the brave call forth sympathy's sigh,
Or swell with sweet anguish humanity's eye :
Here and there in a page if a blemish appear,
(And what page, or what life, from a blemish is clear?)
TRIM and TOBY with soft intercession attend ;
LE FEVRE intreats you to pardon his friend ;
MARIA too pleads for her fav'rite distress'd ;
As you feel for her sorrows, oh grant her request !—
Should these advocates fail, I've another to call,
One tear of his MONK shall obliterate all.
Favoured pupil of Nature and Fancy, of yore,
Whom from Humour's embrace sweet Philanthropy bore,—
While the Graces and Loves scatter flowers on thy urn,
And wit weeps the blossom too hastily torn,—
This meed too, kind Spirit ! unoffended receive,
From a youth, next to Shakespeare's, who honours thy grave !

mony ; and his *Sermons* throughout (though sometimes, perhaps, chargeable with a levity not entirely becoming the pulpit) breathe the kindest spirit of *Philanthropy*, of *good-will towards men*. For the few exceptional parts of his works, those small blemishes

> *Quas aut incuria fudit,*
> *Aut humana parum cavit natura—*

suffer them, kind Critic, to rest with his ashes !

The above eulogium will, I doubt not, appear to you (and perhaps also to many others) much too high for the literary character of STERNE. I have not, at present, either leisure or inclination to enter into argument upon the question ; but, in truth, I consider myself as largely his debtor for the tears and the laughter he so frequently excited, and was desirous to leave behind me (for so long at least as this trifle shall remain) some small memorial of my gratitude. I will even add that although I regard the memory of *Shakespeare* with a veneration little short of idolatry, I esteem the *Monk's horn-box* a relic "as devoutly to be wished," as a pipe-stopper a walking-stick, or even an inkstand of the *mulberry-tree.*

THE

LIFE AND OPINIONS

OF

TRISTRAM SHANDY, Gent.

Ταράσσει τοὺς Ἀνθρώπους οὐ τὰ Πράγματα,
Ἀλλὰ τὰ περὶ τῶν Πραγμάτων, Δόγματα.

VOL. I. ORIG. EDIT.

VOL. I.   A*

TO

TO

THE RIGHT HON. MR. PITT.

Sir,

NEVER poor wight of a Dedicator had less hopes 'from his Dedi-cation than I have from this of mine ; for it is written in a bye-corner of the kingdom, and in a retir'd thatch'd house, where I live in a constant endeavour to fence against the infirmities of ill health, and other evils of life, by Mirth ; being firmly persuaded, that every time a man smiles,—but much more so when he laughs,—it adds something to this Fragment of Life.

I humbly beg, Sir, that you will honour this Book by taking it—(not under your Protection,—it must protect itself, but)—into the country with you ; where, if I am ever told it has made you smile, or can conceive it has beguiled you of one moment's pain,—I shall think myself as happy as a Minister of State ;——perhaps, much happier than any one (one only excepted) that I have read or heard of.

I am, GREAT SIR,

(and, what is more to your honour,)

I am, GOOD SIR,

Your Well-wisher, and

most humble Fellow-subject,

THE AUTHOR.

THE

LIFE AND OPINIONS

OF

TRISTRAM SHANDY, Gent.

🍃 CHAPTER I.

 WISH either my father or my mother, or indeed both of them, as they were in duty both equally bound to it, had minded what they were about, when they begot me; had they duly considered how much depended upon what they were then doing;—that not only the production of a rational Being was concerned in it, but that possibly the happy formation and temperature of his body, perhaps his genius and the very cast of his mind,—and, for aught they knew to the contrary, even the fortunes of his whole house, might take their turn from the humours and dispositions which were then uppermost;—Had they duly weighed and considered all this, and proceeded accordingly,—I am verily persuaded I should have made a quite different figure in the world, from that in which the reader is likely to see me.—Believe me, good folks, this is not so inconsiderable a thing as

many of you may think it;—you have all, I dare say, heard of
the animal spirits, as how they are transfused from father to
son, &c., &c.,—and a great deal to that purpose:—Well, you
may take my word, that nine parts in ten of a man's sense
or his nonsense, his successes and miscarriages in this world,
depend upon their motions and activity, and the different
tracks and trains you put them into; so that when they are
once set a-going, whether right or wrong, 'tis not a halfpenny matter,—away they go cluttering like hey-go mad;
and by treading the same steps over and over again, they
presently make a road of it, as plain and as smooth as a
garden walk, which, when they are once used to, the Devil
himself sometimes shall not be able to drive them off it.

Pray, my dear, quoth my mother, *have you not forgot to
wind up the clock?*——*Good G—!* cried my father, making
an exclamation, but taking care to moderate his voice at the
same time,——*Did ever woman, since the creation of the
world, interrupt a man with such a silly question?* Pray,
what was your father saying?——Nothing.

CHAPTER II.

——THEN, positively, there is nothing in the question that
I can see, either good or bad.——Then, let me tell you, Sir,
it was a very unseasonable question at least,—because it
scattered and dispersed the animal spirits, whose business it
was to have escorted and gone hand in hand with the
HOMUNCULUS, and conducted him safe to the place
destined for his reception.

The HOMUNCULUS, Sir, in however low and ludicrous a
light he may appear, in this age of levity, to the eye of folly
or prejudice;—to the eye of reason, in scientific research,
he stands confessed—a BEING guarded and circumscribed
with rights.——The minutest philosophers, who, by the bye,
have the most enlarged understandings (their souls being
inversely as their inquiries), show us, incontestably, that the

HOMUNCULUS is created by the same hand,—engendered in the same course of nature,—endowed with the same locomotive powers and faculties with us;—that he consists, as we do, of skin, hair, fat, flesh, veins, arteries, ligaments, nerves, cartilages, bones, marrow, brains, glands, genitals, humours, and articulations;—is a Being of as much activity,—and, in all senses of the word, as much and as truly our fellow-creature as my Lord Chancellor of England.—He may be benefited,—he may be injured,—he may obtain redress; in a word, he has all the claims and rights of humanity, which Tully, Puffendorf, or the best ethic writers, allow to arise out of that state and relation.

Now, dear Sir, what if any accident had befallen him in his way alone!—or that, through terror of it, natural to so young a traveller, my little gentleman had got to his journey's end miserably spent;—his muscular strength and virility worn down to a thread;—his own animal spirits ruffled beyond description,—and that, in this sad disordered state of nerves, he had lain down a prey to sudden starts, or a series of melancholy dreams and fancies, for nine long, long months together.—I tremble to think what a foundation had been laid for a thousand weaknesses both of body and mind, which no skill of the physician or the philosopher could ever afterwards have set thoroughly to rights.

CHAPTER III.

To my uncle, Mr. Toby Shandy, do I stand indebted for the preceding anecdote; to whom my father, who was an excellent natural philosopher, and much given to close reasoning upon the smallest matters, had oft, and heavily complained of the injury; but once more particularly, as my uncle Toby well remember'd, upon his observing a most unaccountable obliquity (as he call'd it) in my manner of setting up my top, and justifying the principles upon which I had done it,—the old gentleman shook his head, and, in

a tone more expressive by half of sorrow than reproach, he
said his heart all along foreboded, and he saw it verified in
this, and from a thousand other observations he had made
upon me, That I should neither think nor act like any other
man's child.—*But, alas!* continued he, shaking his head a
second time, and wiping away a tear which was trickling
down his cheeks, *My Tristram's misfortunes began nine
months before ever he came into the world.*

—My mother, who was sitting by, looked up, but she
knew no more than her backside what my father meant;—
but my uncle, Mr. Toby Shandy, who had been often informed of the affair, understood him well.

CHAPTER IV.

I KNOW there are readers in the world, as well as many
other good people in it, who are no readers at all,—who find
themselves ill at ease, unless they are let into the whole
secret, from first to last, of everything which concerns you.

It is in pure compliance with this humour of theirs,
and from a backwardness in my nature to disappoint any
one soul living, that I have been so very particular already.
As my life and opinions are likely to make some noise in
the world, and, if I conjecture right, will take in all ranks,
professions, and denominations of men whatever,—be no
less read than the Pilgrim's Progress itself—and, in the
end, prove the very thing which Montaigne dreaded his
Essays should turn out, that is, a book for a parlour
window,—I find it necessary to consult every one a little
in his turn; and therefore must beg pardon for going on
a little farther in the same way: for which cause, right
glad I am that I have begun the history of myself in the
way I have done; and that I am able to go on, tracing
everything in it, as Horace says, *ab ovo.*

Horace, I know, does not recommend this fashion altogether; but that gentleman is speaking only of an epic

poem or a tragedy—(I forget which);—besides, if it was not true, I should beg Mr. Horace's pardon;—~~for in writing what I have set about, I shall confine myself neither to his rules, nor to any man's rules that ever lived.~~

To such, however, as do not choose to go so far back into these things, I can give no better advice than that they skip over the remaining part of this chapter; for I declare beforehand, 'tis wrote only for the curious and inquisitive.

————Shut the door.————I was begot in the night betwixt the first Sunday and the first Monday in the month of March, in the year of our Lord one thousand seven hundred and eighteen. I am positive I was.—But how I came to be so very particular in my account of a thing which happened before I was born, is owing to another small anecdote, known only in our own family, but now made public for the better clearing up this point.

My father, you must know, who was originally a Turkey merchant, but had left off business for some years, in order to retire to, and die upon, his paternal estate in the county of ——, was, I believe, one of the most regular men, in everything he did, whether 'twas matter of business or matter of amusement, that ever lived. As a small specimen of this extreme exactness of his, to which he was in truth a slave, he had made it a rule, for many years of his life,—on the first Sunday night of every month, throughout the whole year,—as certain as ever the Sunday night came,——to wind up a large house-clock, which we had standing on the back stairs' head, with his own hands:—And being somewhere between fifty and sixty years of age at the time I have been speaking of, he had likewise gradually brought some other little family concernments to the same period, in order, as he would often say to my uncle Toby, to get them all out of the way at one time, and be no more plagued and pestered with them the rest of the month.

It was attended with but one misfortune, which, in a great measure, fell upon myself; and the effects of which, I fear, I shall carry with me to my grave; namely, that from an unhappy association of ideas, which have no connection in nature, it so fell out at length, that my poor mother could never hear the said clock wound up——but the thoughts of some other things unavoidably popped into her head—*et vice versa*——which strange combination of ideas, the sagacious Locke, who certainly understood the nature of these things better than most men, affirms to have produced more wry actions than all other sources of prejudice whatever.

But this by the bye.

Now it appears, by a memorandum in my father's pocket-book, which now lies on the table, "That on Lady-day, which was on the 25th of the same month in which I date my geniture,——my father set out upon his journey to London, with my eldest brother Bobby, to fix him at Westminster School;" and, as it appears from the same authority, "That he did not get down to his wife and family till the *second week* in May following,"—it brings the thing almost to a certainty. However, what follows in the beginning of the next chapter puts it beyond all possibility of doubt.

——But pray, Sir, what was your father doing all December, January, and February?——Why, Madam,—he was all that time afflicted with a Sciatica.

CHAPTER V.

On the fifth day of November, 1718, which, to the era fixed on, was as near nine calendar months as any husband could in reason have expected,—was I, Tristram Shandy, Gentleman, brought forth into this scurvy and disastrous world of ours.——I wish I had been born in the Moon, or in any of the planets (except Jupiter or Saturn, because I never could bear cold weather); for it could not well have fared worse with me in any of them (though I will not answer for Venus) than it has in this vile, dirty planet of ours,—which,

o' my conscience, with reverence be it spoken, I take to be
made up of the shreds and clippings of the rest :———not
but the planet is well enough, provided a man could be born
in it to a great title or to a great estate; or could anyhow
contrive to be called up to public charges, and employments
of dignity or power ;———but that is not my case ;———and
therefore every man will speak of the fair as his own market
has gone in it ;———for which cause I affirm it over again to
be one of the vilest worlds that ever was made ;—for I can
truly say, that from the first hour I drew my breath in it,
to this, that I can now scarce draw it at all, for an asthma
I got in skating against the wind in Flanders,—I have been
the continual sport of what the world calls Fortune; and
though I will not wrong her, by saying, she has ever made
me feel the weight of any great or signal evil,———yet, with
all the good temper in the world, I affirm it of her, that, in
every stage of my life, and at every turn and corner where
she could get fairly at me, the ungracious duchess has pelted
me with a set of as pitiful misadventures and cross accidents
as ever small HERO sustained.

CHAPTER VI.

IN the beginning of the last chapter I informed you exactly
when I was born; but I did not inform you *how*. No, that
particular was reserved entirely for a chapter by itself :—
besides, Sir, as you and I are, in a manner, perfect strangers to
each other, it would not have been proper to have let you into
too many circumstances relating to myself all at once.—You
must have a little patience. I have undertaken, you see, to
write not only my life, but my opinions also; hoping and
expecting that your knowledge of my character, and of what
kind of a mortal I am, by the one, would give you a better
relish for the other. As you proceed farther with me, the
slight acquaintance, which is now beginning betwixt us, will
grow into familiarity ; and that, unless one of us is in fault,

will terminate in friendship.—*O diem præclarum !*—then nothing which has touched me will be thought trifling in its nature or tedious in its telling. Therefore, my dear friend and companion, if you should think me somewhat sparing of my narrative on my first setting out—bear with me,—and let me go on, and tell my story my own way:—Or, if I should seem now and then to trifle upon the road, or should sometimes put on a fool's cap with a bell to it, for a moment or two as we pass along,—don't fly off,—but rather courteously give me credit for a little more wisdom than appears upon my outside;—and as we jog on, either laugh with me, or at me, or, in short, do anything—only keep your temper.

CHAPTER VII.

In the same village where my father and my mother dwelt, dwelt also a thin, upright, motherly, notable, good old body of a midwife who, with the help of a little plain good sense, and some years' full employment in her business, in which she had all along trusted little to her own efforts, and a great deal to those of dame Nature,—had acquired, in her way, no small degree of reputation in the world :——by which word *world*, need I in this place inform your worship, that I would be understood to mean no more of it, than a small circle described upon the circle of the great world, of four English miles diameter, or thereabouts, of which the cottage where the good old woman lived is supposed to be the centre ?—She had been left, it seems, a widow in great distress, with three or four small children, in her forty-seventh year ; and as she was at that time a person of decent carriage,—grave deportment,—a woman, moreover, of few words, and withal an object of compassion, whose distress, and silence under it, called out the louder for a friendly lift, —the wife of the parson of the parish was touched with pity ; and, having often lamented an inconvenience to which her husband's flock had been for many years exposed, inasmuch as there was no such thing as a midwife, of any kind or degree, to be got at, let the case have been ever so urgent, within less than six or seven long miles riding; which said seven long miles in dark nights and dismal roads, the country thereabouts being nothing but a deep clay, was almost equal to fourteen; and that, in effect, was sometimes next to having no midwife at all;—it came into her head, that it would be doing as seasonable a kindness to the whole parish, as to the poor creature herself, to get her a little instructed in some of the plain principles of the business, in order to set her up in it. As no woman thereabouts was better qualified to execute the plan she had formed than herself, the gentlewoman very charitably undertook it; and having great influence over the female part of the parish, she found no difficulty in effecting it to the utmost of her wishes. In truth, the parson join'd his interest with his wife's in the whole affair; and in order to do things as they should be, and give the poor soul as good a title by law to practise, as his wife had given by institution,—he cheerfully paid the fees for the ordinary's licence himself, amounting in the whole to the sum of eighteen shillings and fourpence; so that betwixt them both, the good woman was fully invested in the real and corporal possession of her office, together with all its *rights, members, and appurtenances whatsoever.*

These last words, you must know, were not according to the old form in which such licences, faculties, and powers usually ran, which in like cases had heretofore been granted to the sisterhood. But it was according to a neat formula of Didius his own devising, who having a particular turn for taking to pieces, and new framing over again, all kind of instruments in that way, not only hit upon this dainty amendment, but coaxed many of the old licensed matrons in the neighbourhood to open their faculties afresh, in order to have this whim-wham of his inserted.

I own I never could envy Didius in these kinds of fancies of his:—but every man to his own taste. Did not Dr. Kunastrokius, that great man, at his leisure hours, take the greatest delight imaginable in combing of asses' tails, and

plucking the dead hairs out with his teeth, though he had
tweezers always in his pocket? Nay, if you come to that,
Sir, have not the wisest men in all ages, not excepting
Solomon himself,—have they not had their HOBBY-HORSES
—their running-horses,—their coins, and their cockle-shells,
their drums and their trumpets, their fiddles, their pallets,—
their maggots, and their butterflies?—and so long as a man
rides his HOBBY-HORSE peaceably and quietly along the
king's highway, and neither compels you or me to get up
behind him,—pray, Sir, what have either you or I to do
with it?

CHAPTER VIII.

—*De gustibus non est disputandum ;*—that is, there is no dis-
puting against HOBBY-HORSES, and for my part, I seldom
do ; nor could I with any sort of grace, had I been an
enemy to them at the bottom, for happening, at certain
intervals and changes of the moon, to be both fiddler and
painter, according as the fly stings,—be it known to you,
that I keep a couple of pads myself, upon which, in their
turns (nor do I care who knows it), I frequently ride out
and take the air ;—though sometimes, to my shame be it
spoken, I take somewhat longer journeys than what a wise
man would think altogether right.—But the truth is,—I am
not a wise man ;—and, besides, am a mortal of so little consequence in the world, it is not much matter what I do : so
I seldom fret or fume at all about it ; nor does it much disturb my rest, when I see such great Lords and tall Personages as hereafter follow,—such, for instance, as my Lord
A, B, C, D, E, F, G, H, I, K, L, M, N, O, P, Q, and so on,
all of a row, mounted upon their several horses ;—some with
large stirrups, getting on in a more grave and sober pace ;——
others, on the contrary, tucked up to their very chins, with
whips across their mouths, scouring and scampering it away
like so many little party-coloured devils astride a mortgage,
—and as if some of them were resolved to break their necks.

——So much the better—say I to myself; for in case the worst should happen, the world will make a shift to do excellently well without them; and for the rest——why——God speed them!——e'en let them ride on without opposition from me; for were their lordships unhorsed this very night —'tis ten to one but that many of them would be worse mounted, by one half, before to-morrow morning.

Not one of these instances therefore can be said to break in upon my rest.——But there is an instance, which I own puts me off my guard, and that is, when I see *one* born for great actions, and what is still more for his honour, whose nature ever inclines him to good ones,—when I behold such a *one*, my Lord, like yourself, whose principles and conduct are as generous and noble as his blood, and whom, for that reason, a corrupt world cannot spare one moment ;—when I see such a *one*, my Lord, mounted, though it is but for a minute beyond the time which my love to my country has prescribed to him, and my zeal for his glory wishes,—then, my Lord, I cease to be a philosopher, and, in the first transport of an honest impatience, I wish the HOBBY-HORSE, with all his fraternity, at the Devil.

       " My Lord,

" I MAINTAIN this to be a Dedication, notwithstanding its singularity in the three great essentials, of matter, form, and place : I beg, therefore, you will accept it as such, and that you will permit me to lay it, with the most respectful humility, at your Lordship's feet,—when you are upon them,—which you can be when you please ; and that is, my Lord, whenever there is occasion for it, and, I will add, to the best purposes too.   I have the honour to be,   .

       " My Lord,

     Your Lordship's most obedient,

       and most devoted,

         and most humble servant,

           TRISTRAM SHANDY."

CHAPTER IX.

I SOLEMNLY declare to all mankind that the above Dedication was made for no one Prince, Prelate, Pope, or Potentate,
—Duke, Marquis, Earl, Viscount, or Baron, of this, or any
other realm in Christendom;——nor has it yet been hawked
about, or offered publicly or privately, directly or indirectly, to
any one person or personage, great or small ; but is honestly
a true Virgin Dedication, untried on, upon any soul living.

I labour this point so particularly, merely to remove any
offence or objection which might arise against it from the
manner in which I propose to make the most of it ; which
is the putting it up fairly to public sale ; which I now do.

——Every author has a way of his own in bringing his
points to bear ;—for my own part, as I hate chaffering and
higgling for a few guineas in a dark entry,—I resolved
within myself, from the very beginning, to deal squarely and
openly with your Great Folks in this affair, and try whether
I should not come off the better by it.

If, therefore, there is any one Duke, Marquis, Earl, Viscount, or Baron, in these his Majesty's dominions, who
stands in need of a tight, genteel Dedication, and whom the
above will suit (for, by the bye, unless it suits in some degree,
I will not part with it),——it is much at his service for fifty
guineas ;——which, I am positive, is twenty guineas less
than it ought to be afforded for, by any man of genius.

My Lord, if you examine it over again, it is far from
being a gross piece of daubing, as some dedications are.
The design, your Lordship sees, is good,—the colouring
transparent,—the drawing, not amiss ;—or, to speak more
like a man of science, and measure my piece in the painter's
scale, divided into 20,—I believe, my Lord, the outlines
will turn out as 12,—the composition as 9,—the colouring
as 6,—the expression 13 and a half,—and the design—if
I may be allowed, my Lord, to understand my own *design*,
and supposing absolute perfection in designing to be as
20—I think it cannot well fall short of 19. Besides all

this,—there is keeping in it; and the dark strokes in the HONNY-HORSE (which is a secondary figure, and a kind of background to the whole) give great force to the principal lights in your own figure, and make it come off wonderfully;——and besides, there is an air of originality in the *tout ensemble.*

Be pleased, my good Lord, to order the sum to be paid into the hands of Mr. Dodsley, for the benefit of the author; and in the next edition, care shall be taken that this chapter be expunged, and your Lordship's titles, distinctions, arms, and good actions, be placed at the front of the preceding chapter; all which, from the words *De gustibus non est disputandum,* and whatever else in this book relates to HONNY-HORSES, but no more, shall stand dedicated to your Lordship.—The rest I dedicate to the MOON, who, by-the-bye, of all the Patrons or Matrons I can think of, has most power to set my book a-going, and make the world run mad after it.

Bright Goddess!

If thou art not too busy with CANDID and Miss CUNEGUND's affairs,—take Tristram Shandy under thy protection also!

———

CHAPTER X.

WHATEVER degree of small merit the act of benignity in favour of the midwife might justly claim, or in whom that claim truly rested,—at first sight seems not very material to this history;——certain however it was that the gentlewoman, the parson's wife, did run away at that time with the whole of it: and yet, for my life, I cannot help thinking but that the parson himself, though he had not the good fortune to hit upon the design first,—yet, as he heartily concurred in it the moment it was laid before him, and as heartily parted with his money to carry it into execution, had a claim to some share of it,—if not to a full half of whatever honour was due to it.

The world at that time was pleased to determine the matter otherwise.

Lay down the book, and I will allow you half a day to give a probable guess at the grounds of this procedure.

Be it known then, that, for about five years before the date of the midwife's licence,—of which you have had so circumstantial an account,—the parson we have .to do with had made himself a country-talk, by a breach of all decorum, which he had committed against himself, his station, and his office ;—and that was in never appearing better, or otherwise mounted, than upon a lean, sorry, jack-ass of a horse, value about one pound fifteen shillings ; who, to shorten all description of him, was full brother to Rosinante : as far as similitude congenial could make him, for he answered his description to a hairbreadth in everything,—except that I do not remember 'tis anywhere said, that Rosinante was broken-winded ; and that moreover, Rosinante, as is the happiness of most Spanish horses, fat or lean, was undoubtedly a horse at all points.

I know well that Hero's horse was a horse of chaste deportment, which may have given grounds for the contrary opinion ; but it is as certain, at the same time, that Rosinante's continency (as may be demonstrated from the adventure of the Yanguesian carriers) proceeded from no bodily defect or cause whatsoever, but from the temperance and orderly current of his blood.—And let me tell you, Madam, there is a great deal of very good chastity in the world, in behalf of which you could not say more for your life.

Let that be as it may ;—as my purpose is to do exact justice to every creature brought upon the stage of this dramatic work,—I could not stifle this distinction in favour of.Don Quixote's horse ;——in all other points, the parson's horse, I say, was just such another ; for he was as lean, and as lank, and as sorry a jade as Humility herself could have bestrided.

In the estimation of here and there a man of weak judgment, it was greatly in the parson's power to have helped the figure of this horse of his,—for he was master of a very handsome demi-peak'd saddle, quilted on the seat w... pressing plush, garnished with a double row of silver-headed ... his and a noble pair of shining brass stirrups, with a housi... f altogether suitable of grey superfine cloth, with an edging of black lace, terminating in a deep, black, silk fringe, *poudré d'or ;*—all which he had purchased in the pride and prime of his life, together with a grand embossed bridle, ornamented at all points as it should be.——But not caring to banter his beast, he had hung all these up behind his study door ; and, in lieu of them, had seriously befitted him with just such a bridle and such a saddle, as the figure and value of such a steed might well and truly deserve.

In the several sallies about his parish, and in the neighbouring visits to the gentry who lived around him,——you will easily comprehend that the parson, so appointed, would both hear and see enough to keep his philosophy from rusting. To speak the truth, he never could enter a village but he caught the attention of both old and young.——Labour stood still as he passed,—the bucket hung suspended in the middle of the well,—the spinning-wheel forgot its round,— even chuck-farthing and shufflecap themselves stood gaping till he had got out of sight ; and as his movement was not of the quickest, he had generally time enough upon his hands to make his observations,—to hear the groans of the serious,—and the laughter of the light-hearted ; all which he bore with excellent tranquillity.—His character was,—he loved a jest in his heart ; and as he saw himself in the true point of ridicule, he would say he could not be angry with others for seeing him in a light in which he so strongly saw himself : so that to his friends, who knew his foible was not the love of money, and who therefore made the less scruple in bantering the extravagance of his humour,—instead of giving the true cause,—he chose rather to join in the laugh against himself ; and as he never carried one single ounce of flesh upon his own bones, being altogether as spare a figure as his beast,—he would sometimes insist upon it, that the horse was as good as the rider deserved ;—that they were, centaur-like,—both of a piece. At other times, and in other

The word *when his spirits were above the temptation of false
matter* he would say, he found himself going off fast in a
La sumption; and, with great gravity, would pretend he
gir could not bear the sight of a fat horse, without a dejection
of heart, and a sensible alteration in his pulse; and that he
had made choice of the lean one he rode upon, not only to
keep himself in countenance, but in spirits.

At different times he would give fifty humorous and
apposite reasons for riding a meek-spirited jade of a broken-
winded horse, preferably to one of mettle;—for on such a
one he could sit mechanically, and meditate as delightfully
de vanitate mundi et fugâ sæculi, as with the advantage of a
death's head before him;—that, in all other exercitations,
he could spend his time, as he rode slowly along, to as much
account as in his study;—that he could draw up an argument in his sermon, or a hole in his breeches, as steadily on
the one as in the other;—that brisk trotting and slow argumentation, like wit and judgment, were two incompatible
movements.—But that upon his steed—he could unite and
reconcile everything;—he could compose his sermon,—he
could compose his cough,——and in case nature gave a call
that way, he could likewise compose himself to sleep.—In
short, the parson, upon such encounters, would assign any
cause but the true cause;—and he withheld the true one,
only out of a nicety of temper, because he thought it did
honour to him.

But the truth of the story was as follows:—In the first
years of this gentleman's life, and about the time when the
superb saddle and bridle were purchased by him, it had been
his manner, or vanity, or call it what you will,—to run into
the opposite extreme.—In the language of the country where
he dwelt, he was said to have loved a good horse, and
generally had one of the best in the whole parish standing
in his stable always ready for saddling; and as the nearest
midwife, as I told you, did not live nearer to the village
than seven miles, and in a vile country,—it so fell out that
the poor gentleman was scarce a whole week together without
some piteous application for his beast; and, as he was not

an unkind-hearted man, and every case was more pressing and more distressful than the last,—as much as he loved his beast he had never a heart to refuse him; the upshot of which was generally this, that his horse was either clapp'd, or spavin'd, or greas'd;—or he was twitter-bon'd, or broken-winded, or something, in short, or other had befallen him, which would let him carry no flesh;—so that he had every nine or ten months a bad horse to get rid of,—and a good horse to purchase in his stead.

What the loss in such a balance might amount to, *communibus annis*, I would leave to a special jury of sufferers in the same traffic to determine;—but let it be what it would, the honest gentleman bore it for many years without a murmur, till, at length, by repeated ill-accidents of the kind, he found it necessary to take the thing under consideration: and, upon weighing the whole, and summing it up in his mind, he found it not only disproportioned to his other expenses, but withal so heavy an article in itself, as to disable him from any other act of generosity in his parish: besides this, he considered that with half the sum thus galloped away, he could do ten times as much good;—and what still weighed more with him than all other considerations put together, was this, that it confined all his charity into one particular channel, and where, as he fancied, it was the least wanted, namely, to the child-bearing and child-getting part of his parish; reserving nothing for the impotent,—nothing for the aged,—nothing for the many comfortless scenes he was hourly called forth to visit, where poverty, and sickness, and affliction dwelt together.

For these reasons he resolved to discontinue the expense; and there appeared but two possible ways to extricate him clearly out of it;—and these were, either to make it an irrevocable law never more to lend his steed upon any application whatever,—or else be content to ride the last poor devil, such as they had made him, with all his aches and infirmities, to the very end of the chapter.

As he dreaded his own constancy in the first, he very cheerfully betook himself to the second; and though he

could very well have explained it, as I said, to his honour,—
yet, for that very reason, he had a spirit above it; choosing
rather to bear the contempt of his enemies, and the laughter
of his friends, than undergo the pain of telling a story which
might seem a panegyric upon himself.

I have the highest idea of the spiritual and refined sentiments of this reverend gentleman, from this single stroke in
his character, which I think comes up to any of the honest
refinements of the peerless knight of La Mancha, whom,
by-the-bye, with all his follies, I love more, and would
actually have gone farther to have paid a visit to, than the
greatest hero of antiquity.

But this is not the moral of my story. The thing I had
in view was to show the temper of the world in the whole
of this affair.—For you must know that so long as this explanation would have done the parson credit,—the devil a
soul could find it out:—I suppose his enemies would not,
and that his friends could not.——But no sooner did he
bestir himself in behalf of the midwife, and pay the expenses
of the ordinary's licence to set her up,—but the whole secret
came out; every horse he had lost, and two horses more
than ever he had lost, with all the circumstances of their
destruction, were known and distinctly remembered.—The
story ran like wild-fire:—"The parson had a returning fit
of pride which had just seized him; and he was going to
be well mounted once again in his life; and if it was so,
'twas plain as the sun at noonday, he would pocket the
expense of the licence ten times told, the very first year:—
so that everybody was left to judge what were his views
in this act of charity."

What were his views in this, and in every other action of
his life,—or rather what were the opinions which floated in
the brains of other people concerning it, was a thought
which too much floated in his own, and too often broke in
upon his rest, when he should have been found asleep.

About ten years ago, this gentleman had the good fortune
to be made entirely easy upon that score,—it being just so
long since he left his parish,—and the whole world at the

same time behind him ;—and stands accountable to a Judge,
of whom he will have no cause to complain.

But there is a fatality attends the actions of some men':
order them as they will, they pass thro' a certain medium,
which so twists and refracts them from their true directions
——that, with all the titles to praise which a rectitude of
heart can give, the doers of them are nevertheless forced to
live and die without it.

Of the truth of which this gentleman was a painful
example.——But to know by what means this came to pass,
—and to make that knowledge of use to you, I insist upon
it that you read the two following chapters, which contain
such a sketch of his life and conversation, as will carry its
moral along with it. When this is done, if nothing stops
us in our way, we will go on with the midwife.

CHAPTER XI.

YORICK was this parson's name, and, what is very remarkable in it (as appears from a most ancient account of the
family, wrote upon strong vellum, and now in perfect preservation), it had been exactly so spelt for near—I was
within an ace of saying nine hundred years ;—but I would
not shake my credit in telling an improbable truth, however
indisputable in itself ;——and therefore I shall content myself with only saying——it had been exactly so spelt, without the least variation or transposition of a single letter, for
I do not know how long; which is more than I would venture to say of one half of the best surnames in the kingdom ;
which, in a course of years, have generally undergone as
many chops and changes as their owners.—Has this been
owing to the pride, or to the shame of the respective pro-
prietors ?—In honest truth, I think sometimes to the one,
and sometimes to the other, just as the temptation has
wrought. But a villanous affair it is, and will one day so
blend and confound us all together, that no one shall be able

to stand up and swear, "That his own great grandfather was the man who did either this or that."

This evil had been sufficiently fenced against by the prudent care of the Yorick family, and their religious preservation of these records I quote, which do farther inform us, that the family was originally of Danish extraction, and had been transplanted into England as early as in the reign of Horwendillus, king of Denmark, in whose court, it seems, an ancestor of this Mr. Yorick, and from whom he was lineally descended, held a considerable post to the day of his death. Of what nature this considerable post was, this record saith not—it only adds, That, for near two centuries, it had been totally abolished, as altogether unnecessary, not only in that court, but in every other court of the Christian world.

It has often come into my head, that this post could be no other than that of the king's chief jester;—and that Hamlet's Yorick, in our Shakspeare, many of whose plays, you know, are founded upon authenticated facts, was certainly the very man.

I have not the time to look into Saxo-Grammaticus's Danish history, to know the certainty of this;—but if you have leisure, and can easily get at the book, you may do it full as well yourself.

I had just time, in my travels through Denmark with Mr. Noddy's eldest son, whom, in the year 1741, I accompanied as governor, riding along with him at a prodigious rate through most parts of Europe, and of which original journey, performed by us two, a most delectable narrative will be given in the progress of this work—I had just time, I say, and that was all, to prove the truth of an observation made by a long sojourner in that country; namely, "That Nature was neither very lavish, nor was she very stingy in her gifts of genius and capacity to its inhabitants;—but, like a discreet parent, was moderately kind to them all; observing such an equal tenor in the distribution of her favours, as to bring them, in those points, pretty near to a level with each other; so that you will meet with few instances in that kingdom of refined parts; but a great deal

of good plain household understanding amongst all ranks
of people, of which everybody has a share;" which is, I
think, very right.

With us, you see, the case is quite different:—we are all
ups and downs in this matter;—you are a great genius;—
or 'tis fifty to one, Sir, you are a great dunce and a blockhead :—not that there is a total want of intermediate steps ;
—no,—we are not so irregular as that comes to ;—but the
two extremes are more common, and in a greater degree in
this unsettled island, where Nature, in her gifts and dispositions of this kind, is most whimsical and capricious ; Fortune
herself not being more so, in the bequest of her goods and
chattels, than she.

This is all that ever staggered my faith in regard to
Yorick's extraction, who, by what I can remember of him,
and by all the accounts I could ever get of him, seemed not
to have had one single drop of Danish blood in his whole
crasis ; in nine hundred years it might possibly have run
out :———I will not philosophise one moment with you about
it ; for happen how it would, the fact was this:—That instead of that cold phlegm, and exact regularity of sense and
humours, you would have looked for in one so extracted, he
was, on the contrary, as mercurial and sublimated a composition,—as heteroclite a creature in all his declensions,
———with as much life and whim, and *gaieté de cœur* about
him, as the kindliest climate could have engendered and put
together. With all this sail, poor Yorick carried not one
ounce of ballast ; he was utterly unpractised in the world,
and at the age of twenty-six, knew just about as well how
to steer his course in it, as a romping, unsuspicious girl of
thirteen : so that, upon his first setting out, the brisk gale of
his spirits, as you will imagine, ran him foul ten times in a
day of somebody's tackling ; and as the grave and more
slow-paced were oftenest in his way,———you may likewise
imagine, 'twas with such he had generally the ill-luck to get
the most entangled. For aught I know, there might be
some mixture of unlucky wit at the bottom of such *fracas :*
———for, to speak the truth, Yorick had an invincible dislike

and opposition in his nature to gravity;—not a gravity as
such;—for where gravity was wanted, he would be the most
grave or serious of mortal men for days and weeks together;
—but he was an enemy to the affectation of it, and declared
open war against it, only as it appeared a cloak for ignorance, or for folly : and then, whenever it fell in his way,
however sheltered and protected, he seldom gave it much
quarter.

Sometimes, in his wild way of talking, he would say, that
Gravity was an arrant scoundrel; and he would add,—of
the most dangerous kind too,—because a sly one; and that
he verily believed more honest, well-meaning people were
bubbled out of their goods and money by it in one twelvemonth, than by pocket-picking and shop-lifting in sever.
In the naked temper which a merry heart discovered, he
would say, there was no danger,—but to itself:—whereas
the very essence of gravity was design, and consequently
deceit;—'twas a taught trick, to gain credit of the world for
more sense and knowledge than a man was worth; and that,
with all its pretensions,—it was no better, but often worse,
than what a French wit had long ago defined it,—viz. *A*
mysterious carriage of the body to cover the defects of the
mind;—which definition of gravity, Yorick, with great im-
prudence, would say, deserved to be wrote in letters of gold.

But, in plain truth, he was a man unhackneyed and unpractised in the world, and was altogether as indiscreet and
foolish on every other subject of discourse where policy is
wont to impress restraint. Yorick had no impression but
one, and that was what arose from the nature of the deed
spoken of; which impression he would usually translate into
plain English without any periphrasis;—and too oft without
much distinction of either person, time, or place;—so that
when mention was made of a pitiful or an ungenerous proceeding——he never gave himself a moment's time to reflect
who was the hero of the piece,——what his station,——or
how far he had power to hurt him hereafter;——but if it
was a dirty action,—without more ado,—The man was a
dirty fellow,—and so on.—And as his comments had usually

the ill fate to be terminated either in a *bon mot*, or to be enlivened throughout with some drollery or humour of expression, it gave wings to Yorick's indiscretion. In a word, though he never sought, yet, at the same time, as he seldom shunned occasions of saying what came uppermost, and without much ceremony;——he had but too many temptations in life of scattering his wit and his humour, his gibes and his jests about him.——They were not lost for want of gathering.

What were the consequences, and what was Yorick's catastrophe thereupon, you will read in the next chapter.

———

CHAPTER XII.

The Mortgager and Mortgagée differ the one from the other, not more in length of purse, than the Jester and Jestée do, in that of memory. But in this the comparison between them runs, as the scholiasts call it, upon all-four; which, by-the-bye, is upon one or two legs more than some of the best of Homer's can pretend to;—namely, That the one raises a sum, and the other a laugh, at your expense, and thinks no more about it. Interest, however, still runs on in both cases;—the periodical or accidental payments of it, just serving to keep the memory of the affair alive; till, at length, in some evil hour,—pop comes the creditor upon each, and, by demanding principal upon the spot, together with full interest to the very day, makes them both feel the full extent of their obligations.

As the reader (for I hate your *ifs*) has a thorough knowledge of human nature, I need not say more to satisfy him, that my Hero could not go on at this rate without some slight experience of these incidental mementos. To speak the truth, he had wantonly involved himself in a multitude of small book-debts of this stamp, which, notwithstanding Eugenius's frequent advice, he too much disregarded; thinking, that as not one of them was contracted thro' any malignancy,—but, on the contrary, from an honesty of mind, and a mere jocundity of humour, they would all of them be crossed out in course.

Eugenius would never admit this; and would often tell him, that one day or other he would certainly be reckoned with; and he would often add, in an accent of sorrowful apprehension,—to the uttermost mite. To which Yorick, with his usual carelessness of heart, would as often answer with a pshaw!—and if the subject was started in the fields, —with a hop, skip, and jump at the end of it: but if close pent up in the social chimney-corner, where the culprit was barricadoed in with a table and a couple of arm-chairs, and could not so readily fly off in a tangent,— Eugenius would then go on with his lecture upon discretion, in words to this purpose, though somewhat better put together:—

Trust me, dear Yorick, this unweary pleasantry of thine will sooner or later bring thee into scrapes and difficulties, which no after-wit can extricate thee out of.——In these sallies, too oft, I see, it happens, that a person laughed at, considers himself in the light of a person injured, with all the rights of such a situation belonging to him; and when thou viewest him in that light too, and reckonest up his friends, his family, his kindred and allies,——and musterest up with them the many recruits which will list under him from a sense of common danger,——'tis no extravagant arithmetic to say, that for every ten jokes—thou hast got an hundred enemies: and till thou hast gone on, and raised a swarm of wasps about thine ears, and art half stung to death by them, thou wilt never be convinced it is so.

I cannot suspect it in the man whom I esteem, that there is the least spur from spleen or malevolence of intent in these sallies;—I believe and know them to be truly honest and sportive:—but consider, my dear lad, that fools cannot distinguish this,—and that knaves will not: and that thou knowest not what it is, either to provoke the one, or to make merry with the other:——whenever they associate for mutual defence, depend upon it, they will carry on the war in such a manner against thee, my dear friend, as to make thee heartily sick of it, and of thy life too.

Revenge, from some baneful corner, shall level a tale of dishonour at thee, which no innocence of heart or integrity of conduct shall set right.——The fortunes of thy house shall totter;—thy character, which led the way to them, shall bleed on every side of it ;—thy faith questioned,—thy works belied,—thy wit forgotten,—thy learning trampled on. To wind up the last scene of thy tragedy, CRUELTY and COWARDICE, twin ruffians, hired and sent on by MALICE in the dark, shall strike together at all thy infirmities and mistakes ;——the best of us, my dear lad, lie open there, ——and trust me,——trust me, Yorick, *when, to gratify a private appetite, it is once resolved upon that an innocent and an helpless creature shall be sacrificed, 'tis an easy matter to pick up sticks enough from any thicket where it has strayed, to make a fire to offer it up with.*

Yorick scarce ever heard this sad vaticination of his destiny read over to him, but, with a tear stealing from his eye, and a promissory look attending it, that he was resolved, for the time to come, to ride his tit with more sobriety.—But, alas, too late !—a grand confederacy, with ***** and ***** at the head of it, was formed before the first prediction of it.—The whole plan of attack, just as Eugenius had foreboded, was put in execution all at once,—with so little mercy on the side of the allies,—and so little suspicion in Yorick of what was carrying on against him,—that when he thought, good easy man! full surely preferment was o' ripening, they had smote his root, and then he fell, as many a worthy man had fallen before him.

Yorick, however, fought it out with all imaginable gallantry for some time ; till, overpowered by numbers, and worn out at length by the calamities of the war,—but more so by the ungenerous manner in which it was carried on,—he threw down the sword; and, though he kept up his spirits in appearance to the last, he died, nevertheless, as was generally thought, quite broken-hearted.

What inclined Eugenius to the same opinion was as follows :—

A few hours before Yorick breathed his last, Eugenius stept in, with an intent to take his last sight and last farewell of him. Upon his drawing Yorick's curtain, and asking how he felt himself, Yorick, looking up in his face, took hold of his hand,—and, after thanking him for the many tokens of his friendship to him,—for which, he said, if it was their fate to meet hereafter, he would thank him again and again,—he told him, he was within a few hours of giving his enemies the slip for ever.—I hope not! answered Eugenius, with tears trickling down his cheeks, and with the tenderest tone that ever man spoke—I hope not, Yorick ! said he.——Yorick replied, with a look up, and a gentle squeeze of Eugenius's hand, and that was all; but it cut Eugenius to his heart.—Come, come, Yorick, quoth Eugenius, wiping his eyes, and summoning up the man within him,—my dear lad, be comforted, let not all thy spirits and fortitude forsake thee at this crisis when thou most want'st them ;——who knows what resources are in store, and what the power of God may yet do for thee !——Yorick laid his hand upon his heart, and gently shook his head.——For my part, continued Eugenius, crying bitterly as he uttered the words,—I declare I know not, Yorick, how to part with thee ; and would gladly flatter my hopes, added Eugenius, cheering up his voice, that there is still enough left of thee to make a bishop, and that I may live to see it.——I beseech thee, Eugenius, quoth Yorick, taking off his night-cap as well as he could with his left hand,——his right being still grasped close in that of Eugenius,——I beseech thee to take a view of my head.—I see nothing that ails it, replied Eugenius.—Then, alas ! my friend, said Yorick, let me tell you, that 'tis so bruised and mis-shapen with the blows which ****** and *****, and some others, have so unhandsomely given me in the dark, that I might say with Sancho Pança, that, should I recover, and "Mitres thereupon be suffered to rain down from heaven as thick as hail, not one of them would fit it."——Yorick's last breath was hanging

upon his trembling lips, ready to depart as he uttered this:
——yet still it was uttered with something of a Cervantic
tone;——and as he spoke it, Eugenius could perceive a
stream of lambent fire lighted up for a moment in his eyes:
——faint picture of those flashes of his spirit, which (as
Shakspeare said of his ancestor) were wont to set the table
in a roar!

Eugenius was convinced from this, that the heart of his
friend was broke: he squeezed his hand,——and then walked
softly out of the room, weeping as he walked. Yorick followed Eugenius with his eyes to the door,—he then closed
them,—and never opened them more.

He lies buried in the corner of his churchyard, in the
parish of ——, under a plain marble slab, which his friend
Eugenius, by leave of his executors, laid upon his grave, with
no more than these three words of inscription, serving both
for his epitaph and elegy :—

| Alas, poor YORICK! |

Ten times a day has Yorick's ghost the consolation to
hear his monumental inscription read over with such a
variety of plaintive tones, as denote a general pity and
esteem for him:——a foot-way crossing the churchyard,
close by the side of his grave,—not a passenger goes by
without stopping to cast a look upon it,—and sighing, as he
walks on,

Alas, poor YORICK!

CHAPTER XIII.

IT is so long since the reader of this rhapsodical work has been parted from the midwife, that it is high time to mention her again to him, merely to put him in mind that there is such a body still in the world, and whom, upon the best judgment I can form upon my own plan at present, I am going to introduce to him for good and all; but as fresh matter may be started, and much unexpected business fall out betwixt the reader and myself, which may require immediate despatch,—'twas right to take care that the poor woman should not be lost in the meantime;—because, when she is wanted, we can no way do without her.

I think I told you that this good woman was a person of no small note and consequence throughout our whole village and township;—that her fame had spread itself to the very out-edge and circumference of that centre of importance, of which kind every soul living, whether he has a shirt to his back or no,——has one surrounding him ;——which said circle, by the way, whenever 'tis said that such a one is of great weight and importance in the *world*,——I desire may be enlarged or contracted in your Worship's fancy, in a compound ratio of the station, profession, knowledge, abilities, height and depth (measuring both ways) of the personage brought before you.

In the present case, if I remember, I fixed it about four or five miles ; which not only comprehended the whole parish; but extended itself to two or three of the adjacent hamlets in the skirts of the next parish; which made a considerable thing of it. I must add, that she was, moreover, very well looked on at one large grange-house, and some other odd houses and farms within two or three miles, as I said, from the smoke of her own chimney :——But I must here, once for all, inform you, that all this will be more exactly deline- ated and explained in a map, now in the hands of the engraver, which, with many other pieces and developments of this work, will be added to the end of the twentieth volume,—

not to swell the work,—I detest the thought of such a thing ;—but by way of commentary, scholium, illustration, and key to such passages, incidents, or innuendos as shall be thought to be either of private interpretation, or of dark and doubtful meaning, after my Life and my Opinions shall have been read over (now don't forget the meaning of the word) by all the *world*;——which, betwixt you and me, and in spite of all the gentlemen-reviewers in Great Britain, and of all that their Worships should undertake to write or say to the contrary,—I am determined shall be the case.—I need not tell your Worship that all this is spoke in confidence.

CHAPTER XIV.

Upon looking into my mother's marriage-settlement, in order to satisfy myself and reader in a point necessary to be cleared up, before we could proceed any farther in this history,—I had the good fortune to pop upon the very thing I wanted before I had read a day and a half straight forwards :—it might have taken me up a month ;—which shews plainly, that when a man sits down to write a history,—though it be but the History of Jack Hickathrift or Tom Thumb, he knows no more than his heels what lets and confounded hindrances he is to meet with in his way,—or what a dance he may be led, by one excursion or another, before all is over. Could an historiographer drive on his history, as a muleteer drives on his mule,—straight forward;——for instance, from Rome all the way to Loretto, without ever once turning his head aside, either to the right hand or to the left——he might venture to foretell you to an hour when he should get to his journey's end ;——but the thing is, morally speaking, impossible : for, if he is a man of the least spirit, he will have fifty deviations from a straight line to make with this or that party as he goes along, which he can no ways avoid. He will have views and prospects to him-

self perpetually soliciting his eye, which he can no more
help standing still to look at than he can fly; he will, moreover, have various

Accounts to reconcile;

Anecdotes to pick up;

Inscriptions to make out;

Stories to weave in;

Traditions to sift;

Personages to call upon;

Panegyrics to paste up at this door;

Pasquinades at that:——All which both the man and the
mule are exempt from.   To sum up all; There are archives
at every stage to be look'd into, and rolls, records, documents,
and endless genealogies, which justice ever and anon calls
him back to stay the reading of:——In short, there is no
end of it——for my own part, I declare I have been at it
these six weeks, making all the speed I possibly could,—and
am not yet born:—I have just been able, and that's all, to
tell you *when* it happen'd, but not *how*;—so that you see
the thing is yet far from being accomplished.

These unforeseen stoppages, which I own I had no conception of when I first set out;—but which I am convinced
now will rather increase than diminish as I advance,—have
struck out a hint which I am resolved to follow,——and
that is,—not to be in a hurry;—but to go on leisurely,
writing and publishing two volumes of my life every year;
——which, if I am suffered to go on quietly, and can make
a tolerable bargain with my bookseller, I shall continue to
do as long as I live.

CHAPTER XV.

THE article in my mother's marriage-settlement, which I
told the reader I was at the pains to search for, and which,
now that I have found it, I think proper to lay before him,
—is so much more fully express'd in the deed itself than ever

I can pretend to do it, that it would be barbarity to take it out of the lawyer's hand:—It is as follows:—

"𝔄𝔫𝔡 𝔱𝔥𝔦𝔰 𝔍𝔫𝔡𝔢𝔫𝔱𝔲𝔯𝔢 𝔣𝔲𝔯𝔱𝔥𝔢𝔯 𝔴𝔦𝔱𝔫𝔢𝔰𝔰𝔢𝔱𝔥, That the said Walter Shandy, merchant, in consideration of the said intended marriage to be had, and, by God's blessing, to be well and truly solemnized and consummated between the said Walter Shandy and Elizabeth Mollineux aforesaid, and divers other good and valuable causes and considerations him thereunto specially moving,—doth grant, covenant, condescend, consent, conclude, bargain, and fully agree to and with John Dixon and James Turner, esqrs., the above-named Trustees, &c., &c.,—to wit,—That in case it should hereafter so fall out, chance, happen, or otherwise come to pass, That the said Walter Shandy, merchant, shall have left off business before the time or times that the said Elizabeth Mollineux shall, according to the course of nature or otherwise, have left off bearing and bringing forth children;—and that, in consequence of the said Walter Shandy having so left off business, he shall, in despite, and against the free-will, consent, and good-liking of the said Elizabeth Mollineux,—make a departure from the city of London, in order to retire to, and dwell upon, his estate at Shandy Hall, in the county of ——, or at any other country-seat, castle, hall, mansion-house, messuage, or grange-house, now purchased, or hereafter to be purchased, or upon any part or parcel thereof:—That then, and as often as the said Elizabeth Mollineux shall happen to be enceint with child or children severally and lawfully begot, or to be begotten, upon the body of the said Elizabeth Mollineux, during her said coverture,—he the said Walter Shandy shall, at his own proper costs and charges, and out of his own proper moneys, upon good and reasonable notice, which is hereby agreed to be within six weeks of her the said Elizabeth Mollineux's full reckoning, or time of supposed and computed delivery,—pay, or cause to be paid, the sum of one hundred and twenty pounds of good and lawful money, to John Dixon and James Turner, esqrs. or assigns,—upon TRUST and confidence, and for and unto the use and uses, intent, end, and purpose following:

—**That is to say,**—That the said sum of one hundred and twenty pounds shall be paid into the hands of the said Elizabeth Mollineux, or to be otherwise applied by them, the said Trustees, for the well and truly hiring of one coach, with able and sufficient horses, to carry and convey the body of the said Elizabeth Mollineux, and the child or children which she shall be then and there enceint and pregnant with,—unto the city of London; and for the further paying and defraying of all other incidental costs, charges, and expenses whatsoever,—in and about, and for and relating to her said intended delivery and lying-in, in the said city or suburbs thereof: And that the said Elizabeth Mollineux shall and may, from time to time, and at all such time and times as are here covenanted and agreed upon,—peaceably and quietly hire the said coach and horses, and have free ingress, egress, and regress throughout her journey, in and from the said coach, according to the tenor, true intent, and meaning of these presents, without any let, suit, trouble, disturbance, molestation, discharge, hindrance, forfeiture, eviction, vexation, interruption, or incumbrance whatsoever:—And that it shall moreover be lawful to and for the said Elizabeth Mollineux, from time to time, and as oft or often as she shall well and truly be advanced in her said pregnancy, to the time heretofore stipulated and agreed upon,—to live and reside in such place or places, and in such family or families, and with such relations, friends, and other persons within the said city of London, as she at her own will and pleasure, notwithstanding her present coverture, and as if she was a *femme sole* and unmarried,—shall think fit.—**And this Indenture further witnesseth,** That for the more effectually carrying of the said covenant into execution, the said Walter Shandy, merchant, doth hereby grant, bargain, sell, release, and confirm unto the said John Dixon and James Turner, esqrs., their heirs, executors, and assigns, in their actual possession now being, by virtue of an indenture of bargain and sale for a year to them the said John Dixon and James Turner, esqrs., by him the said Walter Shandy, merchant, thereof made; which said bargain and sale for a year, bears date the day next before the date of these presents, and by force and virtue of the statute for transferring of uses into possession,—All that the manor and lordship of Shandy, in the county of ——, with all the rights, members, and appurtenances thereof; and all and every the messuages, houses, buildings, barns, stables, orchards, gardens, backsides, tofts, crofts, garths, cottages, lands, meadows, feedings, pastures, marshes, commons, woods, underwoods, drains, fisheries, waters, and water-courses;—together with all rents, reversions, services, annuities, fee-farms, knights' fees, views of frankpledge, escheats, reliefs, mines, quarries, goods and chattels of felons and fugitives, felons of themselves, and put in exigent, deodands, fee-warrens, and all other royalties and seigniories, rights and jurisdictions, privileges and hereditaments whatsoever.——And also the advowson, donation, presentation, and free disposition of the rectory or parsonage of Shandy aforesaid, and all and every the tenths, tithes, glebe lands."—In three words,——My mother was to lie-in (if she chose it) in London.

But, in order to put a stop to the practice of any unfair play on the part of my mother, which a marriage-article of this nature too manifestly opened a door to, and which indeed had never been thought of at all, but for my uncle Toby Shandy,—a clause was added in security of my father, which was this:—"That in case my mother hereafter should, at any time, put my father to the trouble and expense of a London journey, upon false cries and tokens,——that for every such instance, she should forfeit all the right and title which the covenant gave her to the next turn;——but no more,—and so on, *toties quoties*, in as effectual a manner as if such a covenant betwixt them had not been made."—This, by the way, was no more than what was reasonable;—and yet, as reasonable as it was, I have ever thought it hard that the whole weight of the article should have fallen entirely, as it did, upon myself.

But I was begot and born to misfortunes;—for my poor mother, whether it was wind or water—or a compound of both,—or neither;—or whether it was simply the mere swell

of imagination and fancy in her; or how far a strong wish
and desire to have it so, might mislead her judgment :—in
short, whether she was deceived or deceiving in this matter,
it no way becomes me to decide. The fact was this, That
in the latter end of September 1717, which was the year
before I was born, my mother having carried my father up
to town much against the grain,—he peremptorily insisted
upon the clause;—so that I was doom'd, by marriage-
articles, to have my nose squeez'd as flat to my face, as if
the Destinies had actually spun me without one.

How this event came about,—and what a train of vexatious disappointments, in one stage or other of my life, have
pursued me, from the mere loss, or rather compression, of
this one single member,—shall be laid before the reader all
in due time.

CHAPTER XVI.

My father, as anybody may naturally imagine, came down
with my mother into the country, in but a pettish kind of a
humour. The first twenty or five-and-twenty miles he did
nothing in the world but fret and tease himself, and indeed
my mother too, about the cursed expense, which he said
might every shilling of it have been saved.—Then, what
vexed him more than everything else was, the provoking
time of year,—which, as I told you, was towards the end of
September, when his wall-fruit, and green-gages especially,
in which he was very curious, were just ready for pulling.—
"Had he been whistled up to London, upon a Tom Fool's
errand, in any other month of the whole year, he should not
have said three words about it."

For the next two whole stages, no subject would go down,
but the heavy blow he had sustained from the loss of a son,
whom he seems he had fully reckon'd upon in his mind, and
register'd down in his pocket-book, a second staff for his old
age, in case Bobby should fail him. "The disappointment

of this (he said) was ten times more to a wise man than all the money which the journey, &c., had cost him, put together :—rot the hundred and twenty pounds,——he did not mind it a rush!"

From Stilton, all the way to Grantham, nothing in the whole affair provoked him so much as the condolences of his friends, and the foolish figure they should both make at church, the first Sunday;——of which, in the satirical vehemence of his wit, now sharpened a little by vexation, he would give so many humorous and provoking descriptions,—and place his rib and self in so many tormenting lights and attitudes in the face of the whole congregation,— that my mother declared, these two stages were so truly tragicomical, that she did nothing but laugh and cry in a breath, from one end to the other of them all the way.

From Grantham, till they had cross'd the Trent, my father was out of all kind of patience at the vile trick and imposition which he fancied my mother had put upon him in this affair.—" Certainly," he would say to himself, over and over again, " the woman could not be deceived herself——if she could,——what weakness!"—tormenting word!—which led his imagination a thorny dance, and, before all was over, play'd the deuce and all with him;—for sure as ever the word *weakness* was uttered, and struck full upon his brain, so sure it set him upon running divisions upon how many kinds of weaknesses there were;——that there was such a thing as weakness of the body,——as well as weakness of the mind ;—and then he would do nothing but syllogise within himself, for a stage or two together, How far the cause of all these vexations might, or might not, have arisen out of himself.

In short, he had so many little subjects of disquietude springing out of this one affair, all fretting successively in his mind as they rose up in it, that my mother, whatever was her journey up, had but an uneasy journey of it down. ——In a word, as she complained to my uncle Toby, he would have tired out the patience of any flesh alive. .

CHAPTER XVII. '''

THOUGH my father travelled homewards, as I told you, in none of the best of moods,—pshawing and pishing all the way down,—yet he had the complaisance to keep the worst part of the story still to himself;—which was the resolution he had taken of doing himself the justice, which my uncle Toby's clause in the marriage-settlement empowered him : nor was it till the very night in which I was begot, which was thirteen months after, that she had the least intimation of his design ; when my father, happening, as you remember, to be a little chagrined and out of temper,——took occasion, as they lay chatting gravely in bed afterwards, talking over what was to come,——to let her know that she must accommodate herself as well as she could to the bargain made between them in their marriage-deeds; which was, to lie-in of her next child in the country, to balance the last year's journey.

My father was a gentleman of many virtues ;—but he had a strong spice of that in his temper, which might, or might not, add to the number.—'Tis known by the name of Perseverance, in a good cause ;—and of Obstinacy, in a bad one : of this my mother had so much knowledge, that she knew 'twas to no purpose to make any remonstrance ; so she e'en resolved to sit down quietly, and make the most of it.

CHAPTER XVIII.

As the point was that night agreed, or rather determined, that my mother should lie-in of me in the country, she took her measures accordingly; for which purpose, when she was three days, or thereabouts, gone with child, she began to cast her eyes upon the midwife, whom you have so often heard me mention ; and before the week was well got round, as the famous Dr. Manningham was not to be had, she had come to a final determination in her mind,——notwithstand-

ing there was a scientific operator within so near a call as
eight miles of us, and who, moreover, had expressly wrote a
five-shilling book upon the subject of midwifery, in which
he had exposed, not only the blunders of the sisterhood itself,
—but had likewise superadded many curious improvements
for the quicker extraction of the fœtus in cross births, and
some other cases of danger which belay us in getting into
the world : notwithstanding all this, my mother, I say, was
absolutely determined to trust her life, and mine with it,
into no soul's hand but this old woman's only.—Now this I
like ;—when we cannot get at the very thing we wish,
——never to take up with the next best in degree to it.
No; that's pitiful beyond description.—It is no more than
a week from this very day, in which I am now writing this
book for the edification of the world,—which is March 9,
1759,——that my dear, dear Jenny, observing I looked a
little grave, as she stood cheapening a silk of five-and-twenty
shillings a yard,—told the mercer, she was sorry she had
given him so much trouble;—and immediately went and
bought herself a yard-wide stuff of ten-pence a yard.—'Tis
the duplication of one and the same greatness of soul : only,
what lessened the honour of it somewhat in my mother's
case, was, that she could not heroine it into so violent and
hazardous an extreme, as one in her situation might have
wished ; because the old midwife had really some little claim
to be depended upon,—as much, at least, as success could
give her; having, in the course of her practice of near twenty
years in the parish, brought every mother's son of them into
the world without any one slip or accident which could
fairly be laid to her account.

These facts, though they had their weight, yet did not
altogether satisfy some few scruples and uneasinesses which
hung upon my father's spirits, in relation to this choice.—
To say nothing of the natural workings of humanity and
justice—or of the yearnings of parental and connubial
love, all which prompted him to leave as little to hazard
as possible in a case of this kind,——he felt himself concerned in a particular manner, that all should go right

in the present case, from the accumulated sorrow he lay open
to, should any evil betide his wife and child in lying-in at
Shandy Hall.——He knew the world judged by events; and
would add to his afflictions in such a misfortune, by loading
him with the whole blame of it.——'Alas o' day!—had
Mrs. Shandy (poor gentlewoman!) had but her wish in
going up to town just to lie-in and come down again;
which, they say, she begged and prayed for upon her bare
knees,——and which, in my opinion,—considering the
fortune which Mr. Shandy got with her,—was no such
mighty matter to have complied with, the lady and her
babe might both of them have been alive at this hour."

This exclamation, my father knew, was unanswerable;—
and yet, it was not merely to shelter himself,—nor was it
altogether for the care of his offspring and wife that he
seemed so extremely anxious about this point;—my father
had extensive views of things, and stood moreover, as he
thought, deeply concerned in it for the public good, from
the dread he entertained of the bad uses an ill-fated instance
might be put to.

He was very sensible that all political writers upon the
subject had unanimously agreed and lamented, from the
beginning of Queen Elizabeth's reign down to his own time,
that the current of men and money towards the metropolis,
upon one frivolous errand or another,—set in so strong,—as
to become dangerous to our civil rights;—though, by the bye,
——a *current* was not the image he took most delight in,—
a *distemper* was here his favourite metaphor, and he would
run it down into a perfect allegory, by maintaining it was
identically the same in the body national as in the body
natural, where the blood and spirits were driven up into the
head faster than they could find their ways down;—a stop-
page of circulation must ensue, which was death in both cases.

There was little danger, he would say, of losing our liber-
ties by French politics or French invasions;——nor was he
so much in pain of a consumption from the mass of corrupted
matter and ulcerated humours in our constitution, which he
hoped was not so bad as it was imagined;—but he verily

feared that, in some violent push, we should go off, all at
once, in a state-apoplexy;—and then, he would say, *The
Lord have mercy upon us all!*

My father was never able to give the history of this distemper,—without the remedy along with it.

"Was I an absolute prince," he would say, pulling up
his breeches with both his hands, as he rose from his arm-
chair, " I would appoint able judges, at every avenue of my
metropolis, who should take cognizance of every fool's
business who came there;—and if, upon a fair and candid
hearing, it appeared not of weight sufficient to leave his own
home, and come up, bag and baggage, with his wife and
children, farmer's sons, &c., &c., at his backside, they should
be all sent back, from constable to constable, like vagrants
as they were, to the place of their legal settlements. By
this means I should take care that my metropolis totter'd not
through its own weight;—that the head be no longer too
big for the body,—that the extremes, now wasted and pinn'd
in, be restored to their due share of nourishment, and regain
with it their natural strength and beauty:—I would effectually provide, That the meadows and cornfields of my
dominions should laugh and sing;—that good cheer and
hospitality flourish once more;—and that such weight and
influence be put thereby into the hands of the Squirality of
my kingdom, as should counterpoise what I perceive my
Nobility are now taking from them."

"Why are there so few palaces and gentlemen's seats,"
he would ask, with some emotion, as he walked across the
room, "throughout so many delicious provinces in France?
Whence is it that the few remaining *châteaus* amongst them
are so dismantled,—so unfurnished, and in so ruinous and
desolate a condition?——Because, Sir," (he would say) " in
that kingdom no man has any country-interest to support;
—the little interest of any kind which any man has anywhere in it, is concentrated in the court, and the looks of
the Grand Monarch: by the sunshine of whose countenance,
or the clouds which pass across it, every Frenchman lives
or dies.".

Another political reason which prompted my father so
strongly to guard against the least evil accident in my
mother's lying-in in the country,——was, That any such
instance would infallibly throw a balance of power, too
great already, into the weaker vessels of the gentry, in his
own, or higher stations;——which, with the many other
usurped rights which that part of the constitution was
hourly establishing,—would, in the end, prove fatal to the
monarchical system of domestic government established in
the first creation of things by God.

In this point he was entirely of Sir Robert Filmer's
opinion, That the plans and institutions of the greatest
monarchies in the eastern parts of the world were, originally,
all stolen from that admirable pattern and prototype of this
household and paternal power;—which, for a century, he
said, and more, had gradually been degenerating away into
a mix'd government;——the form of which, however desir-
able in great combinations of the species,——was very
troublesome in small ones,—and seldom produced anything,
that he saw, but sorrow and confusion.

For all these reasons, private and public, put together,—
my father was for having the man mid-wife, by all means,
—my mother, by no means.   My father begg'd and intreated
she would for once recede from her prerogative in this
matter, and suffer him to choose for her:—my mother, on
the contrary, insisted upon her privilege in this matter, to
choose for herself,—and have no mortal's help but the old
woman's.—What could my father do?   He was almost at
his wits' end;——talked it over with her in all moods;—
placed his arguments in all lights;—argued the matter with
her like a Christian,—like a Heathen,—like a husband,—
like a father,—like a patriot,—like a man:—My mother
answered everything only like a woman; which was a little
hard upon her;—for as she could not assume and fight it out
behind such a variety of characters,—'twas no fair match :—
'twas seven to one.—What could my mother do?——She
had the advantage (otherwise she had been certainly overpowered) of a small reinforcement of chagrin personal at the

bottom, which bore her up, and enabled her to dispute the affair with my father with so equal an advantage,—that both sides sung *Te Deum.* In a word, my mother was to have the old woman,—and the operator was to have licence to drink a bottle of wine with my father and my uncle Toby Shandy in the back parlour,—for which he was to be paid five guineas.

I must beg leave, before I finish this chapter, to enter a caveat in the breast of my fair reader;—and it is this,—Not to take it absolutely for granted, from an unguarded word or two which I have dropped in it——"That I am a married man."—I own, the tender appellation of my dear, dear Jenny,—with some other strokes of conjugal knowledge, interspersed here and there, might, naturally enough, have misled the most candid judge in the world into such a determination against me.—All I plead for, in this case, Madam, is strict justice; and that you do so much of it, to me as well as to yourself,—as not to prejudge, or receive such an impression of me, till you have better evidence, than, I am positive, at present can be produced against me.—Not that I can be so vain or unreasonable, Madam, as to desire you should therefore think that my dear, dear Jenny is my kept mistress;—no,—that would be flattering my character in the other extreme, and giving it an air of freedom, which, perhaps, it has no kind of right to. All I contend for, is the utter impossibility, for some volumes, that you, or the most penetrating spirit upon earth, should know how this matter really stands.—It is not impossible, but that my dear, dear Jenny! tender as the appellation is, may be my child.——Consider,—I was born in the year eighteen.—Nor is there anything unnatural or extravagant in the supposition, that my dear Jenny may be my friend!—Friend!—My friend.—Surely, Madam, a friendship between the two sexes may subsist, and be supported, without——Fy! Mr. Shandy—Without anything, Madam, but that tender and delicious sentiment which ever mixes in friendship, where there is a difference of sex. Let me intreat you to study the pure and sentimental parts of the best French Romances;—it will really, Madam, astonish you to see with what a variety of chaste expressions this delicious sentiment, which I have the honour to speak of, is dressed out.

CHAPTER XIX.

I WOULD sooner undertake to explain the hardest problem in geometry, than pretend to account for it, that a gentleman of my father's great good sense,——knowing, as the reader must have observed him, and curious too in philosophy,—wise also in political reasoning,—and in polemical (as he will find) no way ignorant,—could be capable of entertaining a notion in his head, so out of the common track,—that I fear the reader, when I come to mention it to him, if he is the least of a choleric temper, will immediately throw the book by; if mercurial, he will laugh most heartily at it; —and if he is of a grave and saturnine cast, he will, at first sight, absolutely condemn as fanciful and extravagant; and that was in respect to the choice and imposition of Christian names, on which he thought a great deal more depended than what superficial minds were capable of conceiving.

His opinion in this matter was, That there was a strange kind of magic bias, which good or bad names, as he called them, irresistibly impressed upon our characters and conduct.

The hero of Cervantes argued not the point with more seriousness,—nor had he more faith,—or more to say on the powers of necromancy in dishonouring his deeds,—or on Dulcinea's name, in shedding lustre upon them, than my father had on those of Trismegistus or Archimedes, on the one hand,—or of Nyky and Simkin, on the other. How many Cæsars and Pompeys, he would say, by mere inspiration of the names, have been rendered worthy of them! And how many, he would add, are there, who might have done exceeding well in the world had not their characters and spirits been totally depressed and Nicodemus'd into nothing!

I see plainly, Sir, by your looks (or as the case happened), my father would say—that you do not heartily subscribe to this opinion of mine,—which, to those, he would add, who have not carefully sifted it to the bottom,—I own has an air more of fancy than of solid reasoning in it;—and yet, my dear Sir, if I may presume to know your character, I am morally assured, I should hazard little in stating a case to you, not as a party in the dispute,—but as a judge, and trusting my appeal upon it to your own good sense and candid disquisition in this matter;——you are a person free from as many narrow prejudices of education as most men; —and, if I may presume to penetrate farther into you,—of a liberality of genius above bearing down an opinion, merely because it wants friends. Your son,—your dear son,— from whose sweet and open temper you have so much to expect,—your Billy, Sir!—would you, for the world, have called him JUDAS?—Would you, my dear son, he would say, laying his hand upon your breast, with the genteelest address, —and in that soft and irresistible *piano* of voice which the nature of the *argumentum ad hominem* absolutely requires, —Would you, Sir, if a *Jew* of a godfather had proposed the name of your child, and offered you his purse along with it, would you have consented to such a desecration of him? ——O my God! he would say, looking up, if I know your temper right, Sir,—you are incapable of it;—you would have trampled upon the offer;—you would have thrown the temptation at the tempter's head with abhorrence.

Your greatness of mind in this action, which I admire, with that generous contempt of money, which you show me in the whole transaction, is really noble;—and what renders it more so, is the principle of it;—the workings of a parent's love upon the truth and conviction of this very hypothesis, namely, That was your son called Judas,—the sordid and treacherous idea, so inseparable from the name, would have accompanied him through life like his shadow, and, in the end, made a miser and a rascal of him, in spite, Sir, of your example.

I never knew a man able to answer this argument.——

But, indeed, to speak of my father as he was;—he was
certainly irresistible;—both in his orations and disputations;
—he was born an orator;—Θεοδίδακτος.—Persuasion hung
upon his lips, and the elements of Logic and Rhetoric were
so blended up in him,—and, withal, he had so shrewd a
guess at the weaknesses and passions of his respondent,—
that NATURE might have stood up and said,—"This man
is eloquent."—In short, whether he was on the weak or the
strong side of the question, 'twas hazardous in either case to
attack him :—and yet, 'tis strange, he had never read Cicero
nor Quintilian de Oratore, nor Isocrates, nor Aristotle, nor
Longinus, amongst the ancients;—nor Vossius, nor Skiop-
pius, nor Ramus, nor Farnaby, amongst the moderns;—
and, what is more astonishing, he had never in his whole
life the least light or spark of subtilty struck into his mind
by one single lecture upon Crackenthorp or Burgersdicius
or any Dutch logician or commentator;—he knew not so
much as in what the difference of an argument *ad igno-
rantiam*, and an argument *ad hominem* consisted; so that I
well remember, when he went up along with me to enter
my name at Jesus' College in * * * *,—it was a matter of
just wonder with my worthy tutor, and two or three fellows
of that learned society,—that a man who knew not so much
as the names of his tools, should be able to work after that
fashion with them.

To work with them in the best manner he could, was
what my father was, however, perpetually forced upon;——
for he had a thousand little sceptical notions of the comic·
kind to defend,—most of which notions, I verily believe, at
first entered upon the footing of mere whims, and of a *vive
la bagatelle;* and as such, he would make merry with them
for half an hour or so, and, having sharpened his wit upon
them, dismiss them till another day.

I mention this, not only as a matter of hypothesis or conjecture upon the progress and establishment of my father's
many odd opinions,—but as a warning to the learned reader
against the indiscreet reception of such guests, who, after a
free and undisturbed entrance, for some years, into our

brains,—at length claim a kind of settlement there,——
working sometimes like yeast ;—but more generally after the
manner of the gentle passion, beginning in jest, but ending
in downright earnest.

Whether this was the case of the singularity of my
father's notions—or that his judgment, at length, became
the dupe of his wit ;—or how far, in many of his notions, he
might, though odd, be absolutely right ;——the reader, as
he comes at them, shall decide. All that I maintain here is,
that in this one, of the influence of Christian names, however it gained footing, he was serious ;—he was all uni-
formity ;—he was systematical, and, like all systematic
reasoners, he would move both heaven and earth, and twist
and torture everything in nature to support his hypothesis.
In a word, I repeat it over again,—he was serious ; and, in
consequence of it, he would lose all kind of patience whenever he saw people, especially of condition, who should have
known better,—as careless and as indifferent about the name
they imposed upon their child, or more so, than in the
choice of Ponto or Cupid for their puppy-dog.

This, he would say, look'd ill ;—and had, moreover, this
particular aggravation in it ; viz., That when once a vile
name was wrongfully or injudiciously given, 'twas not like
the case of a man's character, which, when wrong'd, might
hereafter be cleared ;——and possibly, some time or other,
if not in the man's life, at least after his death,—be, somehow or other, set to rights with the world : but the injury
of this, he would say, could never be undone ;—nay, he
doubted even whether an Act of Parliament could reach it :
——He knew as well as you, that the legislature assumed a
power over surnames ; but for very strong reasons, which he
could give, it had never yet adventured, he would say, to go
a step farther.

It was observable, that though my father, in consequence
of this opinion, had, as I have told you, the strongest likings
and dislikings towards certain names,—that there were still
numbers of names which hung so equally in the balance
before him, that they were absolutely indifferent to him.

Jack, Dick, and Tom were of this class: these my father called neutral names;—affirming of them, without a satire, that there had been as many knaves and fools at least, as wise and good men, since the world began, who had indifferently borne them;—so that, like equal forces acting against each other in contrary directions, he thought they mutually destroyed each other's effects; for which reason he would often declare, He would not give a cherry-stone to choose amongst them.   Bob, which was my brother's name, was another of these neutral kinds of Christian names, which operated very little either way; and as my father happen'd to be at Epsom when it was given him,—he would oft-times thank Heaven it was no worse.   Andrew was something like a negative quantity in Algebra with him;—'twas worse, he said, than nothing.—William stood pretty high:——Numps again was low with him:—and Nick, he said, was the *Devil*.

But of all the names in the universe, he had the most unconquerable aversion for *Tristram*:—he had the lowest and most contemptible opinion of it of anything in the world, thinking it could possibly produce nothing in *rerum naturâ*, but what was extremely mean and pitiful; so that in the midst of a dispute on the subject,—in which, by the bye, he was frequently involved,——he would sometimes break off in a sudden and spirited *Epiphonema*, or rather *Erotesis*, raised a third, and sometimes a full fifth above the key of the discourse,——and demand it categorically of his antagonist, Whether he would take upon him to say, he had ever remembered,——whether he had ever read,—or even whether he had ever heard tell of a man, called Tristram, performing anything great or worth recording?—No,—he would say, *Tristram!*—The thing is impossible.

What could be wanting in my father but to have wrote a book to publish this notion of his to the world?   Little boots it to the subtle speculatist to stand single in his opinions,—unless he gives them proper vent:—It was the identical thing which my father did:—for in the year sixteen, which was two years before I was born, he was at the pains of writing an express *Dissertation* simply upon the word Tristram,—shewing the world, with great candour and modesty, the grounds of his great abhorrence to the name.

When this story is compared with the title-page,—will not the gentle reader pity my father from his soul?—to see an orderly and well-disposed gentleman, who tho' singular, yet inoffensive in his notions,—so played upon in them by cross purposes!——to look down upon the stage, and see him baffled and overthrown in all his little systems and wishes! to behold a train of events perpetually falling out against him, and in so critical and cruel a way, as if they had purposely been plann'd and pointed against him, merely to insult his speculations!—In a word, to behold such a one, in his old age, ill-fitted for troubles, ten times in a day suffering sorrow!—ten times in a day calling the child of his prayers *Tristram!*—Melancholy dissyllable of sound! which, to his ears, was unison to Nincompoop, and every name vituperative under heaven.—By his ashes, I swear it,—if ever malignant spirit took pleasure, or busied itself in traversing the purposes of mortal man,—it must have been here!—and if it was not necessary I should be born before I was christened, I would this moment give the reader an account of it.

CHAPTER XX.

——How could you, Madam, be so inattentive in reading the last chapter? I told you in it, *That my mother was not a Papist.*——Papist! You told me no such thing, Sir.—— Madam, I beg leave to repeat it over again, that I told you, as plain, at least, as words, by direct inference, could tell you such a thing.—Then, Sir, I must have miss'd a page.—No, Madam,—you have not miss'd a word.——Then I was asleep, Sir.—My pride, Madam, cannot allow you that refuge.—Then I declare, I know nothing at all about the matter.—That, Madam, is the very fault I lay to your charge; and, as a punishment for it, I do insist upon it, that you immediately turn back, that is, as soon as you get to the next full stop, and read the whole chapter over again. I have imposed this penance upon the lady neither out of wantonness nor cruelty, but from the best of motives; and therefore shall make her no apology for it when she returns back.—'Tis to rebuke a vicious taste, which has crept into thousands besides herself,—of reading straight forwards, more in quest of the adventures than of the deep erudition and knowledge which a book of this cast, if read over as it should be, would infallibly impart with them.——The mind should be accustomed to make wise reflections, and draw curious conclusions as it goes along; the habitude of which made Pliny the Younger affirm, "That he never read a book so bad, but he drew some profit from it." The stories of Greece and Rome, run over without this turn and application, do less service, I affirm it, than the history of Parismus and Parismenus, or of the Seven Champions of England, read with it.

——But here comes my fair lady. Have you read over again the chapter, Madam, as I desired you?—You have: and did you not observe the passage, upon the second reading, which admits the inference?——Not a word like it! Then, Madam, be pleased to ponder well the last line but one of the chapter, where I take upon me to say, "It was *necessary* I should be born before I was christen'd." Had my mother, Madam, been a Papist, that consequence did not follow.*

---

* The Romish Rituals direct the baptizing of the child, in cases of danger *before* it is born ;—but upon this proviso, That some part or other of the child's body be seen by the baptizer.——But the Doctors of the Sorbonne, by a deliberation held amongst them, April 10, 1733, have enlarged the powers of the midwives, by determining, that though no part of the child's body should appear, that baptism shall, nevertheless, be administered to it by injection, —*par le moyen d'une petite canule,*—Anglicè, *a squirt.*——'Tis very strange that St. Thomas Aquinas, who had so good a mechanical head, both for tying and untying the knots of school-divinity, should, after so much pains bestowed upon this, give up the point at last, as a second *La chose impossible.*—"Infantes in maternis uteris existentes" (quoth St. Thomas !) "baptisari possunt *nullo modo.*"—O Thomas ! Thomas !

If the reader has the curiosity to see the question upon baptism *by injection,*

It is a terrible misfortune for this same book of mine, but more so to the Republic of Letters;—so that my own is quite swallowed up in the consideration of it,—that this

as presented to the Doctors of the Sorbonne, with their consultation thereupon, it is as follows :—

MÉMOIRE PRÉSENTÉ À MESSIEURS LES DOCTEURS DE SORBONNE.[*]

Un Chirurgien Accoucheur, représente à Messieurs les Docteurs de Sorbonne, qu'il y a des cas, quoique très rares, où une mère ne sçauroit accoucher, et même où l'enfant est tellement renfermé dans le sein de sa mère, qu'il ne fait paroître aucune partie de son corps, ce qui seroit un cas, suivant les Rituels, de lui conférer, du moins sous condition, le baptême. Le Chirurgien, qui consulte, prétend, par le moyen d'une petite canule, de pouvoir baptiser immediatement l'enfant, sans faire aucun tort à la mère.——Il demand si ce moyen, qu'il vient de proposer, est permis et légitime, et s'il peut s'en servir dans les cas qu'il vient d'exposer.

RÉPONSE.

Le Conseil estime, que la question proposée souffre de grandes difficultés. Les Théologiens posent d'un coté pour principe, que le baptême, qui est une naissance spirituelle, suppose une première naissance; il faut être né dans le monde, pour renaître en Jesus Christ, comme ils l'enseignent. S. Thomas 3 *part. quæst.* 88, *artic.* 11, suit cette doctrine comme une verité constante ; l'on ne peut, dit ce S. Docteur, baptiser les enfans qui sont renfermés dans le sein de leurs mères, et S. Thomas est fondé sur ce, que les enfans ne sont point nés et ne peuvent être comptés parmi les autres hommes ; d'ou il conclut, qu'ils ne peuvent être l'objet d'une action extérieure pour reçevoir par leur ministère les sacremens nécessaires au salut : *Pueri in maternis uteris existentes nondum prodierunt in lucem ut cum aliis hominibus vitam ducant ; unde non possunt subjici actioni humanæ, ut per eorum ministerium sacramenta recipiant ad salutam.* Les rituels ordonnent dans la pratique ce que les théologiens ont établi sur les mêmes matières, et ils defendent tous d'une manière uniforme, de baptiser les enfans qui sont renfermés dans le sein de leurs mères, s'ils ne font paroître quelque partie de leurs corps. Le concours des théologiens, et des rituels, qui sont les règles des diocèses, paroit former une autorité qui termine la question présente ; cependant le conseil de conscience considérant d'un coté, que le raisonnement des théologiens est uniquement fondé sur une raison de convenance, et que la defense des rituels suppose que l'on ne peut baptiser immediatement les enfans ainsi renfermés dans le sein de leurs mères, ce qui est contre la supposition presente ; et d'un autre côté, considérant que les mêmes théologiens enseignent, que l'on peut risquer les sacremens que Jesus Christ a établis comme des moyens faciles, mais nécessaires pour sanctifier les hommes ; et d'ailleurs estimant, que les enfans renfermés dans le sein de leurs mères, pourroient être capables de salut, parcequ'ils sont

[*] *Vide* Deventer, Paris edit. 4to, 1734, p. 366.

self-same vile pruriency for fresh adventures in all things, has got so strongly into our habit and humour,—and so wholly intent are we upon satisfying the impatience of our concupiscence that way,—that nothing but the gross and

capables de damnation ;—pour ces considérations, et en égard à l'exposé, suivant lequel on assure avoir trouvé un moyen certain de baptiser ces enfans ainsi renfermés, sans faire aucun tort à la mère, le Conseil estime que l'on pourroit se servir du moyen proposé, dans la confiance qu'il a, que Dieu n'a point laissé ces sortes d'enfans sans aucuns secours, et supposant, comme il est exposé, que le moyen dont il s'agit est propre à leur procurer le baptême ; cependant comme il s'agiroit, en autorisant la pratique proposée, de changer une règle universellement établie, le Conseil croit que celui qui consulte doit s'adresser à son évêque, et à qui il appartient de juger de l'utilité, et du danger du moyen proposé, et comme, sous le bon plaisir de l'évêque, le Conseil estime qu'il faudroit recourir au Pape, qui a le droit d'expliquer les régles de l'église, et d'y déroger dans le cas, ou la loi ne sçauroit obliger, quelque sage et quelque utile que paroisse la manière de baptiser dont il s'agit, le Conseil ne pourroit l'approver sans le concours de ces deux autorités. On conseille, au moins à celui qui consulte, de s'adresser à son évêque, et de lui faire part de la présente décision, afin que, si le prelat entre dans les raisons sur lesquelles les docteurs soussignés s'appuyent, il puisse être autorisé, dans le cas de nécessité, ou il risqueroit trop d'attendre que la permission fût demandée et accordée d'employer le moyen qu'il propose si avantageux au salut de l'enfant. Au reste, le Conseil, en estimant que l'on pourroit s'en servir, croit cependant, que si les enfans dont il s'agit, venoient au monde, contre l'espérance de ceux qui se seroient servis du même moyen, il seroit nécessaire de les baptiser *sous condition ;* et en cela le Conseil se conforme à tous les rituels, qui en autorisant le baptême d'un enfant qui fait paroître quelque partie de son corps, enjoignent néanmoins, et ordonnent de le baptiser *sous condition*, s'il vient heureusement au monde.|

Délibéré en Sorbonne, le 10 Avril, 1733.

A. Le Moyne.
L. De Romigny.
De Marcilly.

Mr. Tristram Shandy's compliments to Messrs. Le Moyne, De Romigny, and De Marcilly ; hopes they all rested well the night after so tiresome a consultation.—He begs to know, whether, after the ceremony of marriage, and before that of consummation, the baptising all the *Homunculi* at once, slapdash, by *injection*, would not be a shorter and safer cut still ; on condition, as above, That if the *Homunculi* do well, and come safe into the world after this, that each and every of them shall be baptised again (*sous condition*).—And provided, in the second place, That the thing can be done, which Mr. Shandy apprehends it may, *par le moyen d'une* petite canule, and *sans faire aucun tort au père ?*

more carnal parts of a composition will go down :—the subtle hints and sly communications of science fly off, like spirits upwards,——the heavy moral escapes downwards ; and both the one and the other are as much lost to the world, as if they were still left in the bottom of the ink-horn.

I wish the male reader has not pass'd by many a one, as quaint and curious as this one, in which the female reader has been detected. I wish it may have its effects ;—and that all good people, both male and female, from example, may be taught to think as well as read.

CHAPTER XXI.

——I wonder what's all that noise, and running back-wards and forwards for, above stairs ! quoth my father, addressing himself, after an hour and a half's silence, to my uncle Toby,——who, you must know, was sitting on the opposite side of the fire, smoking his social pipe all the time, in mute contemplation of a new pair of black plush breeches which he had got on :—What can they be doing, brother ? —quoth my father,—we can scarce hear ourselves talk.

I think, replied my uncle Toby, taking his pipe from his mouth, and striking the head of it two or three times upon the nail of his left thumb as he began his sentence,——I think, says he,—— But to enter rightly into my uncle Toby's sentiments upon this matter, you must be made to enter first a little into his character, the outlines of which I shall just give you ; and then the dialogue between him and my father will go on as well again.

Pray, what was that man's name,—for I write in such a hurry, I have no time to recollect or look for it,——who first made the observation, " That there was great incon-stancy in our air and climate ? " Whoever he was, 'twas a just and good observation in him.—But the corollary

drawn from it, namely, "That it is this which has furnished us with such a variety of odd and whimsical characters;"—that was not his;—it was found out by another
man, at least a century and a half after him. Then again
—That this copious store-house of original materials is the
true and natural cause, that our comedies are so much
better than those of France, or any others that either have
been, or can be wrote upon the Continent:——that discovery was not fully made till about the middle of King
William's reign,—when the great Dryden, in writing one
of his long prefaces (if I mistake not) most fortunately hit
upon it. Indeed, toward the latter end of Queen Anne,
the great Addison began to patronise the notion, and more
fully explained it to the world in one or two of his Specta-
tors;—but the discovery was not his.—Then, fourthly and
lastly, That this strange irregularity in our climate, producing
so strange an irregularity in our characters,——doth thereby,
in some sort, make us amends, by giving us somewhat to make
us merry with when the weather will not suffer us to go
out of doors;—that observation is my own;—and was struck
out by me this very rainy day, March 26, 1759, and betwixt
the hours of nine and ten in the morning.

Thus—thus, my fellow-labourers and associates in this
great harvest of our learning, now ripening before our eyes;
thus it is, by slow steps of casual increase, that our knowledge
physical, metaphysical, physiological, polemical, nautical,
mathematical, enigmatical, technical, biographical, romantical,
chemical, and obstetrical, with fifty other branches of it (most
of 'em ending as these do, in *ical*), have, for these two last
centuries and more, gradually been creeping upwards towards
that 'Ακμὴ of their perfections, from which, if we may form
a conjecture from the advances of these last seven years, we
cannot possibly be far off.

When that happens, it is to be hoped, it will put an end
to all kind of writings whatsoever;—the want of all kind of
writing will put an end to all kind of reading;—and that, in
time,—*As war begets poverty; poverty peace*,—must, in
course, put an end to all kind of knowledge;——and then

———we shall have all to begin over again; or, in other words, be exactly where we started.

——Happy! thrice happy times! I only wish that the æra of my begetting, as well as the mode and manner of it, had been a little altered,——or that it could have been put off, with any convenience to my father or mother, for some twenty or five-and-twenty years longer, when a man in the literary world might have stood some chance.——

But I forget my uncle Toby, whom all this while we have left knocking the ashes out of his tobacco-pipe.

His humour was of that particular species, which does honour to our atmosphere: and I should have made no scruple of ranking him amongst one of the first-rate productions of it, had not there appeared too many strong lines in it of a family likeness, which showed that he derived the singularity of his temper more from blood, than either wind or water, or any modifications or combinations of them whatever: And I have, therefore, oft-times wondered, that my father, tho' I believe he had his reasons for it, upon his observing some tokens of eccentricity in my course when I was a boy,—should never once endeavour to account for them in this way: for all the Shandy family were of an original character throughout:——I mean the males,—the females had no character at all,—except, indeed, my great-aunt Dinah, who, about sixty years ago, was married and got with child by the coachman, for which my father, according to his hypothesis of Christian names, would often say, She might thank her godfathers and godmothers.

It will seem very strange,——and I would as soon think of dropping a riddle in the reader's way, which is not my interest to do, as set him upon guessing how it could come to pass, that an event of this kind, so many years after it had happened, should be reserved for the interruption of the peace and unity, which otherwise so cordially subsisted, between my father and my uncle Toby. One would have thought, that the whole force of the misfortune should have spent and wasted itself in the family at first,—as is generally the case.—But nothing ever wrought with our family after the ordinary way.   Possibly at the very time this happened, it might have something else to afflict it; and as afflictions are sent down for our good, and that as this had never done the Shandy Family any good at all, it might lie waiting till apt times and circumstances should give it an opportunity to discharge its office.——Observe, I determine nothing upon this.——My way is ever to point out the curious, different tracts of investigation, to come at the first springs of the events I tell;—not with a pedantic Fescue,—or in the decisive manner of Tacitus, who outwits himself and his reader;—but with the officious humility of a heart devoted to the assistance merely of the inquisitive:—to them I write, ——and by them I shall be read,—if any such reading as this could be supposed to hold out so long, to the very end of the world.

Why this cause of sorrow, therefore, was thus reserved for my father and uncle, is undetermined by me.   But how and in what direction it exerted itself so as to become the cause of dissatisfaction between them, after it began to operate, is what I am able to explain with great exactness, and is as follows:

My uncle, Toby Shandy, Madam, was a gentleman, who, with the virtues which usually constitute the character of a man of honour and rectitude,——possessed one in a very eminent degree, which is seldom or never put into the catalogue; and that was a most extreme and unparalleled modesty of nature;——though I correct the word Nature, for this reason, that I may not prejudge a point which must shortly come to a hearing, and that is, Whether this modesty of his was natural or acquired?——Whichever way my uncle Toby came by it, 'twas nevertheless modesty in the truest sense of it; and that is, Madam, not in regard to words, for he was so unhappy as to have very little choice in them,—but to things;—and this kind of modesty so possessed him, and it arose to such a height in him, as almost to equal, if such a thing could be, even the modesty of a woman: that female nicety, Madam, and inward cleanliness of mind and fancy, in your sex, which makes you so much the awe of ours.

You will imagine, Madam, that my uncle Toby had contracted all this from this very source;—that he had spent a
great part of his time in converse with your sex; and that,
from a thorough knowledge of you, and the force of imitation, which such fair examples render irresistible, he had
acquired this amiable turn of mind.

I wish I could say so;—for unless it was with his sister-in
law, my father's wife and my mother,——my uncle Toby
scarce exchanged three words with the sex in as many years.
—No; he got it, Madam, by a blow.——A blow!——Yes,
Madam, it was owing to a blow from a stone, broke off by
a ball from the parapet of a horn-work at the siege of
Namur, which struck full upon my uncle Toby's groin.——
Which way could that effect it ?—The story of that, Madam,
is long and interesting;—but it would be running my
history all upon heaps to give it you here.——'Tis for an
episode hereafter; and every circumstance relating to it, in
its proper place, shall be faithfully laid before you :—Till
then, it is not in my power to give farther light into
this matter, or say more than what I have said already,
——That my uncle Toby was a gentleman of unparalleled
modesty, which happening to be somewhat subtilised and
rarefied by the constant heat of a little family pride,——
they both so wrought together with him, that he could
never bear to hear the affair of my aunt Dinah touched upon,
but with the greatest emotion.——The least hint of it was
enough to make the blood fly into his face ;—but when my
father enlarged upon the story in mixed companies, which
the illustration of his hypothesis frequently obliged him to
do,—the unfortunate blight of one of the fairest branches of
the family would set my uncle Toby's honour and modesty
o' bleeding ; and he would often take my father aside, in the
greatest concern imaginable, to expostulate and tell him, he
would give him anything in the world, only to let the story
rest.

My father, I believe, had the truest love and tenderness
for my uncle Toby, that ever one brother bore towards
another ; and would have done anything in nature, which

one brother in reason could have desired of another, to have
made my uncle Toby's heart easy in this, or any other
point.   But this lay out of his power.

——My father, as I told you, was a philosopher in grain.
—speculative,—systematical ;—and my aunt Dinah's affair
was a matter of as much consequence to him, as the retro-
gradation of the planets to Copernicus :—the backslidings
of Venus in her orbit fortified the Copernican system, called
so after his name ; and the backslidings of my aunt Dinah
in her orbit, did the same service in establishing my father's
system, which, I trust, will for ever hereafter be called the
SHANDEAN SYSTEM, after this.

In any other family dishonour, my father, I believe, had
as nice a sense of shame as any man whatever ;——and
neither he, nor, I daresay, Copernicus would have divulged
the affair in either case, or have taken the least notice of it
to the world, but for the obligations they owed, as they
thought, to truth.—*Amicus Plato,*—my father would say,
construing the words to my uncle Toby, as he went along,
Amicus Plato ;—that is, Dinah was my aunt ;—*sed magis
amica veritas*—but Truth is my sister.

This contrariety of humours betwixt my father and my
uncle was the source of many a fraternal squabble.   The
one could not bear to hear the tale of family disgrace re-
corded,——and the other would scarce ever let a day pass to
an end without some hint at it.

For God's sake, my uncle Toby would cry,——and for
my sake, and for all our sakes, my dear brother Shandy,—
do let this story of our aunt's, and her ashes, sleep in peace !
—How can you—how can you have so little feeling and
compassion for the character of our family ?——What is
the character of a family to an hypothesis? my father
would reply.——Nay, if you come to that—what is the life
of a family ?——The life of a family !—my uncle Toby
would say, throwing himself back in his arm-chair, and
lifting up his hands, his eyes, and one leg.——Yes, the life,
——my father would say, maintaining his point.   How
many thousands of 'em are there, every year that come,

cast away (in all civilised countries at least)——and considered as nothing but common air, in competition of an hypothesis! In my plain sense of things, my uncle Toby would answer——every such instance is downright Murder, let who will commit it.——There lies your mistake, my father would reply;——for, in *foro Scientiæ*, there is no such thing as Murder;——'tis only Death, brother.

My uncle Toby would never offer to answer this by any other kind of argument than that of whistling half-a-dozen bars of Lillibullero.——You must know, it was the usual channel thro' which his passions got vent, when anything shocked or surprised him :——but especially when anything which he deemed very absurd was offered.

As not one of our logical writers, nor any of the commentators upon them, that I remember, have thought proper to give a name to this particular species of argument, —I here take the liberty to do it myself, for two reasons: first, That, in order to prevent all confusion in disputes, it may stand as much distinguished, for ever, from every other species of argument——as the *Argumentum ad Verecundiam, ex Absurdo, ex Fortiori,* or any other argument whatsoever:—and, secondly, That it may be said, by my children's children, when my head is laid to rest,——that their learn'd grandfather's head had been busied to as much purpose once, as other people's :—That he had invented a name, and generously thrown it into the Treasury of the *Ars Logica,* for one of the most unanswerable arguments in the whole science : and, if the end of disputation is more to silence than convince,—they may add, if they please,—for one of the best arguments too.

I do therefore, by these presents, strictly order and command, That it be known and distinguished by the name and title of the *Argumentum Fistulatorium,* and no other;—and that it rank hereafter with the *Argumentum Baculinum* and the *Argumentum ad Crumenam,* and for ever hereafter be treated of in the same chapter.

As for the *Argumentum Tripodium,* which is never used but by the woman against the man ;—and the *Argumentum ad Rem*, which, contrariwise, is made use of by the man only against the woman ;—as these two are enough in conscience for one lecture ;——and, moreover, as the one is the best answer to the other,—let them likewise be kept apart, and be treated of in a place by themselves.

———

CHAPTER XXII.

THE learned Bishop Hall, I mean the famous Dr. Joseph Hall, who was Bishop of Exeter in King James the First's reign, tells us, in one of his Decades, at the end of his Divine Art of Meditation, imprinted in London, in the year 1610, by John Beal, dwelling in Aldersgate-street, " That it is an abominable thing for a man to commend himself :" ——and I really think it is so.

And yet, on the other hand, when a thing is executed in a masterly kind of a fashion, which thing is not likely to be found out;—I think it as full as abominable, that a man should lose the honour of it, and go out of the world with the conceit of it rotting in his head.

This is precisely my situation.

For in this long digression which I was accidently led into, as in all my digressions (one only excepted), there is a master-stroke of digressive skill, the merit of which has all along, I fear, been overlooked by my reader,—not for want of penetration in him,—but because 'tis an excellence seldom looked for, or expected indeed, in a digression ;—and it is this : That, though my digressions are all fair, as you observe, —and that I fly off from what I am about, as far, and as often too, as any writer in Great Britain,—yet I constantly take care to order affairs so, that my main business does not stand still in my absence.

I was just going, for example, to have given you the great outlines of my uncle Toby's most whimsical character ;— when my aunt Dinah and the coachman came across us, and led us a vagary some millions of miles into the very heart of the planetary system : notwithstanding all this, you perceive that the drawing of my uncle Toby's character went on gently all the time;—not the great contours of it,—that was impossible,—but some familiar strokes and faint designations of it, were here and there touch'd on, as he went along; so that you are much better acquainted with my uncle Toby now than you was before.

By this contrivance, the machinery of my work is of a species by itself; two contrary motions are introduced into it, and reconciled, which were thought to be at variance with each other. In a word, my work is digressive, and it is progressive too,—and at the same time.

This, Sir, is a very different story from that of the earth's moving round her axis in her diurnal rotation, with her progress in her elliptic orbit, which brings about the year, and constitutes that variety and vicissitude of seasons we enjoy;—though I own it suggested the thought,—as I believe the greatest of our boasted improvements and discoveries have come from such trifling hints.

Digressions, incontestably, are the sunshine;——they are the life, the soul of reading! take them out of this book, for instance—you might as well take the book along with them;—one cold eternal winter would reign in every page of it: restore them to the writer; he steps forth like a bridegroom;—bids All-hail; brings in variety, and forbids the appetite to fail.

All the dexterity is in the good cookery and management of them, so as to be not only for the advantage of the reader, but also of the author, whose distress in this matter is truly pitiable; for if he begins a digression,—from that moment, I observe, his whole work stands stock still;—and if he goes on with his main work,—then there is an end of his digression.

——This is vile work.—For which reason, from the beginning of this, you see, I have constructed the main work, and the adventitious parts of it, with such intersections, and have so complicated and involved the digressive and progressive movements, one wheel within another, that the whole machine, in general, has been kept a-going;—and what's more, it shall be kept a-going these forty years, if it pleases the Fountain of Health to bless me so long with life and good spirits.

———

CHAPTER XXIII.

I HAVE a strong propensity in me to begin this chapter very nonsensically; and I will not baulk my fancy:—accordingly I set off thus:

If the fixture of Momus's glass in the human breast, according to the proposed emendation of that arch critic, had taken place,—first, This foolish consequence would certainly have followed:—That the very wisest and very gravest of us all, in one coin or other, must have paid window-money every day of our lives;

And, secondly, That had the said glass been there set up, nothing more would have been wanting, in order to have taken a man's character, but to have taken a chair and gone softly, as you would to a dioptrical beehive, and look'd in, —viewed the soul stark-naked;—observed all her motions, —her machinations;—traced all her maggots, from their first engendering to their crawling forth;—watched her loose in her frisks, her gambols, her capricios; and after some notice of her more solemn deportment, consequent upon such frisks, &c.,——then taken your pen and ink and set down nothing but what you had seen, and could have sworn to.—But this is an advantage not to be had by the biographer in this planet;—in the planet Mercury (belike) it may be so; if not, better still for him;——for there, the intense heat of the country, which is proved by computators, from its vicinity to the Sun, to be more than equal to that of red-hot iron,—must, I think, long ago have vitrified the bodies of the inhabitants (as the efficient cause) to suit them for the climate (which is the final cause); so that, betwixt them both, all the tenements of their souls, from top to

bottom, may be nothing else, for aught the soundest philosophy can shew to the contrary, but one fine transparent
body of clear gloss (bating the umbilical knot)—so that, till
the inhabitants grow old and tolerably wrinkled, whereby
the rays of light, in passing through them, become so
monstrously refracted,—or return reflected from their sur-
faces in such tranverse lines to the eye, that a man cannot
be seen through,—his soul might as well, unless for mere
ceremony, or the trifling advantage which the umbilical
point gave her,—might, upon all other accounts, I say, as
well play the fool out o' doors as in her own house.

But this, as I said before, is not the case of the inhabitants of this earth;—our minds shine not through the body,
—but are wrapt up here in a dark covering of uncrystallised
flesh and blood; so that, if we would come to the specific
characters of them, we must go some other way to work.

Many, in good truth, are the ways which human wit has
been forced to take, to do this thing with exactness.

Some, for instance, draw all their characters with wind
instruments.—Virgil takes notice of that way, in the affair
of Dido and Æneas;—but it is as fallacious as the breath of
fame;—and, moreover, bespeaks a narrow genius. I am not
ignorant that the Italians pretend to a mathematical exactness in their designations of one particular sort of character
among them, from the *forte* or *piano* of a certain wind-
instrument they use, which they say is infallible.—I dare
not mention the name of the instrument in this place;—'tis
sufficient we have it amongst us,—but never think of making a drawing by it:—this is enigmatical, and intended to
be so, at least *ad populum:*—and therefore, I beg, Madam,
when you come here, that you read on as fast as you can,
and never stop to make any inquiry about it.

There are others, again, who will draw a man's character
from no other helps in the world, but merely from his
evacuations;—but this often gives a very incorrect outline,
—unless, indeed, you take a sketch of his repletions too;
and by correcting one drawing from the other, compound
one good figure out of them both.

I should have no objection to this method, but that I think it must smell too strong of the lamp,—and be render'd still more operose, by forcing you to have an eye to the rest of his non-naturals.——Why the most natural actions of a man's life should be called his Non-naturals,—is another question.

There are others, fourthly, who disdain every one of these expedients;—not from any fertility of their own, but from the various ways of doing it, which they have borrowed from the honourable devices which the Pentagraphic Brethren * of the Brush have shown in taking copies.— These, you must know, are your great historians.

One of these you will see drawing a full-length character *against the light;*—that's illiberal,—dishonest,—and hard upon the character of the man who sits.

Others, to mend the matter, will make a drawing of you in the *Camera;*—that is most unfair of all, because *there* you are sure to be represented in some of your most ridiculous attitudes.

To avoid all and every one of these errors in giving you my uncle Toby's character, I am determined to draw it by no mechanical help whatever;——nor shall my pencil be guided by any one wind-instrument which ever was blown upon, either on this or on the other side of the Alps;—nor will I consider either his repletions or his discharges,—or touch upon his non-naturals; but, in a word, I will draw my uncle Toby's character from his HOBBY-HORSE.

CHAPTER XXIV.

IF I was not morally sure that the reader must be out of all patience for my uncle Toby's character,—I would here previously have convinced him that there is no instrument

* Pentagraph, an instrument to copy prints and pictures mechanically, and in any proportion.

so fit to draw such a thing with, as that which I have pitched upon.

A man and his HOBBY-HORSE, tho' I cannot say that they act and re-act exactly after the same manner in which the soul and body do upon each other; yet, doubtless, there is a communication between them, of some kind; and my opinion rather is, that there is something in it more of the manner of electrified bodies;—and that, by means of the heated parts of the rider, which come immediately into contact with the HOBBY-HORSE,—by long journeys and much friction, it so happens, that the body of the rider is at length fill'd as full of HOBBY-HORSICAL matter as it can hold;——so that if you are able to give but a clear description of the nature of the one, you may form a pretty exact notion of the genius and character of the other.

Now the HOBBY-HORSE which my uncle Toby always rode upon was, in my opinion, an HOBBY-HORSE well worth giving a description of, if it was only upon the score of his great singularity;—for you might have travelled from York to Dover,—from Dover to Penzance in Cornwall, and from Penzance to York back again, and not have seen such another upon the road; or if you had seen such a one, whatever haste you had been in, you must infallibly have stopp'd to have taken a view of him. Indeed, the gait and figure of him was so strange, and so utterly unlike was he, from his head to his tail, to any one of the whole species, that it was now and then made a matter of dispute whether he was really a HOBBY-HORSE or no: but as the philosopher would use no other argument to the sceptic, who disputed with him against the reality of motion, save that of rising up upon his legs, and walking across the room; —so would my uncle Toby use no other argument to prove his HOBBY-HORSE was a HOBBY-HORSE indeed, but by getting upon his back and riding him about;— leaving the world, after that, to determine the point as it thought fit.

In good truth, my uncle Toby mounted him with so much pleasure, and he carried my uncle Toby so well,——that he

troubled his head very little with what the world either said
or thought about it.

It is now high time, however, that I give you a description of him :—but, to go on regularly, I only beg you will
give me leave to acquaint you first, how my uncle Toby
came by him.

————

CHAPTER XXV.

THE wound in my uncle Toby's groin, which he received at
the siege of Namur, rendering him unfit for the service, it
was thought expedient he should return to England, in order,
if possible, to be set to rights.

He was four years totally confined,—part of it to his bed,
and all of it to his room : and in the course of his cure,
which was all that time in hand, suffered unspeakable
miseries,—owing to a succession of exfoliations from the *os
pubis,* and the outward edge of that part of the *coxendix,*
called the *os ilium;*——both which bones were dismally
crushed, as much by the irregularity of the stone, which I
told you was broken off the parapet,—as by its size,—
(though it was pretty large) which inclined the surgeon all
along to think, that the great injury which it had done my
uncle Toby's groin, was more owing to the gravity of the
stone itself, than to the projectile force of it ;—which he
would often tell him was a great happiness.

My father at that time was just beginning business in
London, and had taken a house ;—and as the truest friendship and cordiality subsisted between the two brothers,—
and that my father thought my uncle Toby could nowhere
be so well nursed and taken care of as in his own house,—
he assigned him the very best apartment in it :—and, what
was a much more sincere mark of his affection still, he would
never suffer a friend or an acquaintance to step into the house
on any occasion, but would take him by the hand, and lead
him upstairs to see his brother Toby, and chat an hour by
his bed-side.

The history of a soldier's wound beguiles the pain of it;—
my uncle's visitors at least thought so; and in their daily
calls upon him, from the courtesy arising out of that belief,
they would frequently turn the discourse to that subject;—
and from that subject the discourse would generally roll on to
the siege itself.

These conversations were infinitely kind; and my uncle
Toby received great relief from them, and would have
received much more but that they brought him into some
unforeseen perplexities, which, for three months together,
retarded his cure greatly; and if he had not hit upon an
expedient to extricate himself out of them, I verily believe
they would have laid him in his grave.

What these perplexities of my uncle Toby were,——'tis
impossible for you to guess:—if you could,—I should blush;
not as a relation,—not as a man,—nor even as a woman,—
but I should blush as an author; inasmuch as I set no small
store by myself upon this very account, that my reader has
never yet been able to guess at anything: and in this, Sir, I
am of so nice and singular a humour, that if I thought you
was able to form the least judgment, or probable conjecture
to yourself of what was to come in the next page,—I would
tear it out of my book.

THE

LIFE AND OPINIONS

OF

TRISTRAM SHANDY, Gent.

VOL. II. ORIG. EDIT.

Ταράσσει τοὺς Ἀνθρώπους οὐ τὰ Πράγματα,
Ἀλλὰ τὰ περὶ τῶν Πραγμάτων, Δόγματα.

CHAPTER I.

 HAVE begun the new book, on purpose that I might have room enough to explain the nature of the perplexities in which my uncle Toby was involved, from the many discourses and interrogations about the siege of Mamur, where he received his wound.

I must remind the reader, in case he has read the history of King William's wars;—but if he has not,—I then inform him that one of the most memorable attacks in that siege, was that which was made by the English and Dutch upon the point of the advanced counter-scarp, between the gate of St. Nicholas, which enclosed the great sluice or water-stop, where the English were terribly exposed to the shot of the counter-guard and demi-bastion of St. Roch: the issue of which hot dispute, in three words, was this: That the Dutch lodged themselves upon the counter-guard—and that the English made themselves masters of the covered-way before St. Nicholas'-gate, notwithstanding the gallantry of the French officers, who exposed themselves upon the glacis sword in hand.

As this was the principal attack of which my uncle Toby was an eye-witness at Namur,——the army of the besiegers being cut off, by the confluence of the Maes and Sambre, from seeing much of each other's operations,——my uncle Toby was generally more eloquent and particular in his account of it; and the many perplexities he was in, arose out of the almost insurmountable difficulties he found in telling his story intelligibly, and giving such clear ideas of the differences and distinctions between the scarp and counter-scarp, —the glacis and covered-way,—the half-moon and ravelin, —as to make his company fully comprehend where and what he was about.

Writers themselves are too apt to confound these terms; so that you will the less wonder, if, in his endeavours to explain them, and in opposition to many misconceptions, that my uncle Toby did oft-times puzzle his visitors, and sometimes himself too.

To speak the truth, unless the company my father led upstairs were tolerably clear-headed, or my uncle Toby was in one of his explanatory moods, 'twas a difficult thing, do what he could, to keep the discourse free from obscurity.

What rendered the account of this affair the more intricate to my uncle Toby, was this,—that in the attack of the counter-scarp, before the gate of St. Nicholas, extending itself from the bank of the Maes, quite up to the great water-stop,—the ground was cut and cross-cut with such a multitude of dykes, drains, rivulets, and sluices, on all sides,—and he would get so sadly bewildered, and set fast amongst them, that frequently he could neither get backwards or forwards to save his life; and was oft-times obliged to give up the attack upon that very account only.

These perplexing rebuffs gave my uncle Toby Shandy more perturbations than you would imagine; and as my father's kindness to him was continually dragging up fresh friends and enquirers,——he had but a very uneasy task of it.

No doubt my uncle Toby had great command of himself,
—and could guard appearances, I believe, as well as most
men ;—yet, any one may imagine, that when he could not
retreat out of the ravelin without getting into the half-
moon, or get out of the covered-way without falling down
the counter-scarp, nor cross the dyke without danger of
slipping into the ditch, but that he must have fretted and
fumed inwardly.—He did so ;—and the little and hourly
vexations, which may seem trifling and of no account to
the man who has not read Hippocrates ; yet, whoever has
read Hippocrates, or Dr. James Mackenzie, and has considered well the effects which the passions and affections of
the mind have upon the digestion—(Why not of a wound
as well as of a dinner?) may easily conceive what sharp
paroxysms and exacerbations of his wound my uncle Toby
must have undergone upon that score only.

—My uncle Toby could not philosophise upon it ;—'twas
enough he felt it so :—and having sustained the pain and
sorrows of it for three months together, he was resolved,
some way or other, to extricate himself.

He was one morning lying upon his back in his bed, the
anguish and nature of the wound upon his groin suffering
him to lie in no other position, when a thought came into
his head, that if he could purchase such a thing, and have
it pasted down upon a board, as a large map of the fortification of the town and citadel of Namur, with its environs,
it might be a means of giving him ease.—I take notice of
his desire to have the environs along with the town and
citadel, for this reason,—because my uncle Toby's wound
was got in one of the traverses, about thirty toises from the
returning angle of the trench, opposite to the salient angle
of the demi-bastion of St. Roch :——so that he was pretty
confident he could stick a pin upon the identical spot of
ground where he was standing when the stone struck him.

All this succeeded to his wishes ; and not only freed him
from a world of sad explanations, but, in the end, it proved
the happy means, as you will read, of procuring my uncle
Toby his Hobby-Horse.

CHAPTER II.

THERE is nothing so foolish, when you are at the expense
of making an entertainment of this kind, as to order things
so badly, as to let your critics and gentry of refined taste
run it down : nor is there anything so likely to make them
do it, as that of leaving them out of the party, or, what is
full as offensive, of bestowing your attention upon the rest
of your guests in so particular a way, as if there was no
such thing as a critic (by occupation) at table.

——I guard against both ; for, in the first place, I have
left half-a-dozen places purposely open for them ;—and in
the next place, I pay them all court.—Gentlemen, I kiss
your hands. I protest, no company could give me half the
pleasure :—by my soul, I am glad to see you.——I beg only
you will make no strangers of yourselves, but sit down,
without any ceremony, and fall on heartily.

I said I had left six places, and I was upon the point of
carrying my complaisance so far, as to have left a seventh
open for them,—and in this very spot I stand on ; but
being told by a critic (tho' not by occupation,—but by
nature) that I had acquitted myself well enough, I shall fill
it up directly, hoping, in the meantime, that I shall be able
to make a great deal of more room next year.

——How, in the name of wonder ! could your uncle
Toby, who, it seems, was a military man, and whom you
have represented as no fool,——be at the same time such a
confused, pudding-headed, muddle-headed fellow, as——
Go look.

So, Sir Critic, I could have replied ; but I scorn it.—'Tis
language unurbane,—and only befitting the man who cannot give clear and satisfactory accounts of things, or dive
deep enough into the first causes of human ignorance and
confusion. It is, moreover, the reply valiant,—and therefore I reject it; for tho' it might have suited my uncle
Toby's character as a soldier excellently well,—and had he
not accustomed himself, in such attacks, to whistle the

Lillibullero,* as he wanted no courage, 'tis the very answer
he would have given; yet it would by no means have done
for me. You see as plain as can be, that I write as a man
of erudition;—that even my similes, my allusions, my
illustrations, my metaphors, are erudite,—and that I must
sustain my character properly, and contrast it properly too,
—else what would become of me?——Why, Sir, I should
be undone;—at the very moment that I am going here to
fill up one place against a critic,—I should have made an
opening for a couple.

——Therefore I answer thus:—

Pray, Sir, in all the reading which you have ever read,
did you ever read such a book as Locke's " Essay upon the
Human Understanding?"——Don't answer me rashly,—
because many, I know, quote the book, who have not read
it,—and many have read it who understand it not.—If
either of these is your case, as I write to instruct, I will tell
you in three words what the book is.—It is a history.—A
history! of who? what? where? when? Don't hurry yourself,——It is a history-book, Sir, (which may possibly
recommend it to the world) of what passes in a man's own
mind; and if you will say so much of the book, and no
more, believe me, you will cut no contemptible figure in a
metaphysic circle.

But this by the way.

Now if you will venture to go along with me, and look
down into the bottom of this matter, it will be found that
the cause of obscurity and confusion in the mind of a man,
is threefold.

Dull organs, dear sir, in the first place. Secondly, Slight
and transient impressions made by the objects, when the
said organs are not dull; and, Thirdly, A memory like unto
a sieve; not able to retain what it has received.—Call down
Dolly, your chamber-maid, and I will give you my cap and
bell along with it, if I make not this matter so plain that
Dolly herself should understand it as well as Malbranch.
——When Dolly has indited her epistle to Robin, and has

* See page 78 for " Lillibullero."

thrust her arm into the bottom of her pocket hanging by
her right side,—take that opportunity to recollect, that the
organs and faculties of perception can, by nothing in this
world, be so aptly typified and explained as by that one
thing which Dolly's hand is in search of.—Your organs are
not so dull that I should inform you,—'tis an inch, Sir, of
red seal-wax.

When this is melted and dropped upon the letter, if
Dolly fumbles too long for her thimble, till the wax is over-
hardened, it will not receive the mark of her thimble from
the usual impulse which was wont to imprint it. Very
well. If Dolly's wax, for want of better, is bees-wax, or of
a temper too soft,—though it may receive,—it will not
hold the impression, how hard soever Dolly thrusts against
it ; and, last of all, Supposing the wax good, and eke the
thimble, but applied thereto in careless haste, as her mistress
rings the bell ;—in any one of these three cases, the print
left by the thimble will be as unlike the prototype as a
brass-jack.

Now you must understand, that not one of these was the
true cause of the confusion in my uncle Toby's discourse ;
and it is for that very reason I enlarge upon them so long,
after the manner of great physiologists,—to show the world,
what it did *not* arise from.

What it *did* arise from, I have hinted above ; and a
fertile source of obscurity it is,—and ever will be,—and that
is, the unsteady uses of words, which have perplexed the
clearest and most exalted understandings.

It is ten to one (at Arthur's) whether you have ever read
the literary histories of past ages ;—if you have, what terrible
battles, yclept logomachies, have they occasioned, and per-
petuated with so much gall and ink-shed,—that a good-
natured man cannot read the accounts of them without
tears in his eyes.

Gentle critic ! when thou hast weighed all this, and considered within thyself how much of thy own knowledge,
discourse, and conversation has been pestered and disordered, at one time or the other, by this, and this only :—

what a pudder and racket in Councils about οὐσία and ὑπόστασις; and in the Schools of the learned about power and about spirit;—about essences, and about quintessences;—about substances, and about space;——what confusion in greater Theatres from words of little meaning, and as indeterminate a sense! when thou considerest this, thou wilt not wonder at my uncle Toby's perplexities,—thou wilt drop a tear of pity upon his scarp and his counter-scarp;—his glacis and his covered-way;—his ravelin, and his half-moon: 'twas not by ideas,—by Heavens! his life was put in jeopardy by words.

CHAPTER III.

WHEN my uncle Toby got his map of Namur to his mind, he began immediately to apply himself, and with the utmost diligence, to the study of it; for nothing being of more importance to him than his recovery, and his recovery depending, as you have read, upon the passions and affections of his mind, it behoved him to take the nicest care to make himself so far master of his subject, as to be able to talk upon it without emotion.

In a fortnight's close and painful application, which, by the bye, did my Uncle Toby's wound upon his groin no good,—he was enabled, by the help of some marginal documents at the feet of the elephant, together with Gobesius's military architecture and pyroballogy, translated from the Flemish, to form his discourse with passable perspicuity; and before he was two full months gone,—he was right eloquent upon it, and could make not only the attack of the advanced counter-scarp with great order;——but having by that time gone much deeper into the art than what his first motive made necessary, my uncle Toby was able to cross the Maes and Sambre; make diversions as far as Vauban's line, the abbey of Salsines, &c.; and give his visitors as distinct a history of each of their attacks as of

that of the gate of St. Nicholas, where he had the honour
to receive his wound.

But desire of knowledge, like the thirst of richness, increases
ever with the acquisition of it.   The more my uncle Toby
pored over his map, the more he took a liking to it !—by
the same process and electrical assimilation, as I told you,
through which, I ween, the souls of connoisseurs themselves,
by long friction and incumbition, have the happiness, at
length, to get all be-virtued,—be-pictured,—be-butterflied,
and be-fiddled.

The more my uncle Toby drank of this sweet fountain of
science, the greater was the heat and impatience of his
thirst ; so that before the first year of his confinement had
well gone round, there was scarce a fortified town in Italy
or Flanders, of which, by one means or other, he had not
procured a plan, reading over as he got them, and carefully
collating therewith the histories of their sieges, their demoli-
tions, their improvements, and new works ; all which he
would read with that intense application and delight, that
he would forget himself, his wound, his confinement, his
dinner.

In the second year, my uncle Toby purchased " Ramelli "
and " Cataneo," translated from the Italian :—likewise
" Stevinus," " Moralis," the " Chevalier de Ville," " Lorini,"
" Coehorn," " Sheeter," the " Count de Pagon," the " Mar-
shal Vauban," " Mons. Blondel," with almost as many more
books of military architecture as Don Quixote was found
to have of chivalry, when the curate and barber invaded his
library. ¡

Towards the beginning of the third year, which was in
August, ninety-nine, my uncle Toby found it necessary to
understand a little of projectiles :—and having judged it
best to draw his knowledge from the fountain-head, he
began with N. Tartaglia, who it seems was the first man
who detected the imposition of a cannon-ball's doing all
that mischief under the notion of a right line.—This, N.
Tartaglia proved, to my uncle Toby, to be an impossible
thing.

——Endless is the search of truth.

No sooner was my uncle Toby satisfied which road the cannon-ball *did not* go, but he was insensibly led on, and resolved in his mind to inquire and find out which road the ball *did* go: for which purpose he was obliged to set off afresh with old Maltus, and studied him devoutly.—He proceeded next to Galileo and Torricellius, wherein, by certain geometrical rules, infallibly laid down, he found the precise path to be a Parabola,—or else an Hyperbola,—and that the parameter, or *latus rectum*, of the conic section of the said path, was to the quantity and amplitude in a direct *ratio*, as the whole line to the sine of double the angle of incidence, formed by the breech upon an horizontal plane;—and that the semiparameter,——Stop! my dear uncle Toby,——stop!—go not one foot farther into this thorny and bewildered track :—intricate are the steps! intricate are the mazes of this labyrinth! intricate are the troubles which the pursuit of this bewitching phantom Knowledge will bring upon thee!—O, my uncle, fly—fly—fly from it, as from a serpent!——Is it fit, good-natured man! thou should'st sit up, with the wound upon thy groin, whole nights, baking thy blood with hectic watchings?——Alas! 'twill exasperate thy symptoms—check thy perspirations—evaporate thy spirits—waste thy animal strength—dry up thy radical moisture—bring thee into a costive habit of body—impair thy health—and hasten all the infirmities of thy old age.——O my uncle! my uncle Toby!

MY UNCLE TOBY'S WHISTLE.

LILLIBULLERO.

The Ballad* to this tune was written in the year 1686, on account of King James II. nominating to the Lieutenancy of Ireland, General Talbot, newly created Earl of Tyrconnel, a furious Papist, who had recommended himself to his bigoted master by his arbitrary treatment of the Protestants in the preceding year, when only Lieutenant-General; and whose subsequent conduct fully justified his expectations and their fears.

This foolish Ballad, treating the Papists, and chiefly the Irish, in a very ridiculous manner, had a burden, said to be Irish words, " Lero, lero, lillibullero; " and made an impression on the (King's) army, more powerful than either the Philippics of Demosthenes or Cicero. The whole army, and at last the people, both in city and country, were singing it perpetually. Perhaps never had so slight a thing so great an effect, for it contributed not a little towards the Revolution in 1688.†

LILLIBULLERO, and BULLEN-A-LAH, are said to have been the watch-words used among the Irish papists, in their massacre of the Protestants, in 1641.

* See Percy's "Reliques of Ancient English Poetry," vol. ii. p. 358.
† See Bishop Burnet's "History of his own Times ;" and King's "State of the Protestants in Ireland," 1691. 4to.

LILLIBULLERO.

CHAPTER IV.

I WOULD not give a groat for that man's knowledge in pen-craft, who does not understand this :——That the best plain narrative in the world, tacked very close to the last spirited apostrophe to my uncle Toby,——would have felt both cold and vapid upon the reader's palate ;—therefore I forthwith put an end to the chapter, though I was in the middle of my story.

——Writers of my stamp have one principle in common with painters. Where an exact copying makes our picture less striking, we choose the less evil ; deeming it even more pardonable to trespass against truth than beauty. This is to be understood *cum grano salis :* but be it as it will,——as the parallel is made more for the sake of letting the apostrophe cool, than anything else,—'tis not very material whether, upon any other score, the reader approves of it or not.

In the latter end of the third year, my uncle Toby perceiving that the parameter and semiparameter of the conic section angered his wound, he left off the study of projectiles in a kind of a huff, and betook himself to the practical part of fortification only ; the pleasure of which, like a spring held back, returned upon him with redoubled force.

It was in this year that my uncle began to break in upon the daily regularity of a clean shirt,——to dismiss his barber unshaven,——and to allow his surgeon scarce time sufficient to dress his wound, concerning himself so little about it, as not to ask him once in seven times dressing, how it went on : when, lo !—all of a sudden, for the change was as quick as lightning, he began to sigh heavily for his recovery,—— complained to my father, grew impatient with the surgeon : ——and one morning, as he heard his foot coming upstairs, he shut up his books, and thrust aside his instruments, in order to expostulate with him upon the protraction of the cure, which, he told him, might surely have been accomplished at least by that time :—He dwelt long upon the miseries he had undergone, and the sorrows of his four years' melancholy imprisonment;——adding, that had it not been for the kind looks and fraternal cheerings of the best of brothers, —he had long since sunk under his misfortunes.——My father was by. My uncle Toby's eloquence brought tears into his eyes;——'twas unexpected:——My uncle Toby, by nature, was not eloquent;—it had the greater effect:——The surgeon was confounded;—not that there wanted grounds for such, or greater marks of impatience,—but 'twas unexpected too. In the four years he had attended him, he had never seen anything like it in my uncle Toby's carriage; he had never once dropped one fretful or discontented word;——he had been all patience,—all submission.

——We lose the right of complaining, sometimes, by forbearing it;—but we often treble the force:—The surgeon was astonished; but much more so, when he heard my uncle Toby go on, and peremptorily insist upon his healing up the wound directly,—or sending for Monsieur Ronjat, the king's serjeant-surgeon, to do it for him.

The desire of life and health is implanted in man's nature; ——the love of liberty and enlargement is a sister-passion to it: These my uncle Toby had in common with his species ——and either of them had been sufficient to account for his earnest desire to get well, and out of doors;——but I have told you before, that nothing wrought with our family after the common way;——and from the time and manner in which this eager desire shewed itself in the present case, the penetrating reader will suspect there was some other cause or crotchet for it in my uncle Toby's head:——There was so, and 'tis the subject of the next chapter to set forth what that cause and crotchet was. I own, when that's done, 'twill be time to return back to the parlour fireside, where we left my uncle in the middle of his sentence.

———

CHAPTER V.

WHEN a man gives himself up to the government of a ruling passion,—or, in other words, when his HOBBY-HORSE grows headstrong,—— farewell cool reason and fair discretion!

My uncle Toby's wound was near well! and as soon as the surgeon recovered his surprise, and could get leave to say as much——he told him, 'twas just beginning to incarnate; and that if no fresh exfoliation happened,—which there was no sign of, it would be dried up in five or six weeks. The sound of as many Olympiads, twelve hours before, would have conveyed an idea of shorter duration to my uncle Toby's mind.——The succession of his ideas was now rapid,—he broiled with impatience to put his design in execution ;——and so, without consulting farther with any soul living,—which, by the bye, I think is right, when you are predetermined to take no one soul's advice,——he privately ordered Trim, his man, to pack up a bundle of lint and dressings, and hire a chariot-and-four to be at the door exactly by twelve o'clock .that day, when he knew my father would be upon 'Change.——So leaving a bank-note upon the table for the surgeon's care of him, and a letter of tender thanks for his brother's—he packed up his maps, his books of fortification, his instruments, &c., and, by the help of a crutch on one side, and Trim on the other,——my uncle Toby embarked for Shandy-Hall.

The reason, or rather the rise of this sudden emigration, was as follows :

The table in my uncle Toby's room, and at which, the night before this change happened, he was sitting with his maps, &c., about him—being somewhat of the smallest, for that infinity of great and small instruments of knowledge which usually lay crowded upon it—he had the accident, in reaching over for his tobacco-box, to throw down his compasses ; and in stooping to take the compasses up, with his sleeve he threw down his case of instruments and snuffers ; and as the dice took a run against him, in his endeavouring to catch the snuffers in falling,——he thrust Monsieur Blondel off the table, and Count de Pagon o'top of him.

'Twas to no purpose for a man, lame as my uncle Toby was, to think of redressing these evils by himself,—he rung his bell for his man Trim;——Trim, quoth my uncle Toby, prithee see what confusion I have here been making—I must have some better contrivance, Trim.——Canst not thou take my rule, and measure the length and breadth of this table, and then go and bespeak me one as big again?——Yes, an' please your honour, replied Trim, making a bow; but I hope your Honour will be soon well enough to get down to your country-seat, where—as your Honour takes so much pleasure in fortification—we could manage this matter to a T.

I must here inform you, that this servant of my uncle Toby's, who went by the name of Trim, had been a corporal in my uncle's own company;—his real name was James Butler,—but having got the nickname of Trim, in the regiment, my uncle Toby, unless when he happened to be very angry with him, would never call him by any other name.

The poor fellow had been disabled for the service, by a wound on his left knee by a musket-bullet, at the battle of Landen, which was two years before the affair of Namur;—and as the fellow was well-beloved in the regiment, and a handy fellow into the bargain, my uncle Toby took him for his servant; and of an excellent use was he, attending my uncle Toby, in the camp and in his quarters, as a valet, groom, barber, cook, sempster, and nurse; and indeed, from first to last, waited upon him and served him with great fidelity and affection.

My uncle Toby loved the man in return; and what attached him more to him still, was the similitude of their knowledge.——For Corporal Trim (for so, for the future, I shall call him) by four years' occasional attention to his Master's discourse upon fortified towns, and the advantage of prying and peeping continually into his Master's plans, &c., exclusive and besides what he gained HOBBY-HORSI-

CALLY, as a body-servant, *Non Hobby Horsical per se ;*——
had become no mean proficient in the science; and was
thought, by the cook and chamber-maid, to know as much
of the nature of strongholds as my uncle Toby himself.

I have but one more stroke to give, to finish Corporal
Trim's character,——and it is the only dark line in it.—The
fellow loved to advise, or rather, to hear himself talk ; his
carriage, however, was so perfectly respectful, 'twas easy to
keep him silent when you had him so ; but set his tongue
a-going,—you had no hold of him—he was voluble ;—the
eternal interlardings of *your Honour*, with the respectfulness
of Corporal Trim's manner, interceding so strong in behalf
of his elocution,—that though you might have been incom-
moded,——you could not well be angry. My uncle Toby
was seldom either the one or the other with him,—or, at
least, this fault, in Trim, broke no squares with them. My
uncle Toby, as I said, loved the man ;——and besides, as
he ever looked upon a faithful servant,—as an humble friend,
—he could not bear to stop his mouth.——Such was Corporal Trim.

If I durst presume, continued Trim, to give your Honour
my advice, and speak my opinion in this matter.—Thou art
welcome, Trim, quoth my uncle Toby——speak,——speak
what thou thinkest upon the subject, man, without fear.—
Why then, replied Trim (not hanging his ears and scratching his head like a country-lout, but) stroking his hair back
from his forehead, and standing erect as before his division,
—I think, quoth Trim, advancing his left, which was his
lame leg, a little forwards,—and pointing with his right
hand open towards a map of Dunkirk, which was pinned
against the hangings,——I think, quoth Corporal Trim,
with humble submission to your Honour's better judgment,
——that these ravelins, bastions, curtains, and hornworks
make but a poor, contemptible, fiddle-faddle piece of work
of it here upon paper, compared to what your Honour and
I could make of it, were we in the country by ourselves, and
had but a rood, or a rood and a half of ground to do what
we pleased with. As summer is coming on, continued

Trim, your Honour might sit out of doors, and give me the nography—(Call it ichnography, quoth my uncle)——of the town or citadel your Honour was pleased to sit down before, and I will be shot by your Honour upon the glacis of it, if I did not fortify it to your Honour's mind.——I dare say thou would'st, Trim, quoth my uncle.—For if your Honour, continued the corporal, could but mark me the polygon, with its exact lines and angles—That I could do very well, quoth my uncle.—I would begin with the fossé; and if your Honour could tell me the proper depth and breadth—I can to a hair's breadth, Trim, replied my uncle—I would throw out the earth upon this hand towards the town for the scarp,—and on that hand towards the campaign for the counter-scarp—(Very right, Trim, quoth my uncle Toby)——And when I had sloped them to your mind, ——an' please your Honour, I would face the glacis, as the finest fortifications are done in Flanders, with sods—(and as your Honour knows they should be)—and I would make the walls and parapets with sods too.——The best engineers call them Gazons, Trim, said my uncle Toby.——Whether they are gazons or sods, is not much matter, replied Trim; your Honour knows they are ten times beyond a facing either of brick or stone.——I know, they are, Trim, in some respects,——quoth my uncle Toby, nodding his head;—for a cannon-ball enters into the gazon right onwards, without bringing any rubbish down with it, which might fill the fossé (as was the case at St. Nicholas's gate), and facilitate the passage over it.

Your Honour understands these matters, replied Corporal Trim, better than any officer in his Majesty's service;—— but would your Honour please to let the bespeaking of the table alone, and let us but go into the country, I would work, under your Honour's directions, like a horse, and make fortifications for you something like a tansy, with all their batteries, saps, ditches, and palisadoes, that it should be worth all the world's riding twenty miles to go and see it.

My uncle Toby blushed as red as scarlet, as Trim went

on;—but it was not a blush of guilt,—of modesty, or of
anger;—it was a blush of joy;—he was fired with Corporal
Trim's project and description.——Trim! said my uncle
Toby, thou hast said enough.——We might begin the campaign, continued Trim, on the very day that his Majesty
and the Allies take the field, and demolish them town by
town, as fast as—(Trim, quoth my uncle Toby, say no
more!) Your Honour, continued Trim, might sit in your
arm-chair (pointing to it) this fine weather, giving me your
orders, and I would——(Say no more, Trim! quoth my
uncle Toby)——Besides, your Honour would get not only
pleasure and good pastime,—but good air, and good exercise,
and good health,—and your Honour's wound would be well
in a month. Thou hast said enough, Trim,—quoth my
uncle Toby (putting his hand into his breeches-pocket)—I
like thy project mightily.—And if your Honour pleases, I'll
this moment go and buy a pioneer's spade, to take down
with us; and I'll bespeak a shovel and a pick-axe, and a
couple of——Say no more, Trim, quoth my uncle Toby,
leaping up upon one leg, quite overcome with rapture,—and
thrusting a guinea into Trim's hand—Trim, said my uncle
Toby, say no more;—but go down, Trim, this moment, my
lad, and bring up my supper this instant.

Trim ran down and brought up his master's supper,——to
no purpose:—Trim's plan of operation ran so in my uncle
Toby's head, he could not taste it.—Trim, quoth my uncle
Toby, get me to bed.—'Twas all one. Corporal Trim's
description had fired his imagination,—my uncle Toby could
not shut his eyes.—The more he considered it, the more
bewitching the scene appeared to him;—so that, two full
hours before daylight, he had come to a final determination,
and had concerted the whole plan of his and Corporal
Trim's decampment.

My uncle Toby had a little neat country-house of his own,
in the village where my father's estate lay at Shandy, which
had been left him by an old uncle, with a small estate of
about one hundred pounds a-year. Behind this house, and
contiguous to it, was a kitchen-garden of about half an

acre; and at the bottom of the garden, and cut off from it by a tall yew hedge, was a bowling-green, containing just about as much ground as Corporal Trim wished for;—so that as Trim uttered the words, "A rood and a half of ground, to do what they would with,"—this identical bowling-green instantly presented itself and became curiously painted, all at once, upon the retina of my uncle Toby's fancy;—which was the physical cause of making him change colour, or at least of heightening his blush, to that immoderate degree I spoke of.

Never did lover post down to a beloved mistress with more heat and expectation than my uncle Toby did, to enjoy this selfsame thing in private;—I say in private;—for it was sheltered from the house, as I told you, by a tall yew hedge, and was covered on the other three sides, from mortal sight, by rough holly and thick-set flowering shrubs; so that the idea of not being seen, did not a little contribute to the idea of pleasure preconceived in my uncle Toby's mind.—Vain thought! however thick it was planted about,—or private soever it might seem,—to think, dear uncle Toby, of enjoying a thing which took up a whole rood and a half of ground,——and not have it known!

How my uncle Toby and Corporal Trim managed this matter,——with the history of their campaigns, which were no way barren of events,——may make no uninteresting under-plot in the epitasis and working-up of this drama.—At present, the scene must drop,—and change for the parlour fire-side.

———

CHAPTER VI.

——What can they be doing, brother? said my father.—I think, replied my uncle Toby,—taking, as I told you, his pipe from his mouth, and striking the ashes out of it as he began his sentence;——I think, replied he,—it would not be amiss, brother, if we rung the bell.

'Pray, what's all that racket over our heads, Obadiah?
——quoth my father:——my brother and I can scarce hear
ourselves speak.

Sir, answered Obadiah, making a bow towards his left
shoulder,—my Mistress is taken very badly.—And where's
Susannah running down the garden there, as if they were
going to ravish her?——Sir, she is running the shortest cut
into the town, replied Obadiah, to fetch the old midwife.—
Then saddle a horse, quoth my father, and do you go
directly for Dr. Slop, the man-midwife, with all our services,
——and let him know your mistresss is fallen into labour,
——and that I desire he will return with you with all speed.

It is very strange, says my father, addressing himself to
my uncle Toby, as Obadiah shut the door,——as there is
so expert an operator as Dr. Slop so near,—that my
wife should persist to the very last in this obstinate humour
of hers, in trusting the life of my child, who has had one
misfortune already, to the ignorance of an old woman;——
and not only the life of my child, brother,——but her own
life, and with it the lives of all the children I might, peradventure, have begot out of her hereafter.

Mayhap, brother, replied my uncle Toby, my sister does
it to save the expense:—A pudding's end,—replied my
father,——the Doctor must be paid the same for inaction as
action,—if not better,—to keep him in temper.

——Then it can be out of nothing in the whole world,
quoth my uncle Toby, in the simplicity of his heart,—but
Modesty.—My sister, I dare say, added he, does not care to
let a man come so near her ——. I will not say whether
my uncle Toby had completed the sentence or not;—'tis
for his advantage to suppose he had,——as, I think he could
have added no ONE WORD which would have improved it.

If, on the contrary, my uncle Toby had not fully arrived
at the period's end—then the world stands indebted to the
sudden snapping of my father's tobacco-pipe for one of the
neatest examples of that ornamental figure in oratory, which
Rhetoricians style the *Aposiopesis*.——Just Heaven! how
does the *Poco piu* and the *Poco meno* of the Italian artists;

—the insensible MORE or LESS, determine the precise line of
beauty in the sentence, as well as in the statue! How do
the slight touches of the chisel, the pencil, the pen, the
fiddle-stick, *et cætera*, give the true swell,—which gives the
true pleasure!—O my countrymen!—be nice; be cautious
of your language;—and never, O! never let it be forgotten
upon what small particles your eloquence and your fame
depend.

——"My sister, mayhap," quoth my uncle Toby, "does
not choose to let a man come so near her ——" Make this
dash, 'tis an Aposiopesis;—Take the dash away, and write
Backside,——'tis bawdy.—Scratch Backside out, and put
Cover'd-way in, 'tis a Metaphor;—and, I dare say, as fortification ran so much in my uncle Toby's head, that if he
had been left to have added one word to the sentence,——
that word was it.

But whether that was the case, or not the case;—or
whether the snapping of my father's tobacco-pipe, so
critically, happened through accident or anger, will be seen
in due time.

CHAPTER VII.

Tho' my father was a good natural philosopher,—yet he
was something of a moral philosopher too; for which reason,
when his tobacco-pipe snapp'd short in the middle,—he had
nothing to do, as such, but to have taken hold of the two
pieces, and thrown them gently upon the back of the fire.
——He did no such thing;——he threw them with all the
violence in the world;—and to give the action still more
emphasis,—he started upon both legs to do it.

This looked something like heat;—and the manner of
his reply to what my uncle Toby was saying, proved it was
so.

—"Not choose," quoth my father, (repeating my uncle
Toby's words) "to let a man come so near her ——!" By
Heaven, brother Toby! you would try the patience of

Job ;—and I think I have the plagues of one already without
it. ——Why ? ——Where ? ——Wherein ? ——Wherefore ?
——Upon what account ? replied my uncle Toby, in the
utmost astonishment.—To think, said my father, of a man
living to your age, brother, and knowing so little about
women !——I know nothing at all about them,—replied my
uncle Toby :   And I think, continued he, that the shock
I received the year after the demolition of Dunkirk, in my
affair with Widow Wadman ; which shock you know I
should not have received, but from my total ignorance of
the sex,—has given me just cause to say, That I neither
know, nor do pretend to know, anything about 'em, or their
concerns either.—Methinks, brother, replied my father, you
might, at least, know so much as the right end of a woman
from the wrong.

It is said in Aristotle's Master-Piece, " That when a man
doth think of anything which is past,——he looketh down
upon the ground ;——but that when he thinketh of something that is to come, he looketh up towards the heavens."

My uncle Toby, I suppose, thought of neither, for he
look'd horizontally.—Right end ! quoth my uncle Toby,
muttering the two words low to himself, and fixing his two
eyes insensibly, as he muttered them, upon a small crevice,
formed by a bad joint in the chimney-piece——Right end
of a woman ?——I declare, quoth my uncle, I know no
more which it is than the man in the moon ;——and if I
was to think, continued my uncle Toby (keeping his eyes
still fixed upon the bad joint), this month together, I am
sure I should not be able to find it out.

Then, brother Toby, replied my father, I will tell you.

Everything in this world, continued my father (filling a
fresh pipe)—everything in this world, my dear brother
Toby, has two handles.——Not always, quoth my uncle
Toby.——At least, replied my father, every one has two
hands,——which comes to the same thing.——Now, if a
man was to sit down coolly, and consider within himself
the make, the shape, the construction, come-at-ability, and
convenience of all the parts which constitute the whole of

that animal, called Woman, and compare them analogically
——I never understood rightly the meaning of that word,
—quoth my uncle Toby.—

ANALOGY, replied my father, is the certain relation and
agreement which different——Here, a devil of a rap at the
door snapped my father's definition (like his tobacco-pipe)
in two,—and, at the same time, crushed the head of as
notable and curious a dissertation as ever was engendered
in the womb of speculation ;—it was some months before
my father could get an opportunity to be safely delivered of
it :—And, at this hour, it is a thing full as problematical as
the subject of the dissertation itself—(considering the confusion and distresses of our domestic misadventures, which
are now coming thick one upon the back of another)
whether I shall be able to find a place for it in the third
volume or not.

CHAPTER VIII.

IT is about an hour and a half's tolerable good reading
since my uncle Toby rung the bell, when Obadiah was
ordered to saddle a horse, and go for Dr. Slop, the man-
midwife ;—so that no one can say, with reason, that I have
not allowed Obadiah time enough, poetically speaking, and
considering the emergency too, both to go and come ;——
though, morally and truly speaking, the man perhaps has
scarce had time to get on his boots.

If the hypercritic will go upon this ; and is resolved after
all, to take a pendulum, and measure the true distance betwixt the ringing of the bell, and the rap at the door ;—and
after finding it to be no more than two minutes, thirteen
seconds, and three-fifths,—should take upon him to insult
over me for such a breach in the unity, or rather probability
of time ;—I would remind him, that the idea of duration,
and of its simple modes, is got merely from the train and succession of our ideas——and is the true scholastic pendulum,
and by which, as a scholar, I will be tried in this matter,—

abjuring and detesting the jurisdiction of all other pendu-
lums whatever.

I would therefore desire him to consider that it is but
poor eight miles from Shandy-Hall to Dr. Slop, the man-
midwife's house:—and that whilst Obadiah has been going
those said miles and back, I have brought my uncle Toby
from Namur, quite across all Flanders, into England :—
That I have had him ill upon my hands near four years ;—
and have since travelled him and Corporal Trim, in a
chariot-and-four, a journey of near two hundred miles down
into Yorkshire ;——all which, put together, must have
prepared the reader's imagination for the entrance of Dr.
Slop upon the stage,—as much, at least (I hope) as a dance,
a song, or a concerto between the acts.

If my hypercritic is intractable, alleging, that two
minutes and thirteen seconds are no more than two
minutes and thirteen seconds, when I have said all I can
about them ; and that this plea, though it might save me
dramatically, will damn me biographically, rendering my
book from this very moment a professed Romance, which
before, was a book apocryphal :——If I am thus pressed—
I then put an end to the whole objection and controversy
about it all at once,—by acquainting him, that Obadiah
had not got above threescore yards from the stable-yard
before he met with Dr. Slop ;—and indeed he gave a dirty
proof that he had met with him, and was within an ace
giving a tragical one too.

Imagine to yourself——But this had better begin a new
chapter.

––––––

CHAPTER IX.

IMAGINE to yourself a little squat, uncourtly figure of a
Dr. Slop, of about four feet and a half perpendicular height,
with a breadth of back, and a sesquipedality of belly, which
might have done honour to a sergeant in the horse-guards.

Such were the outlines of Doctor Slop's figure, which—

if you have read *Hogarth's* analysis of beauty, and if you
have not, I wish you would;——you must know, may as
certainly be caricatured, and conveyed to the mind by three
strokes as three hundred.

Imagine such a one,——for such, I say, were the outlines
of Dr. Slop's figure, coming slowly along, foot by foot,
waddling through the dirt upon the *vertebræ* of a little
diminutive pony, of a pretty colour——but of strength——
alack !——scarce able to have made an amble of it, under
such a fardel, had the roads been in an ambling condition.——They were not.——Imagine to yourself, Obadiah
mounted upon a strong monster of a coach-horse, pricked
into a full gallop, and making all practicable speed the
adverse way.

Pray, Sir, let me interest you a moment in this description.

Had Dr. Slop beheld Obadiah a mile off, posting in a
narrow lane directly towards him, at that monstrous rate,—
splashing and plunging like a devil thro' thick and thin, as
he approached, would not such a phenomenon, with such a
vortex of mud and water moving along with it, round its
axis,—have been a subject of juster apprehension to Dr.
Slop in his situation, than the *worst* of Whiston's comets?
—To say nothing of the Nucleus; that is, of Obadiah and
the coach-horse.—In my idea, the vortex alone of 'em was
enough to have involved and carried, if not the doctor, at
least the doctor's pony, quite away with it. What then do
you think must the terror and hydrophobia of Dr. Slop
have been, when you read (which you are just going to do)
that he was advancing thus warily along towards Shandy-
Hall, and had approached to within sixty yards of it, and
within five yards of a sudden turn, made by an acute angle
of the garden-wall,—and in the dirtiest part of a dirty lane,
—when Obadiah and his coach-horse turned the corner,
rapid, furious,—pop,—full upon him !—Nothing, I think,
in nature, can be supposed more terrible than such a ren-
counter,—so imprompt ! so ill prepared to stand the shock
of it as Dr. Slop was.

What could Dr. Slop do?—— he crossed himself ✠—

Pugh!—but the doctor, Sir, was a Papist.—No matter; he had better have kept hold of the pommel.—He had so;—nay, as it happened, he had better have done nothing at all; for in crossing himself he let go his whip,——and in attempting to save his whip betwixt his knee and his saddle's skirt, as it slipped, he lost his stirrup,——in losing which he lost his seat;——and in the multitude of all these losses (which, by the bye, shews what little advantage there is in crossing) the unfortunate doctor lost his presence of mind. So that without waiting for Obadiah's onset, he left his pony to its destiny, tumbling off it diagonally, something in the style and manner of a pack of wool, and without any other consequence from the fall, save that of being left (as it would have been) with the broadest part of him sunk about twelve inches deep in the mire.

Obadiah pull'd off his cap twice to Dr. Slop;—once as he was falling,—and then again when he saw him seated.——Ill-timed complaisance;—had not the fellow better have stopped his horse, and got off and help'd him?—Sir, he did all that his situation would allow;—but the *momentum* of the coach-horse was so great, that Obadiah could not do it all at once; he rode in a circle three times round Dr. Slop, before he could fully accomplish it any how;—and at the last, when he did stop his beast, 'twas done with such an explosion of mud, that Obadiah had better have been a league off. In short, never was a Dr. Slop so beluted, and so transubstantiated, since that affair came into fashion.

CHAPTER X.

WHEN Dr. Slop entered the back parlour, where my father and my uncle Toby were discoursing upon the nature of women,——it was hard to determine whether Dr. Slop's figure, or Dr. Slop's presence, occasioned more surprise to them; for as the accident happened so near the house, as not to make it worth while for Obadiah to remount him,

——Obadiah had led him in as he was, *unwiped, un-appointed, unannealed,* with all his stains and blotches on him.—He stood like *Hamlet's* ghost, motionless, and speechless, for a full minute and a half at the parlour-door (Obadiah still holding his hand) with all the majesty of mud :—his hinder parts, upon which he had received his fall, totally besmeared ;——and in every other part of him, blotched over in such a manner with Obadiah's explosion, that you would have sworn (without mental reservation) that every grain of it had taken effect.

Here was a fair opportunity for my uncle Toby to have triumphed over my father, in his turn ;—for no mortal, who had beheld Dr. Slop in that pickle, could have dissented from so much, at least, of my uncle Toby's opinion, " That mayhap his sister might not care to let such a Dr. Slop come so near her ——." But it was the *argumentum ad hominem ;* and if my uncle Toby was not very expert at it, you may think he might not care to use it.——No ; the reason was, 'twas not his nature to insult.

Dr. Slop's presence at that time was no less problematical than the mode of it ; tho' it is certain, one moment's reflection in my father might have solved it ; for he had apprised Dr. Slop but the week before, that my mother was at her full reckoning ; and as the doctor had heard nothing since, 'twas natural and very political too in him, to have taken a ride to Shandy-Hall, as he did, merely to see how matters went on.

But my father's mind took, unfortunately, a wrong turn in the investigation ; running like the hypercritic's, altogether upon the ringing of the bell and the rap upon the door, —measuring their distance, and keeping his mind so intent upon the operation, as to have power to think nothing else ——common-place infirmity of the greatest of mathematicians ! working with might and main at the demonstration, and so wasting all their strength upon it, that they have none left in them to draw the corollary to do good with.

The ringing of the bell and the rap upon the door struck likewise strong upon the *sensorium* of my uncle Toby,— but it excited a very different train of thoughts ;—the two irreconcileable pulsations instantly brought Stevinus, the great engineer, along with them, into my uncle Toby's mind. What business Stevinus had in this affair, is the greatest problem of all:——It shall be solved ;—but not in the next chapter.

CHAPTER XI.

WRITING, when properly managed (as you may be sure I think mine is), is but a different name for conversation. As no one, who knows what he is about in good company, would venture to talk all;——so no author, who understands the just boundaries of decorum and good-breeding, would presume to think all ! the truest respect which you can pay to the reader's understanding, is to halve this matter amicably, and leave him something to imagine, in his turn, as well as yourself.

For my own part, I am eternally paying him compliments of this kind, and do all that lies in my power to keep his imagination as busy as my own.

'Tis his turn now ;—I have given an ample description of Dr. Slop's sad overthrow, and of his sad appearance in the back-parlour ;—his imagination must now go on with it for a while.

Let the reader imagine then, that Dr. Slop has told his tale—and in what words, and with what aggravations, his fancy chooses ; let him suppose, that Obadiah had told his tale also, and with such rueful looks of affected concern, as he thinks best will contrast the two figures as they stand by each other.——Let him imagine, that my father had stepped upstairs to see my mother :—and to conclude this work of imagination, let him imagine the doctor washed,—rubbed down and condoled,—felicitated, got into a pair of Obadiah's pumps, stepping forward towards the door, upon the very point of entering upon action.

Truce !—truce, good Dr. Slop !—stay thy obstetric hand ; ——return it safe into thy bosom, to keep it warm ;——

little dost thou know what obstacles,——little dost thou think what hidden causes retard its operation!——Hast thou, Dr. Slop, hast thou been intrusted with the secret articles of the solemn treaty which has brought thee into this place?—Art thou aware that, at this instant, a daughter of Lucina is put obstetrically over thy head?—Alas! 'tis too true.—Besides, great son of Pilumnus! what canst thou do?—Thou hast come forth unarm'd;—thou hast left thy *tire-tête*—thy new-invented *forceps*,—thy *crotchet*,—thy *squirt*, and all thy instruments of salvation and deliverance, behind thee:—By Heaven! at this moment they are hanging up in a green baize bag, betwixt thy two pistols, at the bed's head!—Ring;—call;—send Obadiah back upon the coach-horse, to bring them with all speed.

——Make great haste, Obadiah, quoth my father, and I'll give thee a crown! and quoth my uncle Toby, I'll give him another!

CHAPTER XII.

You sudden and unexpected arrival, quoth my uncle Toby, addressing himself to Dr. Slop (all three of them sitting down to the fire together, as my uncle Toby began to speak)—instantly brought the great Stevinus into my head, who, you must know, is a favourite author with me.—Then, added my father, making use of the argument *ad crumenam,* —I will lay twenty guineas to a single crown-piece (which will serve to give away to Obadiah when he gets back) that this same Stevinus was some engineer or other,—or has wrote something or other, either directly or indirectly, upon the science of fortification.

He has so,—replied my uncle Toby.—I knew it, said my father; though, for the soul of me, I cannot see what kind of connection there can be betwixt Dr. Slop's sudden coming, and a discourse upon fortification;—yet I fear'd it.—Talk of what we will, brother,——or let the occasion be never so foreign or unfit for the subject,—you are sure to bring it in.

I would not, brother Toby, continued my father,——I
declare I would not have my head so full of curtains and
horn-works.—That I dare say you would not! quoth Dr.
Slop, interrupting him, and laughing most immoderately at
his pun.

Dennis the critic could not detest and abhor a pun, or
the insinuation of a pun, more cordially than my father;—
he would grow testy upon it at any time;—but to be broke
in upon by one, in a serious discourse, was as bad, he would
say, as a fillip upon the nose;——he saw no difference.

Sir, quoth my uncle Toby, addressing himself to Dr.
Slop,—the curtains my brother Shandy mentions here, have
nothing to do with bedsteads;—tho' I know Du Cange says,
"That bed-curtains, in all probability, have taken their
name from them;"—nor have the horn-works he speaks of
anything in the world to do with the horn-works of cuckol-
dom: But the *curtain*, Sir, is the word we use in fortification
for that part of the wall or rampart which lies between the
two bastions, and joins them.—Besiegers seldom offer to
carry on their attacks directly against the curtain, for this
reason because they are so well *flanked*. ('Tis the case of
other curtains, quoth Dr. Slop, laughing.) However, continued my uncle Toby, to make them sure, we generally
choose to place ravelins before them, taking care only to
extend them beyond the fossé or ditch:——The common
men, who know very little of fortification, confound the
ravelin and the half-moon together,—tho' they are very
different things;—not in their figure or construction, for we
make them exactly alike, in all points; for they always
consist of two faces, making a salient angle, with the gorges,
not straight, but in form of a crescent.——Where then lies
the difference? (quoth my father, a little testily.)—In their
situations, answered my uncle Toby:—for when a ravelin,
brother, stands before the curtain, it is a ravelin; and when
a ravelin stands before a bastion, then the ravelin is not a
ravelin;—it is a half-moon;—a half-moon likewise is a half-
moon, and no more, so long as it stands before its bastion;
—but was it to change place, and get before the curtain,—

'twould be no longer a half-moon; a half-moon, in that case, is not a half-moon;—'tis no more than a ravelin.——I think, quoth my father, that the noble science of defence has its weak sides as well as others.

—As for the horn-work (heigh! ho! sighed my father) which, continued my uncle Toby, my brother was speaking of, they are a very considerable part of an outwork;——they are called by the French engineers, *Ouvrage à corne*, and we generally make them to cover such places as we suspect to be weaker than the rest;——'tis formed by two epaulments or demi-bastions—they are very pretty,——and if you will take a walk, I'll engage to show you one well worth your trouble.——I own, continued my uncle Toby, when we crown them, they are much stronger, but then they are very expensive, and take up a great deal of ground, so that, in my opinion, they are most of use to cover or defend the head of a camp; otherwise the double *tenaille*——By the mother who bore us!——brother Toby, quoth my father, not able to hold out any longer,——you would provoke a saint;——here have you got us, I know not how, not only souse into the middle of the old subject again, but so full is your head of these confounded works, that though my wife is this moment in the pains of labour, and you hear her cry out, yet nothing will serve you but to carry off the man-mid-wife.——*Accoucheur*,—if you please, quoth Dr. Slop.—— With all my heart! replied my father; I don't care what they call you;—but I wish the whole science of fortification, with all its inventors, at the devil;—it has been the death of thousands,—and it will be mine in the end.—I would not, I would not, brother Toby, have my brains so full of saps, mines, blinds, gabions, palisadoes, ravelins, half-moons, and such trumpery, to be proprietor of Namur, and of all the towns in Flanders with it.

My uncle Toby was a man patient of injuries;—not from want of courage;—I have told you in a former chapter, " that he was a man of courage:"—and will add here, that where just occasions presented, or called it forth,—I know no man under whose arm I would have sooner taken shelter;

——nor did this arise from any insensibility or obtuseness of his intellectual parts,—for he felt this insult of my father's as feelingly as a man could do;—but he was of a peaceful, placid nature—no jarring element in it—all was mixed up so kindly within him; my uncle Toby had scarce a heart to retaliate upon a fly.

—Go,—says he one day at dinner, to an overgrown one which had buzzed about his nose, and tormented him cruelly all dinner-time,—and which, after infinite attempts, he had caught at last, as it flew by him;—I'll not hurt thee, says my uncle Toby rising from his chair, and going across the room with the fly in his hand,——I'll not hurt a hair of thy head;—Go,—says he, lifting up the sash, and opening his hand as he spoke, to let it escape;—go, poor devil, get thee gone; why should I hurt thee?——This world surely is wide enough to hold both thee and me.

I was but ten years old when this happened; but whether it was, that the action itself was more in unison to my nerves at that age of pity, which instantly set my whole frame into one vibration of most pleasurable sensation;—or how far the manner and expression of it might go towards it;—or in what degree or by what secret magic,—a tone of voice and harmony of movement, attuned by mercy, might find a passage to my heart, I know not;—this I know that the lesson of universal good-will then taught and imprinted by my uncle Toby has never since been worn out of my mind: and tho' I would not depreciate what the study of the *literæ humaniores,* at the University, have done for me in that respect, or discredit the other helps of an expensive education bestowed upon me, both at home and abroad, since;—yet I often think that I owe one half of my philanthropy to that one accidental impression.

This is to serve for parents and governors, instead of a whole volume upon the subject.

I could not give the reader this stroke in my uncle Toby's picture, by the instrument by which I drew the other parts of it—that taking in no more than the mere HOBBY-HORSICAL likeness:——this is a part of his moral character.

My father, in this patient endurance of wrongs, which I mention, was very different, as the reader must long ago have noted ; he had a much more acute and quick sensibility of nature, attended with a little soreness of temper ; tho' this never transported him to anything which looked like malignancy :—yet in the little rubs and vexations of life, 'twas apt to show itself in a drollish and witty kind of peevishness.

——He was, however, frank and generous in his nature ;——at all times open to conviction ; and in the little ebullitions of this subacid humour towards others, but particularly towards my uncle Toby, whom he truly loved,——he would feel more pain, ten times told (except in the affair of my aunt Dinah, or where an hypothesis was concerned) than what he ever gave.

The characters of the two brothers, in this view of them, reflected light upon each other, and appeared with great advantage in this affair which rose about Stevinus.

I need not tell the reader, if he keeps a Honny-Horse,——that a man's Honny-Horse is as tender a part as he has about him ; and that these unprovoked strokes at my uncle Toby's could not be unfelt by him.——No :——as I said above, my uncle Toby did feel them, and very sensibly too.

Pray, Sir, what said he ?—How did he behave ?—O, Sir! —it was great : for as soon as my father had done insulting his Honny-Horse,——he turned his head without the least emotion, from Dr. Slop, to whom he was addressing his discourse, and looking up into my father's face, with a countenance spread over with so much good-nature ;——so placid——so fraternal——so inexpressibly tender towards him ;—it penetrated my father to his heart : He rose up hastily from his chair, and, seizing hold of both my uncle Toby's hands as he spoke :—Brother Toby, said he,—I beg thy pardon ;——forgive, I pray thee, this rash humour which my mother gave me.——My dear, dear brother, answered my uncle Toby, rising up by my father's help, say no more about it ;——you are heartily welcome, had it been ten times as much, brother. But 'tis ungenerous,

replied my father, to hurt any man;——a brother worse ;
——but to hurt a brother of such gentle manners,——so
unprovoking, — and so unresenting;——'tis base :——by
Heaven, 'tis cowardly !—You are heartily welcome, brother,
quoth my uncle Toby,——had it been fifty times as much.
——Besides, what have I to do, my dear Toby, cried my
father, either with your amusements or your pleasures,
unless it was in my power (which it is not) to increase their
measure ?

——Brother Shandy, answered my uncle Toby, looking
wistfully in his face,——you are much mistaken in this
point :—for you do increase my pleasure very much, in
begetting children for the Shandy family at your time of
life.— But, by that, Sir, quoth Dr. Slop, Mr. Shandy
increases his own.——Not a jot, quoth my father.

CHAPTER XIII.

My brother does it, quoth my uncle Toby, out of *principle*.
——In a family way, I suppose, quoth Dr. Slop.——Pshaw !
said my father,—'tis not worth talking of.

CHAPTER XIV.

At the end of the last chapter, my father and my uncle
Toby were left both standing, like Brutus and Cassius, at
the close of the scene, making up their accounts.

As my father spoke the three last words,——he sat
down ; — my uncle Toby exactly followed his example;
only, that before he took his chair, he rung the bell, to
order Corporal Trim, who was in waiting, to step home for
Stevinus :——my uncle Toby's house being no farther off
than the opposite side of the way.

Some men would have dropped the subject of Stevinus ;

but my uncle Toby had no resentment in his heart, and he went on with the subject, to show my father that he had none.

Your sudden appearance, Dr. Slop, quoth my uncle, resuming the discourse, instantly brought Stevinus into my head. (My father, you may be sure, did not offer to lay any more wagers upon Stevinus's head.)——Because, continued my uncle Toby, the celebrated sailing chariot, which belonged to Prince Maurice, and was of such wonderful contrivance, and velocity, as to carry half-a-dozen people thirty German miles, in I don't know how few minutes, ——was invented by Stevinus, that great mathematician and engineer.

You might have spared your servant the trouble, quoth Dr. Slop, (as the fellow is lame) of going for Stevinus's account of it; because, in my return from Leyden thro' the Hague, I walked as far as Schevling, which is two long miles, on purpose to take a view of it.

That's nothing, replied my uncle Toby, to what the learned Peireskius did, who walked a matter of five hundred miles, reckoning from Paris to Schevling, and from Schevling to Paris back again, in order to see it,—and nothing else.

Some men cannot bear to be out-gone.

The more fool Peireskius! replied Dr. Slop. But mark, 'twas out of no contempt of Peireskius at all;——but that Peireskius's indefatigable labour in trudging so far on foot, out of love for the sciences, reduced the exploit of Dr. Slop, in that affair, to nothing:—the more fool Peireskius! said he again.—Why so?—replied my father, taking his brother's part, not only to make reparation as fast as he could for the insult he had given him, which sat still upon my father's mind;——but partly, that my father began really to interest himself in the discourse.——Why so?——said he. Why is Peireskius, or any man else, to be abused for an appetite for that, or any other morsel of sound knowledge? for notwithstanding I know nothing of the chariot in question, continued he, the inventor of it must have had a very mechanical head;—and tho' I cannot guess upon what principles of philosophy he has achieved it;—yet certainly his machine has been constructed upon solid ones, be they what they will, or it could not have answered at the rate my brother mentions.

It answered, replied my uncle Toby, as well, if not better; for, as Peireskius elegantly expresses it, speaking of the velocity of its motion, *Tam citus erat, quam erat ventus:* which, unless I have forgotten my Latin, is, *that it was as swift as the wind itself.*

But pray, Dr. Slop, quoth my father, interrupting my uncle (tho' not without begging pardon for it at the same time), upon what principles was this self-same chariot set a-going?—Upon very pretty principles to be sure, replied Dr. Slop:—and I have often wondered, continued he, evading the question, why none of our gentry, who live upon large plains like this of ours,—(especially they whose wives are not past child-bearing) attempt nothing of this kind; for it would not only be infinitely expeditious upon sudden calls, to which the sex is subject,—if the wind only served,—but would be excellent good husbandry to make use of the winds, which cost nothing, and which eat nothing, rather than horses, which (the devil take 'em) both cost and eat a great·deal.

For that very reason, replied my father, "Because they cost nothing, and because they eat nothing,"—the scheme is bad;—it is the consumption of our products, as well as the manufacture of them, which gives bread to the hungry, circulates trade, brings in money, and supports the value of our lands;—and tho', I own, if I was a Prince, I would generously recompense the scientific head which brought forth such contrivances;—yet I would as peremptorily suppress the use of them.

My father here had got into his element,——and was going on as prosperously with his dissertation upon trade, as my uncle Toby had, before, upon his of fortification;—but to the loss of much sound knowledge, the Destinies in the morning had decreed that no dissertation of any kind should be spun by my father that day,——for as he opened his mouth to begin the next sentence—

CHAPTER XV.

In popped Corporal Trim with Stevinus:—But 'twas too late,—all the discourse had been exhausted without him, and was running into a new channel.

—You may take the book home again, Trim, said my uncle Toby, nodding to him.

But prithee, Corporal, quoth my father, drolling,—look first into it, and see if thou canst spy aught of a sailing chariot in it.

Corporal Trim, by being in the service, had learned to obey,—and not to remonstrate;—so taking the book to a side-table, and running over the leaves: An' please your Honour, said Trim, I can see no such thing;—however, continued the Corporal, drolling a little in his turn, I'll make sure work of it, an' please your Honour:—so taking hold of the two covers of the book, one in each hand, and letting the leaves fall down as he bent the covers back, he gave the book a good sound shake.

There is something fallen out, however, said Trim, an' please your Honour;—but it is not a chariot, or anything like one.—Prithee, Corporal, said my father, smiling, what is it then?—I think, answered Trim, stooping to take it up, ——'tis more like a sermon, for it begins with a text of scripture, and the chapter and verse;—and then goes on, not as a chariot, but like a sermon directly.

The company smiled.

I cannot conceive how it is possible, quoth my uncle Toby, for such a thing as a sermon to have got into my Stevinus.

I think 'tis a sermon, replied Trim;—but if it please your Honours, as it is a fair hand, I will read you a page;—for Trim, you must know, loved to hear himself read almost as well as talk.

I have ever a strong propensity, said my father, to look into things which cross my way by such strange fatalities as these;—and as we have nothing better to do, at least till Obadiah gets back, I shall be obliged to you, brother, if Dr.

Slop has no objection to it, to order the Corporal to give us a page or two of it,—if he is as able to do it as he seems willing. An' it please your Honour, quoth Trim, I officiated two whole campaigns, in Flanders, as clerk to the chaplain of the regiment.——He can read it, quoth my uncle Toby, as well as I can.——Trim, I assure you, was the best scholar in my company, and should have had the next halberd, but for the poor fellow's misfortune. Corporal Trim laid his hand upon his heart, and made an humble bow to his master;—then, laying down his hat upon the floor, and taking up the sermon in his left hand, in order to have his right at liberty,——he advanced, nothing doubting, into the middle of the room, where he could best see, and be best seen by his audience.

CHAPTER XVI.

—If you have any objection,—said my father, addressing himself to Dr. Slop.—Not in the least, replied Dr. Slop;— for it does not appear on which side of the question it is wrote,——it may be a composition of a divine of our Church, as well as yours,—so that we run equal risques.——'Tis wrote upon neither side, quoth Trim, for 'tis only upon *Conscience*, an' please your Honours.

Trim's reason put his audience into good humour,—all but Dr. Slop, who, turning his head about towards Trim, looked a little angry.

Begin, Trim,—and read distinctly, quoth my father.—I will, an' please your Honour, replied the Corporal, making a bow, and bespeaking attention with a slight movement of his right hand.

CHAPTER XVII.

——But before the Corporal begins, I must first give you a description of his attitude;——otherwise he will naturally

stand represented, by your imagination, in an uneasy posture,
—stiff,—perpendicular,—dividing the weight of his body
equally upon both legs;——his eye fixed, as if on duty;—
his look determined;—clenching the sermon in his left hand,
like his fire-lock.——In a word, you would be apt to paint
Trim as if he was standing in his platoon, ready for action.
—His attitude was as unlike all this as you can conceive.

He stood before them with his body swayed, and bent
forwards just so far as to make an angle of 85 degrees and a
half upon the plane of the horizon;—which sound orators,
to whom I address this, know very well to be the true per-
suasive angle of incidence :—in any other angle you may talk
and preach;—'tis certain;—and it is done every day;—but
with what effect,—I leave the world to judge!

The necessity of this precise angle of 85 degrees and a half,
to a mathematical exactness,——does it not show us, by the
way, how the arts and sciences mutually befriend each
other?

How the deuce Corporal Trim, who knew not so much as
an acute angle from an obtuse one, came to hit it so exactly;
——or whether it was chance or nature, or good sense, or
imitation, &c., shall be commented upon in that part of the
Cyclopædia of Arts and Sciences, where the instrumental
parts of the eloquence of the senate, the pulpit, and the bar,
the coffee-house, the bedchamber, and fireside, fall under
consideration.

He stood,—for I repeat it, to take the picture of him in
at one view, with his body swayed, and somewhat bent forwards,—his right leg from under him, sustaining seven-
eighths of his whole weight,——the foot of his left leg, the
defect of which was no disadvantage to his attitude,
advanced a little,—not laterally, nor forwards, but in a line
betwixt them;—his knee bent, but that not violently,—but
so as to fall within the limits of the line of beauty;—and I
add, of the line of science too;—for, consider, it had one-
eighth part of his body to bear up;—so that in this case the
position of the leg is determined,—because the foot could be
no farther advanced, or the knee more bent, than what

would allow him mechanically to receive an eighth part of his whole weight under it, and to carry it too.

☞ *This I recommend to painters:—need I add, to orators?—I think not; for, unless they practise it,——they must fall upon their noses.*

So much for Corporal Trim's body and legs.——He held the sermon loosely, not carelessly, in his left hand, raised something above his stomach, and detached a little from his breast;——his right arm falling negligently by his side, as nature and the laws of gravity ordered it,——but with the palm of it open and turned towards his audience, ready to aid the sentiment, in case it stood in need.

Corporal Trim's eyes and the muscles of his face were in full harmony with the other parts of him ;—he looked frank, —unconstrained,—something assured,—but not bordering upon assurance.

Let not the critic ask how Corporal Trim could come by all this.——I've told him it should be explained ;—but so he stood before my father, my uncle Toby, and Dr. Slop,—so swayed his body, so contracted his limbs, and with such an oratorical sweep throughout the whole figure,——a statuary might have modelled from it ;—nay, I doubt whether the oldest Fellow of a College,—or the Hebrew Professor himself, could have much mended it.

Trim made a bow, and read as follows :—

·

THE SERMON.

HEBREWS xiii. 18.
——*For, we* trust, *we have a good Conscience.*

"TRUST !——Trust we have a good conscience !"

[Certainly, Trim, quoth my father, interrupting him, you give that sentence a very improper accent; for you curl up your nose, man, and read it with such a sneering tone, as if the Parson was going to abuse the Apostle.

He is, an' please your Honour, replied Trim. Pugh ! said my father, smiling.

Sir, quoth Dr. Slop, Trim is certainly in the right; for the writer (who I perceive is a Protestant), by the snappish manner in which he takes up the apostle, is certainly going to abuse him;—if this treatment of him has not done it already. But from whence, replied my father, have you concluded so soon, Dr. Slop, that the writer is of our Church?—for aught I can see yet, he may be of any Church. —Because, answered Dr. Slop, if he was of ours, he durst no more take such a licence, than a bear by his beard:—If, in our communion, Sir, a man was to insult an apostle,——a saint,——or even the paring of a saint's nail,—he would have his eyes scratched out.—What, by the saint? quoth my uncle Toby.—No, replied Dr. Slop, he would have an old house over his head.—Pray is the Inquisition an ancient building, answered my uncle Toby, or is it a modern one? —I know nothing of architecture, replied Dr. Slop.—An', please your Honours, quoth Trim, the Inquisition is the vilest——Prithee spare thy description, Trim, I hate the very name of it, said my father.—No matter for that, answered Dr. Slop,—it has its uses; for tho' I'm no great advocate for it, yet, in such a case as this, he would soon be taught better manners; and I can tell him, if he went on at that rate, would be flung into the Inquisition for his pains. God help him then! quoth my uncle Toby.—Amen! added Trim; for Heaven above knows, I have a poor brother who has been fourteen years a captive in it.—I never heard one word of it before, said my uncle Toby, hastily:—How came he there, Trim?——O, Sir, the story will make your heart bleed,—as it has made mine a thousand times;—but it is too long to be told now;—your Honour shall hear it, from first to last, some day when I am working beside you in our fortifications;—but the short of the story is this;—That my brother Tom went over a servant to Lisbon,—and then married a Jew's widow, who kept a small shop, and sold sausages, which, somehow or other, was the cause of his being taken in the middle of the night out of his bed, where he was lying with his wife and two small children, and carried directly to the Inquisition, where, God help him!

continued Trim, fetching a sigh from the bottom of his heart,—the poor honest lad lies confined at this hour. He was as honest a soul, added Trim, (pulling out his handkerchief) as ever blood warmed.——

The tears trickled down Trim's cheeks faster than he could well wipe them away.—A dead silence in the room ensued for some minutes.—Certain proof of pity !

Come, Trim, quoth my father, after he saw the poor fellow's grief had got a little vent,—read on,—and put this melancholy story out of thy head :—I grieve that I interrupted thee; but prithee begin the sermon again; for if the first sentence in it is matter of abuse, as thou sayest, I have a great desire to know what kind of provocation the apostle has given.

Corporal Trim wiped his face, and returned his handkerchief into his pocket, and, making a bow as he did it,—he began again.]

THE SERMON.

HEBREWS xiii. 18.

——For, we trust, we have a good Conscience.——

"TRUST !—trust we have a good conscience ! Surely if there is anything in this life which a man may depend upon, and to the knowledge of which he is capable of arriving upon the most indisputable evidence, it must be this very thing,—whether he has a good conscience or no."

[I am positive I am right, quoth Dr. Slop.]

"If a man thinks at all, he cannot well be a stranger to the true state of this account :——he must be privy to his own thoughts and desires ;—he must remember his past pursuits, and know certainly the true springs and motives, which, in general, have governed the actions of his life."

[I defy him, without an assistant, quoth Dr. Slop.]

"In other matters we may be deceived by false appearances; and, as the wise man complains, *hardly do we guess aright at the things that are upon the earth, and with labour do we find the things that are before us.* But here the mind has all the evidence and facts within herself;——is conscious of the web she has wove;——knows its texture and fineness, and the exact share which every passion has had in working upon the several designs which virtue or vice has planned before her."

[The language is good, and I declare Trim reads very well, quoth my father.]

"Now,—as conscience is nothing else but the knowledge which the mind has within herself of this; and the judgment, either of approbation or censure, which it unavoidably makes upon the successive actions of our lives; 'tis plain you will say, from the very terms of the proposition,—whenever this inward testimony goes against a man, and he stands self-accused, that he must necessarily be a guilty man.—And, on the contrary, when the report is favourable on his side, and his heart condemns him not, that it is not a matter of *trust*, as the apostle intimates, but a matter of *certainty* and fact, that the conscience is good, and that the man must be good also."

[Then the apostle is altogether in the wrong, I suppose, quoth Dr. Slop, and the Protestant divine is in the right.—Sir, have patience, replied my father, for I think it will presently appear that St. Paul and the Protestant divine are both of an opinion.—As nearly so, quoth Dr. Slop, as east is to west;—but this, continued he, lifting both hands, comes from the liberty of the press!

It is no more at the worst, replied my uncle Toby, than the liberty of the pulpit; for it does not appear that the sermon is printed, or ever likely to be.

Go on, Trim, quoth my father.]

"At first sight this may seem to be a true state of the case: and I make no doubt but the knowledge of right and wrong is so truly impressed upon the mind of man,—that did no such thing ever happen, as that the conscience of a man, by long habits of sin, might (as the scripture assures it may) insensibly become hard;—and, like some tender parts of his body, by much stress and continual hard usage, lose by degrees that nice sense and perception with which God and nature endowed it :—did this never happen ;—or was it certain that self-love could never hang the least bias upon the judgment ;—or that the little interests below could rise up and perplex the faculties of our upper regions, and encompass them about with clouds and thick darkness :——Could no such thing as favour and affection enter this sacred court :—Did Wit disdain to take a bribe in it; or was ashamed to show its face as an advocate for an unwarrantable enjoyment :—Or, lastly, were we assured that Interest stood always unconcerned whilst the cause was hearing—and that Passion never got into the judgment-seat, and pronounced sentence in the stead of Reason, which is supposed always to preside and determine upon the case :—Was this truly so, as the objection must suppose ;—no doubt, then, the religious and moral state of a man would be exactly what he himself esteemed it :—and the guilt or innocence of every man's life could be known, in general, by no better measure, than the degrees of his own approbation and censure.

"I own, in one case, whenever a man's conscience does accuse him (as it seldom errs on that side), that he is guilty; and unless in melancholy and hypochondriac cases, we may safely pronounce upon it, that there is always sufficient grounds for the accusation.

" But the converse of the proposition will not hold true ;——namely, that whenever there is guilt, the conscience must accuse; and if it does not, that a man is therefore innocent.——This is not fact.——So that the common consolation which some good Christian or other is hourly administering to himself, that he thanks God his mind does not misgive him ; and that, consequently, he has a good conscience, because he hath a quiet one,—is fallacious ;—and as current as the inference is, and as infallible as the rule appears at first sight, yet when you look nearer to it, and try the truth of this rule upon plain facts,——you see it liable to so much error from a false application ; the principle upon which it goes so often perverted;——the whole force of it lost, and sometimes so vilely cast away, that it is painful to produce the common examples from human life, which confirm the account.

"A man shall be vicious and utterly debauched in his principles;—exceptionable in his conduct to the world; shall live shameless, in the open commission of a sin which no reason or pretence can justify,——a sin by which, contrary to all the workings of humanity, he shall ruin for ever the deluded partner of his guilt;—rob her of her best dowry; and not only cover her own head with dishonour, —but involve a whole virtuous family in shame and sorrow for her sake. Surely, you will think conscience must lead such a man a troublesome life; he can have no rest night or day from its reproaches.

"Alas Conscience had something else to do all this time, than break in upon him; as Elijah reproached the god Baal,——this domestic god *was either talking, or pursuing, or was on a journey, or peradventure he slept, and could not be awoke.*

"Perhaps He was gone out in company with Honour, to fight a duel; to pay off some debt at play;——or dirty annuity, the bargain of his lust. Perhaps Conscience all this time was engaged at home, talking aloud against petty larceny, and executing vengeance upon some such puny crimes, as his fortune and rank of life secured him against all temptation of committing; so that he lives as merrily," ——[If he was of our Church, tho', quoth Dr. Slop, he could not]—"sleeps as soundly in his bed;—and at last meets death as unconcernedly; perhaps much more so, than a much better man."

[All this is impossible with us, quoth Dr. Slop, turning to my father;—the case could not happen in our Church. —It happens in ours, however, replied my father, but too often.——I own, quoth Dr. Slop, (struck a little with my father's frank acknowledgment)—that a man in the Romish Church may live as badly;—but then he cannot easily die so.——'Tis little matter, replied my father, with an air of

indifference,—how a rascal dies.—I mean, answered Dr.
Slop, he would be denied the benefits of the last sacraments.
—Pray how many have you in all? said my uncle Toby,
——for I always forget.——Seven, answered Dr Slop.——
Humph!—said my uncle Toby, tho' not accented as a
note of acquiescence,—but as an interjection of that
particular species of surprise, when a man, in looking into
a drawer, finds more of a thing than he expected.—Humph
replied my uncle Toby. Dr. Slop, who had an ear, understood my uncle Toby as well as if he had wrote a whole
volume against the seven sacraments.——Humph! replied
Dr. Slop, (stating my uncle Toby's argument over again to
him)——Why, Sir, are there not seven cardinal virtues?
——Seven mortal sins?——Seven golden candlesticks?
——Seven heavens?——'Tis more than I know, replied my
uncle Toby.——Are there not seven wonders of the world?
——Seven days of the creation?——Seven planets?——
Seven plagues?——That there are, quoth my father, with a
most affected gravity. But prithee, continued he, go on
with the rest of thy characters, Trim.]

"Another is sordid, unmerciful," (here Trim waved his
right hand,) a strait-hearted, selfish wretch, incapable either
of private friendship or public spirit. Take notice how he
passes by the widow and orphan in their distress, and sees
all the miseries incident to human life without a sigh or a
prayer, [An' please your Honours, cried Trim, I think this
a viler man than the other.]

"Shall not conscience rise up and sting him on such occasions? No; thank God there is no occasion! *I pay every
man his own; I have no fornication to answer to my conscience ;—no faithless vows or promises to make up ;—I have
debauched no man's wife or child : thank God, I am not as
other men, adulterers, unjust, or even as this libertine, who
stands before me !*

"A third is crafty and designing in his nature. View his
whole life ;—'tis nothing but a cunning contexture of dark
arts and unequitable subterfuges, basely to defeat the true
intent of all laws,——plain dealing, and the safe enjoyment

of our several properties.——You will see such a one working out a frame of little designs upon the ignorance and perplexities of the poor and needy man;—shall raise a fortune upon the inexperience of a youth, or the unsuspecting temper of his friend, who would have trusted him with his life.

"When old age comes on, and repentance calls him to look back upon his black account, and state it over again with his conscience——CONSCIENCE looks into the STATUTES AT LARGE;—finds no express law broken by what he has done;—perceives no penalty or forfeiture of goods and chattels incurred;—sees no scourge waving over his head, or prison opening its gates upon him:—What is there to affright his conscience?—Conscience has got safely entrenched behind the Letter of the Law : sits there invulnerable, fortified with **Cases and Reports** so strongly on all sides, that it is not preaching can dispossess it of its hold."

[Here Corporal Trim and my uncle Toby exchanged looks with each other.—Aye, aye, Trim! quoth my uncle Toby, shaking his head,——these are but sorry fortifications, Trim.——O! very poor work, answered Trim, to what your Honour and I make of it.——The character of this last man, said Dr. Slop, interrupting Trim, is more detestable than all the rest; and seems to have been taken from some pettifogging Lawyer amongst you. Amongst us, a man's conscience could not possibly continue so long *blinded :*——three times in a year, at least, he must go to confession.—Will that restore it to sight? quoth my uncle Toby.——Go on, Trim, quoth my father, or Obadiah will have got back before thou hast got to the end of thy sermon.——'Tis a very short one, replied Trim.——I wish it was longer! quoth my uncle Toby, for I like it hugely.— Trim went on.]

"A fourth man shall want even this refuge; shall break through all the ceremony of slow chicane;——scorns the doubtful workings of secret plots and cautious trains to bring about his purpose:——See the barefaced villain, how he cheats, lies, perjures, robs, murders!—Horrid!—But in-

deed much better was not to be expected in the present
case—the poor man was in the dark !——his priest had get
the keeping of his conscience ;——and all he would let him
know of it, was, That he must believe in the Pope ;—go to
Mass ;—cross himself ;—tell his beads ;—be a good Catholic;
and that this, in all conscience, was enough to carry him to
heaven.—What !—If he perjures ?—Why, he had a mental
reservation in it.—But if he is so wicked and abandoned a
wretch as you represent him ;—if he robs,—if he stabs, will
not conscience, on every such act, receive a wound itself?—
Aye,—but the man has carried it to confession ;——the
wound digests there, and will do well enough, and in a
short time be quite healed up by absolution. O Popery!
what hast thou to answer for !——when not content with
the too many natural and fatal ways, thro' which the heart
of man is every day thus treacherous to itself above all
things,—thou hast wilfully set open the wide gate of deceit,
before the face of this unwary traveller,—too apt, God
knows, to go astray of himself, and confidently speak peace
to himself, when there is no peace.

   " Of this, the common instances which I have drawn out
of life, are too notorious to require much evidence. If any
man doubts the reality of them, or thinks it impossible for
a man to be such a bubble to himself,—I must refer him a
moment to his own reflections, and will then venture to
trust my appeal with his own heart.

   " Let him consider in how different a degree of detestation,
numbers of wicked actions stand there, tho' equally bad and
vicious in their own natures ;——he will soon find, that such
of them as strong inclination and custom have prompted
him to commit, are generally dressed out and painted with
all the false beauties which a soft and a flattering hand can
give them ;—and that the others, to which he feels no propensity, appear at once naked and deformed, surrounded
with all the true circumstances of folly and dishonour.

   " When David surprised Saul sleeping in the cave, and cut
off the skirt of his robe,—we read that his heart smote him
for what he had done :—but in the matter of Uriah, where

a faithful and gallant servant, whom he ought to have loved and honoured, fell to make way for his lust,—where conscience had so much greater reason to take the alarm, his heart smote him not. A whole year had almost passed from the first commission of that crime, to the time Nathan was sent to reprove him ; and we read not once of the least sorrow or compunction of heart which he testified, during all that time, for what he had done.

" Thus conscience, this once able monitor,—placed on high as a judge within us, and intended by our Maker as a just and equitable one too,—by an unhappy train of causes and impediments, takes often such imperfect cognizance of what passes, —does its office so negligently,—sometimes so corruptly, that it is not to be trusted alone ; and therefore we find there is a necessity, an absolute necessity, of joining another principle with it, to aid, if not govern, its determinations.

" So that, if you would form a just judgment of what is of infinite importance to you not to be misled in,—namely, in what degree of real merit you stand, either as an honest man, a useful citizen, a faithful subject to your king, or a good servant to your God,—call in religion and morality. Look : What is written in the law of God ?——How readest thou ?—Consult calm reason and the unchangeable obligations of justice and truth !—what say they ?

" Let CONSCIENCE determine the matter upon these reports ;—and then if thy heart condemns thee not, which is the case the apostle supposes,—the rule will be infallible ; " —[Here Dr. Slop fell asleep]—" *thou wilt have confidence towards God;* that is, have just grounds to believe the judgment thou hast passed upon thyself, is the judgment of God ; and nothing else but an anticipation of that righteous sentence which will be pronounced upon thee hereafter by that Being to whom thou art finally to give an account of thy actions.

" *Blessed is the man,* indeed, then, as the author of the book of Ecclesiasticus expresses it, *who is not pricked with the multitude of his sins : blessed is the man whose heart hath not condemned him : whether he be rich, or whether he be poor, if he have a good heart* (a heart thus guided and informed) *he shall at all times rejoice in a cheerful countenance ; his mind shall tell him more than seven watchmen that sit above upon a tower on high.*"—[A tower has no strength, quoth my uncle Toby, unless 'tis flanked.]—" In the darkest doubts it shall conduct him safer than a thousand casuists, and give the state he lives in a better security for his behaviour than all the causes and restrictions put together, which law-makers are forced to multiply :—*forced*, I say, as things stand ; human laws not being a matter of original choice, but of pure necessity, brought in to fence against the mis-chievous effects of those consciences which are no law unto themselves ; well intending, by the many provisions made,—that in all such corrupt and misguided cases, where principles and the checks of conscience will not make us upright,—to supply their force,—and, by the terrors of gaols and halters, oblige us to it."

[I see plainly, said my father, that this sermon has been composed to be preached at the Temple,—or at some Assize. —I like the reasoning,—and am sorry that Dr. Slop has fallen asleep before the time of his conviction ;—for it is now clear, that the Parson, as I thought at first, never in-sulted St. Paul in the least ;—nor has there been, brother, the least difference between them.——A great matter, if they had differed, replied my uncle Toby !—the best friends in the world may differ sometimes.——True,—brother Toby, quoth my father, shaking hands with him ;—we'll fill our pipes, brother, and then Trim shall go on.

Well,—what dost thou think of it ? said my father, speaking to Corporal Trim, as he reached his tobacco-box.

I think, answered the Corporal, that the seven watchmen upon the tower,—who, I suppose, are all sentinels there, are more, an' please your Honour, than were necessary ;— and to go on at that rate, would harass a regiment all to pieces, which a commanding-officer, who loves his men, will never do, if he can help it ; because two sentinels, added the Corporal, are as good as twenty.—I have been a commanding-officer myself in the *Corps de Garde* a hun-

dred times, continued Trim, rising an inch higher in his
figure, as he spoke ;—and all the time I had the honour to
serve his Majesty King William, in relieving the most considerable posts, I never left more than two in my life.——
Very right, quoth my uncle Toby; but you do not consider,
Trim, that the towers, in Solomon's days, were not such
things as our bastions, flanked and defended by other works.
This, Trim, was an invention since Solomon's death; nor
had they horn-works, or ravelins before the curtain, in his
time ;—or such a fosse as we make with a cuvette in the
middle of it, and with covered ways and counter-scarps,
palisadoed along it, to guard against a *coup de main :*—so
that the seven men upon the tower were a party, I dare
say, from the *Corps de Garde*, set there not only to look out,
but to defend it.——They could be no more, an' please your
Honour, than a Corporal's guard.——My father smiled
inwardly, but not outwardly ;—the subject being rather too
serious, considering what had happened, to make a jest of ;
—so putting his pipe into his mouth, which he had just
lighted,—he contented himself with ordering Trim to read
on. He read on as follows :—]

"To have the fear of God before our eyes, and in our
mutual dealings with each other, to govern our actions by
the eternal measures of right and wrong ;—the first of these
will comprehend the duties of religion ;—the second, those
of morality, which are so inseparably connected together,
that you cannot divide these two *tables*, even in imagination, (though the attempt is often made in practice) without
breaking and mutually destroying them both.

" I said the attempt is often made ; and so it is ;—there
being nothing more common than to see a man who has no
sense at all of religion, and indeed has so much honesty as
to pretend to none, who would take it as the bitterest affront,
should you but hint at a suspicion of his moral character,—
or imagine he was not conscientiously just and scrupulous
to the uttermost mite.

" When there is some appearance that it is so,—tho' one
is unwilling even to suspect the appearance of so amiable a

virtue as moral honesty, yet were we to look into the grounds of it, in the present case, I am persuaded we should find little reason to envy such a one the honour of his motive.

"Let him declaim as pompously as he chooses upon the subject, it will be found to rest upon no better foundation than either his interest, his pride, his ease, or some such little and changeable passion as will give us but small dependence upon his actions in matters of great distress.

"I will illustrate this by an example.

"I know the banker I deal with, or the physician I usually call in,"—[There is no need, cried Dr. Slop, waking, to call in any physician in this case]—"to be neither of them men of much religion. I hear them make jest of it every day, and treat all its sanctions with so much scorn, as to put the matter past doubt. Well;—notwithstanding this, I put my fortune into the hands of the one;—and, what is dearer still to me, I trust my life to the honest skill of the other.

"Now, let me examine what is my reason for this great confidence. Why, in the first place, I believe there is no probability that either of them will employ the power I put into their hands to my disadvantage;—I consider that honesty serves the purposes of this life;—I know their success in the world depends upon the fairness of their characters. —In a word, I'm persuaded that they cannot hurt me without hurting themselves more.

"But put it otherwise; namely, that interest lay, for once, on the other side; that a case should happen, wherein the one, without stain to his reputation, could secrete my fortune, and leave me naked in the world;—or that the other could send me out of it, and enjoy an estate by my death, without dishonour to himself or his art;—in this case, what hold have I of either of them?—Religion, the strongest of all motives, is out of the question;—interest, the next most powerful motive in the world, is strongly against me.——What have I left to cast into the opposite scale, to balance this temptation?——Alas! I have nothing —nothing but what is lighter than a bubble:——I must lie

at the mercy of Honour, or some such capricious principle,
—strait security for two of the most valuable blessings!—
my property and my life.

" As, therefore, we can have no dependence upon morality
without religion;—so, on the other hand,—there is nothing
better to be expected from religion without morality : nevertheless, 'tis no prodigy to see a man whose real moral
character stands very low, who yet entertains the highest
notion of himself in the light of a religious man.

" He shall not only be covetous, revengeful, implacable,—
but even wanting in points of common honesty ; yet, inasmuch as he talks aloud against the infidelity of the age,—is
zealous for some points of religion,—goes twice a day to
church,—attends the sacraments, and amuses himself with a
few instrumental parts of religion,—shall cheat his conscience into a judgment that, for this, he is a religious man,
and has discharged truly his duty to God : and you will find
that such a man, through force of this delusion, generally
looks down with spiritual pride upon every other man who
has less affectation of piety,—though, perhaps, ten times
more real honesty than himself.

" *This likewise is a sore evil under the sun ;* and, I believe,
there is no one mistaken principle, which, for its time, has
wrought more serious mischiefs.——For a general proof of
this,—examine the history of the Romish Church ; "—[Well,
what can you make of that ? cried Dr. Slop]—" see what
scenes of cruelty, murder, rapine, bloodshed "—[They may
thank their own obstinacy, cried Dr. Slop]—" have all been
sanctified by a religion not strictly governed by morality !

" In how many kingdoms of the world "—[Here Trim
kept waving his right hand from the sermon to the extent
of his arm, returning it backwards and forwards to the conclusion of the paragraph].

" In how many kingdoms of the world has the crusading
sword of this misguided saint-errant spared neither age, nor
merit, nor sex, nor condition ?—and, as he fought under the
banners of a religion which set him loose from justice and
humanity, he showed none ; mercilessly trampled upon both,

——heard neither the cries of the unfortunate, nor pitied
their distresses ! "

[I have been in many a battle, an' please your Honour,
quoth Trim, sighing, but never in so melancholy a one as
this :—I would not have drawn a trigger in it against these
poor souls,—to have been made a general officer.——Why?
what do you understand of the affair? said Dr. Slop, looking
towards Trim, with something more of contempt than the
Corporal's honest heart deserved.——What do you know,
friend, about this battle you talk of?——I know, replied
Trim, that I never refused quarter in my life to any man
who cried out for it :—but to a woman or a child, continued
Trim, before I would level my musket at them, I would lose
my life a thousand times.——Here's a crown for thee, Trim,
to drink with Obadiah to-night, quoth my uncle Toby ; and
I'll give Obadiah another too.——God bless your Honour !
replied Trim ;—I had rather these poor women and children
had it.——Thou art an honest fellow, quoth my uncle Toby
——My father nodded his head, as much as to say,—And
so he is.——

But prithee, Trim, said my father, make an end,—for I
see thou hast but a leaf or two left.

Corporal Trim read on.]

" If the testimony of past centuries in this matter is not
sufficient,—consider, at this instant, how the votaries of
that religion are every day thinking to do service and
honour to God, by actions which are a dishonour and
scandal to themselves !

" To be convinced of this, go with me for a moment into
the prisons of the Inquisition."—[God help my poor
brother Tom !]—" Behold Religion, with Mercy and Justice
chained down under her feet,—there sitting ghastly upon a
black tribunal, propped up with racks and instruments of
torment. Hark ;—hark ! what a piteous groan ! "—[Here
Trim's face turned as pale as ashes.]——" See the melancholy wretch, who uttered it "—[Here the tears began to
trickle down] —— " just brought forth to undergo the
anguish of a mock trial, and endure the utmost pains that a

studied system of cruelty has been able to invent."——
[D—n them all! quoth Trim, his colour returning into his
face as red as blood.]—Behold this helpless victim delivered
up to his tormentors,—his body so wasted with sorrow and
confinement!"—[Oh! 'tis my brother! cried poor Trim, in
a most passionate exclamation, dropping the sermon upon
the ground, and clapping his hands together—I fear 'tis
poor Tom!——My father's and my uncle Toby's heart
yearned with sympathy for the poor fellow's distress; even
Slop himself acknowledged pity for him.——Why, Trim,
said my father, this is not a history,—'tis a sermon thou art
reading; prithee begin the sentence again.]——" Behold
this helpless victim delivered up to his tormentors,—his
body so wasted with sorrow and confinement, you will see
every nerve and muscle as it suffers!

"Observe the last movement of that horrid engine!"—
[I would rather face a cannon! quoth Trim, stamping.]—
" See what convulsions it has thrown him into!—Consider
the nature of the posture in which he now lies stretched!—
what exquisite tortures he endures by it!"—[I hope 'tis not
in Portugal!]—"'Tis all nature can bear! Good God! see
how it keeps his weary soul hanging upon his trembling
lips!"—[I would not read another line of it, quoth Trim,
for all this world!—I fear, an' please your Honours, all this
is in Portugal, where my poor brother Tom is!——I tell
thee, Trim, again, quoth my father, 'tis not an historical
account,—'tis a description.—'Tis only a description,
honest man, quoth Slop; there is not a word of truth in it.
——That's another story, replied my father.—However, as
Trim reads it with so much concern,—'tis cruelty to force
him to go on with it.—Give me hold of the sermon, Trim,
—I'll finish it for thee, and thou may'st go.——I must stay
and hear it too, replied Trim, if your Honour will allow me;
—tho' I would not read it myself for a Colonel's pay.——
Poor Trim, quoth my uncle Toby.——My father went on.]

" ——Consider the nature of the posture in which he now
lies stretched!—what exquisite tortures he endures by it!
—'Tis all nature can bear! Good God! see how it keeps

his weary soul hanging upon his trembling lips, willing to take its leave,—but not suffered to depart!—Behold the unhappy wretch led back to his cell!"——[Then, thank God, however, quoth Trim, that they have not killed him!] "See him dragged out of it again, to meet the flames, and the insults in his last agonies, which this principle——this principle, that there can be religion without mercy, has prepared for him!"——[Then, thank God, he is dead! quoth Trim,—he is out of his pain,—and they have done their worst at him.—O Sirs!——Hold your peace, Trim! said my father, going on with the sermon, lest Trim should incense Dr. Slop,—we shall never have done at this rate.]

"The surest way to try the merit of any disputed notion, is, to trace down the consequences such a notion has produced, and compare them with the spirit of. Christianity; ——'tis the short and decisive rule which our Saviour hath left us for these and such like cases, and it is worth a thousand arguments—*By their fruits ye shall know them.*

"I will add no farther to the length of this sermon, than by two or three short and independent rules deducible from it.

"*First*, Whenever a man talks loudly against religion, always suspect that it is not his reason, but his passions, which have got the better of his CREED. A bad life and a good belief are disagreeable and troublesome neighbours; and where they separate, depend upon it, 'tis for no other cause but quietness' sake.

"*Secondly*, When a man, thus represented, tells you in any particular instance,—That such a thing goes against his conscience,—always believe he means exactly the same thing as when he tells you such a thing goes against his stomach; —a present want of appetite being generally the true cause of both.

"In a word,—trust that man in nothing, who has not a CONSCIENCE in everything.

"And, in your own case, remember this plain distinction, a mistake in which has ruined thousands,—That your conscience is not a law:—no, God and reason made the law, and have placed conscience within you to determine;—not, like an Asiatic Cadi, according to the ebbs and flows of his own passions,—but like a British judge in this land of liberty and good sense, who makes no new law, but faithfully declares that law which he knows already written."

THOU hast read the sermon extremely well, Trim, quoth my father.——If he had spared his comments, replied Dr. Slop,—he would have read it much better.——I should have read it ten times better, Sir, answered Trim, but that my heart was so full.——That was the very reason, Trim, replied my father, which has made thee read the sermon as well as thou hast done; and if the clergy of our Church, continued my father, addressing himself to Dr. Slop, would take part in what they deliver, as deeply as this poor fellow has done,—as their compositions are fine;—[I deny it, quoth Dr. Slop]—I maintain it,—that the eloquence of our pulpits, with such subjects to inflame it, would be a model for the whole world:—But, alas! continued my father, and I own it, Sir, with sorrow, that, like French politicians, in this respect, what they gain in the cabinet they lose in the field.——'Twere a pity, quoth my uncle, that this should be lost!——I like the sermon well, replied my father, 'tis dramatic;—and there is something in that way of writing, when skilfully managed, which catches the attention.—— We preach much in that way with us, said Dr. Slop.—— I know that very well, said my father,—but in a tone and manner which disgusted Dr. Slop, full as much as his assent, simply, could have pleased him.——But in this, added Dr. Slop, a little piqued, our sermons have greatly the advantage, that we never introduce any character into them below a patriarch or a patriarch's wife, or a martyr, or a saint.— There are some very bad characters in this, however, said my father; and I do not think the sermon a jot the worse

for 'em.——But pray, quoth my uncle Toby,—whose can
this be?—How could it get into my Stevinus:——A man
must be as great a conjurer as Stevinus, said my father, to
resolve the second question. The first, I think, is not so
difficult;—for, unless my judgment greatly deceives me,—I
know the author, for 'tis wrote, certainly, by the parson of
the parish.

The similitude of the style and manner of it, with those
my father constantly had heard preached in his parish-
church, was the ground of his conjecture,—proving it as
strongly as an argument *à priori* could prove such a thing
to a philosophic mind, That it was Yorick's, and no one's
else.—It was proved to be so *à posteriori*, the day after,
when Yorick sent a servant to my uncle Toby's house to
enquire after it.

It seems that Yorick, who was inquisitive after all kinds
of knowledge, had borrowed Stevinus of my uncle Toby,
and had carelessly popped his sermon, as soon as he had
made it, into the middle of Stevinus; and by an act of
forgetfulness to which he was ever subject, he had sent
Stevinus home, and his sermon to keep him company.

Ill-fated sermon! Thou wast lost, after this recovery of
thee, a second time, dropped thro' an unsuspected fissure in
thy master's pocket down into a treacherous and tattered
lining,—trod deep into the dirt, by the left hind-foot of his
Rosinante inhumanly stepping upon thee as thou falledst;
—buried ten days in the mire,—raised up out of it by a
beggar,—sold for a halfpenny to a parish-clerk, transferred
to his parson,—lost for ever to thy own, the remainder of
his days,—nor restored to his restless manes till this very
moment that I tell the world the story.

Can the reader believe that this sermon of Yorick's was
preached at an assize, in the cathedral of York, before a
thousand witnesses, ready to give oath of it, by a certain
prebendary of that church, and actually printed by him
when he had done?—and within so short a space as two
years and three months after Yorick's death?—Yorick,
indeed, was never better served in his life;——but it was a

little hard to maltreat him after, and plunder him after he was laid in his grave.

However, as the gentleman who did it was in perfect charity with Yorick,—and, in conscious justice, printed but a few copies to give away, and that, I am told, he could moreover have made as good a one himself, had he thought fit,—I declare I would not have published this anecdote to the world;—nor do I publish it with an intent to hurt his character and advancement in the Church;—I leave that to others;—but I find myself impelled by two reasons, which I cannot withstand.

The first is, That in doing justice, I may give rest to Yorick's ghost;—which,—as the country-people, and some others, believe,—*still walks.*

The second reason is, That, by laying open this story to the world, I gain an opportunity of informing it,—That in case the character of Parson Yorick, and the sample of his sermons, is liked,—there are now in the possession of the Shandy family, as many as will make a handsome volume, at the world's service;—and much good may they do it!

CHAPTER XVIII.

Obadiah gained the two crowns without dispute; for he came in jingling, with all the instruments in a green-baize bag we spoke of, slung across his body, just as Corporal Trim went out of the room.

It is now proper, I think, quoth Dr. Slop (clearing up his looks), as we are in a condition to be of some service to Mrs. Shandy, to send upstairs, to know how she goes on.

I have ordered, answered my father, the old midwife to come down to us upon the least difficulty;—for you must know, Dr. Slop, continued my father, with a perplexed kind of a smile upon his countenance, that, by express treaty, solemnly ratified between me and my wife, you are no more than an auxiliary in this affair,—and not so much as that,—

unless the lean old mother of a midwife above stairs cannot
do without you.—Women have their particular fancies; and
in points of this nature, continued my father, where they
bear the whole burden, and suffer so much acute pain, for
the advantage of our families, and the good of the species,
—they claim a right of deciding, *en Souveraines,* in whose
hands, and in what fashion, they choose to undergo it.

They are in the right of it,—quoth my uncle Toby.——
But, Sir, replied Dr. Slop, not taking notice of my uncle
Toby's opinion, but turning to my father,—they had better
govern in other points;—and a father of a family, who wishes
its perpetuity, in my opinion, had better exchange this prerogative with them, and give up some other rights in lieu of
it.——I know not, quoth my father, answering a little too
testily to be quite dispassionate in what he said,—I know
not, quoth he, what we have left to give up in lieu of who
shall bring our children into the world, unless that, of who
shall beget them.——One would almost give up anything,
replied Dr. Slop.——I beg your pardon,—answered my
uncle Toby.——Sir, replied Dr. Slop, it would astonish you
to know what improvements we have made of late-years, in
all branches of obstetrical knowledge, but particularly in
that one single point of the safe and expeditious extraction
of the *fœtus,*—which has received such lights, that, for my
part (holding up his hands) I declare, I wonder how the
world has——.   I wish, quoth my uncle Toby, you had
seen what prodigious armies we had in Flanders!

———

CHAPTER XIX.

I HAVE dropped the curtain over this scene for a minute,—
to remind you of one thing,—and to inform you of another.

What I have to inform you, comes, I own, a little out of
its due course;—for it should have been told a hundred and
fifty pages ago, but that I foresaw then 'twould come in pat
hereafter, and be of more advantage here than elsewhere.—

Writers had need look before them, to keep up the spirit and connection of what they have in hand.

When these two things are done,—the curtain shall be drawn up again; and my uncle Toby, my father, and Dr. Slop, shall go on with their discourse, without any more interruption.

First, then, the matter which I have to remind you of, is this :—That from the specimens of singularity in my father's notions in the point of Christian names, and that other previous point thereto,—you was led, I think, into an opinion,—(and I am sure I said as much) that my father was a gentleman altogether as odd and whimsical in fifty other opinions. In truth, there was not a stage in the life of man, from the very first act of his begetting,—down to the lean and slippered pantaloon in his second childishness, but he had some favourite notion to himself, springing out of it, as sceptical, and as far out of the highway of thinking, as these two which have been explained.

—Mr. Shandy, my father, Sir, would see nothing in the light in which others placed it ;—he placed things in his own light ;—he would weigh nothing in' common scales :—no, he was too refined a researcher to lie open to so gross an imposition.—To come at the exact weight of things in the scientific steel-yard, the *fulcrum*, he would say, should be almost invisible, to avoid all friction from popular tenets ;—without this, the *minutiæ* of philosophy, which would always turn the balance, will have no weight at all. Knowledge, like matter, he would affirm, was divisible *in infinitum* ;—that the grains and scruples were as much a part of it, as the gravitation of the whole world.—In a word, he would say, error was error—no matter where it fell—whether in a fraction—or a pound, 'twas alike fatal to Truth ; and she was kept down at the bottom of her well, as inevitably by a mistake in the dust of a butterfly's wing,—as in the disk of the sun, the moon, and all the stars of Heaven put together.

He would often lament that it was for want of considering this properly, and of applying it skilfully to civil matters, as well as to speculative truths, that so many things in this world were out of joint;—that the political arch was giving way;—and that the very foundations of our excellent constitution, in Church and State, were so sapped as estimators had reported.

You cry out, he would say, we are a ruined, undone people. Why? he would ask, making use of the sorites or syllogism of Zeno and Chrysippus, without knowing it belonged to them.—Why? why are we a ruined people?— Because we are corrupted.—Whence is it, dear Sir, that we are corrupted?—Because we are needy;—our poverty, and not our wills, consent:—and wherefore, he would add, are we needy?—From the neglect, he would answer, of our pence—and our halfpence:—our banknotes, Sir, our guineas: nay, our shillings take care of themselves.

'Tis the same, he would say, throughout the whole circle of the sciences;—the great, the established points of them, are not to be broke in upon.—The laws of nature will defend themselves;—but error—(he would add, looking earnestly at my mother)—error, Sir, creeps in thro' the minute holes and small crevices which human nature leaves unguarded.

This turn of thinking in my father is what I had to remind you of:—the point you are to be informed of, and which I have reserved for this place, is as follows:—

Amongst the many and excellent reasons with which my father had urged my mother to accept of Dr. Slop's assistance preferably to that of the old woman,—there was one of a very singular nature; which when he had done arguing the matter with her as a Christian, and came to argue it over again with her as a philosopher, he had put his whole strength to, depending indeed upon it as his sheet-anchor.
——It failed him, tho' from no defect in the argument itself; but that, do what he could, he was not able for his soul to make her comprehend the drift of it.——Cursed luck! said he to himself, one afternoon, as he walked out of the room, after he had been stating it for an hour and a · half to her, to no manner of purpose;—cursed luck! said he, biting his lip as he shut the door,—for a man to be

master of one of the finest chains of reasoning in nature
—and have a wife at the same time with such a headpiece,
that he cannot hang up a single inference within-side of it,
to save his soul from destruction !

This argument, though, it was entirely lost upon my
mother,—had more weight with him than all his other
arguments joined together :—I will therefore endeavour to
do it justice,—and set it forth with all the perspicuity I am
master of.

My father set out upon the strength of these two following axioms :—

First, That an ounce of a man's own wit was worth a ton
of other people's ; and,

Secondly, (which, by the bye, was the groundwork of
the first axiom,—tho' it comes last) That every man's wit
must come from every man's own soul,—and no other
body's.

Now, as it was plain to my father, that all souls were by
nature equal,—and that the great difference between the
most acute and the most obtuse understanding,—was from
no original sharpness or bluntness of one thinking substance above or below another,—but arose merely from the
lucky or unlucky organisation of the body, in that part
where the soul principally took up her residence,—he had
made it the subject of his enquiry to find out the identical
place.

Now, from the best accounts he had been able to get of
this matter, he was satisfied it could not be where Des Cartes
had fixed it, upon the top of the *pineal* gland of the brain ;
which, as he philosophised, formed a cushion for her about
the size of a marrow-pea; tho', to speak the truth, as so
many nerves did terminate all in that one place,—'twas no
bad conjecture ;—and my father had certainly fallen with
that great philosopher plumb into the centre of the mistake
had it not been for my uncle Toby, who rescued him out of
it, by a story he told him of a Walloon officer at the battle
of Landen, who had one part of his brain shot away by a
musket-ball,—and another part of it taken out after by a

French surgeon ; and after all, recovered, and did his duty very well without it.

If death, said my father, reasoning with himself, is nothing but the separation of the soul from the body ;—and if it is true that people can walk about and do their business without brains,—then certes the soul does not inhabit there. Q. E. D.

As for that certain, very thin, subtle, and very fragrant juice which Coglionissimo Borri, the great Milanese physician, affirms, in a Letter to Bartholine, to have discovered in the *cellulæ* of the *occipital* parts of the *cerebellum*, and which he likewise affirms to be the principal seat of the reasonable soul (for, you must know, in these latter and more enlightened ages, there are two souls in every man living,—the one, according to the great Metheglingius, being called the *Animus;* the other, the *Anima;*)—as for the opinion, I say, of Borri,—my father could never subscribe to it by any means ; the very idea of so noble, so refined, so immaterial, and so exalted a being as the *Anima*, or even the *Animus*, taking up her residence and sitting dabbling, like a tadpole, all day long, both summer and winter, in a puddle, —or in a liquid of any kind, how thick or thin soever, he would say, shocked his imagination ; he would scarce give the doctrine a hearing.

What therefore seemed the least liable to objections of any, was, that the chief *sensorium*, or headquarters of the soul, and to which place all intelligences were referred, and from whence all her mandates were issued,—was in, or near, the *cerebellum*,—or rather somewhere about the *medulla oblongata*, wherein it was generally agreed by Dutch anatomists, that all the minute nerves from all the organs of the seven senses concentred, like streets and winding alleys, into a square.

So far there was nothing singular in my father's opinion, —he had the best of philosophers, of all ages and climates, to go along with him.——But here he took a road of his own, setting up another Shandean hypothesis upon these corner-stones they had laid for him ;—and which said hypothesis equally stood its ground; whether the subtilty and fineness of the soul depended upon the temperature and clearness of the said liquor, or of the finer network and texture in the *cerebellum* itself; which opinion he favoured.

He maintained, that next to the due care to be taken in the act of propagation of each individual, which required all the thought in the world, as it laid the foundation of this incomprehensible contexture, in which wit, memory, fancy, eloquence, and what is usually meant by the name of good natural parts, do consist ;—that next to this and his Christian name, which were the two original and most efficacious causes of all ;—that the third cause, or rather what logicians call the *Causa sine quâ non*, and without which all that was done was of no manner of significance, —was the preservation of this delicate and fine-spun web, from the havoc which was generally made in it by the violent compression and crush which the head was made to undergo, by the nonsensical method of bringing us into the world by that foremost.

——This requires explanation.

My father, who dipped into all kinds of books, upon looking into *Lithopædus Senonesis de Portu difficili*,* published by Adrianus Smelvgot, had found out, that the lax and pliable state of a child's head in parturition, the bones of the *cranium* having no sutures at that time, was such,— that by force of the woman's efforts, which, in strong labour-pains, was equal, upon an average, to the weight of 470 pounds avoirdupois acting perpendicularly upon it,—it so happened, that in forty-nine instances out of fifty, the said head was compressed and moulded into the shape of an oblong conical piece of dough, such as a pastry-cook

---

* The author is here twice mistaken ; for *Lithopædus* should be wrote thus, *Lithopædii Senonensis Icon.* The second mistake is, that this *Lithopædus* is not an author, but a drawing of a petrified child. The account of this, published by Athosius 1580, may be seen at the end of Cordæus's works in Spachius. Mr. Tristram Shandy has been led into this error, either from seeing *Lithopædus's* name of late in a catalogue of learned writers in Dr. ——, or by mistaking *Lithopædus* for *Trinecavellius*,—from the too great similitude of the names.

generally rolls up, in order to make a pie of.—Good God !
—cried my father, what havoc and destruction must this
make in the infinitely fine and tender texture of the *cerebellum !*—Or if there is such a juice as Borri pretends,—is
it not enough to make the clearest liquid in the world both
feculent and mothery ?

But how great was his apprehension, when he further
understood, that this force, acting upon the very vertex of
the head, not only injured the brain itself, or *cerebrum*,—but
that it necessarily squeezed and propelled the *cerebrum*
towards the *cerebellum*, which was the immediate seat of
the understanding !——Angels and ministers of grace defend
us ! cried my father. Can any soul withstand this shock ?
—No wonder the intellectual web is so rent and tattered as
we see it ; and that so many of our best heads are no better
than a puzzled skein of silk,—all perplexity,—all confusion
withinside.

But when my father read on, and was let into the secret,
that when a child was turned topsy-turvy, which was easy
for an operator to do, and was extracted by the feet ;——
that instead of the *cerebrum* being propelled towards the
cerebellum, the *cerebellum*, on the contrary, was propelled
simply towards the *cerebrum*, where it could do no manner
of hurt :——By Heavens ! cried he, the world is in conspiracy to drive out what little wit God has given us,—and
the professors of the obstetric art are listed into the same
conspiracy.—What is it to me which end of my son comes
foremost into the world, provided all goes right after, and
his *cerebellum* escapes uncrushed?

It is the nature of an hypothesis, when once a man has
conceived it, that it assimilates everything to itself, as
proper nourishment ; and, from the first moment of your
begetting it, it generally grows the stronger by everything
you see, hear, read, or understand.   This is of great use.

When my father was gone with this about a month there
was scarce a phenomenon of stupidity or of genius, which
he could not readily solve by it :——it accounted for the
eldest son being the greatest blockhead in the family.——

Poor devil! he would say,—he made way for the capacity of his younger brothers.——It unriddled the observations of drivellers and monstrous heads,—showing *à priori*, it could not be otherwise,—unless *** I don't know what. It wonderfully explained and accounted for the *acumen* of the Asiatic genius; and that sprightlier turn, and a more penetrating intuition of minds, in warmer climates; not from the loose and commonplace solution of a clearer sky, and a more perpetual sunshine, &c.—which, for aught he knew, might as well rarefy and dilute the faculties of the soul into nothing, by one extreme, as they are condensed in colder climates, by the other;—but he traced the affair up to its spring-head;—showed, that in warmer climates, nature had laid a lighter tax upon the fairest parts of the creation; their pleasures more; the necessity of their pains less, insomuch that the pressure and resistance upon the vertex was so slight, that the whole organisation of the *cerebellum* was preserved; nay, he did not believe, in natural births, that so much as a single thread of the network was broke or displaced,—so that the soul might just act as she liked.

When my father had got so far,——what a blaze of light did the accounts of the Cæsarian section, and of the towering geniuses who had come safe into the world by it, cast upon this hypothesis! Here you see, he would say, there was no injury done to the *sensorium;*—no pressure of the head against the *pelvis;*—no propulsion of the *cerebrum* towards the *cerebellum,* either by *os pubis* on this side, or the *os coxygis* on that;——and pray, what were the happy consequences?—Why, Sir, your Julius Cæsar, who gave the operation a name;—and your Hermes Trismegistus, who was born so before ever the operation had a name;——your Scipio Africanus; your Manlius Torquatus; our Edward the Sixth,—who, had he lived, would have done the same honour to the hypothesis:——These, and many more who figured high in the annals of fame,—all came *side-way*, Sir, into the world.

The incision of the *abdomen* and *uterus* ran for six weeks together in my father's head; he had read, and was satisfied, that wounds in the *epigastrium*, and those in the *matrix* were not mortal;—so that the belly of the mother might be opened extremely well to give a passage to the child.—He mentioned the thing one afternoon to my mother,——merely as a matter of fact; but seeing her turn as pale as ashes at the very mention of it, as much as the operation flattered his hopes, he thought it as well to say no more of it,—contenting himself with admiring—what he thought was to no purpose to propose.

This was my father, Mr. Shandy's hypothesis; concerning which I have only to add, that my brother Bobby did as great honour to it (whatever he did to the family) as any one of the great heroes we spoke of; for happening not only to be christened, as I told you, but to be born too, when my father was at Epsom,—being moreover my mother's first child,—coming into the world with his head *foremost*,—and turning out afterwards a lad of wonderful slow parts,—my father spelt all these together into his opinion; and as he had failed at one end,—he was determined to try the other.

This was not to be expected from one of the sisterhood, who are not easily to be put out of their way;—and was therefore one of my father's great reasons in favour of a man of science,——whom he could better deal with.

Of all men in the world, Dr. Slop was the fittest for my father's purpose;—for tho' his new-invented forceps was the armour he had proved, and what he maintained to be the safest instrument of deliverance, yet, it seems, he had scattered a word or two in his book, in favour of the very thing which ran in my father's fancy;—tho' not with a view to the soul's good in extracting by the feet, as was my father's system,—but for reasons merely obstetrical.

This will account for the coalition betwixt my father and Dr. Slop, in the ensuing discourse, which went a little hard against my uncle Toby.——In what manner a plain man, with nothing but common sense, could bear up against two such allies in science, is hard to conceive.—You may conjecture upon it, if you please;—and whilst your imagination is in motion, you may encourage it to go on, and discover by what causes and effects in nature it could come to pass, that my uncle Toby got his modesty by the wound he received upon his groin.—You may raise a system to account for the loss of my nose by marriage-articles,—and show the world how it could happen, that I should have the misfortune to be called Tristram, in opposition to my father's hypothesis, and the wish of the whole family, godfathers and godmothers not excepted.—These, with fifty other points left yet unravelled, you may endeavour to solve, if you have time ;—but I tell you beforehand it will be in vain ; for not the sage Alquise, the magician in Don Belianis of Greece, nor the no less famous Urganda the sorceress, his wife, (were they alive) could pretend to come within a league of the truth.

The reader will be content to wait for a full explanation of these matters till the next year,—when a series of things will be laid open which he little expects.

THE

LIFE AND OPINIONS

OF

TRISTRAM SHANDY, Gent.

VOL. III. ORIG. EDIT.

Multitudinis imperitæ non formido judicia, meis tamen, rogo, parcant opus-
culis—in quibus fuit propositi semper, à jocis ad seria, in seriis vicissim ad
jocos transire.

—Joan. Saresberiensis, *Episcopus Lugdun.*

CHAPTER I.

 WISH, Dr. Slop," quoth my uncle Toby (re-
peating his wish for Dr. Slop a second time,
and with a degree of more zeal and earnestness in his manner of wishing than he had
wished at first *)——" I wish, Dr. Slop,"
quoth my uncle Toby, " you had seen what prodigious
armies we had in Flanders!"

My uncle Toby's wish did Dr. Slop a disservice, which his
heart never intended any man;—Sir, it confounded him,—
and thereby putting his ideas first into confusion, and then
to fight, he could not rally them again for the soul of him.

In all disputes—male or female,—whether for honour, for
profit, or for love,—it makes no difference in the case;—
nothing is more dangerous, Madam, than a wish coming

* *Vide* page 128.

sideways in this unexpected manner upon a man. The safest way, in general, to take off the force of the wish is, for the party wished at, instantly to get upon his legs,—and wish the *wisher* something-in return, of pretty near the same value ;—so balancing the account upon the spot, you stand as you were ;—nay, sometimes gain the advantage of the attack by it.

This will be fully illustrated to the world in my chapter of wishes.—

Dr. Slop did not understand the nature of this defence ;— he was puzzled with it, and it put an entire stop to the dispute for four minutes and a half ;—five had been fatal to it : —My father saw the danger ;—the dispute was one of the most interesting disputes in the world : " Whether the child of his prayers and endeavours should be born without a head or with one."—He waited to the last moment, to allow Dr. Slop, in whose behalf the wish was made, his right of returning it ; but perceiving, I say, that he was confounded, and continued looking with that perplexed vacuity of eye which puzzled souls generally stare with,—first in my uncle Toby's face,—then in his,—then up,—then down,—then east,— east and by east,—and so on,—coasting it along by the plinth of the wainscot till he had got to the opposite point of the compass,—and that he had actually begun to count the brass nails upon the arm of his chair,—my father thought there was no time to be lost with my uncle Toby ; so took up the discourse as follows :—

CHAPTER II.

—" WHAT prodigious armies you had in Flanders ! "——

Brother Toby, replied my father, taking his wig from off his head with his right hand, and with his *left* pulling out a striped India handkerchief from his right coat-pocket, in order to rub his head, as he argued the point with my uncle Toby.——

——Now, in this I think my father was much to blame; and I will give you my reasons for it.

Matters of no more seeming consequence in themselves than, "Whether my father should have taken off his wig with his right hand or with his left,"—have divided the greatest kingdoms, and made the crowns of the monarchs who governed them to totter upon their heads.——But need I tell you, Sir, that the circumstances with which everything in this world is begirt, give everything in this world its size and shape,——and, by tightening it, or relaxing it, this way or that, make the thing to be what it is,—great,—little,—good,—bad,—indifferent or not indifferent, just as the case happens?

As my father's India handkerchief was in his right coat-pocket, he should by no means have suffered his right hand to have got engaged: on the contrary, instead of taking off his wig with it, as he did, he ought to have committed that entirely to the left; and then, when the natural exigency my father was under of rubbing his head, called out for his handkerchief, he would have had nothing in the world to have done, but to have put his right hand into his right coat-pocket and taken it out;—which he might have done without any violence, or the least ungraceful twist in any one tendon or muscle of his whole body.

In this case (unless, indeed, my father had been resolved to make a fool of himself by holding the wig stiff in his left hand,—or by making some nonsensical angle or other at his elbow-joint, or arm-pit)—his whole attitude had been easy, —natural, — unforced. Reynolds himself, as great and graceful as he paints, might have painted him as he sat.

Now, as my father managed this matter,—consider what a devil of a figure my father made of himself.

In the latter end of Queen Anne's reign, and in the beginning of the reign of King George the First,—" Coat-pockets were cut very low down in the skirt."—I need say no more ;—the father of mischief, had he been hammering at it a month, could not have contrived a worse fashion for one in my father's situation.

CHAPTER III.

It was not an easy matter in any king's reign (unless you were as lean a subject as myself) to have forced your hand, diagonally, quite across your whole body, so as to gain the bottom of your opposite coat-pocket.——In the year one thousand seven hundred and eighteen, when this happened, it was extremely difficult; so that when my uncle Toby discovered the transverse zig-zaggery of my father's approaches towards it, it instantly brought into his mind those he had done duty in, before the gate of St. Nicholas;—the idea of which drew off his attention so entirely from the subject in debate, that he had got his right hand to the bell to ring up Trim to go and fetch his map of Namur, and his compasses and sector along with it, to measure the returning angles of the transverses of that attack,—but particularly of that one where he received his wound upon his groin.

My father knit his brows, and, as he knit them, all the blood in his body seemed to rush up into his face :—my uncle Toby dismounted immediately.

—I did not apprehend your uncle Toby was on horseback.——

CHAPTER IV.

A man's body and his mind, with the utmost reverence to both I speak it, are exactly like a jerkin,—and a jerkin's lining;—rumple the one,—you rumple the other. There is one certain exception, however, in this case, and that is, when you are so fortunate a fellow as to have had your jerkin made of gum-taffeta, and the body-lining to it of a sarcenet, or thin Persian.

Zeno, Cleanthes, Diogenes Babylonius, Dionysius, Heracleotes, Antipater, Panætius, and Possidonius, amongst the Greeks ; — Cato, and Varro, and Seneca, amongst the Romans ; — Pantenus, and Clemens Alexandrinus, and

Montaigne, amongst the Christians; and a score and a half of good, honest, unthinking Shandean people as ever lived, whose names I can't recollect,—all pretended that their jerkins were made after this fashion;—you might have rumpled and crumpled, and doubled and creased, and fretted and fridged the outside of them all to pieces;—in short, you might have played the very devil with them, and, at the same time, not one of the insides of them would have been one button the worse, for all you had done to them.

I believe in my conscience that mine is made up somewhat after this sort:—for never poor jerkin has been tickled off at such a rate as it has been these last nine months together;—and yet I declare, the lining to it,—as far as I am a judge of the matter,—is not a threepenny piece the worse;—pell-mell, helter-skelter, ding-dong, cut-and-thrust, back stroke and fore stroke, side way and long way, have they been trimming it for me. Had there been the least gumminess in my lining, by Heaven! it had all of it, long ago, been frayed and fretted to a thread.

——You Messrs. the Monthly Reviewers:——how could you cut and slash my jerkin as you did?—how did you know but you would cut my lining too?

Heartily and from my soul, to the protection of that Being who will injure none of us, do I recommend you and your affairs,—so God bless you!—only next month, if any one of you should gnash his teeth, and storm and rage at me, as some of you did last May (in which I remember the weather was very hot)—don't be exasperated if I pass it by again with good temper,—being determined, as long as I live or write (which, in my case, means the same thing) never to give the honest gentleman a worse word or a worse wish than my uncle Toby gave the fly which buzzed about his nose all dinner-time:——" Go,—go, poor devil," quoth he;—"get thee gone:—why should I hurt thee! This world is surely wide enough to hold thee and me."

CHAPTER V.

ANY man, Madam, reasoning upwards, and observing the prodigious suffusion of blood in my father's countenance,— by means of which (as all the blood in his body seemed to rush into his face, as I told you) he must have reddened, pictorically and scientifically speaking, six whole tints and a half, if not a full octave above his natural colour;—any man, Madam, but my uncle Toby, who had observed this,— together with the violent knitting of my father's brows, and the extravagant contortion of his body during the whole affair,—would have concluded my father in a rage; and, taking that for granted,—had he been a lover of such kind of concord as arises from two such instruments being put in exact tune,—he would instantly have screwed up his to the same pitch;—and then the devil and all had broke loose —the whole piece, Madam, must have been played off like the sixth of Avison Scarlatti—*con furia,*—like mad.—Grant me patience!—What has *con furia,*—*con strepito,*—or any other hurly-burly whatever to do with harmony?

Any man, I say, Madam, but my uncle Toby, the benignity of whose heart interpreted every motion of the body in the kindest sense the motion would admit of, would have concluded my father angry, and blamed him too. My uncle Toby blamed nothing but the tailor who cut the pocket hole ;—so, sitting still till my father had got his handkerchief out of it, and looking all the time up in his face with inexpressible good-will,—my father at length went on as follows :—

CHAPTER VI.

" WHAT prodigious armies you had in Flanders !"

——Brother Toby, quoth my father, I do believe thee to be as honest a man, and with as good and as upright a heart as ever God created ;—nor is it thy fault if all the children

which have been, may, can, shall, will, or ought to be
begotten, come with their heads foremost into the world :—
but believe me, dear Toby, the accidents which unavoidably
way-lay them, not only in the article of our begetting 'em,
—though these, in my opinion, are well worth considering,
—but the dangers and difficulties our children are beset
with, after they are got forth into the world, are enow ;—
little need is there to expose them to unnecessary ones in
their passage to it.——Are these dangers, quoth my uncle
Toby, laying his hand upon my father's knee, and looking
up seriously in his face for an answer,—are these dangers
greater now-a-days, brother, than in times past ?——Brother
Toby, answered my father, if a child was but fairly begot,
and born alive, and healthy, and the mother did well after
it,—our forefathers never looked farther.—My uncle Toby
instantly withdrew his hand from off my father's knee,
reclined his body gently back in his chair, raised his head
till he could just see the cornice of the room, and then
directing the buccinatory muscles along his cheeks, and the
obicular muscles 'around his lips, to do their duty, he
whistled *Lillibullero.*

CHAPTER VII.

WHILST my uncle Toby was whistling *Lillibullero* to my
father,—Dr. Slop was stamping, and cursing and damning
at Obadiah at a most dreadful rate.——It would have done
your heart good, and cured you, Sir, for ever of the vile sin
of swearing, to have heard him. I am determined, therefore, to relate the whole affair to you.

When Dr. Slop's maid delivered the green-baize bag, with
her master's instruments in it, to Obadiah, she very sensibly
exhorted him to put his head and one arm through the
strings, and ride with it slung across his body. So undoing
the bow-knot, to lengthen the strings for him, without any
more ado she helped him on with it. However, as this, in

some measure, unguarded the mouth of the bag; lest anything should bolt out in galloping back, at the speed
Obadiah threatened, they consulted to take it off again : and
in the great care and caution of their hearts, they had taken
the two strings and tied them close (pursing up the mouth
of the bag first) with half-a-dozen hard knots, each of which
Obadiah, to make all safe, had twitched and drawn together
with all the strength of his body.

This answered all that Obadiah and the maid intended;
but was no remedy against some evils which neither he nor
she foresaw.   The instruments, it seems, as tight as the bag
was tied above, had so much room to play in it, towards the
bottom, (the shape of the bag being conical,) that Obadiah
could not make a trot of it, but with such a terrible jingle,
what with the *tiretête, forceps,* and *squirt,* as would have
been enough, had Hymen been taking a jaunt that way, to
have frightened him out of the country ; but when Obadiah
accelerated his motion, and from a plain trot assayed to
prick his coach-horse into a full gallop,—by Heaven ! Sir,
the jingle was incredible.

As Obadiah had a wife and three children,—the turpitude
of fornication, and the many other political ill consequences
of this jingling, never once entered his brain ; he had however his objection, which came home to himself, and weighed
with him, as it has oftentimes done with the greatest patriots
—"The poor fellow, Sir, was not able to hear himself
whistle."

CHAPTER VIII.

As Obadiah loved wind-music preferably to all the instrumental music he carried with him,—he very considerately
set his imagination to work, to contrive and to invent by
what means he should put himself in a condition of
enjoying it.

In all distresses (except musical) where small cords are

wanted, nothing is so apt to enter a man's head as his hat-band :——the philosophy of this is so near the surface,—I scorn to enter into it.

As Obadiah's was a mixed case ;——mark, Sirs,—I say, a mixed case; for it was obstetrical,—*scriptical,* squirtical, papistical—and, as far as the coach-horse was concerned in it,—Cabalistical, and only partly musical ;—Obadiah made no scruple of availing himself of the first expedient which offered : so taking hold of the bag and instruments, and gripping them hard together, with one hand, and with the finger and thumb of the other putting the end of the hat-band betwixt his teeth, and then slipping his hand down to the middle of it,—he tied and cross-tied them all fast together, from one end to the other (as you would cord a trunk), with such a multiplicity of roundabouts and intricate cross turns, with a hard knot at every intersection or point where the strings met,—that Dr. Slop must have had three-fifths of Job's patience at least to have unloosed them. —I think, in my conscience, that had Nature been in one of her nimble moods, and in humour for such a contest,—and she and Dr. Slop both fairly started together,—there is no man living who had seen the bag with all that Obadiah had done to it,—and known likewise the great speed the Goddess can make when she thinks proper, who would have had the least doubt remaining in his mind—which of the two would have carried off the prize. My mother, Madam, had been delivered sooner then the green bag infallibly—at least by twenty knots.—Sport of small accidents, Tristram Shandy ! that thou art, and ever will be ! had that trial been made for thee, and it was fifty to one but it had,—thy affairs had not been so depress'd (at least by the depression of thy nose) as they have been ; nor had the fortunes of thy house and the occasions of making them, which have so often presented themselves in the course of thy life, to thee, been so often, so vexatiously, so tamely, so irrecoverably abandoned —as thou hast been forced to leave them :—but 'tis over,— all but the account of 'em, which cannot be given to the curious till I am got into the world.

CHAPTER IX.

GREAT wits jump:—for the moment Dr. Slop cast his eyes upon his bag (which he had not done till the dispute with my uncle Toby about midwifery put him in mind of it) the very same thought occurred.—'Tis God's mercy, quoth he (to himself), that Mrs. Shandy has had so bad a time of it! else she might have been brought to bed, seven times told, before one-half of these knots could have been got untied. —But here you must distinguish:—the thought floated only in Dr. Slop's mind, without sail or ballast to it, as a simple proposition; millions of which, as your worship knows, are every day swimming quietly in the middle of the thin juice of a man's understanding, without being carried backwards or forwards, till some little gusts of passion or interest drive them to one side.

A sudden trampling in the room above, near my mother's bed, did the proposition the very service I am speaking of. By all that's unfortunate, quoth Dr. Slop, unless I make haste, the thing will actually befall me, as it is!

CHAPTER X.

IN the case of knots; by which, in the first place, I would not be understood to mean slip-knots,—because, in the course of my life and opinions,—my opinions concerning them will come in more properly when I mention the catastrophe of my great uncle, Mr. Hammond Shandy,— a little man,—but of high fancy;—he rushed into the Duke of Monmouth's affair:—nor, secondly, in this place, do I mean that particular species of knots called Bow-knots;— there is so little address, or skill, or patience required in the unloosing them, that they are below my giving any opinion at all about them.—But by the knots I am speaking of, may it please your Reverences to believe, that I mean good,

honest, devilish tight, hard knots, made *bonâ fide* as Obadiah
made his;—in which there is no quibbling provision made
by the duplication and return of the two ends of the strings
thro' the annulus or noose made by the second implication
of them,—to get them slipp'd and undone by.—I hope you
apprehend me!

In the case of these knots then, and of the several obstruc-
tions, which, may it please your Reverences, such knots
cast in our way in getting through life,—every hasty man
can whip out his penknife and cut through them.—'Tis
wrong. Believe me, Sirs, the most virtuous way, and which
both reason and conscience dictate,—is to take our teeth
or our fingers to them.—Dr. Slop had lost his teeth—his
favourite instrument, by extracting in a wrong direction, or
by some misapplication of it, unfortunately slipping, he had
formerly, in a hard labour, knock'd out three of the best of
them with the handle of it:——he tried his fingers;—alas!
the nails of his fingers and thumbs were cut close.—The
deuce take it! I can make nothing of it, either way! cried
Dr. Slop.—The trampling overhead, near my mother's
bedside, increased.—Pox take the fellow! I shall never get
the knots untied, as long as I live!—My mother gave a
groan.——Lend me your penknife!—I must e'en cut the
knots at last.—Pugh!—psha! Lord!—I have cut my
thumb quite across, to the very bone.—Curse the fellow!—
if there was not another man-midwife within fifty miles—I
am undone for this bout.—I wish the scoundrel hang'd!—I
wish he was shot!—I wish all the devils in hell had him for
a blockhead!——

My father had a great respect for Obadiah, and could
not bear to hear him disposed of in such a manner:—he
had, moreover, some little respect for himself,—and could
as ill bear with the indignity offered to himself in it.

Had Dr. Slop cut any part about him but his thumb,—
my father had pass'd it by—his prudence had triumphed:—
as it was, he was determined to have his revenge.

Small curses, Dr. Slop, upon great occasions, quoth my
father (condoling with him first upon the accident), are but

so much waste of our strength and soul's health to no
manner of purpose.——I own it, replied Dr. Slop.——They
are like sparrow-shot, quoth my uncle Toby (suspending his
whistling) fired against a bastion.——They serve, continued
my father, to stir the humours—but carry off none of their
acrimony :—for my own part, I seldom swear or curse at all
—I hold it bad ;—but if I fall into it by surprise, I generally
retain so much presence of mind (right! quoth my uncle
Toby) as to make it answer my purpose ;—that is, I swear
on till I find myself easy.   A wise and a just man, however,
would always endeavour to proportion the vent given to
these humours, not only to the degree of them stirring
within himself,—but to the size and ill intent of the offence
upon which they are to fall.—"Injuries come only from
the heart," quoth my uncle Toby.——For this reason, continued my father, with the most Cervantic gravity, I have
the greatest veneration in the world for that gentleman,
who, in distrust of his own discretion in this point, sat
down and composed (that is at his leisure) fit forms of
swearing suitable to all cases, from the lowest to the
highest provocations which could possibly happen to him ;
—which forms being well considered by him,—and such,
moreover, as he could stand to, he kept them ever by him
on the chimney-piece, within his reach, ready for use.——I
never apprehended, replied Dr. Slop, that such a thing was
ever thought of,—much less executed.—I beg your pardon!
answered my father : I was reading, though not using, one
of them to my brother Toby this morning, whilst he pour'd
out the tea :—'tis here upon the shelf over my head ;——
but if I remember right, 'tis too violent for a cut of the
thumb.——Not at all, quoth Dr. Slop—the devil take the
fellow !——Then, answered my father, 'tis much at your
service, Dr. Slop,—on condition you read it aloud.—So
rising up and reaching down a form of excommunication of
the Church of Rome, a copy of which my father (who was
curious in his collections) had procured out of the ledger-
book of the church of Rochester, writ by Ernulphus the
bishop,—with a most affected seriousness of look and voice,

which might have cajoled Ernulphus himself,—he put it into Dr. Slop's hands.——Dr. Slop wrapt his thumb up in the corner of his handkerchief, and with a wry face, though without any suspicion, read aloud, as follows,—my uncle Toby whistling *Lillibullero* as loud as he could, all the time.

TEXTUS DE ECCLESIA ROFFENSI, PER

ERNULFUM EPISCOPUM.

CAP. XI.

EXCOMMUNICATIO.

Ex auctoritate Dei Omnipotentis, Patris, et Filij, et Spiritus Sancti, et sanctorum canonum, sanctæque et intemeratæ Virginis Dei genetricis Mariæ,—

——Atque omnium cœlestium virtutum, angelorum, archangelorum, thronorum, dominationum, potestatuum, cherubim ac seraphim, et sanctorum patriarcharum, prophetarum, et omnium apostolorum et evangelistarum, et sanctorum innocentum, qui in conspectu Agni Santi digni inventi sunt canticum cantare novum, et sanctorum martyrum, et sanctorum confessorum, et sanctarum virginum, atque omnium simul sanctorum et electorum Dei,—Excommunicamus, et anathe-
       vel os   s   *vel* os   s
matizamus hunc furem, vel hunc malefactorem, N. N. et à liminibus sanctæ Dei ecclesiæ sequestramus, et æternis sup-
       vel i   n
pliciis excruciandus, mancipetur, cum Dathan et Abiram, et cum his qui dixerunt Domino Deo, Recede à nobis, scientiam

As the genuineness of the consultation of the *Sorbonne* upon the question of Baptism was doubted by some and denied by others,—'twas thought proper to print the original of this Excommunication : for the copy of which Mr. Shandy returns thanks to the Chapter-clerk of the Dean and Chapter of Rochester.

CHAPTER XI.

" By the authority of God Almighty, the Father, Son, and
Holy Ghost, and of the holy canons, and of the undefiled
Virgin Mary, mother and patroness of our Saviour,"—[I
think there is no necessity, quoth Dr. Slop, dropping the
paper down to his knee, and addressing himself to my father,
—as you have read it over, Sir, so lately to read it aloud;—
and as Captain Shandy seems to have no great inclination
to hear it,—I may as well read it to myself.——That's contrary to treaty, replied my father.—Besides there is something so whimsical, especially in the latter part of it, I should
grieve to lose the pleasure of a second reading.——Dr. Slop
did not altogether like it;—but my uncle Toby offering at
that instant to give over whistling, and read it himself to
them, Dr. Slop thought he might as well read it, under the
cover of my uncle Toby's whistling—as suffer my uncle
Toby to read it alone;—so raising up the paper to his face,
and holding it quite parallel to it, in order to hide his chagrin,
—he read it aloud, as follows,—my uncle Toby whistling
Lillibullero, though not quite so loud as before :—]

" By the authority of God Almighty, the Father, Son, and
Holy Ghost, and of the undefiled Virgin Mary, mother and
patroness of our Saviour, and of all the celestial virtues,
angels, archangels, thrones, dominions, powers, cherubim
and seraphim, and of all the holy patriarchs, prophets, and
of all the apostles and evangelists, and of the holy innocents,
who in the sight of the Holy Lamb are found worthy
to sing the new song of the holy martyrs and holy confessors,
and of the holy virgins, and of all the saints together, with
the holy and elect of God,—May he " (Obadiah) " be
damn'd ! " (for tying these knots)—" We excommunicate and
anathematise him; and from the thresholds of the holy
Church of God Almighty we sequester him, that he may be
tormented, disposed, and delivered over with Dathan, and
Abiram, and with those who say unto the Lord God,
' Depart from us, we desire none of thy ways.' And as fire

viarum tuarum nolumus: et sicut aquâ ignis extinguitur, sic
                vel eorum   n
extinguatur, lucerna ejus in secula seculorum nisi respuerit,
                      n
et ad satisfactionem venerit!   Amen.

            os
    Maledicat illum Deus Pater qui hominem creavit!   Male-
      os
dicat illum Dei Filius qui pro homine passus est!   Maledicat
os
illum Spiritus Sanctus qui in baptismo effusus est!   Male-
        os
dicat illum sancta crux, quam Christus pro nostrâ salute
hostem triumphans ascendit!

                os
    Maledicat illum sancta Dei genetrix et perpetua Virgo
                          os
Maria!   Maledicat illum sanctus Michael, animarum sus-
                          os
ceptor sacrarum.   Maledicant illum omnes angeli et archangeli, principatus et potestates, omnesque militia coelestes!

            os
    Maledicat illum patriarcharum et prophetarum laudabilis
          os
numerus!   Maledicant illum sanctus Johannes Præcursor et
Baptista Christi, et sanctus Petrus, et sanctus Paulus, atque
sanctus Andreas, omnesque Christi apostoli, simul et cæteri
discipuli, quatuor quoque evangelistæ, qui sua prædicatione
                                          os
mundum universum converterunt! Maledicat illum cuneus
martyrum et confessorum mirificus, qui Deo bonis operibus
placitus inventus est!

              os
    Maledicant illum sacrarum virginum chori, quæ mundi
vana causa honoris Christi respuenda contempserunt!
          os
Maledicant illum omnes sancti qui ab initio mundi usque
in finem seculi Deo dilecti inveniuntur!

is quenched with water, so let the light of him be put out for evermore, unless it shall repent him" (Obadiah, of the knots which he has tied) "and make satisfaction" (for them)! "Amen."

"May the Father who created man, curse him!—May the Son who suffered for us, curse him!——May the Holy Ghost, who was given to us in baptism, curse him!" (Obadiah)——May the holy cross, which Christ, for our salvation, triumphing over his enemies, ascended, curse him!"

"May the holy and eternal Virgin Mary, mother of God, curse him!——May St. Michael, the advocate of holy souls, curse him!——May all the angels, and archangels, principalities and powers, and all the heavenly armies, curse him!" [Our armies swore terribly in Flanders, cried my uncle Toby,—but nothing to this!——For my own part, I could not have a heart to curse my dog so.]

"May the praiseworthy multitude of patriarchs and prophets, curse him!

"May St. John the Præcursor, and St. John the Baptist, and St. Peter, and St. Paul, and St. Andrew, and all other Christ's apostles, together curse him! And may the rest of his disciples and four evangelists, who by their preaching converted the universal world, and may the holy and wonderful company of martyrs and confessors, who by their holy works are found pleasing to God Almighty, curse him!" (Obadiah.)

"May the holy choir of the holy virgins, who for the honour of Christ have despised the things of the world, damn him!—May all the saints who, from the beginning of the world to everlasting ages, are found to be beloved of God, damn him!—May the heavens, and earth, and all the holy things remaining therein, damn him," (Obadiah) "or her!" (or whoever else had a hand in tying these knots.)

os
Maledicant illum cœli et terra, et omnia sancta in eis manentia!

i   n   n
Maledictus sit ubicunque, fuerit, sive in domo, sive in agro, sive in viâ, sive in semitâ, sive in silvâ, sive in aquâ, sive in ecclesiâ!

i   n
Maledictus sit vivendo, moriendo,—

manducando, bibendo, esuriendo, sitiendo, jejunando, dormitando, dormiendo, vigilando, ambulando, stando, sedendo, jacendo, operando, quiescendo, mingendo, cacando, flebotomando!

i   n
Maledictus sit in totis viribus corporis!

i   n
Maledictus sit intus et exterius!

i   n   i   n
Maledictus sit in capillis! maledictus sit in cerebro!

i   n
Maledictus sit in vertice, in temporibus, in fronte, in auriculis, in superciliis, in oculis, in genis, in maxillis, in naribus, in dentibus, mordacibus, in labris sive molibus, in labiis, in gutture, in humeris, in carpis, in brachiis, in manibus, in digitis, in pectore, in corde, et in omnibus, interioribus stomacho tenus, in renibus, in inguine, in femore, in genitalibus, in coxis, in genibus, in cruribus, in pedibus, et in unguibus!

i   n
Maledictus sit in totis compagibus membrorum, á vertice capitis, usque ad plantam pedis!—Non sit in eo sanitas!

os
Maledicat illum Christus Filius Dei vivi toto suæ majestatis imperio——

"May he (Obadiah) be damn'd, wherever he be,—whether in the house or the stables, the garden or the field, or the highway, or in the path, or in the wood, or in the water, or in the church!——May he be cursed in living, in dying!" [Here my uncle Toby, taking the advantage of a *minim* in the second bar of his tune, kept whistling one continued note to the end of the sentence,—Dr. Slop, with his division of curses moving under him, like a running bass all the way.] "May he be cursed in eating and drinking; in being hungry, in being thirsty, in fasting, in sleeping, in slumbering, in waking, in walking, in standing, in sitting, in lying, in working, in resting, in pissing, in shitting, and in blood-letting.

"May he (Obadiah) be cursed in all the faculties of his body!

"May he be cursed inwardly and outwardly!——May he be cursed in the hair of his head!——May he be cursed in his brains, and in his vertex," (that is a sad curse! quoth my father) "in his temples, in his forehead, in his ears, in his eyebrows, in his cheeks, in his jaw-bones, in his nostrils, in his fore-teeth and grinders, in his lips, in his throat, in his shoulders, in his wrists, in his arms, in his hands, in his fingers!

May he be damn'd in his mouth, in his breast, in his heart and purtenance, down to the very stomach!

"May he be cursed in his reins, and in his groin," (God in heaven forbid! quoth my uncle Toby) "in his thighs, in his genitals" (my father shook his head) "and in his hips, and in his knees, his legs, and feet, and toe-nails!

"May he be cursed in all the joints and articulations of his members, from the top of his head to the sole of his foot! May there be no soundness in him!

"May the Son of the living God, with all the glory of his Majesty"——[Here my uncle Toby, throwing back his head, gave a monstrous, long, loud Whew—w—w——; something betwixt the interjectional whistle of *Hey-day!* and the word itself.——

——By the golden beard of Jupiter,—and of Juno (if her

——et insurgat adversus illum cœlum cum omnibus virtu-
tibus quæ in eo moventur ad *damnandum* eum, nisi pœnituerit
et ad satisfactionem venerit. Amen. Fiat, fiat! Amen.

majesty wore one), and by the beards of the rest of your Heathen Worships, which, by the bye, was no small number; since, what with the beards of your celestial gods, and gods aërial and aquatic,—to say nothing of the beards of town-gods and country-gods, of the celestial goddesses your wives, or of the infernal goddesses your whores and concubines (that is, in case they wore them)——all which beards, as Varro tells me, upon his word and honour, when mustered up together, made no less than thirty thousand effective beards upon the Pagan establishment;—every beard of which claimed the rights and privileges of being stroken and sworn by:—by all these beards together then,—I vow and protest, that of the two bad cassocks I am worth in the world, I would have given the better of them, as freely as ever Cid Hamet offered his,—only to have stood by, and heard my uncle Toby's accompaniment ‖

——"curse him!" continued Dr. Slop,—"and may Heaven, with all the powers which move therein, rise up against him, curse and damn him" (Obadiah), "unless he repent and make satisfaction! Amen. So be it,—so be it! Amen."

I declare, quoth my uncle Toby, my heart would not let me curse the Devil himself with so much bitterness.——He is the father of curses, replied Dr. Slop.——So am not I, replied my uncle.——But he is cursed and damned already, to all eternity, replied Dr. Slop.

✓ I am sorry for it, quoth my uncle Toby.

Dr. Slop drew up his mouth, and was just beginning to return my uncle Toby the compliment of his Whu—u—u—, or interjectional whistle,—when the door hastily opening in the next chapter but one,—put an end to the affair.

CHAPTER XII.

Now don't let us give ourselves a parcel of airs, and pretend that the oaths we make free with in this land of liberty of

ours are our own ; and, because we have the spirit to swear
them,—imagine that we have had the wit to invent them too.

I'll undertake this moment to prove it to any man in the
world, except to a connoisseur ;——though I declare I object only to a connoisseur in swearing,—as I would do to a
connoisseur in painting, &c., &c., the whole set of 'em are
so hung round and *befetish'd* with the bobs and trinkets of
criticism,—or, to drop my metaphor, which by the bye is a
pity,—for I have fetched it as far as from the coast of
Guinea,—their heads, Sir, are stuck so full of rules and
compasses, and have that eternal propensity to apply them
upon all occasions, that a work of genius had better go to
the Devil at once, than stand to be prick'd and tortur'd to
death by 'em.

—And how did Garrick speak the soliloquy last night ?—
Oh, against all rule, my Lord—most ungrammatically ! betwixt the substantive and the adjective, which should agree
together in *number, case,* and *gender,* he made a breach thus,
—stopping, as if the point wanted settling ;—and betwixt
the nominative case, which, your Lordship knows, should
govern the verb, he suspended his voice in the epilogue a
dozen times, three seconds and three-fifths by a stop-watch,
my Lord, each time.——Admirable grammarian !——But
in suspending his voice,—was the sense suspended likewise ?
—Did no expression of attitude or countenance fill up the
chasm ?—Was the eye silent ?—Did you narrowly look ?
——I looked only at the stop-watch, my Lord.——Excellent observer !

And what of this new book the whole world makes such
a rout about ?——Oh, 'tis out of all plump, my Lord,—
quite an irregular thing !—not one of the angles at the four
corners was a right angle.——I had my rule and compasses,
&c., my Lord, in my pocket.——Excellent critic !

——And for the epic poem your Lordship bid me look
at,—upon taking the length, breadth, height, and depth of
it, and trying them at home, upon an exact scale of Bossu's,
—'tis out, my Lord, in every one of its dimensions.——Admirable connoisseur !

——And did you step in, to take a look at the grand picture in your way back?——'Tis a melancholy daub, my Lord! not one principle of the pyramid in any one group! —and what a price!—for there is nothing of the colouring of Titian—the expression of Rubens—the grace of Raphael —the purity of Dominichino—the *corregiescity* of Corregio —the learning of Poussin—the airs of Guido—the taste of the Caraccis—or the grand contour of Angelo.——Grant me patience, just Heaven! Of all the cants which are canted in this canting world,—though the cant of hypocrites may be the worst,—the cant of criticism is the most tormenting!

I would go fifty miles on foot, for I have not a horse worth riding on, to kiss the hand of that man whose generous heart will give up the reins of his imagination into his author's hands,—be pleased he knows not why, and cares not wherefore.

Great Apollo! if thou art in a giving humour,—give me, —I ask no more, but one stroke of native humour, with a single spark of thy own fire along with it,—and send Mercury, with the *rules and compasses*, if he can be spared, with my compliments to,——no matter.

Now to any one else I will undertake to prove that all the oaths and imprecations which we have been puffing off upon the world for these two hundred and fifty years last past, as originals,—except *St. Paul's thumb*,—*God's flesh* and *God's fish*, which were oaths monarchical, and, considering who made them, not much amiss; and as king's oaths, 'tis not much matter whether they were fish or flesh; —else, I say, there is not an oath, or at least a curse amongst them, which has not been copied over and over again out of Ernulphus a thousand times: but, like all other copies, how infinitely short of the force and spirit of the original!—It is thought to be no bad oath,—and by itself passes very well,—"G—d damn you!"——Set it beside Ernulphus's,—"God Almighty the Father damn you!— God the Son damn you!—God the Holy Ghost damn you!" —you see 'tis nothing.——There is an orientality in his we cannot rise up to: besides, he is more copious in his invention,—possess'd more of the excellences of a swearer,—had such a thorough knowledge of the human frame, its membranes, nerves, ligaments, knittings of the joints, and articulations, — that when Ernulphus cursed, — no part escaped him.——'Tis true, there is something of a *hardness* in his manner,—and, as in Michael Angelo, a want of *grace ;*—but then there is such a greatness of *gusto!*

My father, who generally look'd upon everything in a light very different from all mankind, would, after all, never allow this to be an original.—He considered rather Ernulphus's anathema as an institute of swearing, in which, as he suspected, upon the decline of swearing in some milder pontificate, Ernulphus, by order of the succeeding Pope, had with great learning and diligence collected together all the laws of it ;—for the same reason that Justinian, in the decline of the empire, had ordered his chancellor Tribonian to collect the Roman or civil laws all together into one code or digest—lest, through the rust of time,—and the fatality of all things committed to oral tradition,—they should be lost to the world for ever.

For this reason, my father would oftentimes affirm, there was not an oath, from the great and tremendous oath of William the Conqueror ("By the splendour of God!") down to the lowest oath of the scavenger ("Damn your eyes!") which was not to be found in Ernulphus.——In short, he would add,—I defy a man to swear out of it.

The hypothesis is, like most of my father's, singular and ingenious too ;—nor have I any objection to it, but that it overturns my own.

———

CHAPTER XIII.

——BLESS my soul !—my poor mistress is ready to faint—and her pains are gone—and the drops are done—and the bottle of julap is broke—and the nurse has cut her arm—(and I my thumb, cried Dr. Slop) ; and the child is where it was, continued Susannah,—and the midwife has fallen backwards upon the edge of the fender, and bruised her hip as black as your hat.——I'll look at it, quoth Dr. Slop.—— There is no need of that, replied Susannah,—you had better look at my mistress—but the midwife would gladly first give you an account how things are; so desires you would go upstairs and speak to her, this moment.

Human-nature is the same in all professions.

The midwife had just before been put over Dr. Slop's head;—he had not digested it.—No, replied Dr. Slop, 'twould be full as proper, if the midwife came down to me. ——I like subordination, quoth my uncle Toby,—and but for it, after the reduction of Lisle, I know not what might have become of the garrison of Ghent, in the mutiny for bread, in the year Ten.——Nor, replied Dr. Slop, (parody-ing my uncle Toby's hobby-horsical reflection; though full as hobby-horsical himself)—do I know, Captain Shandy, what might have become of the garrison above stairs, in the mutiny and confusion I find all things are in at present, but for the subordination of fingers and thumbs to ******: —the application of which, Sir, under this accident of mine comes in so *à propos*, that without it, the cut upon my thumb might have been felt by the Shandy family as long as the Shandy family had a name.

CHAPTER XIV.

LET us go back to the ******—in the last chapter.

It is a singular stroke of eloquence (at least it was so when eloquence flourished at Athens and Rome; and would be so now, did orators wear mantles) not to mention the name of a thing, when you had the thing about you *in petto*, ready to produce, pop, in the place you want it. A scar, an axe, a sword, a pink'd doublet, a rusty helmet, a pound and a half of pot-ashes in an urn, or a three-halfpenny pickle-pot;—but above all, a tender infant royally accoutred.

—Tho' if it was too young, and the oration as long as Tully's second Philippic,—it must certainly have beshit the orator's mantle.—And then again if too old,—it must have been unwieldy and incommodious to his action,—so as to make him lose by his child almost as much as he could gain by it. —Otherwise, when a state-orator has hit the precise age to a minute,—hid his BAMBINO in his mantle so cunningly that no mortal could smell it,—and produced it so critically that no soul could say it came in by head and shoulders, —Oh, Sir, it has done wonders!—it has opened the sluices, and turn'd the brains, and shook the principles, and un-hinged the politics of half a nation.

These feats, however, are not to be done, except in those states and times, I say, where orators wore mantles,—and pretty large ones too, my brethren, with some twenty or five-and-twenty yards of good purple, superfine, marketable cloth in them,—with large flowing folds and doubles, and in a great style of design.—All which plainly shows, may it please your Worships, that the decay of eloquence, and the little good service it does at present, both within and with-out doors, is owing to nothing else in the world but short coats and the disuse of trunk-hose.——We can conceal nothing under ours, Madam, worth shewing.

* * *

CHAPTER XV.

DR. SLOP was within an ace of being an exception to all this argumentation : for happening to have his green-baize bag upon his knees when he began to parody my uncle Toby,—'twas as good as the best mantle in the world to him : for which purpose, when he foresaw the sentence would end in his new-invented forceps, he thrust his hand into the bag, in order to have them ready to clap in, when your Reverences took so much notice of the ******, which, had he managed,—my uncle Toby had certainly been overthrown : the sentence and the argument in that case jumping closely in one point, so like the two lines which form the salient angle of a ravelin,—Dr. Slop would never have given them up;—and my uncle Toby would as soon have thought of flying, as taking them by force: but Dr. Slop fumbled so vilely in pulling them out, it took off the whole effect, and, what was a ten times worse evil (for they seldom come alone in this life) in pulling out his forceps, his forceps unfortunately drew out the squirt along with it.

When a proposition can be taken in two senses,—'tis a law in disputation, that the respondent may reply to which of the two he pleases, or finds most convenient for him.— This threw the advantage of the argument quite on my uncle Toby's side,——" Good God !" cried my uncle Toby, *" are children brought into the world with a squirt ?"*

———————

CHAPTER XVI.

—Upon my honour, Sir, you have tore every bit of skin quite off the back of both my hands with your forceps, cried my uncle Toby :—and you have crush'd all my knuckles into the bargain with them to a jelly.——'Tis your own fault, said Dr. Slop ;—you should have clinch'd your two fists together into the form of a child's head, as I told you, and sat firm.——I did so, answered my uncle Toby.——Then the points of my forceps have not been sufficiently arm'd, or the rivet wants closing,—or else the cut on my thumb has made me a little awkward,—or possibly——'Tis well, quoth my father, interrupting the detail of possibilities—that the experiment was not first made upon my child's headpiece.——It would not have been a cherry-stone the worse, answered Dr. Slop.——I maintain it, said my uncle Toby, it would have broke the *cerebellum* (unless indeed the skull had been as hard as a granado) and turn'd it all into a perfect posset.——Pshaw ! replied Dr. Slop, a child's head is naturally as soft as the pap of an apple ;—the sutures give way ;—and besides, I could have extracted by the feet after.——Not you, said she.——I rather wish you would begin that way, quoth my father.

Pray do, added my uncle Toby.

CHAPTER XVII.

——AND pray, good woman, after all, will you take upon you to say, it may not be the child's hip, as well as the child's head ?—('Tis most certainly the head, replied the midwife.) Because, continued Dr. Slop (turning to my father), as positive as these old ladies generally are,—'tis a point very difficult to know,—and yet of the greatest consequence to be known ;——because, Sir, if the hip is mistaken for the head,—there is a possibility (if it is a boy) that the forceps * * *

——What the possibility was, Dr. Slop whispered very low to my father, and then to my uncle Toby.——There is no such danger, continued he, with the head.——No, in truth, quoth my father ;—but when your possibility has taken place at the hip,—you may as well take off the head too.

——It is morally impossible that the reader should understand this—'Tis enough Dr. Slop understood it ;—so taking the green-baize bag in his hand, with the help of Obadiah's pumps, he tripp'd pretty nimbly, for a man of his size, across the room to the door ;—and from the door was shown the way, by the good old midwife, to my mother's apartments.

CHAPTER XVIII.

IT is two hours and ten minutes,—and no more,—cried my father, looking at his watch, since Dr. Slop and Obadiah arrived ;—and I know not how it happens, brother Toby,—but, to my imagination,—it seems almost an age.

——Here—pray, Sir, take hold of my cap :—nay, take the bell along with it, and my pantoufles too.

Now, sir, they are all at your service ; and I freely make you a present of 'em, on condition you give me all your attention to this chapter.

Though my father said, " *He knew not how it happen'd,*" —yet he knew very well how it happen'd ;—and at the instant he spoke it, was predetermined in his mind to give my uncle Toby a clear account of the matter, by a metaphysical dissertation upon the subject of *duration and its simple modes,* in order to shew my uncle Toby by what mechanism and mensuration in the brain it came to pass, that the rapid succession of their ideas, and the eternal scampering of the discourse from one thing to another, since Dr. Slop had come into the room, had lengthened out so short a period to so inconceivable an extent.——" I know not how it happens," cried my father ;—" but it seems an age."

——'Tis owing entirely, quoth my uncle Toby, to the succession of our ideas.

My father, who had an itch, in common with all philosophers, of reasoning upon everything which happened, and accounting for it too,—proposed infinite pleasure to himself in this, of the succession of ideas ; and had not the least apprehension of having it snatch'd out of his hands by my uncle Toby, who (honest man !) generally took everything as it happen'd ;—and who of all things in the world troubled his brain the least with abstruse thinking ;—the ideas of time and space,—or how we came by those ideas,—or of what stuff they were made,—or whether they were born with us, or we picked them up afterwards as we went along, —or whether we did it in frocks,—or not till we had got into breeches ;—with a thousand other enquiries and disputes about INFINITY, PRESCIENCE, LIBERTY, NECESSITY, and so forth, upon whose desperate and unconquerable theories so many fine heads have been turned and cracked, —never did my uncle Toby's the least injury at all ; my father knew it,—and was no less surprised than he was disappointed with my uncle's fortuitous solution.

Do you understand the theory of that affair? replied my
father.

Not I, quoth my uncle.

—But you have some ideas, said my father, of what you
talk about?

No more than my horse, replied my uncle Toby.

Gracious Heaven! cried my father, looking upwards, and
clasping his two hands together,—there is a worth in thy
honest ignorance, brother Toby;—'twere almost a pity to
exchange it for a knowledge.—But I'll tell thee.——

To understand what Time is aright, without which we
never can comprehend Infinity, insomuch as one is a portion
of the other,—we ought seriously to sit down and consider
what idea it is we have of *duration,* so as to give a satisfactory account how we came by it.——What is that to anybody? quoth my uncle Toby. * "For if you will turn your
eyes inwards upon your mind," continued my father, "and
observe attentively, you will perceive, brother, that whilst
you and I are talking together, and thinking, and smoking
our pipes, or whilst we receive successively ideas in our
minds, we know that we do exist; and so we estimate the
existence, or the continuation of the existence of ourselves,
or anything else, commensurate to, the succession of any
ideas in our minds, the duration of ourselves, or any such
other thing co-existing with our thinking;—and so, according to that preconceived "——You puzzle me to death,
cried my uncle Toby.

——'Tis owing to this, replied my father, that in our
computations of time we are so used to minutes, hours,
weeks, and months—and of clocks (I wish there was not a
clock in the kingdom) to measure out their several portions
to us, and to those who belong to us,—that 'twill be well if,
in time to come, the *succession of our ideas* be of any use or
service to us at all.

Now, whether we observe it or no, continued my father, in
every sound man's head there is a regular succession of ideas,
of one sort or other, which follow each other in train just

* *Vide* Locke.

like——A train of artillery ? said my uncle Toby——A train of fiddle-stick !—quoth my father—which follow and succeed one another in our minds at certain distances, just like the images in the inside of a lantern turned round by the heat of a candle.—I declare, quoth my uncle Toby, mine are more like a smoke-jack.——Then, brother Toby, I have nothing more to say to you upon the subject, said my father.

CHAPTER XIX.

——What a conjuncture was here lost !——My father, in one of his best explanatory moods,—in eager pursuit of a metaphysical point, into the very region where clouds and thick darkness would soon have encompassed it about ;—my uncle Toby in one of the finest dispositions for it in the world ;—his head like a smoke-jack ;—the funnel unswept, and the ideas whirling round and round about in it, all obfuscated and darkened over with fuliginous matter.—— By the tombstone of Lucian !—if it is in being ;—if not, why then by his ashes ! by the ashes of my dear Rabelais, and dearer Cervantes !——my father and my uncle Toby's discourse upon TIME and ETERNITY,—was a discourse devoutly to be wished for ! and the petulancy of my father's humour, in putting a stop to it as he did, was a robbery of the *Ontologic Treasury* of such a jewel, as no coalition of great occasions and great men are ever likely to restore to it again.

CHAPTER XX.

Tho' my father persisted in not going on with the discourse, —yet he could not get my uncle Toby's smoke-jack out of his head,—piqued as he was at first with it ;—there was something in the comparison at the bottom which hit his fancy ; for which purpose, resting his elbow on the table, and reclining the right side of his head upon the palm of his hand,—but looking first steadfastly in the fire,—he began to commune with himself, and philosophise about it : but his spirits being worn out with the fatigues of investigating new tracts, and the constant exertion of his faculties upon that variety of subjects which had taken their turn in the discourse,—the idea of the smoke-jack soon turned all his ideas upside down,—so that he fell asleep almost before he knew what he was about.

As for my uncle Toby, his smoke-jack had not made a dozen revolutions before he fell asleep also.——Peace be with them both !——Dr. Slop is engaged with the midwife and my mother, above stairs.——Trim is busy in turning an old pair of jack-boots into a couple of mortars, to be employed in the siege of Messina next summer ;—and is this instant boring the touch-holes with the point of a hot poker. ——All my heroes are off my hands ;—'tis the first time I have had a moment to spare,—and I'll make use of it, and write my Preface.

THE AUTHOR'S PREFACE.

No, I'll not say a word about it ;—here it is.—In publishing it,—I have appealed to the world,—and to the world I leave it ;—it must speak for itself.

All I know of the matter is, when I sat down, my intent was to write a good book ; and as far as the tenuity of my understanding would hold out,—a wise, ay, and a discreet ; taking care only, as I went along, to put into it all the wit and the judgment (be it more or less) which the great Author and Bestower of them had thought fit originally to give me ; —so that, as your Worships see,—'tis just as God pleases.

Now, Agalastes (speaking dispraisingly) saith, That there may be some wit in it, for aught he knows,—but no judgment at all : and Triptolemus and Phutatorius agreeing thereto, ask, How is it possible there should ? for that wit and judgment in this world never go together ; inasmuch as they are two operations differing from each other as wide as east from west.—So says Locke:—so are farting and hickuping, say I. But in answer to this, Didius the great church-lawyer, in his code *de fartendi et illustrandi fallaciis*, doth maintain and make fully appear, That an illustration is no argument:—nor do I maintain the wiping of a looking-glass clean to be a syllogism;—but you all, may it please your Worships, see the better for it;—so that the main good these things do, is only to clarify the understanding previous to the application of the argument itself, in order to free it from any little motes, or specks of *opacular* matter, which, if left swimming therein, might hinder a conception, and spoil all.

Now, my dear anti-Shandeans, and thrice able critics and fellow-labourers (for to you I write this Preface)—and to you, most subtle statesmen and discreet doctors (do,—pull off your beards) renowned for gravity and wisdom;—Monopolus, my politician;—Didius, my counsel;—Kysarcius, my friend;—Phutatorius, my guide;—Gastripheres, the preserver of my life;—Somnolentius, the balm and repose of it,—not forgetting all others, as well sleeping as waking, ecclesiastical as civil, whom for brevity, but out of no resentment to you, I lump all together.——Believe me, Right Worthy,

My most zealous wish and fervent prayer in your behalf, and in my own too, in case the thing is not done already for us,——is, That the great gifts and endowments both of wit and judgment, with everything which usually goes along with them:—such as memory, fancy, genius, eloquence, quick parts, and what not, may this precious moment, without stint or measure, let or hindrance, be poured down warm as each of us could bear it,—scum and sediment and all (for I would not have a drop lost) into the several receptacles, cells, cellules, domiciles, dormitories, refectories, and spare places of our brains,——in such sort, that they might continue to be injected and tunn'd into, according to the true intent and meaning of my wish, until every vessel of them; both great and small, be so replenished, saturated, and filled up therewith, that no more, would it save a man's life, could possibly be got either in or out.

Bless us!—what noble work we should make!—how should I tickle it off!—and what spirits should I find myself in, to be writing away for such readers!—and you,—just Heaven!—with what raptures would you sit and read!—but oh!—'tis too much!—I am sick,—I faint away deliciously at the thoughts of it!—'tis more than nature can bear!— lay hold of me,—I am giddy,—I am stone blind,—I am dying,—I am gone.——Help! Help! Help!—But hold,—I grow something better again, for I am beginning to foresee, when this is over, that as we shall all of us continue to be great wits,—we should never agree amongst ourselves one day to an end:—there would be so much satire and sarcasm, —scoffing and flouting, with rallying and reparteeing of it, —thrusting and parrying in one corner or another,—there would be nothing but mischief among us.——Chaste stars! what biting and scratching, and what a racket and a clatter we should make, what with breaking of heads, rapping of knuckles, and hitting of sore places,—there would be no such thing as living for us.

But then again, as we should all of us be men of great judgment, we should make up matters as fast as ever they went wrong; and though we should abominate each other ten times worse than so many devils or devilesses, we should nevertheless, my dear creatures, be all courtesy and kindness, milk and honey;—'twould be a second land of promise —a paradise upon earth, if there was such a thing to be had; so that, upon the whole, we should have done well enough.

All I fret and fume at, and what most distresses my invention at present, is how to bring the point itself to bear; for, as your Worships well know, that of these heavenly emanations of *wit* and *judgment*, which I have so bountifully wished both for your Worships and myself,—there is but a certain *quantum* stored up for us all, for the use and behoof of the whole race of mankind; and such small *modicums* of 'em are only sent forth into this wide world, circulating here and there in one by-corner or another,—and in such narrow streams, and at such prodigious intervals from each other, that one would wonder how it holds out, or could be sufficient for the wants and emergencies of so many great states and populous empires.

Indeed, there is one thing to be considered: That in Nova Zembla, North Lapland, and in all those cold and dreary tracks of the globe which lie more directly under the arctic and antarctic circles, where the whole province of a man's concernments lies, for near nine months together within the narrow compass of his cave,—where the spirits are compressed almost to nothing,—and where the passions of a man, with everything which belongs to them, are as frigid as the zone itself;—there the least quantity of *judgment* imaginable does the business;—and of *wit*,—there is a total and an absolute saving,—for, as not one spark is wanted,—so not one spark is given. Angels and ministers of grace defend us! what a dismal thing would it have been to have governed a kingdom, to have fought a battle, or made a treaty, or run a match, or wrote a book, or got a child, or held a provincial chapter there, with so *plentiful a lack* of wit and judgment about us!—For mercy's sake, let us think no more about it, but travel on as fast as we can southwards into Norway,—crossing over Swedeland, if you please, through the small triangular province of Angermania, to the Lake of Bothnia; coasting along it through East and West Bothnia, down to Carelia, and so on, through all those states and provinces which border upon the far side of the Gulf of Finland, and the north-east of the Baltic, up to Petersburg, and just stepping into Ingria;—then stretching over directly from thence through the north parts of the Russian empire, leaving Siberia a little upon the left hand till we got into the very heart of Russia and Asiatic Tartary.

Now through this long tour which I have led you, you observe the good people are better off by far, than in the polar countries which we have just left:——for if you hold your hand over your eyes, and look very attentively, you may perceive some small glimmerings (as it were) of wit, with a comfortable provision of good, plain, household judgment, which, taking the quality and quantity of it together, they make a very good shift with;—and had they more of either the one or the other, it would destroy the proper balance betwixt them; and I am satisfied, moreover, they would want occasions to put them to use.

Now, Sir, if I conduct you home again into this warmer and more luxuriant island, where, you perceive, the spring-tide of our blood and humours runs high;—where we have more ambition, and pride, and envy, and lechery, and other whoreson passions upon our hands to govern and subject to reason,—the *height* of our wit, and the *depth* of our judgment, you see, are exactly proportioned to the *length* and *breadth* of our necessities;—and accordingly we have them sent down amongst us in such a flowing kind of decent and creditable plenty, that no one thinks he has any cause to complain.

It must, however, be confessed, on this head, that, as our air blows hot and cold,—wet and dry, ten times in a day, we have them in no regular and settled way;—so that sometimes, for near half a century together, there shall be very little wit or judgment either to be seen or heard of amongst us:—the small channels of them shall seem quite dried up;—then all of a sudden the sluices shall break out, and take a fit of running again like fury,—you would think they would never stop:——and then it is that, in writing, and fighting, and twenty other gallant things, we drive all the world before us.

It is by these observations, and a wary reasoning by analogy in that kind of argumentative process which Suidas calls *dialectic induction*,—that I draw and set up this position as most true and veritable:

That of these two luminaries, so much of their irradiations are suffered from time to time to shine down upon us, as He, whose infinite wisdom, which dispenses everything in exact weight and measure, knows will just serve to light us on our way in this night of our obscurity; so that your Reverences and Worships now find out, nor is it a moment longer in my power to conceal it from you, That the fervent wish in your behalf with which I set out was no more than the first insinuating *How d'ye* of a caressing prefacer, stifling his reader, as a lover sometimes does a coy mistress, into silence. For, alas! could this effusion of light have been as easily procured as the exordium wished it,—I tremble to think how many thousands for it, of benighted travellers (in the learned sciences at least) must have groped and blundered on in the dark, all the nights of their lives,—running their heads against posts, and knocking out their brains, without ever getting to their journey's end ;—some falling with their noses perpendicularly into sinks ;—others horizontally, with their tails into kennels : Here one half of a learned profession tilting *full butt* against the other half of it ; and then tumbling and rolling one over the other in the dirt, like hogs :— Here the brethren of another profession, who should have run in opposition to each other, flying, on the contrary, like a flock of wild geese, all in a row the same way.—What confusion !—what mistakes !—fiddlers and painters judging by their eyes and ears—admirable !—trusting to the passions excited,—in an air sung, or a story painted to the heart,— instead of measuring them by a quadrant !

In the foreground of this picture, a *statesman* turning the political wheel, like a brute, the wrong way round—*against* the stream of corruption,—by Heaven! instead of *with* it !

In this corner a son of the divine Esculapius, writing a book against predestination; perhaps worse,—feeling his patient's pulse, instead of his apothecary's :—a brother of the Faculty in the background upon his knees, in tears,— drawing the curtains of a mangled victim, to beg his forgiveness ;—offering a fee, instead of taking one.

In that spacious HALL, a coalition of the gown, from all the bars of it, driving a damn'd, dirty, vexatious cause before them, with all their might and main, the wrong way !— kicking it *out* of the great doors, instead of *in !*—and with such fury in their looks, and such a degree of inveteracy in their manner of kicking it, as if the laws had been originally made for the peace and preservation of mankind :——perhaps

a more enormous mistake committed by them still,—a liti-
gated point fairly hung up;—for instance, Whether *John
o' Nokes* his nose could stand in *Tom o' Stiles* his face, without
a trespass, or not?—rashly determined by them in five-and-
twenty minutes, which, with the cautious pro's and con's
required in so intricate a proceeding, might have taken up as
many months;—and if carried on upon a military plan, as
your Honours know an ACTION should be, with all the strata-
gems practicable therein,—such as feints,—forced marches,
—surprises,—ambuscades,—mask-batteries, and a thousand
other strokes of generalship, which consist in catching at all
advantages on both sides,—might reasonably have lasted
them as many years, finding food and raiment all that term
for a centumvirate of the profession.

As for the Clergy,—No;—if I say a word against them,
I'll be shot.——I have no desire; and besides, if I had,—I
durst not for my soul touch upon the subject. With such
weak nerves and spirits, and in the condition I am in at
present, 'twould be as much as my life was worth, to deject
and contrist myself with so bad and melancholy an account;
—and therefore 'tis safer to draw a curtain across, and hasten
from it as fast as I can, to the main and principal point I
have undertaken to clear up;—and that is, How it comes to
pass, that your men of least *wit* are reported to be men of
most *judgment?*—But mark—I say, *reported to be;*—for it
is no more, my dear Sirs, than a report, and which, like
twenty others taken up every day upon trust, I maintain to
be a vile and malicious report into the bargain.

This, by the help of the observation already premised, and
I hope already weighed and perpended by your Reverences
and Worships, I shall forthwith make appear.

I hate set dissertations;—and, above all things in the
world, 'tis one of the silliest things in one of them, to darken
your hypothesis by placing a number of tall, opaque words,
one before another, in a right line, betwixt your own and
your reader's conception,—when, in all likelihood, if you
had looked about, you might have seen something standing,
or hanging up, which would have cleared the point at once

—"for what hindrance, hurt, or harm doth the laudable desire of knowledge bring to any man, if even from a sot, a pot, a fool, a stool, a winter-mittain, a truckle for a pulley, the lid of a goldsmith's crucible, an oil-bottle, an old slipper, or a cane-chair?"—I am this moment sitting upon one. Will you give me leave to illustrate this affair of wit and judgment, by the two nobs on the top of the back of it?— they are fastened on, you see, with two pegs stuck slightly into two gimlet-holes, and will place what I have to say in so clear a light, as to let you see through the drift and meaning of my whole preface, as plainly as if every point and particle of it was made up of sunbeams.

I enter now directly upon the point.

—Here stands *wit*—and there stands *judgment*, close beside it, just like the two knobs I'm speaking of, upon the back of this selfsame chair on which I am sitting.

—You see, they are the highest and most ornamental parts of its *frame*,—as wit and judgment are of *ours*,—and, like them too, indubitably both made and fitted to go together, in order, as we say in all such cases of duplicated embellishments,—*to answer one another.*

Now, for the sake of an experiment, and for the clearer illustrating this matter,—let us for a moment take off one of these two curious ornaments (I care not which) from the point or pinnacle of the chair it now stands on;—nay, don't laugh at it,—but did you ever see, in the whole course of your lives, such a ridiculous business as this has made of it? —Why, 'tis as miserable a sight as a sow with one ear; and there is just as much sense and symmetry in the one as in the other.——Do,—pray, get off your seats, only to take a view of it.—Now, would any man, who valued his character a straw, have turned a piece of work out of his hand in such a condition?—Nay, lay your hands upon your hearts, and answer this plain question, Whether this one single knob which now stands here like a blockhead by itself, can serve any purpose upon earth, but to put one in mind of the want of the other?—and let me further ask, in case the chair was your own, if you would not in your consciences think, rather than be as it is, that it would be ten times better without any knob at all?

Now these two knobs,—or top-ornaments of the mind of man, which crown the whole entablature,—being, as I said, wit and judgment, which, of all others, as I have proved it, are the most needful,—the most priz'd,—the most calamitous to be without, and consequently the hardest to come at;—for all these reasons put together, there is not a mortal among us who is so destitute of a love of good fame or feeding,—or so ignorant of what will do him good therein,—who does not wish and steadfastly resolve in his own mind, to be, or to be thought at least, master of the one or the other, and indeed of both of them, if the thing seems any way feasible, or likely to be brought to pass.

Now, your graver gentry having a little or no kind of chance in aiming at the one,—unless they laid hold of the other,—pray what do you think would become of them?— Why, Sirs, in spite of all their *gravities*, they must e'en have been contented to have gone with their insides naked:—this was not to be borne, but by an effort of philosophy not to be supposed in the case we are upon;—so that no one could well have been angry with them, had they been satisfied with what little they could have snatched up and secreted under their cloaks and great periwigs, had they not raised a *hue* and *cry* at the same time against the lawful owner.

I need not tell your Worships, that this was done with so much cunning and artifice,—that the great Locke, who was seldom outwitted by false sounds,—was nevertheless bubbled here.——The cry, its seems, was so deep and solemn a one, and, what with the help of great wigs, grave faces, and other implements of deceit, was rendered so general a one against the *poor wits* in this matter, that the philosopher himself was deceived by it:—it was his glory to free the world from the lumber of a thousand vulgar errors;—but this was not of the number; so that, instead of sitting down coolly, as such a philosopher should have done, to have examined the matter of fact before he philosophised upon it,—on the contrary, he took the fact for granted, and so joined in with the cry, and halloo'd it as boisterously as the rest.

This has been made the Magna Charta of stupidity ever since:—but your Reverences plainly see, it has been obtained in such a manner, that the title to it is not worth a groat:——which, by the bye, is one of the many and vile impositions which gravity and grave folks have to answer for hereafter.

As for great wigs, upon which I may be thought to have spoken my mind too freely,—I beg leave to qualify whatever has been unguardedly said to their dispraise or prejudice, by one general declaration.—That I have no abhorrence whatever, nor do I detest and abjure either great wigs or long beards any farther than when I see they are bespoke and let grow on purpose to carry on this selfsame imposture,—for any purpose.—Peace be with them!—☞ Mark only,—I write not for them.

CHAPTER XXI.

EVERY day, for at least ten years together, did my father resolve to have it mended:—'tis not mended yet.—No family but ours would have borne with it an hour;—and what is most astonishing, there was not a subject in the world upon which my father was so eloquent, as upon that of door-hinges:——and yet at the same time he was certainly one of the greatest bubbles to them, I think, that history can produce: his rhetoric and conduct were at perpetual handicuffs.——Never did the parlour-door open, but his philosophy or his principles fell a victim to it.—Three drops of oil with a feather, and a smart stroke of a hammer, had saved his honour for ever.

——Inconsistent soul that man is!—languishing under wounds, which he has the power to heal!—his whole life a contradiction to his knowledge!—his reason, that precious gift of God to him,—(instead of pouring in oil) serving but to sharpen his sensibilities,—to multiply his pains, and render him melancholy and more uneasy under them!—Poor unhappy creature, that he should do so!—Are not the necessary causes of misery in this life enough, but he must add voluntary ones to his stock of sorrow!—struggle against evils which cannot be avoided! and submit to others, which a tenth part of the trouble they create him would remove from his heart for ever!

By all that is good and virtuous, if there are three drops of oil to be got, and a hammer to be found within ten miles of Shandy-Hall, the parlour door-hinge shall be mended this reign.

CHAPTER XXII.

WHEN Corporal Trim had brought his two mortars to bear, he was delighted with his handiwork above measure; and knowing what a pleasure it would be to his master to see them, he was not able to resist the desire he had of carrying them directly into his parlour.

Now, next to the moral lesson I had in view, in mentioning the affair of *hinges*, I had a speculative consideration arising out of it, and it is this:

Had the parlour-door opened and turn'd upon its hinges as a door should do,—

Or, for example, as cleverly as our government has been turning upon its hinges,—(that is, in case things have all along gone well with your Worship,—otherwise I give up my simile)—in this case, I say, there had been no danger, either to master or man, in Corporal Trim's peeping in: the moment he had beheld my father and my uncle Toby fast asleep,—the respectfulness of his carriage was such, he would have retired as silent as death, and left them both in their arm-chairs, dreaming as happy as he had found them: but the thing was, morally speaking, so very impracticable, that for the many years in which this hinge was suffered to be out of order, and amongst the hourly grievances my father submitted to upon its account,—this was one; that he never folded his arms to take his nap after dinner, but the thoughts of being unavoidably awakened by the first person who should open the door, was always uppermost in his imagination, and so incessantly stepp'd in betwixt him and the first balmy presage of his repose, as to rob him, as he often declared, of the whole sweets of it.

"When things move upon bad hinges, an' please your Worships, how can it be otherwise?"

Pray what's the matter? Who is there? cried my father, waking, the moment the door began to creak.——I wish the smith would give a peep at that confounded hinge!—— 'Tis nothing, an' please your Honour, said Trim, but two mortars I am bringing in.——They sha'n't make a clatter with them here! cried my father hastily.——If Dr. Slop has any drugs to pound, let him do it in the kitchen.——May it please your Honour, cried Trim, they are two mortar-pieces for a siege next summer, which I have been making out of a pair of jack-boots, which Obadiah told me your Honour had left off wearing.——By Heaven! cried my father, springing out of his chair, as he swore,—I have not one appointment belonging to me which I have set so much store by, as I do by these jack-boots:—they were our great-grandfather's, brother Toby:—they were *hereditary.*——Then I fear, quoth my uncle Toby, Trim has cut off the entail.——I have only cut off the tops, an' please your Honour, cried Trim.——I hate *perpetuities* as much as any man alive, cried my father,—but these jack-boots, continued he (smiling, though very angry at the same time), have been in the family, brother, ever since the civil wars:—Sir Roger Shandy wore them at the battle of Marston-Moor.—I declare I would not have taken ten pounds for them.——I'll pay you the money, brother Shandy, quoth my uncle Toby, looking at the two mortars with infinite pleasure, and putting his hand into his breeches-pocket as he viewed them—I'll pay you the ten pounds this moment, with all my heart and soul!——

Brother Toby, replied my father, altering his tone, you

care not what money you dissipate and throw away, provided, continued he, 'tis but upon a SIEGE.——Have I not
one hundred and twenty pounds a year, besides my half-
pay? cried my uncle Toby.——What is that,—replied my
father hastily,—to ten pounds for a pair of jack-boots?—
twelve guineas for your *pontoons ?*—half as much for your
Dutch drawbridge?—to say nothing of the train of little
brass artillery you bespoke last week, with twenty other pre-
parations for the siege of Messina! Believe me, dear brother
Toby, continued my father, taking him kindly by the hand,
—these military operations of yours are above your strength:
—you mean well, brother, but they carry you into greater
expenses than you were at first aware of;—and take my
word, dear Toby, they will in the end quite ruin your fortune, and make a beggar of you.——What signifies it if
they do, brother, replied my uncle Toby, so long as we know
'tis for the good of the nation ?——

My father could not help smiling, for his soul :—his anger
at the worst was never more than a spark ;—and the zeal
and simplicity of Trim,—and the generous (though hobby-
horsical) gallantry of my uncle Toby, brought him into perfect good humour with them in an instant.

Generous souls !—God prosper you both, and your mortar-
pieces too! quoth my father to himself.

CHAPTER XXIII.

ALL is quiet and hush, cried my father, at least above stairs :
I hear not one foot stirring.—Prithee, Trim, who's in the
kitchen?——There is no one soul in the kitchen, answered
Trim, making a low bow as he spoke, except Dr. Slop.——
Confusion! cried my father (getting up upon his legs a
second time) not one single thing has gone right this day!
Had I faith in astrology, brother, (which, by the bye, my
father had), I would have sworn some retrograde planet was
hanging over this unfortunate house of mine, and turning

every individual thing in it out of its place. Why, I thought Dr. Slop had been above stairs with my wife; and so said you.—What can the fellow be puzzling about in the kitchen!——He is busy, an' please your Honour, replied Trim, in making a bridge.——'Tis very obliging in him, quoth my uncle Toby:—pray, give my humble service to Dr. Slop, Trim, and tell him I thank him heartily.

You must know, my uncle Toby mistook the bridge,—as widely as my father mistook the mortars:—but to understand how my uncle Toby could mistake the bridge,—I fear I must give you an exact account of the road which led to it;—or, to drop my metaphor (for there is nothing more dishonest in an historian than the use of one)—in order to conceive the probability of this error in my uncle Toby aright, I must give you some account of an adventure of Trim's, though much against my will: I say much against my will, only because the story, in one sense, is certainly out of its place here; for by right, it should come in, either amongst the anecdotes of my uncle Toby's amours with Widow Wadman, in which Corporal Trim was no mean actor,—or else in the middle of his and my uncle Toby's campaigns on the bowling-green, for it will do very well in either place;—but then, if I reserve it for either of those parts of my story,—I ruin the story I'm upon;—and if I tell it here,—I anticipate matters, and ruin it there.

—What would your Worships have me to do in this case?

Tell it, Mr. Shandy, by all means.——You are a fool, Tristram, if you do.

O ye Powers! (for Powers ye are, and great ones too)—which enable mortal man to tell a story worth the hearing,—that kindly show him where he is to begin it,—and where he is to end it,—what he is to put into it,—and what he is to leave out,—how much of it he is to cast into a shade,—and whereabouts he is to throw his light!—Ye, who preside over this vast empire of biographical freebooters, and see how many scrapes and plunges your subjects hourly fall into,—will you do one thing?

I beg and beseech you (in case you will do nothing better for us), that wherever, in any part of your dominions, it so falls out, that three several roads meet in one point, as they have done just here—that at least you set up a guide-post in the centre of them, in mere charity, to direct an uncertain devil which of the three he is to take.

CHAPTER XXIV.

THO' the shock my uncle Toby received the year after the demolition of Dunkirk, in his affair with Widow Wadman, had fixed him in a resolution never more to think of the sex,—or of aught which belonged to it;—yet Corporal Trim had made no such bargain with himself.—Indeed, in my uncle Toby's case there was a strange and unaccountable concurrence of circumstances, which insensibly drew him in, to lay siege to that fair and strong citadel.—In Trim's case there was a concurrence of nothing in the world, but of him and Bridget in the kitchen;—though, in truth, the love and veneration he bore his master was such, and so fond was he of imitating him in all he did, that had my uncle Toby employed his time and genius in tagging of points,—I am persuaded that the honest Corporal would have laid down his arms, and followed his example with pleasure. When, therefore, my uncle Toby sat down before the mistress,—Corporal Trim incontinently took ground before the maid.

Now, my dear friend Garrick, whom I have so much cause to esteem and honour—(why, or wherefore, 'tis no matter)—can it escape your penetration,—I defy it,—that so many playwrights, and opificers of chitchat, have ever since been working upon Trim's and my uncle Toby's pattern?—I care not what Aristotle, or Pacuvius, or Bossu, or Ricaboni say—(though I never read one of them)—there is not a greater difference between a single-horse chair and Madam Pompadour's *vis-à-vis*, than betwixt a single amour and an amour thus nobly doubled, and going upon all four, prancing throughout a grand drama.—Sir, a simple, single silly affair of that kind,—is quite lost in five acts;—but that is neither here nor there.

After a series of attacks and repulses in a course of nine months on my uncle Toby's quarter, a most minute account of every particular of which shall be given in its proper place, my uncle Toby, honest man! found it necessary to draw off his forces, and raise the siege somewhat indignantly.

Corporal Trim, as I said, had made no such bargain, either with himself,—or with any one else:—the fidelity however of his heart not suffering him to go into a house which his master had forsaken with disgust,—he contented himself with turning his part of the siege into a blockade; —that is, he kept others off;—for though he never after went to the house, yet he never met Bridget in the village but he would either nod, or wink, or smile, or look kindly at her,—or (as circumstances directed) he would shake her by the hand,—or ask her lovingly how she did,—or would give her a ribbon,—and now and then, though never but when it could be done with decorum, would give Bridget a ——

Precisely in this situation did these things stand for five years; that is, from the demolition of Dunkirk in the year thirteen, to the latter end of my uncle Toby's campaign in the year eighteen, which was about six or seven weeks before the time I'm speaking of,——when Trim, as his custom was, after he had put my uncle Toby to bed, going down one moon-shiny night to see that everything was right at his fortifications,—in the lane separated from the bowling-green with flowering shrubs and holly,—he espied his Bridget.

As the Corporal thought there was nothing in the world so well worth showing as the glorious works which he and my uncle Toby had made, Trim courteously and gallantly took her by the hand, and led her in. This was not done so privately, but that the foul-mouth'd trumpet of Fame carried it from ear to ear, till at length it reach'd my father's, with this untoward circumstance along with it, that my uncle Toby's curious drawbridge, constructed and painted after the Dutch fashion, and which went quite across the ditch,—was broke down, and somehow or other crushed all to pieces that very night.

My father, as you have observed, had no great esteem for my uncle Toby's HOBBY-HORSE; he thought it the most ridiculous horse that ever gentleman mounted; and indeed, unless my uncle Toby vexed him about it, could never think of it once, without smiling at it; so that it could never get lame, or happen any mischance, but it tickled my father's imagination beyond measure: but this being an accident much more to his humour than any one which had yet befallen it, it proved an inexhaustible fund of entertainment to him.—Well,—but, dear Toby! my father would say, do tell me seriously how this affair of the bridge happened?—— How can you tease me so much about it? my uncle Toby would reply;—I have told it you twenty times, word for word as Trim told it me.——Prithee, how was it then, Corporal? my father would cry, turning to Trim.——It was a mere misfortune, an' please your Honour;—I was shewing Mrs. Bridget our fortifications; and in going too near the edge of the *fossé*, I unfortunately slipp'd in.——Very well, Trim! my father would cry—(smiling mysteriously, and giving a nod,—but without interrupting him)——and being link'd fast, an' please your Honour, arm in arm with Mrs. Bridget, I dragg'd her after me; by means of which she fell backwards, soss against the bridge;—and Trim's foot (my uncle Toby would cry, taking the story out of his mouth) getting into the cuvette, he tumbled full against the bridge too.——It was a thousand to one, my uncle Toby would add, that the poor fellow did not break his leg.——Ay, truly, my father would say;—a limb is soon broke, brother Toby, in such encounters.——And so, an' please your Honour, the bridge, which your Honour knows was a very slight one, was broke down betwixt us, and splintered all to pieces.

At other times, but especially when my uncle Toby was

so unfortunate as to say a syllable about cannons, bombs, or petards,—my father would exhaust all the stores of his eloquence (which indeed were very great) in a panegyric upon the battering-rams of the ancients—the vinea which Alexander made use of at the siege of Troy.—He would tell my uncle Toby of the *catapultæ* of the Syrians, which threw such monstrous stones so many hundred feet, and shook the strongest bulwarks from their very foundations :—he would go on and describe the wonderful mechanism of the *ballista*, which Marcellinus makes so much rout about !—the terrible effects of the *pyraboli*, which cast fire ;—the danger of the *terebra* and *scorpio*, which cast javelins.—But what are these, would he say, to the destructive machinery of Corporal Trim ? Believe me, brother Toby, no bridge, or bastion, or sally-port, that ever was constructed in this world, can hold out against such artillery.

My uncle Toby would never attempt any defence against the force of this ridicule, but that of redoubling the vehemence of smoking his pipe: in doing which, he raised so dense a vapour one night after supper, that it set my father, who was a little phthisical, into a suffocating fit of violent coughing: my uncle Toby leap'd up, without feeling the pain upon his groin,—and, with infinite pity, stood beside his brother's chair, tapping his back with one hand, and holding his head with the other, and from time to time wiping his eyes with a clean cambric handkerchief, which he pulled out of his pocket.—The affectionate and endearing manner in which my uncle Toby did these little offices—cut my father thro' his reins, for the pain he had just been giving him.—May my brains be knocked out with a battering-ram or a catapulta, I care not which, quoth my father to himself,—if ever I insult this worthy soul more !

———

CHAPTER XXV.

THE drawbridge being held irreparable, Trim was ordered
directly to set about another,——but not upon the same
model : for Cardinal Alberoni's intrigues at that time being
discovered, and my uncle Toby rightly foreseeing that a
flame would inevitably break out betwixt Spain and the
Empire, and that the operations of the ensuing campaign
must in all likelihood be either in Naples or Sicily,—he
determined upon an Italian bridge—my uncle Toby, by the
bye, was not far out of his conjectures) ;—but my father,
who was infinitely the better politician, and took the lead
as far of my uncle Toby in the cabinet, as my uncle Toby
took it of him in the field,—convinced him, that if the King
of Spain and the Emperor went together by the ears,—
England, France, and Holland must, by force of their
pre-engagements, all enter the lists too ;—and if so, he would
say, the combatants, brother Toby, as sure as we are alive,
will fall to it again, pell-mell, upon the old prize-fighting
stage of Flanders !—then what will you do with your
Italian bridge ?

—We will go on with it, then, upon the old model ; cried
my uncle Toby.

When Corporal Trim had about half-finished it in that
style,—my uncle Toby found out a capital defect in it,
which he had never thoroughly considered before.   It
turned, it seems, upon hinges at both ends of it, opening in
the middle ; one half of which turning to one side of the
fossé, and the other to the other; the advantage of which
was this, that by dividing the weight of the bridge into two
equal portions, it empowered my uncle Toby to raise it up
or let it down with the end of his crutch, and with one
hand, which, as his garrison was weak, was as much as he
could well spare :—but the disadvantages of such a construction were insurmountable ;—for by this means, he
would say, I leave one half of my bridge in my enemy's
possession ; and pray, of what use is the other ?

The natural remedy for this was, no doubt, to have his bridge fast only at one end with hinges, so that the whole might be lifted up together, and stand bolt upright;—but that was rejected, for the reason given above.

For a whole week after, he was determined in his mind to have one of that particular construction which is made to draw back horizontally, to hinder a passage; and to thrust forwards again, to gain a passage,—of which sorts your Worships might have seen three famous ones at Spires before its destruction—and one now at Brisac, if I mistake not:—but my father advising my uncle Toby, with great earnestness, to have nothing more to do with thrusting bridges,—and my uncle foreseeing, moreover, that it would but perpetuate the memory of the Corporal's misfortune, he changed his mind for that of the Marquis d'Hôpital's invention, which the younger Bernouilli has so well and learnedly described, as your Worships may see—*Act. Erud. Lips.* an. 1695:—to these a lead weight is an eternal balance, and keeps watch as well as a couple of sentinels, inasmuch as the construction of them was a curve line approximating to a cycloid——if not a cycloid itself.

My uncle Toby understood the nature of a parabola, as well as any man in England;—but was not quite such a master of the cycloid:—he talked however about it every day——the bridge went not forwards.——We'll ask somebody about it, cried my uncle Toby to Trim.

CHAPTER XXVI.

WHEN Trim came in, and told my father that Dr. Slop was in the kitchen, and busy in making a bridge,—my uncle Toby——the affair of the jack-boots having just then raised a train of military ideas in his brain——took it instantly for granted that Dr. Slop was making a model of the Marquis d'Hôpital's bridge.——'Tis very obliging in

him, quoth my uncle Toby ;—pray give my humble service
to Dr. Slop, Trim, and tell him I thank him heartily.

Had my uncle Toby's head been a Savoyard's box, and
my father peeping in all the time at one end of it,—it could
not have given him a more distinct conception of the
operations of my uncle Toby's imagination than what he
had ; so, notwithstanding the catapulta and battering-ram,
and his bitter imprecation about them, he was just beginning
to triumph,—

When Trim's answer, in an instant, tore the laurel from
his brows, and twisted it to pieces.

CHAPTER XXVII.

——THIS unfortunate drawbridge of yours, quoth my
father,——God bless your Honour, cried Trim, 'tis a bridge
for master's nose !—In bringing him into the world with
his vile instruments, he has crushed his nose, Susannah says,
as flat as a pancake to his face ; and he is making a false
bridge, with a piece of cotton, and a thin piece of whalebone
out of Susannah's stays, to raise it up.

——Lead me, brother Toby, cried my father, to my room
this instant !

CHAPTER XXVIII.

FROM the first moment I sat down to write my life for the
amusement of the world, and my opinions for its instruction,
has a cloud insensibly been gathering over my father.—A
tide of little evils and distresses has been setting in against
him.—Not one thing, as he observed himself, has gone
right ; and now is the storm thicken'd and going to break,
and pour down full upon his head.

I enter upon this part of my story in the most pensive

and melancholy frame of mind that ever sympathetic breast was touched with.—My nerves relax as I tell it.—Every line I write, I feel an abatement of the quickness of my pulse, and of that careless alacrity with it, which every day of my life prompts me to say and write a thousand things I should not:—and this moment, that I last dipp'd my pen into my ink, I could not help taking notice what a cautious air of sad composure and solemnity there appear'd in my manner of doing it.—Lord! how different from the rash jerks and hare-brain'd squirts thou art wont, Tristram, to transact it with in other humours,—dropping thy pen,—spurting thy ink about thy table and thy books,—as if thy pen and thy ink, thy books and thy furniture, cost thee nothing!

CHAPTER XXIX.

——I won't go about to argue the point with you:—'tis so;—and I am persuaded of it, Madam, as much as can be, "That both man and woman bear pain or sorrow (and, for aught I know, pleasure too) best in a horizontal position."

The moment my father got up into his chamber, he threw himself prostrate across his bed in the wildest disorder imaginable, but at the same time in the most lamentable attitude, of a man borne down with sorrows, that ever the eye of pity dropp'd a tear for.—The palm of his right hand, as he fell upon the bed, receiving his forehead, and covering the greatest part of both his eyes, gently sunk down with his head (his elbow giving way backwards) till his nose touch'd the quilt;—his left arm hung insensibly over the side of the bed, his knuckles reclining upon the handle of the chamber-pot, which peep'd out beyond the valance;—his right leg (his left being drawn up towards his body) hung half over the side of the bed, the edge of it pressing upon his shin-bone.—He felt it not. A fix'd, inflexible sorrow took possession of every line of his face.—He sigh'd once,—heav'd his breast often,—but uttered not a word.

An old set-stitch'd chair, valanced and fringed around with parti-coloured worsted bobs, stood at the bed's head, opposite to the side where my father's head reclined.—My uncle Toby sat him down in it.

Before an affliction is digested,—consolation ever comes too soon;—and after it is digested,—it comes too late :—so that you see, Madam, there is but a mark between these two, as fine almost as a hair, for a comforter to take aim at. —My uncle Toby was always either on this side or on that of it; and would often say, he believed in his heart he could as soon hit the longitude:—for this reason, when he sat down in the chair, he drew the curtain a little forwards, and, having a tear at every one's service,—he pull'd out a cambric handkerchief,—gave a low sigh, but held his peace.

———

CHAPTER XXX.

——" ALL is not gain that is got into the purse."—So that, notwithstanding my father had the happiness of reading the oddest books in the universe, and had moreover, in himself, the oddest way of thinking that ever man in it was bless'd with, yet it had this drawback upon him after all,———That it laid him open to some of the oddest and most whimsical distresses; of which this particular one, which he sank under at present, is as strong an example as can be given.

No doubt, the breaking down of the bridge of a child's nose, by the edge of a pair of forceps,—however scientifically applied,—would vex any man in the world who was at so much pains in begetting a child as my father was;—yet, it will not account for the extravagance of his affliction, nor will it justify the unchristian manner he abandoned and surrendered himself up to.

To explain this, I must leave him upon the bed for half an hour,—and my uncle Toby in his old fringed chair, sitting beside him.

CHAPTER XXXI.

—— I THINK it a very unreasonable demand,—cried my great-grandfather, twisting up the paper, and throwing it upon the table.——By this account, Madam, you have but two thousand pounds fortune, and not a shilling more;—and you insist upon having three hundred pounds a year jointure for it.——

—"Because," replied my great-grandmother, "you have little or no nose, Sir."——

Now, before I venture to make use of the word *Nose* a second time,—to avoid all confusion in what will be said upon it, in this interesting part of my story, it may not be amiss to explain my own meaning, and define, with all possible exactness and precision, what I would willingly be understood to mean by the term; being of opinion, that 'tis owing to the negligence and perverseness of writers in despising this precaution,—and to nothing else,—that all the polemical writings in divinity are not as clear and demonstrative as those upon *a Will o' the Wisp*, or any other sound part of philosophy and natural pursuit; in order to which, what have you to do, before you set out,—unless you intend to go puzzling on to the day of judgment,—but to give the world a good definition, and stand to it, of the main word you have most occasion for,—changing it, Sir, as you would a guinea, into small coin?—which done,—let the father of confusion puzzle you, if he can; or put a different idea either into your head, or your reader's head, if he knows how.

In books of strict morality and close reasoning,—such as this I am engaged in,—the neglect is inexcusable; and Heaven is witness how the world has revenged itself upon me for leaving so many openings to equivocal strictures,—and for depending so much as I have done all along, upon the cleanliness of my readers' imaginations.

——Here are two senses, cried Eugenius, as we walked along, pointing with the forefinger of his right hand to the word *crevice*, in the one hundred and sixteenth page of this first volume of this book of books;——here are two senses, —quoth he.——And here are two roads, replied I, turning short upon him,—a dirty and a clean one,—which shall we take?——The clean, by all means, replied Eugenius.—— Eugenius, said I, stepping before him, and laying my hand upon his breast,—to define—is to distrust.—Thus I triumphed over Eugenius;—but I triumphed over him, as I always do, like a fool.—'Tis my comfort, however, I am not an obstinate one: therefore,

I define a nose as follows,—entreating only, beforehand, and beseeching my readers, both male and female, of what age, complexion, and condition soever, for the love of God and their own souls, to guard against the temptations and suggestions of the Devil, and suffer him by no art or wile to put any other ideas into their minds than what I put into my definition;—for, by the word *Nose*, throughout all this long chapter of Noses, and in every other part of my work where the word *Nose* occurs,—I declare, by that word, I mean a nose, and nothing more or less.

CHAPTER XXXII.

——"BECAUSE," quoth my great-grandmother, repeating the words again,—"you have little or no nose, Sir."——

S'death! cried my great-grandfather, clapping his hand upon his nose;—'tis not so small as that comes to;—'tis a full inch longer than my father's.——Now, my great-grandfather's nose was, for all the world, like unto the noses of all the men, women, and children whom Pantagruel found dwelling upon the island of Ennasin.—By the way, if you would know the strange way of getting akin amongst so flat-nosed a people, you must read the book:—find it out yourself you never can.——

—'Twas shaped, Sir, like an ace of clubs.

——'Tis a full inch, continued my grandfather, pressing

up the ridge of his nose with his finger and thumb; and repeating his assertion,—'Tis a full inch longer, Madam, than my father's.——You must mean your uncle's, replied my great-grandmother.

——My great-grandfather was convinced.—He untwisted the paper, and signed the article.

CHAPTER XXXIII.

——WHAT an unconscionable jointure, my dear, do we pay out of this small estate of ours! quoth my grandmother to my grandfather.——

My father, replied my grandfather, had no more nose, my dear, saving the mark, than there is upon the back of my hand.——

Now, you must. know, that my great-grandmother outlived my grandfather twelve years; so that my father had the jointure to pay a hundred and fifty pounds half-yearly—(on Michaelmas and Lady-Day)—during all that time.

No man discharged pecuniary obligations with a better grace than my father;—and, as far as a hundred pounds went, he would fling it upon the table, guinea by guinea, with that spirited jerk of an honest welcome, which generous souls, and generous souls only, are able to fling down money; but, as soon as ever he entered upon the odd fifty, —he generally gave a loud *hem !* rubbed the side of his nose leisurely with the flat part of his forefinger,—inserted his hand cautiously betwixt his head and the cawl of his wig,—looked at both sides of every guinea as he parted with it,—and seldom could get to the end of the fifty pounds without pulling out his handkerchief, and wiping his temples.

Defend me, gracious Heaven! from those persecuting spirits who make no allowances for these workings within us.—Never, oh never, may. I lay down in their tents, who cannot relax the engine, and feel pity for the force of education, and the prevalence of opinions long derived from ancestors!

For three generations at least, this *tenet* in favour of long noses had gradually been taking root in our family.—TRADITION was all along on its side, and INTEREST was every half-year stepping in to strengthen it; so that the whimsicality of my father's brain was far from having the whole honour of this, as it had of almost all his other strange notions;—for, in a great measure, he might be said to have suck'd this in with his mother's milk. He did his part, however.—If education planted the mistake (in case it was one), my father watered it, and ripened it to perfection.

He would often declare, in speaking his thoughts upon the subject, that he did not conceive how the greatest family in England could stand it out against an uninterrupted succession of six or seven short noses.—And, for the contrary reason, he would generally add, That it must be one of the greatest problems in civil life, where the same number of long and jolly noses, following one another in a direct line, did not raise and hoist it up into the best vacancies in the kingdom.—He would often boast that the Shandy family rank'd very high in king Harry the VIIIth's time; but owed its rise to no state engine,—he would say,—but to that only;—but that, like other families,—he would add,— it had felt the turn of the wheel, and had never recovered the blow of my great-grandfather's nose.—It was an ace of clubs indeed! he would cry, shaking his head;—and as vile a one for an unfortunate family as ever turn'd up trumps.

——Fair and softly, gentle reader! where is thy fancy carrying thee!—If there is truth in man, by my great-grandfather's nose, I mean the external organ of smelling, or that part of man which stands prominent in his face,— and which painters say, in good jolly noses and well-proportioned faces, should comprehend a full third;—that is, measured downwards from the setting on of the hair.—

——What a life of it has an author, at this pass!

CHAPTER XXXIV.

It is a singular blessing, that nature has formed the mind of man with the same happy backwardness and renitency against conviction, which is observed in old dogs,—" of not learning new tricks."

What a shuttlecock of a fellow would the greatest philosopher that ever existed be whisk'd into at once, did he read such books, and observe such facts, and think such thoughts, as would eternally be making him change sides!

Now, my father, as I told you last year, detested all this:—He pick'd up an opinion, Sir, as a man in a state of nature picks up an apple;—it becomes his own;—and if he is a man of spirit, he would lose his life rather than give it up.

I am aware that Didius, the great civilian, will contest this point, and cry out against me, Whence comes this man's right to this apple? *ex confesso*, he will say,—things were in a state of nature;—the apple is as much Frank's apple as John's.—Pray, Mr. Shandy, what patent has he to show for it? and how did it begin to be his? was it when he set his heart upon it? or when he gathered it? or when he chewed it? or when he roasted it? or when he peel'd it, or when he brought it home? or when he digested?—or when he——?—For 'tis plain, Sir, if the first picking up of the apple made it not his, that no subsequent act could.

Brother Didius, Tribonius will answer—(now Tribonius the civilian and church lawyer's beard being three inches and a half and three-eights longer than Didius his beard,—I'm glad he takes up the cudgels for me; so I give myself no farther trouble about the answer)—Brother Didius, Tribonius will say, it is a decreed case, as you may find it in the fragments of Gregorius and Hermogenes' codes, and in all the codes from Justinian's down to the codes of Louis and Des Eaux,—That the sweat of a man's brow, and the exsudations of a man's brains, are as much a man's own property as the breeches upon his backside;—which said exsudations, &c., being dropp'd upon the said apple by the labour

of finding it, and picking it up; and being moreover indissolubly wasted, and as indissolubly annex'd, by the picker
up, to the thing pick'd up, carried home, roasted, peel'd,
eaten, digested, and so on,—'tis evident that the gatherer
of the apple, in so doing, has mix'd up something which was
his own, with the apple which was not his own; by which
means he has acquired a property;—or, in other words, the
apple is John's apple.

By the same learned chain of reasoning, my father stood
up for all his opinions: he had spared no pains in picking
them up; and the more they lay out of the common way,
the better still was his title.—No mortal claimed them; they
had cost him, moreover, as much labour in cooking and
digesting as in the case above; so that they might well and
truly be said to be of his own goods and chattels.—Accordingly, he held fast by 'em both by teeth and claws,—would
fly to whatever he could lay his hands on,—and, in a word,
would intrench and fortify them round with as many cir-
cumvallations and breast-works as my uncle Toby would a
citadel.

There is one plaguy rub in the way of this,—the scarcity
of materials to make anything of a defence with, in case of
a smart attack; inasmuch as few men of great genius has
exercised their parts in writing books upon the subject of
great noses. By the trotting of my lean horse, the thing is
incredible! and I am quite lost in my understanding, when
I am considering what a treasure of precious time and talents
together has been wasted upon worse subjects,—and how
many millions of books, in all languages, and in all possible
types and bindings, have been fabricated on points not half
so much tending to the unity and peace-making of the
world! What was to be had, however, he set the greater
store by; and though my father would ofttimes sport with
my uncle Toby's library,—which, by the bye, was ridiculous
enough,—yet, at the very same time he did it, he collected
every book and treatise which had been systematically wrote
upon noses, with as much care as my honest uncle Toby has
done those upon military architecture.—'Tis true, a much

less table would have held them;—but that was not thy transgression, my dear uncle.—

Here,—but why here,—rather than in any other part of my story?——I am not able to tell:——but here it is——my heart stops me to pay to thee, my dear uncle Toby, once for all, the tribute I owe thy goodness.—Here let me thrust my chair aside, and kneel down upon the ground, whilst I am pouring forth the warmest sentiment of love for thee, and veneration for the excellency of thy character, that ever virtue and nature kindled in a nephew's bosom.—Peace and comfort rest for evermore upon thy head!—Thou enviedst no man's comforts,—insultedst no man's opinions;—thou blackenedst no man's character,—devouredst no man's bread! Gently, with faithful Trim behind thee, didst thou ramble round the little circle of thy pleasures, jostling no creature in thy way: for each one's sorrows thou hadst a tear; for each man's need thou hadst a shilling.

Whilst I am worth one to pay a weeder,—thy path from thy door to thy bowling-green shall never be grown up.—Whilst there is a rood and a half of land in the Shandy family, thy fortifications, my dear uncle Toby, shall never be demolish'd.

———

CHAPTER XXXV.

My father's collection was not great; but, to make amends, it was curious; and consequently he was some time in making it: he had the great fortune, however, to set off well, in getting Bruscambille's prologue upon long noses, almost for nothing;—for he gave no more for Bruscambille than three half-crowns; owing, indeed, to the strong fancy which the stall-man saw my father had for the book, the moment he laid his hands upon it.—There are not three Bruscambilles in Christendom, said the stall-man, except what are chain'd up in the libraries of the curious. My father flung down the money as quick as lightning,—took Bruscambille into his bosom,—hied home from Piccadilly to Coleman Street with it, as he would have hied home with a treasure, without taking his hand once off from Bruscambille all the way.

To those who do not yet know of which gender Bruscambille is,—inasmuch as a prologue upon long noses might easily be done by either,—'twill be no objection against the simile—to say, That when my father got home, he solaced himself with Bruscambille after the manner in which, 'tis ten to one, your Worship solaced yourself with your first mistress;—that is, from morning even unto night: which, by the bye, how delightful soever it may prove to the inamorato,—is of little or no entertainment at all to by-standers.—Take notice, I go no farther with the simile;—my father's eye was greater than his appetite,—his zeal greater than his knowledge;—he cool'd,—his affections became divided;——he got hold of Prignitz,—purchased Scroderus, Andrea Paræus, Bouchet's Evening Conferences, and, above all, the great and learned Hafen Slawkenbergius; of which,—as I shall have much to say by and bye,—I will say nothing now.

CHAPTER XXXVI.

OF all the tracts my father was at the pains to procure and study, in support of his hypothesis, there was not any one wherein he felt a more cruel disappointment at first, than in the celebrated Dialogue between Pamphagus and Cocles, written by the chaste pen of the great and venerable Erasmus, upon the various uses and seasonable applications of long noses.——Now don't let Satan, my dear girl, in this chapter, take advantage of any one spot of rising ground to get astride of your imagination, if you can anyways help it; or, if he is so nimble as to slip on, let me beg of you, like an unback'd filly, to *frisk it, squirt it, to jump it, to rear it, to bound it—and to kick it, with long kicks and short kicks*, till, like Tickletoby's mare, you break a strap or a crupper, and throw his Worship into the dirt.——You need not kill him.—

—And pray, who was Tickletoby's mare?—

—'Tis just as discreditable and unscholar-like a question, Sir, as to have asked what year (*ab Urb. Cond.*) the second Punic war broke out.—Who was Tickletoby's mare!—— Read, read, read, read, my unlearned reader! read,—or, by the knowledge of the great Saint Paraleipomenon,—I tell you beforehand, you had better throw down the book at once; for without *much reading*, by which your Reverence knows I mean *much knowledge*, you will no more be able to penetrate the moral of this marbled page (motley emblem of my work!) than the world, with all its sagacity, has been able to unravel the many opinions, transactions, and truths which still lie mystically hid under the dark veil of the black one.

CHAPTER XXXVII.

" *Nihil me pœnitet.hujus nasi,*" quoth Pamphagus;—that is, —"My nose has been the making of me."——" *Nec est cur pœniteat,*" replies Cocles; that is, " How the deuce should such a nose fail ? "

The doctrine, you see, was laid down by Erasmus, as my father wished it, with the utmost plainness; but my father's disappointment was, in finding nothing more from so able a pen, but the bare fact itself; without any of that speculative subtilty or ambidexterity of argumentation upon it, which Heaven had bestowed upon man, on purpose to investigate Truth, and fight for her on all sides.—My father pish'd and pugh'd, at first, most terribly.——'Tis worth something to have a good name. As the dialogue was of Erasmus, my father soon came to himself, and read it over and over again with great application, studying every word and every syllable of it, thro' and thro', in its most strict and literal interpretation.—He could still make nothing of it, that way. Mayhap, there is more meant than is said in it, quoth my father.—Learned men, brother Toby, don't write dialogues upon long noses for nothing.—I'll study the

mystic and the allegoric sense.—Here is some room to turn
a man's self in, brother.

My father read on.———

Now, I find it needful to inform your Reverences and
Worships, that besides the many nautical uses of long noses
enumerated by Erasmus, the dialogist affirmeth, That a long
nose is not without its domestic conveniences also; for that, in
a case of distress,—and for want of a pair of bellows,—it will
do excellently well, *ad excitandum focum* (to stir up the fire).

Nature had been prodigal in her gifts to my father beyond
measure, and had sown the seeds of verbal criticism as deep
within him, as she had done the seeds of all other knowledge;
—so that he had got out his penknife, and was trying experiments upon the sentence, to see if he could not scratch
some better sense into it.—I've got within a single letter,
brother Toby, cried my father, of Erasmus his mystic meaning.———You are near enough, brother, replied my uncle, in
all conscience.———Pshaw! cried my father, scratching on,
—I might as well be seven miles off.—I've done it!—said
my father, snapping his fingers. See, my dear brother
Toby, how I have mended the sense.———But you have
marr'd a word, replied my uncle Toby.———My father put
on his spectacles,—bit his lip,—and tore out the leaf in a
passion.

CHAPTER XXXVIII.

O SLAWKENBERGIUS! thou faithful analyser of my Dis-
grazias,—thou sad foreteller of so many of the whips and
short turns which in one stage or other of my life have
come slap upon me from the shortness of my nose,—and no
other cause, that I am conscious of,—tell me, Slawkenbergius! what secret impulse was it? what intonation of
voice? whence came it? how did it sound in thy ears?—
art thou sure thou heard'st it?—which first cried out to
thee—Go,—Slawkenbergius! dedicate the labours of thy
life,—neglect thy pastimes,—call forth all the powers and

faculties of thy nature,—macerate thyself in the service of mankind, and write a grand FOLIO for them, upon the subject of their noses.

How the communication was conveyed into Slawkenbergius's sensorium, — so that Slawkenbergius should know whose finger touch'd the key,—and whose hand it was that blew the bellows,—as Hafen Slawkenbergius has been dead and laid in his grave above fourscore and ten years,—we can only raise conjectures.

Slawkenbergius was play'd upon, for aught I know, like one of Whitefield's disciples ;—that is, with such a distinct intelligence, Sir, of which of the two masters it was that had been practising upon his *instrument*,—as to make all reasoning upon it needless.

——For in the account which Hafen Slawkenbergius gives the world of his motives and occasions for writing, and spending so many years of his life upon this one work, —towards the end of his prolegomena; which, by the bye, should have come · first,—but the bookbinder has most injudiciously placed it betwixt the analytical contents of the book and the book itself,—he informs his reader, That ever since he had arrived at the age of discernment, and was able to sit down coolly, and consider within himself the true state and condition of man,—and distinguish the main end and design of his · being ;—or,—to shorten my translation, for Slawkenbergius's book is in Latin, and not a little prolix in this passage ;—ever since I understood, quoth Slawkenbergius, anything,—or rather *what was what*,—and could perceive that the point of long noses had been too loosely handled by all who had gone before,—have I, Slawkenbergius, felt a strong impulse, with a mighty and unresistible call within me, to gird up myself to this undertaking.

And to do justice to Slawkenbergius, he has entered the list with a stronger lance, and taken a much larger career in it, than any one man who had ever entered it before him ;—and indeed, in many respects, deserves to be *en-nich'd* as a prototype for all writers of voluminous works at least, to model their books by ;—for he has taken in, Sir, the

whole subject,—examined every part of it *dialectically*,—
then brought it into full day; dilucidating it with all the
light which either the collision of his own natural parts
could strike,—or the profoundest knowledge of the sciences
had empowered him to cast upon it;—collating, collecting
and compiling;—begging, borrowing, and stealing, as he
went along, all that had been wrote or wrangled thereupon
in the schools and porticos of the learned; so that Slawkenbergius his book may properly be considered, not only as a
model,—but as a thorough-stitched DIGEST and regular
institute of noses, comprehending in it all that is or can be
needful to be known about them.

For this cause it is that I forbear to speak of so many
(otherwise) valuable books and treatises of my father's
collecting, wrote either plump upon noses—or collaterally
touching them;—such, for instance, as Prignitz, now lying
upon the table before me, who with infinite learning, and
from the most candid and scholar-like examination of above
four thousand different skulls, in upwards of twenty charnel-
houses in Silesia, which he had rummaged,—has informed
us, that the mensuration and configuration of the osseous
or bony parts of human noses, in any given tract of country
except Crim Tartary, where they are all crushed down by
the thumb, so that no judgment can be formed upon them,
—are much nearer alike than the world imagines;—the
difference amongst them being, he says, a mere trifle, not
worth taking notice of;—but that the size and jollity of
every individual nose, and by which one nose ranks above
another, and bears a higher price, is owing to the cartila-
ginous and muscular parts of it, into whose ducts and
sinuses the blood and animal spirits being impell'd and
driven by the warmth and force of the imagination, which
is but a step from it (bating the case of idiots, whom
Prignitz, who had lived many years in Turkey, supposes
under the more immediate tutelage of Heaven)—it so
happens, and ever must, says Prignitz, that the excellency
of the nose is in a direct arithmetical proportion to the
excellency of the wearer's fancy.

It is for the same reason; that is, because 'tis all comprehended in Slawkenbergius, that I say nothing likewise of Scroderus (Andrea), who, all the world knows, set himself to oppugn Prignitz with great violence ;—proving it in his own way, first logically, and then by a series of stubborn facts, " That so far was Prignitz from the truth, in affirming that the fancy begat the nose, that, on the contrary,—the nose begat the fancy."

—The learned suspected Scroderus of an indecent sophism in this ;—and Prignitz cried out aloud in the dispute, that Scroderus had shifted the idea upon him ;—but Scroderus went on maintaining his thesis.

My father was just balancing within himself, which of the two sides he should take in this affair; when Ambrose Paræus decided it in a moment, and by overthrowing the systems both of Prignitz and Scroderus, drove my father out of both sides of the controversy at once.

Be witness——

I don't acquaint the learned reader—in saying it,—I mention it only to show the learned, I know the fact myself,——

That this Ambrose Paræus was chief surgeon and nose-mender to Francis the Ninth of France; and in high credit with him and the two preceding, or succeeding kings (I know not which)—and that, except in the slip he made in his story of Taliacotius's noses, and his manner of setting them on,—he was esteemed by the whole college of physicians at that time, as more knowing in matters of noses, than any one who had ever taken them in hand.

Now, Ambrose Paræus convinced my father, that the true and efficient cause of what had engaged so much the attention of the world, and upon which Prignitz and Scroderus had wasted so much learning and fine parts,—was neither this nor that ;—but that the length and goodness of the nose was owing simply to the softness and flaccidity in the nurse's breast,—as the flatness and shortness of *puisne* noses was to the firmness and elastic repulsion of the same organ of nutrition in the hale and lively ;—which, tho'

happy for the woman, was the undoing of the child, inasmuch as his nose was so snubb'd, so rebuft'd, so rebated, and
so refrigerated thereby, as never to arrive *ad mensuram suam
legitimam ;*—but that in case of flaccidity and softness of
the nurse or mother's breast—by sinking into it, quoth
Paraeus, as into so much butter, the nose was comforted,
nourish'd, plump'd up, refresh'd, refocillated, and set a growing for ever.

I have but two things to observe of Paraeus; first, That
he proves and explains all this with the utmost chastity and
decorum of expression :—for which, may his soul for ever
rest in peace !

And, secondly, That besides the systems of Prignitz and
Scroderus, which Ambrose Paraeus his hypothesis effectually
overthrew,—it overthrew at the same time the system of
peace and harmony of our family; and for three days
together, not only embroiled matters between my father
and my mother, but turn'd likewise the whole house and
everything in it, except my uncle Toby, quite upside down.

Such a ridiculous tale of a dispute between a man and his
wife, never surely, in any age or country, got vent through
the keyhole of a street-door.

My mother, you must know,——but I have fifty things
more necessary to let you know first:—I have a hundred
difficulties which I have promised to clear up, and a thousand distresses and domestic misadventures crowding in upon
me thick and threefold, one upon the neck of another. A
cow broke in (to-morrow morning) to my uncle Toby's fortifications, and ate up two rations and a half of dried grass,
tearing up the sods with it, which faced his horn-work and
covered way.——Trim insists upon being tried by a court-
martial,—the cow to be shot,—Slop to be *crucifix'd,*—
myself to be *tristram'd,* and at my very baptism made a
martyr of ;—poor unhappy Devils that we all are !—I want
swaddling ;—but there is no time to be lost in exclamations,
—I have left my father lying across his bed, and uncle Toby
in his old fringed chair, sitting beside him, and promised I
would go back to them in half an hour; and five-and-thirty

minutes are laps'd already.——Of all the perplexities a mortal author was ever seen in,—this certainly is the greatest; for I have Hafen Slawkenbergius's folio, Sir, to finish;—a dialogue between my father and my uncle Toby, upon the solution of Prignitz, Scroderus, Ambrose Paræus, Panocrates, and Grangousier to relate;—a tale out of Slawkenbergius to translate;—and all this in five minutes less than no time at all.—Such a head!—would to Heaven my enemies only saw the inside of it.

CHAPTER XXXIX.

THERE was not any one scene more entertaining in our family;—and to do it justice in this point,—I here put off my cap, and lay it upon the table, close beside my ink-horn, on purpose to make my declaration to the world concerning this one article the more solemn,—That I believe, in my soul, (unless my love and partiality to my understanding blinds me) the hand of the Supreme Maker and First Designer of all things never made or put a family together (in that period at least of it which I have sat down to write the story of)—where the characters of it were cast or contrasted with so dramatic a felicity as ours was, for this end; or in which the capacities of affording such exquisite scenes, and the powers of shifting them perpetually from morning to night, were lodged and intrusted with so unlimited a confidence, as in the Shandy family.

Not any one of these was more diverting, I say, in this whimsical theatre of ours,—than what frequently arose out of this self-same chapter of long noses,—especially when my father's imagination was heated with the enquiry, and nothing would serve him but to heat my uncle Toby's too.

My uncle Toby would give my father all possible fair play in this attempt; and with infinite patience would sit smoking his pipe for whole hours together, whilst my father was

practising upon his head and trying every accessible avenue
to drive Prignitz and Scroderus's solutions into it.

Whether they were above my uncle Toby's reason,—or
contrary to it,—or that his brain was like *damp* timber, and
no spark could possibly take hold; or that it was so full of
saps, mines, blinds, curtains, and such military disqualifica-
tions to his seeing clearly into Prignitz and Scroderus's
doctrines,—I say not:—let schoolmen, scullions,—anatomists,—and engineers fight for it among themselves.——

'Twas some misfortune, I make no doubt, in this affair,
that my father had every word of it to translate for the
benefit of my uncle Toby, and render out of Slawkenbergius's Latin, of which, as he was no great master, his
translation was not always of the purest,—and generally
least so when 'twas most wanted.—This naturally opened
a door to a second misfortune;—that in the warmer paroxysms of his zeal to open my uncle Toby's eyes, my father's
ideas ran on as much faster than the translation, as the
translation outmoved my uncle Toby's:—neither the one
nor the other added much to the perspicuity of my father's
lecture.

CHAPTER XL.

The gift of ratiocination and making syllogisms,—I mean
in man,—for in superior classes of being, such as angels and
spirits, 'tis all done, may it please your Worships, as they
tell me, by INTUITION;—and beings inferior, as your Worships all know,—syllogise by their noses: though there is
an island swimming in the sea (though not altogether at its
ease) whose inhabitants, if my intelligence deceives me not,
are so wonderfully gifted, as to syllogise after the same
fashion, and ofttimes to make very well out too:——but
that's neither here nor there :—

The gift of doing it as it should be, amongst us, or, the
great and principal act of ratiocination in man, as logicians
tell us, is the finding out the agreement or disagreement of

two ideas one with another, by the intervention of a third (called the *medius terminus*); just as a man, as Locke well observes, by a yard, finds two men's nine-pin-alleys to be of the same length, which could not be brought together, to measure their equality, by *juxtaposition.*

Had the same great reasoner looked on, as my father illustrated his systems of noses, and observed my uncle Toby's deportment,—what great attention he gave to every word;—and as oft as he took his pipe from his mouth, with what wonderful seriousness he contemplated the length of it!—surveying it transversely as he held it betwixt his finger and his thumb;—then fore-right,—then this way, and then that, in all its possible directions and fore-shortenings,—he would have concluded my uncle Toby had got hold of the *medius terminus*, and was syllogising and measuring with it the truth of each hypothesis of long noses, in order, as my father laid them before him. This, by the bye, was more than my father wanted:—his aim, in all the pains he was at in these philosophical lectures,—was, to enable my uncle Toby not to *discuss*,—but *comprehend*;—to hold the grains and scruples of learning, not to *weigh* them.—My uncle Toby, as you will read in the next chapter, did neither the one nor the other.

CHAPTER XLI.

'Tis a pity, cried my father, one winter's night, after a three hours' painful translation of Slawkenbergius,—'tis a pity, cried my father, putting my mother's thread-paper into the book for a mark as he spoke,—that Truth, brother Toby, should shut herself up in such impregnable fastnesses, and be so obstinate as not to surrender herself up sometimes upon the closest siege.—

Now it happened then, as indeed it had often done before, that my uncle Toby's fancy, during the time of my father's explanation of Prignitz to him,—having nothing to

stay it there, had taken a short flight to the bowling-green :
—his body might as well have taken a turn there too;—so
that with all the semblance of a deep schoolman intent upon
the *medius terminus*,—my uncle Toby was, in fact, as
ignorant of the whole lecture, and all its pro's and con's, as
if my father had been translating Hafen Slawkenbergius
from the Latin tongue into the Cherokee. But the word
siege, like a talismanic power, in my father's metaphor,
wafting back my uncle Toby's fancy, quick as a note could
follow the touch,—he open'd his ears,—and my father
observing that he took his pipe out of his mouth, and
shuffled his chair nearer the table, as with a desire to profit,
—my father with great pleasure began his sentence again,
—changing only the plan, and dropping the metaphor of
the siege in it, to keep clear of some dangers my father
apprehended from it.

   'Tis a pity, said my father, that truth can only be on one
side, brother Toby,—considering what ingenuity these
learned men have all shown in their solutions of noses.——
Can noses be dissolved ? replied my uncle Toby.

   —My father thrust back his chair,—rose up,—put on his
hat,—took four long strides to the door,—jerked it open,—
thrust his head half-way out,—shut the door again,—took
no notice of the bad hinge,—returned to the table,—pluck'd
my mother's thread-paper out of Slawkenbergius's book,—
went hastily to his bureau,—walked slowly back,—twisted
my mother's thread-paper about his thumb,—unbuttoned
his waistcoat,—threw my mother's thread-paper into the
fire,—bit her satin pin-cushion in two,—filled his mouth with
bran,—confounded it :—but mark !—the oath of confusion
was levell'd at my uncle Toby's brain,—which was e'en
confused enough already ;—the curse came charged only
with the bran ;—the bran, may it please your Honours, was
no more than powder to the ball.

   'Twas well my father's passions lasted not long; for so
long as they did last, they led him a busy life on't ; and it
is one of the most unaccountable problems that ever I met
with in my observations of human nature, that nothing

should prove my father's mettle so much, or make his passions go off so like gunpowder, as the unexpected stroke his science met with from the quaint simplicity of my uncle Toby's questions.——Had ten dozen of hornets stung him behind in so many different places all at one time,—he could not have exerted more mechanical functions in fewer seconds,—or started half so much, as with one single *quære* of three words unseasonably popping in full upon him in his hobby-horsical career.

'Twas all one to my uncle Toby ;—he smoked his pipe on with unvaried composure ;—his heart never intended offence to his brother ;—and as his head could seldom find out where the sting of it lay,—he always gave my father the credit of cooling by himself.——He was five minutes and thirty-five seconds about it in the present case.

By all that's good ! said my father, swearing, as he came to himself, and taking the oath out of Ernulphus's digest of curses—(though, to do my father justice, it was a fault, as he told Dr. Slop in the affair of Ernulphus, which he as seldom committed as any man upon earth)——By all that's good and great ! brother Toby, said my father, if it was not for the aids of philosophy, which befriend one so much as they do,—you would put a man beside all temper.—Why, by the *solutions* of noses, of which I was telling you, I meant, as you might have known, had you favoured me with one grain of attention, the various accounts, which learned men of different kinds of knowledge have given the world of the causes of short and long noses.——There is no cause but one, replied my uncle Toby,—why one man's nose is longer than another's, but because that God pleases to have it so.——That is Grangousier's solution, said my father.—— 'Tis he, continued my uncle Toby, looking up, and not regarding my father's interruption, who makes us all, and frames and puts us together in such forms and proportions, and for such ends, as is agreeable to his infinite wisdom.—— 'Tis a pious account, cried my father, but not philosophical ; —there is more religion in it than sound science. 'Twas no inconsistent part of my uncle Toby's character—that he feared God, and reverenced religion.—So the moment my father finished his remark,—my uncle fell a whistling *Lille-bullero* with more zeal (though more out of tune) than usual.—

What is become of my wife's thread-paper?

CHAPTER XLII.

No matter;—as an appendage to seamstressy, the thread-paper might be of some consequence to my mother;—of none to my father as a mark in Slawkenbergius.—Slawkenbergius, in every page of him, was a rich treasure of inexhaustible knowledge to my father;—he could not open him amiss; and he would often say, in closing the book, That if all the arts and sciences in the world, with the books which treated of them, were lost,—should the wisdom and policies of governments, he would say, through disuse, ever happen to be forgot; and all that statesmen had wrote or caused to be written, upon the strong or the weak sides of courts or kingdoms, should they be forgot also,—and Slawkenbergius only left,—there would be enough in him in all conscience, he would say, to set the world a-going again. A treasure, therefore, was he indeed! an institute of all that was necessary to be known of noses, and everything else:—at matin, noon, and vespers was Hafen Slawkenbergius his recreation and delight: 'twas for ever in his hands:—you would have sworn, Sir, it had been a canon's prayer-book;—so worn, so glazed, so contrited and attrited was it with fingers and with thumbs in all its parts, from one end even unto the other.

I am not such a bigot to Slawkenbergius as my father:—there is a fund in him, no doubt: but, in my opinion, the best, I don't say the most profitable, but the most amusing part of Hafen Slawkenbergius, is his Tales;—and, considering he was a German, many of them told not without fancy.—These take up his second book, containing nearly one-half of his folio, and are comprehended in ten decades; each decade containing ten tales.—Philosophy is not built upon tales; and therefore 'twas certainly wrong in Slawkenbergius to send them into the world by that name!—there are a few of them in his eighth, ninth, and tenth decades, which, I own, seem rather playful and sportive than speculative;—but, in general, they are to be looked upon by the learned as a detail of so many independent facts, all of them turning round, somehow or other, upon the main hinges of his subject, and collected by him with great fidelity, and added to his work as so many illustrations upon the doctrines of noses.

As we have leisure enough upon our hands,—if you give me leave, Madam, I'll tell you the ninth tale of his tenth decade.

SLAWKENBERGII FABELLA.*

VESPERA quâdam frigidulâ, posteriori in parte mensis Augusti, peregrinus, mulo fusco colore incidens, manticâ a tergo, paucis indusiis, binis calceis, braccisque sericis coccineis repleta, Argentoratum ingressus est.

Militi cum percontanti, quum portus intraret, dixit, se apud Nasorum promontorium fuisse, Francofurtum proficisci, et Argentoratum, transitu ad fines Sarmatiæ mensis intervallo, reversurum.

Miles peregrini in faciem suspexit :——Dî boni, novæ forma nasi !

At multum mihi profuit, inquit peregrinus, carpum

* As Hafen Slawkenbergius de Nasis is extremely scarce, it may not be unacceptable to the learned reader to see the specimen of a few pages of his original : I will make no reflection upon it, but that his story-telling Latin is much more concise than his philosophic—and, I think, has more of Latinity in it.

THE

LIFE AND OPINIONS

OF

TRISTRAM SHANDY, Gent.

VOL. IV. ORIG. EDIT.

Multitudinis imperitæ non formido judicia, meis tamen, rogo, parcant opus-
culis—in quibus fuit propositi semper, à jocis ad seria, in seriis vicissim
ad jocos transire. .

—JOAN. SARESBERIENSIS, *Episcopus Lugdun.*

SLAWKENBERGUIS'S TALE.

T was one cool, refreshing evening, at the close
of a very sultry day, in the latter end of the
month of August, when a stranger, mounted
upon a dark mule, with a small cloak-bag behind him, containing a few shirts, a pair of
shoes, and a crimson-satin pair of breeches, entered the
town of Strasburg.

He told the sentinel who questioned him, as he entered
the gates, that he had been at the Promontory of Noses—
was going on to Frankfort——and should be back again at
Strasburg that day month, in his way to the borders of
Crim Tartary.

The sentinel looked up into the stranger's face:——he
never saw such a Nose in his life!

—I have made a very good venture of it, quoth the

amento extrahens, è quo pependit acinaces : Loculo manum inesruit ; et magnâ cum urbanitate, pilei parte anteriore tactâ manu sinistrâ, ut extendit dextram, militi florinum dedit, et processit.

Dolet mihi, ait miles, tympanistam nanum et valgum alloquens, virum adeo urbanum vaginam perdidisse : itinerari haud poterit nudâ acinaci ; neque vaginam toto Argentorato, habilem inveniet.——Nullam unquam habui, respondit peregrinus respiciens——seque comiter inclinans—hoc more gesto, nudam acinacem elevans, mulo lenté progrediente, ut nasum tueri possim.

Non immerito, benigne peregrine, respondit miles.

Nihili æstimo, ait ille tympanista, è pergamenâ factitius est.

Prout christianus sum, inquit miles, nasus ille, ni sexties major sit, meo esset conformis.

Crepitare audivi, ait tympanista.

Mehercule ! sanguinem emisit, respondit miles.

Miseret me, inquit tympanista, qui non ambo tetigimus !

Eodem temporis puncto, quo hæc res argumentata fuit inter militem et tympanistam, disceptabatur ibidem tubicine et uxore suâ, qui tunc accesserunt, et, peregrino prætereunte, restiterunt.

Quantus nasus ! æque longus est, ait tubicina, ac tuba.

Et ex eodem metallo, ait tubicen, velut sternutamento audias.

Tantum abest, respondit illa, quod fistulam dulcedine vincit.

Æneus est, ait tubicen.

Nequaquam, respondit uxor.

Rursum affirmo, ait tubicen, quod æneus est.

stranger; so slipping his wrist out of the loop of a black ribbon, to which a short scymetar was hung, he put his hand into his pocket, and with great courtesy touching the fore-part of his cap with his left hand, as he extended his right, he put a florin into the sentinel's hand, and passed on.

It grieves me, said the sentinel, speaking to a little dwarf-ish bandy-legg'd drummer, that so courteous a soul should have lost his scabbard;—he cannot travel without one to his scymetar; and will not be able to get a scabbard to fit it in all Strasburg.——I never had one, replied the stranger, looking back to the sentinel, and putting his hand up to his cap as he spoke.—I carry it, continued he, thus,—holding up his naked scymetar, his mule moving on slowly all the time,—on purpose to defend my nose.

It is well worth it, gentle stranger, replied the sentinel.

——'Tis not worth a single stiver, said the bandy-legg'd drummer:—'tis a nose of parchment.

As I am a true Catholic,—except that it is six times as big,—'tis a nose, said the sentinel, like my own.

—I heard it crackle, said the drummer.

By Dunder! said the sentinel, I saw it bleed.

What a pity, cried the bandy-legg'd drummer, we did not both touch it.

At the very time that this dispute was maintaining by the sentinel and the drummer,—was the same point debating betwixt a trumpeter and a trumpeter's wife, who were just then coming up, and had stopped to see the stranger pass by.

Benedicity!——What a nose!—'tis as long, said the trumpeter's wife, as a trumpet.

And of the same metal, said the trumpeter, as you hear by its sneezing.

'Tis as soft as a flute, said she.

—'Tis brass, said the trumpeter.

—'Tis a pudding's end, said his wife.

I tell thee again, said the trumpeter, 'tis a brazen nose.

Rem penitus explorabo; prius, enim digito tangam, ait uxor, quam dormivero.

Mulus peregrini gradu lento progressus est, ut unumquodque verbum controversiæ, non tantum inter militem et tympanistam, verum etiam inter tubicinem et uxorem ejus, audiret.

Nequaquam, ait ille, in muli collum fræna demittens, et manibus ambabus in pectus positis (mulo lentè progrediente) nequaquam, ait ille respiciens, non necesse est ut res isthæc dilucidata foret. Minime gentium! meus nasus nunquam tangetur, dum spiritus hos reget artus——Ad quid agendum? ait uxor burgomagistri.

Perigrinus illi non respondit. Votum faciebat tunc temporis Sancto Nicolao; quo facto, in sinum dextrum inserens, e quâ negligenter pependit acinaces, lento gradu processit per plateam Argentorati latam quæ ad diversorium templo ex adversum ducit.

Peregrinus mulo descendens stabulo includi, et manticam inferri jussit: quâ apertâ et coccineis sericis femoralibus extractis cum argenteo laciniato Περιζώματε, his sese induit, statimque, acinaci in manu, ad forum deambulavit.

Quod ubi peregrinus esset ingressus, uxorem tubicinis obviam euntem aspicit; illico, cursum flectit, metuens ne nasus suus exploraretur, atque ad diversorium regressus est —exuit se vestibus; braccus coccineas sericas manticæ impostuit mulumque educi jussit.

I'll know the bottom of it, said the trumpeter's wife, for I will touch it with my finger before I sleep.

The stranger's mule moved on at so slow a rate, that he heard every word of the dispute, not only betwixt the sentinel and the drummer, but betwixt the trumpeter and the trumpeter's wife.

No! said he, dropping his reins upon his mule's neck and laying both his hands upon his breast, the one over the other in a saint-like position (his mule going on easily all the time) — No! said he, looking up, — I am not such a debtor to the world,—slandered and disappointed as I have been,—as to give it that conviction: ——no! said he, my nose shall never be touched whilst Heaven gives me strength——To do what? said a burgomaster's wife.

The stranger took no notice of the burgomaster's wife; —he was making a vow to Saint Nicholas; which done, having uncrossed his arms with the same solemnity with which he crossed them, he took up the reins of his bridle with his left hand, and putting his right hand into his bosom, with the scymetar hanging loosely to the wrist of it, he rode on, as slowly as one foot of the mule could follow another, through the principal streets of Strasburg, till chance brought him to the great inn in the market-place, over-against the church.

The moment the stranger alighted, he ordered his mule to be led into the stable, and his cloak-bag to be brought in; then opening, and taking out of it his crimson-satin breeches, with a silver-fringed—(appendage to them, which I dare not translate)—he put his breeches, with his fringed cod-piece on, and forthwith, with his short scymetar in his hand, walked out to the grand parade.

The stranger had just taken three turns upon the parade, when he perceived the trumpeter's wife at the opposite side of it;—so turning short, in pain lest his nose should be attempted, he instantly went back to his inn,— undressed himself, packed up his crimson-satin breeches, &c., in his cloak-bag, and called for his mule.

Francofurtum proficiscor, ait ille, et Argentoratum quatuor abhinc hebdomadis revertar.

Bene curasti hoc jumentum? (ait) muli faciem manu
demulcens—me, manticamque meam, plus sexcentis mille
passibus portavit.

Longa via est! respondit hospes, nisi plurimum esset
negotii.—Enimvero, ait peregrinus, a Nasorum promontorio
redivi, et nasum speciosissimum, egregiosissimumque quem
unquam quisquam sortitus est, acquisivi.

Dum peregrinus hanc miram rationem de seipso reddit,
hospes et uxor ejus, oculis intentis, peregrini nasum con-
templantur——Per sanctos sanctasque omnes, ait hospitis
uxor, nasis duodecim maximis in toto Argentorato major
est!—estné, ait illa mariti in aurem insusurrans, nonne est
nasus praegrandis?

Dolus inest, anime mî, ait hospes—nasus est falsus.

Verus est, respondit uxor.
Ex abiete factus est, ait ille, terebinthinum olet.
Carbunculus inest, ait uxor.
Mortuus est nasus, respondit hospes.
Vivus est ait illa,—et si ipsa vivam, tangam.

Votum feci Sancto Nicolao, ait peregrinus, nasum meum
intactum fore usque ad——Quodnam tempus? illico respondit illa.

Minimè tangetur, inquit ille, (manibus in pectus com-
positis) usque ad illam horam——Quam horam? ait illa.——
Nullam, respondit peregrinus, donec pervenio ad——Quem
locum,—obsecro? ait illa.——Peregrinus nil respondens
mulo conscenso discessit.

I am going forwards, said the stranger, for Frankfort— and shall be back at Strasburg this day month.

I hope, continued the stranger, stroking down the face of his mule with his left hand as he was going to mount it, that you have been kind to this faithful slave of mine:—it has carried me and my cloak-bag, continued he, tapping the mule's back, above six hundred leagues.

——'Tis a long journey, Sir, replied the master of the inn, —unless a man has great business.——Tut! tut! said the stranger, I have been at the Promontory of Noses; and have got me one of the goodliest and jolliest, thank Heaven! that ever fell to a single man's lot.

Whilst the stranger was giving this odd account of himself, the master of the inn and his wife kept both their eyes fixed full upon the stranger's nose.——By Saint Radagunda, said the innkeeper's wife to herself, there is more of it than in any dozen of the largest noses put together in all Strasburg! Is it not, said she, whispering her husband in his ear, is it not a noble nose?

'Tis an imposture, my dear, said the master of the inn;— 'tis a false nose.

'Tis a true nose, said his wife.

'Tis made of fir-tree, said he; I smell the turpentine.—— There's a pimple on it, said she.

'Tis a dead nose, replied the innkeeper.

'Tis a live nose; and if I am alive myself, said the innkeeper's wife, I will touch it.

I have made a vow to St. Nicholas this day, said the stranger, that my nose shall not be touched till——Here the stranger, suspending his voice, looked up.——Till when? said she hastily.

It never shall be touched, said he, clasping his hands and bringing them close to his breast, till that hour——What hour? cried the innkeeper's wife.——Never!—never! said the stranger, never till I am got——For Heaven's sake! into what place? said she.——The stranger rode away without saying a word.

The stranger had not got half a league on his way towards Frankfort, before all the city of Strasburg was in an uproar about his nose. The Compline bells were just ringing, to call the Strasburgers to their devotions, and shut up the duties of the day in prayer:—no soul in all Strasburg heard 'em;—the city was like a swarm of bees,—men, women, and children, (the Compline bells tinkling all the time) flying here and there,—in at one door and out at another, this way and that way,—long ways and cross ways,—up one street, down another street,—in at this alley, out at that;—did you see it? did you see it? did you see it? O! did you see it? ——who saw it? who did see it? for mercy's sake, who saw it?

Alack-a-day! I was at vespers!—I was washing, I was starching, I was scouring, I was quilting.——God help me! I never saw it—I never touched it!—would I had been a sentinel, a bandy-legged drummer, a trumpeter, a trumpeter's wife! was the general cry and lamentation in every street and corner of Strasburg.

Whilst all this confusion and disorder triumphed throughout the great city of Strasburg, was the courteous stranger going on as gently upon his mule, in his way to Frankfort as if he had no concern at all in the affair,——talking, all the way he rode, in broken sentences, sometimes to his mule, —sometimes to himself,—sometimes to his Julia.

O Julia, my lovely Julia;—nay, I cannot stop to let thee bite that thistle:—that ever the suspected tongue of a rival should have robbed me of enjoyment when I was upon the point of tasting it!——

——Pugh!—'tis nothing but a thistle—never mind it;— thou shalt have a better supper at night.

——Banished from my country,—my friends,—from thee:——

Poor devil, thou'rt sadly tired with the journey!——Come, —get on a little faster—there's nothing in my cloak-bag but two shirts,—a crimson-satin pair of breeches,—and a fringed ——. Dear Julia!

——But why to Frankfort?—is it that there is a hand

unfelt, which secretly is conducting me through these meanders and unsuspected tracts?

——Stumbling! by Saint Nicholas, every step!—Why, at this rate, we shall be all night in getting in——

——To happiness;—or I am to be the sport of fortune and slander?—destined to be driven forth unconvicted,——unheard,——untouched;—if so, why did I not stay at Strasburg, where justice—but I had sworn! Come, thou shalt drink—to St. Nicholas——O Julia!——What dost thou prick up thy ears at?—'tis nothing but a man! &c.

The stranger rode on, communing in this manner with his mule and Julia,—till he arrived at his inn, where, as soon as he arrived, he alighted;—saw his mule, as he had promised it, taken good care of,—took off his cloak-bag, with his crimson-satin breeches, &c., in it;—called for an omelet for his supper, went to his bed about twelve o'clock, and in five minutes fell fast asleep.

It was about the same hour when the tumult in Strasburg being abated for that night,—the Strasburgers had all got quietly into their beds,—but not like the stranger, for the rest either of their minds or bodies. Queen Mab, like an elf as she was, had taken the stranger's nose, and, without reduction of its bulk, had that night been at the pains of slitting and dividing it into as many noses, of different cuts and fashions, as there were heads in Strasburg to hold them. The abbess of Quedlingburg, who, with the four great dignitaries of her chapter, the prioress, the deaness, the subchantress, and senior-canoness, had that week come to Strasburg, to consult the University upon a case of conscience relating to their placket-holes,—was ill all the night.

The courteous stranger's nose had got perched upon the top of the pineal gland of her brain, and made such rousing work in the fancies of the four great dignitaries of her chapter, they could not get a wink of sleep the whole night through for it;—there was no keeping a limb still amongst them:—in short, they got up, like so many ghosts.

The penitentiaries of the third order of Saint Francis,—the nuns of Mount Calvary,—the Præmonstratenses,—the

Clunienses,*—the Carthusians,—and all the severer orders
of nuns, who lay that night in blankets or haircloth, were
still in a worse condition than the abbess of Quedlingberg,
—by tumbling and tossing, and tossing and tumbling from
one side of their beds to the other the whole night long;—
the several sisterhoods had scratched and mauled themselves
all to death;——they got out of their beds almost flay'd
alive;——everybody thought Saint Anthony had visited
them, for probation, with his fire;—they had never once, in
short, shut their eyes the whole night long, from vespers to
matins.

The nuns of Saint Ursula acted the wisest;—they had
never attempted to go to bed at all.

The dean of Strasburg, the prebendaries, the capitulars
and domiciliars, (capitularly assembled in the morning to
consider the case of buttered buns) all wished they had
followed the nuns of Saint Ursula's example.

In the hurry and confusion everything had been in the
night before, the bakers had all forgot to lay their leaven,—
there were no buttered buns to be had for breakfast in all
Strasburg;—the whole close of the cathedral was in one
eternal commotion;——such a cause of restlessness and
disquietude, and such a zealous inquiry into the cause of
that restlessness, had never happened in Strasburg since
Martin Luther, with his doctrines, had turned the city upside down.

If the stranger's nose took this liberty of thrusting himself
thus into the dishes † of religious orders, &c., what a carnival
did his nose make of it in those of the laity!—'tis more
than my pen, worn to the stump as it is, has power to
describe; though, I acknowledge, (*cries* Slawkenbergius,
*with more gaiety of thought than I could have expected from
him*) that there is many a good simile now subsisting in the

* Hafen Slawkenbergius means the Benedictine Nuns of Cluny, founded in
the year 940, by Odo, abbé de Cluny.

† Mr. Shandy's compliments to orators,—is very sensible that Slawkenbergius has here changed his metaphor,—which he is very guilty of;—that
as a translator, Mr. Shandy has all along done what he could to make him
stick to it,—but that here 'twas impossible.

world which might give my countrymen some idea of it; but at the close of such a folio as this, wrote for their sakes, and in which I have spent the greatest part of my life,—tho' I own to them the simile is in being, yet would it not be unreasonable in them to expect I should have either time or inclination to search for it? Let it suffice to say, that the riot and disorder it occasioned in the Strasburgers' fantasies was so general,—such an overpowering mastership had it got of all the faculties of the Strasburgers' minds,—so many strange things, with equal confidence on all sides, and with equal eloquence in all places, were spoken and sworn to concerning it, that turned the whole stream of all discourse and wonder towards it; every soul, good and bad, —rich and poor,—learned and unlearned,—doctor and student,—mistress and maid,—gentle and simple,—nun's flesh and woman's flesh, in Strasburg, spent their time in hearing tidings about it;—every eye in Strasburg languished to see it;—every finger—every thumb in Strasburg—burned to touch it.

Now what might add, if anything may be thought necessary to add, to so vehement a desire, was this,—that the sentinel, the bandy-legged drummer, the trumpeter, the trumpeter's wife, the burgomaster's widow, the master of the inn, and the master of the inn's wife, how widely soever they all differed every one from another in their testimonies and descriptions of the stranger's nose,—they all agreed together in two points,—namely, that he was gone to Frankfort, and would not return to Strasburg till that day month; and secondly, whether his nose was true or false, that the stranger himself was one of the most perfect paragons of beauty,—the finest-made man,—the most genteel! —the most generous of his purse,—the most courteous in his carriage, that had ever entered the gates of Strasburg;—that as he rode, with his scymetar slung loosely to his wrist, through the streets,—and walked with his crimson-satin breeches across the parade,—'twas with so sweet an air of careless modesty, and so manly withal,— as would have put the heart in jeopardy (had his nose not stood in his way) of every virgin who had cast her eyes upon him.

I call not upon that heart which is a stranger to the throbs and yearnings of curiosity, so excited, to justify the abbess of Quedlingberg, the prioress, the deaness, the sub-chantress, for sending at noonday for the trumpeter's wife : she went through the streets of Strasburg with her husband's trumpet in her hand,—the best apparatus the straitness of the time would allow her, for the illustration of her theory, —she stayed no longer than three days.

The sentinel and the bandy-legged drummer !—nothing on this side of old Athens could equal them ! they read their lectures under the city-gates to comers and goers, with all the pomp of a Chrysippus and a Crantor in their porticoes.

The master of the inn, with his hostler on his left hand, read his also in the same style,—under the portico or gate-way of his stable yard ;—his wife, hers more privately in a back room. All flocked to their lectures ; not promiscu-ously,—but to this or that, as is ever the way, as faith and credulity marshalled them. In a word, each Strasburger came crowding for intelligence ;—and every Strasburger had the intelligence he wanted.

'Tis worth remarking, for the benefit of all demonstrators in natural philosophy, &c., that as soon as the trumpeter's wife had finished the abbess of Quedlingberg's private lecture, and had begun to read in public, which she did upon a stool in the middle of the great parade,—she incom-moded the other demonstrators, mainly, by gaining inconti-nently the most fashionable part of the city of Strasburg for her auditory.——But when a demonstrator in philosophy (cries Slawkenbergius) has a trumpet for an apparatus, pray what rival in science can pretend to be heard besides him ?

Whilst the unlearned, through these conduits of intelli-gence, were all busied in getting down to the bottom of the well, where TRUTH keeps her little court,——were the learned in their way as busy in pumping her up thro' the conduits of dialetic induction ;—they concerned themselves not with facts,—they reasoned.——

No one profession had thrown more light upon this subject than the Faculty,—had not all their disputes about it run into the affair of *wens* and œdematous swellings, they could not keep clear of them for their bloods and souls.— The stranger's nose had nothing to do either with wens or œdematous swellings.

It was demonstrated, however, very satisfactorily, that a ponderous mass of heterogeneous matter could not be congested and conglomerated to the nose, whilst the infant was *in utero*, without destroying the statical balance of the fœtus, and throwing it plump upon its head nine months before the time.—

——The opponents granted the theory;—they denied the consequences.

And if a suitable provision of veins, arteries, &c., said they, was not laid in, for the due nourishment of such a nose, in the very first *stamina* and rudiments of its formation, before it came into the world (bating the case of wens), it could not regularly grow and be sustained afterwards.

This was all answered by a dissertation upon nutriment,— and the affect which nutriment had in extending the vessels ; and in the increase and prolongation of the muscular parts to the greatest growth and expansion imaginable.—In the triumph of which theory, they went so far as to affirm, That there was no cause in nature why a nose might not grow to the size of the man himself.

The respondents satisfied the world this event could never happen to them so long as a man had but one stomach and one pair of lungs :—for the stomach, said they, being the only organ destined for the reception of food, and turning it into chyle, and the lungs the only engine of sanguification,—it could possibly work off no more than what the appetite brought it : or, admitting the possibility of a man's overloading his stomach, nature had set bounds however to his lungs,—the engine was of a determined size and strength, and could elaborate but a certain quantity in a given time ; —that is, it could produce just as much blood as was sufficient for one single man, and no more; so that, if there was as much nose as man,—they proved a mortification must necessarily ensue; and forasmuch as there could not be a support for both, that the nose must either fall off from the man, or the man inevitably fall off from the nose.

Nature accommodates herself to these emergencies, cried the opponents,—else what do you say to the case of a whole stomach,—a whole pair of lungs, and but *half* a man, when both his legs have been unfortunately shot off?

He dies of a plethora, said they,—or must spit blood, and in a fortnight or three weeks go off in a consumption.——

——It happens otherwise,—replied the opponents.——

It ought not, said they.

The more curious and intimate enquirers after Nature and her doings, though they went hand in hand a good way together, yet they all divided about the nose at last, almost as much as the Faculty itself.

They amicably laid it down, that there was a just and geometrical arrangement and proportion of the several parts of the human frame to its several destinations, offices, and functions, which could not be transgressed but within certain limits;—that Nature, though she sported,—she sported within a certain circle;—and they could not agree about the diameter of it.

The logician stuck much closer to the point before them than any of the classes of the *literati*;—they began and ended with the word *Nose*: and had it not been for a *petitio principii*, which one of the ablest of them ran his head against in the beginning of the combat, the whole controversy had been settled at once.

A nose, argued the logician, cannot bleed without blood, —and not only blood,—but blood circulating in it to supply the phenomenon with a succession of drops—(a stream being but a quicker succession of drops, that is included, said he.)

——Now death, continued the logician, being nothing but the stagnation of the blood,—

I deny the definition:—death is the separation of the soul from the body, said his antagonist.——Then we don't agree about our weapons, said the logician.——Then there is an end of the dispute, replied the antagonist.——

The civilians were still more concise: what they offered being more in the nature of a decree—than a dispute.——

Such a monstrous nose, said they, had it been a true nose, could not possibly have been suffered in civil society; —and if false, to impose upon society with such false signs and tokens, was a still greater violation of its rights, and must have had still less mercy shown it.

The only objection to this was, that if it proved anything, it proved the stranger's nose was neither true nor false.

This left room for the controversy to go on. It was maintained by the advocates of the ecclesiastic court, that there was nothing to inhibit a decree, since the stranger *ex mero motu* had confessed he had been at the Promontory of Noses, and had got one of the goodliest, &c., &c.——To this it was answered, it was impossible there should be such a place as the Promontory of Noses, and the learned, be ignorant where it lay. The commissary of the Bishop of Strasburg undertook the advocates' part, explained this matter in a treatise upon proverbial phrases, showing them, that the Promontory of Noses was a mere allegoric expression, importing no more than that nature had given him a long nose: in proof of which, with great learning, he cited the under-written authorities,* which had decided the point incontestably, had it not appeared that a dispute about some franchises of dean and chapter-lands had been determined by it nineteen years before.

* Nonnulli ex nostratibus eadem loquendi formula utun. Quinimo & Logistæ & Canonistæ.——Vid. Parce Barne Jas in d. L. Provincial. Constitut. de Conjec. Vid. Vol. lib. 4. Titul. 1. n. 7. qua etiam in re conspir. Om. de Promontorio Nas. Tichmak. ff. d. tit. 3. fol. 189. passim. Vid. Glos. de contrahend. empt. &c. necnon J. Scrudr. in cap. § reful. per totum. Cum his cons. Rever. J. Tubal, Sentent. & Prov. cap. 9. ff. 11, 12, obiter. V. & Librum, cui Tit. de Terris & Phras. Belg. ad. finem, cum comment. N. Bardy Belg. Vid. Scrip. Argentoratens. de Antiq. Ecc. in Episc. Archiv. fid. coll. per Von Jacobum Koinshoven, Folio, Argent. 1583. præcip. ad finem. Quibus add. Rebuff in L. obvenire de Signif. Nom. ff. fol. & de jure Gent. & Civil de protib. aliena feud. per. federa, test. Joha. Luxius in prolegom. quem velim videas, de Analy. Cap. 1, 2, 3. Vid. Idea.

It happened,—I must not say unluckily for Truth, because they were giving her a lift another way in so doing,—that the two universities of Strasburg,—the Lutheran, founded in year 1538 by Jacobus Sturmius, counsellor of the senate, —and the Popish, founded by Leopold, archduke of Austria, were, during all this time, employing the whole depth of their knowledge (except just what the affair of the abbess of Quedlingberg's placket-holes required)—in determining the point of Martin Luther's damnation.

The Popish doctors had undertaken to demonstrate, à priori, that from the necessary influence of the planets on the twenty-second day of October, 1483,—when the moon was in the twelfth house, Jupiter, Mars, and Venus in the third; the Sun, Saturn, and Mercury, all got together in the fourth;—that he must in course, and unavoidably, be a damn'd man; and that his doctrines, by a direct corollary, must be damn'd doctrines too.

By inspection into his horoscope, where five planets were in coition all at once with Scorpio * (in reading this, my father would always shake his head) in the ninth house, which the Arabians allotted to religion,—it appeared that Martin Luther did not care one stiver about the matter;— and that, from the horoscope directed to the conjunction of Mars,—they made it plain likewise he must die cursing and blaspheming;—with the blast of which his soul (being steep'd in guilt) sailed before the wind in the lake of Hell-fire.

The little objection of the Lutheran doctors to this, was, that it must certainly be the soul of another man, born October 22, '83, which was forced to sail down before the wind in that manner,—inasmuch as it appeared from the register of Islaben, in the county of Mansfelt, that Luther

* Hæc mira, satisque horrenda. Planetarum coitio sub Scorpio Asterismo in nona cœli statione, quam Arabes religioni deputabant efficit *Martinum Lutherum* sacrilegium hereticum, Christianæ religionis hostem acerrimum atque prophanum, ex horoscopi directione ad Martis coitum, religiosissimus obiit, ejus Anima scelestissima ad infernos navigavit,—ab Alecto, Tisiphone & Megara flagellis igneis cruciata perenniter.

——Lucas Gaurieus in Tractatu astrologico de præteritis multorum hominum accidentibus per genituras examinatis.

was not born in the year 1483, but in '84; and not on the 22nd day of October, but on the 10th of November, the eve of Martinmas-day, from whence he had the name of Martin.

[——I must break off my translation for a moment; for, if I did not, I know I should no more be able to shut my eyes in bed, than the abbess of Quedlingberg.—It is to tell the reader, that my father never read this passage of Slaw-kenbergius to my uncle Toby, but with triumph,—not over my uncle Toby, for he never opposed him in it,—but over the whole world.

—Now you see, brother Toby, he would say, looking up, "that christian names are not such indifferent things:"—had Luther here been called by any other name but Martin, he would have been damn'd to all eternity;—not that I look upon Martin, he would add, as a good name,—far from it, —'tis something better than a neutral, and but a little;—yet, little as it is, you see it was of some service to him.

My father knew the weakness of this prop to his hypo-thesis, as well as the best logician could show him ;—yet so strange is the weakness of man at the same time, as it fell in his way, he could not for his life but make use of it; and it was certainly for this reason, that though there are many stories in Hafen Slawkenbergius's Decades full as entertain-ing as this I am translating, yet there is not one amongst them which my father read over with half the delight ;—it flattered two of his strangest hypotheses together,—his *Names* and his *Noses.*—I will be bold to say, he might have read all the books in the Alexandrian Library, had not fate taken other care of them, and not have met with a book or passage in one, which hit two such nails as these upon the head at one stroke.]

The two universities of Strasburg were hard tugging at this affair of Luther's navigation. The Protestant doctors had demonstrated, that he had not sailed right before the wind, as the Popish doctors had pretended ; and as every one knew there was no sailing full in the teeth of it,—they were going to settle, in case he had sailed, how many points he was off; whether Martin had doubled the Cape, or had fallen upon a lee-shore; and no doubt, as it was an enquiry of much edification, at least to those who understood this sort of *navigation*, they had gone on with it in spite of the size of the stranger's nose, had not the size of the stranger's nose drawn off the attention of the world from what they were about:—it was their business to follow.

The abbess of Quedlingberg and her four dignitaries were no stop; for the enormity of the stranger's nose running full as much in their fancies as their case of conscience,—the affair of their placket-holes kept cold:—in a word, the printers were ordered to distribute their types:—all controversies dropp'd.

'Twas a square cap with a silver tassel upon the crown of it—to a nutshell,—to have guessed on which side of the nose the two universities would split.

'Tis above reason, cried the doctors on one side.

'Tis below reason, cried the others.

'Tis faith, cried one.

'Tis a fiddlestick, said the other.

'Tis possible, cried one.

'Tis impossible, said the other.

God's power is infinite, cried the Nosarians; he can do anything.

He can do nothing, replied the Antinosarians, which implies contradictions.

He can make matter think, said the Nosarians.

As certainly as you can make a velvet cap out of a sow's ear, replied the Antinosarians.

He cannot make two and two five, replied the Popish doctors.——'Tis false, said their other opponents.

Infinite power is infinite power, said the doctors who maintained the reality of the nose.—It extends only to all possible things, replied the Lutherans.

By God in heaven! cried the Popish doctors, he can make a nose, if he thinks fit, as big as the steeple of Strasburg.

Now the steeple of Strasburg being the biggest and the tallest church-steeple to be seen in the whole world, the Antinosarians denied that a nose of 575 geometrical feet in length could be worn, at least by a middle-siz'd man.—The Popish doctors swore it could:—the Lutheran doctors said No;—it could not.

This at once started a new dispute, which they pursued a great way, upon the extent and limitation of the moral and natural attributes of God.—That controversy led them naturally into Thomas Aquinas; and Thomas Aquinas to the Devil.

The stranger's nose was no more heard of in the dispute; —it just served as a frigate, to launch them into the gulf of School-divinity,—and then they all sailed before the wind.

\ Heat is in proportion to the want of true knowledge. \

The controversy about the attributes, &c., instead of cooling, on the contrary, had inflamed the Strasburgers' imaginations to a most inordinate degree.—The less they understood of the matter, the greater was their wonder about it;—they were left in all the distresses of desire unsatisfied,—saw their doctors, the *Parchmentarians*, the *Brassarians*, 'the *Turpentarians*, on one side,—the Popish doctors on the other, like Pantagruel and his companions in quest of the oracle of the bottle, all embarked out of sight.

——The poor Strasburgers left upon the beach!

——What was to be done?—No delay;—the uproar increased,—every one in disorder,—the city-gates set open.

Unfortunate Strasburgers!—was there in the store-house of nature,—was there in the lumber-rooms of learning,— was there in the great arsenal of chance, one single engine left undrawn forth to torture your curiosities, and stretch your desires, which was not pointed by the hand of Fate to play upon your hearts?—I dip not my pen into my ink to excuse the surrender of yourselves,—'tis to write your panegyric.—Show me a city so macerated with expectation, —who neither ate, nor drank, nor slept, nor prayed, nor hearkened to the calls either of religion or nature, for seven-and-twenty days together, who could have held out one day longer!

On the twenty-eighth the courteous stranger had promised to return to Strasburg.

Seven thousand coaches (Slawkenbergius must certainly have made some mistake in his numerical characters), 7000 coaches,—15,000 single-horse chairs,—20,000 waggons, crowded as full as they could all hold with senators, counsellors, syndics,—beguines, widows, wives, virgins, canons, concubines, all in their coaches:—The abbess of Quedlingberg, with the prioress, the deaness, and sub-chantress, leading the procession in one coach, and the dean of Strasburg, with the four great dignitaries of his chapter, on her left hand,—the rest following higglety-pigglety as they could; some on horseback,—some on foot,—some led, some driven, —some down the Rhine,—some this way,—some that,—all set out at sunrise to meet the courteous stranger on the road.

' Haste we now towards the catastrophe of my tale,—I say catastrophe, (cries Slawkenbergius) inasmuch as a tale, with parts rightly disposed, not only rejoiceth (*gaudet*) in the *Catastrophe* and *Peripetia* of a DRAMA, but rejoiceth moreover in all the essential and integrant parts of it;—it has its *Protasis, Epitasis, Catastasis*, its *Catastrophe* or *Peripetia*, growing one out of the other in it, in the order Aristotle first planted them,—without which a tale had better never be told at all, says Slawkenbergius, but be kept to a man's self.

In all my ten tales, in all my ten decades, have I, Slawkenbergius, tied down every tale of them as tightly to this rule, as I have done this of the stranger and his nose.

—From his first parley with the sentinel to his leaving the city of Strasburg, after pulling off his crimson-satin pair of breeches, is the *Protasis*, or first entrance,—where the characters of the *Personæ Dramatis* are just touched in, and the subject slightly begun.

The *Epitasis*, wherein the action is more fully entered upon and heightened, till it arrives at its state or height, called the *Catastasis*, and which usually takes up the 2nd and 3rd act, is included within that busy period of my tale, betwixt the first night's uproar about the nose, to the conclusion of the trumpeter's wife's lectures upon it in the middle of the grand parade: and from the first embarking of the learned in the dispute—to the doctor's finally sailing away, and leaving the Strasburgers upon the beach in distress, is the *Catastasis*, or the ripening of the incidents and passions for their bursting forth in the 5th act.

This commences with the setting out of the Strasburgers on the Frankfort road, and terminates in unwinding the labyrinth, and bringing the hero out of a state of agitation (as Aristotle calls it) to a state of rest and quietness.

This, says Hafen Slawkenbergius, constitutes the *Catastrophe* or *Peripetia* of my tale;—and that is the part of it I am going to relate.

We left the stranger behind the curtain asleep:—he enters now upon the stage.

—What dost thou prick up thy ears at?—'tis nothing but a man upon a horse,—was the last word the stranger uttered to his mule. It was not proper then to tell the reader that the mule took his master's word for it; and without any more *ifs* or *ands*, let the traveller and his horse pass by.

The traveller was hastening with all diligence to get to Strasburg that night. What a fool am I, said the traveller to himself, when he had rode about a league farther, to think of getting into Strasburg this night!—Strasburg!—the great Strasburg!—Strasburg, the capital of all Alsatia! Strasburg, an imperial city! Strasburg, a sovereign state! Strasburg, garrisoned with five thousand of the best troops in all the world!—Alas! if I was at the gates of Strasburg this moment, I could not gain admittance into it for a ducat, —nay, a ducat and a half:—'tis too much,—better go back to the last inn I have passed,—than lie I know not where, —or give I know not what. The traveller, as he made these reflections in his mind, turned his horse's head about, and, three minutes after the stranger had been conducted into his chamber, he arrived at the same inn.

——We have bacon in the house, said the host, and bread; and till eleven o'clock this night had three eggs in it;—but a stranger, who arrived an hour ago, has had them dressed into an omelet, and we have nothing.—

Alas! said the traveller, harassed as I am, I want nothing

but a bed.——I have one as soft as is in Alsatia, said the host.

—The stranger, continued he, should have slept in it, for 'tis my best bed, but upon the score of his nose.——He has got a defluction, said the traveller.——Not that I know, cried the host.—But 'tis a camp-bed; and Jacinta, said he, looking towards the maid, imagined there was not room in it to turn his nose in.——Why so? cried the traveller, starting back.——It is so long a nose, replied the host.—— The traveller fixed his eyes upon Jacinta, then upon the ground,—kneeled upon his right knee, had just got his hand laid upon his breast——Trifle not with my anxiety, said he, rising up again.——'Tis no trifle, said Jacinta, 'tis the most glorious nose!——The traveller fell upon his knee again,— laid his hand upon his breast,—then, said he, looking up to Heaven, thou hast conducted me to the end of my pilgrimage!—'Tis Diego.

The traveller was the brother of Julia, so often invoked that night by the stranger, as he rode from Strasburg upon his mule; and was come, on her part, in quest of him. He had accompanied his sister from Valladolid across the Pyrenean Mountains through France, and had many an entangled skein to wind off in pursuit of him, through the many meanders and abrupt turnings of a lover's thorny tracks.

——Julia had sunk under it,—and had not been able to get a step farther than to Lyons; where, with the many disquietudes of a tender heart, which all talk of,—but few feel,—she sicken'd, but had just strength to write a letter to Diego! and having conjured her brother never to see her face till he had found him out, and put the letter into his hands, Julia took to her bed.

Fernandez, (for that was her brother's name)—tho' the camp-bed was as soft as any one in Alsace, yet he could not shut his eyes in it.—As soon as it was day, he rose; and hearing Diego was risen too, he entered his chamber, and discharged his sister's commission.

The letter was as follows:

"Seig. Diego,

" Whether my suspicions of your nose were justly excited, or not,—'tis not now to enquire;—it is enough I have not had firmness to put them to farther trial.

" How could I know so little of myself, when I sent my duenna to forbid your coming more under my lattice? or how could I know so little of you, Diego, as to imagine you would have stayed one day in Valladolid to have given ease to my doubts? Was I to be abandoned, Diego, because I was deceived! or was it kind to take me at my word, whether my suspicions were just or no, and leave me, as you did, a prey to much uncertainty and sorrow?

" In what manner Julia has resented this,—my brother, when he puts this letter into your hands, will tell you; he will tell you in how few moments she repented of the rash message she had sent you,—in what frantic haste she flew to her lattice, and how many days and nights together she leaned immovably upon her elbow, looking through it towards the way which Diego was wont to come.

" He will tell you, when she heard of your departure,—how her spirits deserted her,—how her heart sicken'd,—how piteously she mourned,—how long she hung her head. O Diego! how many weary steps has my brother's pity led me by the hand languishing to trace out yours!—how far has desire carried me beyond strength!—and how oft have I fainted by the way, and sunk into his arms, with only power to cry out,—O my Diego!

" If the gentleness of your carriage has not belied your heart, you will fly to me almost as fast as you fled from me: —haste as you will,—you will arrive but to see me expire. ——'Tis a bitter draught, Diego; but ho! 'tis embittered still more by dying un——!"

She could proceed no farther.

Slawkenbergius supposes the word intended was *unconvinced*; but her strength would not enable her to finish her letter.

The heart of the courteous Diego overflowed as he read

the letter :—he ordered his mule forthwith, and Fernandez's
horse, to be saddled ; and as no vent in prose is equal to
that of poetry in such conflicts,—chance, which as often
directs us to remedies as to *diseases,* having thrown a piece
of charcoal into the window,—Diego availed himself of it ;
and, whilst the hostler was getting ready his mule, he eased
his mind against the wall as follows :

ODE.

Harsh and untuneful are the notes of love,
· Unless my Julia strikes the key,
Her hand alone can touch the part,
 Whose dulcet move-
 ment charms the heart,
And governs all the man with sympathetic sway.

2d.

O Julia !

· The lines were very natural,—for they were nothing at all
to the purpose, says Slawkenbergius, and 'tis a pity there
were no more of them ; but whether it was that Seig. Diego
was slow in composing verses,—or the hostler quick in saddling mules,—is not averred : certain it was that Diego's mule
and Fernandez's horse were ready at the door of the inn
before Diego was ready for his second stanza ; so, without
staying to finish his ode, they both mounted, sallied forth,
passed the Rhine, traversed Alsace, shaped their course
towards Lyons ; and, before the Strasburgers and the abbess
of Quedlingberg had set out on their cavalcade, had Fernandez, Diego, and his Julia, crossed the Pyrenean Mountains,
and got safe to Valladolid.

'Tis needless to inform the geographical reader, that, when
Diego was in Spain, it was not possible to meet the courteous
stranger in the Frankfort road : it is enough to say, that
of all restless desires, curiosity being the strongest,—the
Strasburgers felt the full force of it ; and that for three days
and nights they were tossed to and fro in the Frankfort road,
with the tempestuous fury of this passion, before they could
submit to return home ;—when, alas ! an event was prepared

for them, of all others the most grievous that could befall a free people.

As this revolution of the Strasburgers' affairs is often spoken of and little understood, I will, in ten words, says Slawkenbergius, give the world an explanation of it, and with it put an end to my tale.

Everybody knows of the grand system of Universal Monarchy, wrote by order of Monsieur Colbert, and put in manuscript into the hands of Lewis the Fourteenth, in the year 1664.

'Tis as well known, that one branch out of many of that system, was the getting possession of Strasburg, to favour an entrance at all times into Suabia, in order to disturb the quiet of Germany;—and that, in consequence of this plan, Strasburg unhappily fell at length into their hands.

It is the lot of a few to trace out the true springs of this and such-like revolutions;—the vulgar look too high for them,—Statesmen look too low;—Truth (for once) lies in the middle.

What a fatal thing is the popular pride of a free city! cries one historian.—The Strasburgers deemed it a diminution of their freedom to receive an Imperial garrison,—so fell a prey to a French one.

The fate, says another, of the Strasburgers, may be a warning to all free people to save their money.—They anticipated their revenues,—brought themselves under taxes, exhausted their strength, and, in the end, became so weak a people, they had not strength to keep their gates shut; and so the French pushed them open!

Alas! alas! cries Slawkenbergius, 'twas not the French, —'twas *curiosity* pushed them open.—The French, indeed, who are ever upon the catch, when they saw the Strasburgers, men, women, and children, all marched out to follow the stranger's nose,—each man followed his own, and marched in.

Trade and manufactures have decayed and gradually grown down ever since,—but not from any cause which commercial heads have assigned; for it is owing to this only, that

Noses have ever so run in their heads, that the Strasburgers could not follow their business.

Alas! alas! cries Slawkenbergius, making an exclamation, —it is not the first,—and I fear will not be the last fortress that has been either won—or lost by *Noses*.

THE END OF SLAWKENBERGIUS'S TALE.

_____

CHAPTER I.

WITH all this learning upon Noses running perpetually in my father's fancy,—with so many family prejudices,—and ten decades of such tales running on for ever along with them,—how was it possible with such exquisite,—was it a true nose ?—that a man with such exquisite feelings as my father had, could bear the shock at all below stairs,—or, indeed above stairs, in any other posture but the very posture I have described ?

———Throw yourself down upon the bed a dozen times,— taking care only to place a looking-glass first in a chair on one side of it before you do it.—But was the stranger's nose a true nose, or was it a false one ?

To tell that beforehand, Madam, would be to do injury to one of the best tales in the Christian world ; and that is the tenth of the tenth decade, which immediately followed this.

This tale, cried Slawkenbergius, somewhat exultingly, has been reserved by me for the concluding tale of my whole work ; knowing right well, that when I shall have told it, and my reader shall have read it thro',—'twould be even high time for both of us to shut up the book ; inasmuch, continues Slawkenbergius, as I know of no tale which could possibly ever go down after it.

—'Tis a tale indeed !

This sets out with the first interview in the inn at Lyons,

when Fernandez left the courteous stranger and his sister
Julia alone in her chamber, and is overwritten

THE INTRICACIES

OF

DIEGO AND JULIA.

Heavens! thou art a strange creature, Slawkenbergius!
what a whimsical view of the involutions of the heart of
woman hast thou opened! How this can ever be translated,
and yet if this specimen of Slawkenbergius's tales, and the
exquisiteness of his moral, should please the world,—translated shall a couple of volumes be.—Else, how this can ever
be translated into good English, I have no sort of conception.
—There seems, in some passages, to want a sixth sense to
do it rightly.—What can he mean by the lambent pupil-
ability of slow, low, dry chat, five notes below the natural
tone,—which you know, Madam, is little more than a
whisper? The moment I pronounced the words, I could
perceive an attempt towards a vibration in the strings about
the region of the heart.—The brain made no acknowledgment.—There's often no good understanding betwixt 'em :—
I felt as if I understood it.—I had no ideas.—The movement could not be without cause.—I'm lost. I can make
nothing of it,—unless, may it please your Worships, the
voice, in that case being little more than a whisper, unavoidably forces the eyes to approach not only within six inches
of each other,—but to look into the pupils.—Is not that
dangerous?—But it can't be avoided ;—for to look up to the
ceiling, in that case the two chins unavoidably meet ;—and,
to look down into each other's lap, the foreheads come into
immediate contact, which at once puts an end to the con-
ference,—I mean to the sentimental part of it.—What is
left, Madam, is not worth stooping for.

———

CHAPTER II.

My father lay stretched across the bed as still as if the hand of Death had pushed him down, for a full hour and a half, before he began to play upon the floor with the toe of that foot which hung over the bedside.   My uncle Toby's heart was a pound lighter for it.—In a few moments, his left hand, the knuckles of which had all the time reclined upon the handle of the chamber-pot, came to its feeling;—he thrust it a little more within the valance,—drew up his hand, when he had done, into his bosom,—gave a hem! My good uncle Toby, with infinite pleasure, answered it; and full gladly would have ingrafted a sentence of consolation upon the opening it afforded : but having no talents, as I said, that way, and fearing, moreover, that he might set out with something which might make a bad matter worse, he contented himself with resting his chin placidly upon the cross of his crutch.

Now, whether the compression shortened my uncle Toby's face into a more pleasurable oval,—or that the philanthropy of his heart, in seeing his brother beginning to emerge out of the sea of his afflictions, had braced up his muscles,—so that the compression upon his chin only doubled the benignity which was there before, is not hard to decide.—My father, in turning his eyes, was struck with such a gleam of sunshine in his face, as melted down the sullenness of his grief in a moment.

He broke silence as follows :—

———

CHAPTER III.

Did ever man, brother Toby, cried my father, raising himself upon his elbow, and turning himself round to the opposite side of the bed, where my uncle Toby was sitting in his old fringed chair, with his chin resting upon his crutch,—

did ever a poor unfortunate man, brother Toby, cried my father, receive so many lashes?——The most I ever saw given, quoth my uncle Toby (ringing the bell at the bed's head for Trim), was to a grenadier, I think, in Mackay's regiment.

——Had my uncle Toby shot a bullet through my father's heart, he could not have fallen down with his nose upon the quilt more suddenly.

Bless me! said my uncle Toby.

CHAPTER IV.

Was it Mackay's regiment, quoth my uncle Toby, where the poor grenadier was so unmercifully whipp'd at Bruges, about the ducats?——O Christ! he was innocent! cried Trim, with a deep sigh—And he was whipp'd, may it please your Honour, almost to Death's door.—They had better have shot him outright, as he begg'd, and he had gone directly to Heaven; for he was as innocent as your Honour.——I thank thee, Trim! quoth my uncle Toby. ——I never think of his, continued Trim, and my poor brother Tom's misfortunes, for we were all three school-fellows, but I cry like a coward.——Tears are no proof of cowardice, Trim.—I drop them oft-times myself, cried my uncle Toby.——I know your Honour does, replied Trim, and so am not ashamed of it myself.—But to think, may it please your Honour, continued Trim,—a tear stealing into the corner of his eye as he spoke,—to think of two virtuous lads, with hearts as warm in their bodies, and as honest as God could make them,—the children of honest people, going forth with gallant spirits to seek their fortunes in the world,—and fall into such evils,—poor Tom! to be tortured upon a rack for nothing—but marrying a Jew's widow who sold sausages!—honest Dick Johnson's soul to be scourged out of his body, for the ducats another man put into his knapsack!—O!—these are misfortunes,

cried Trim, pulling out his handkerchief,—these are misfortunes, may it please your Honour, worth lying down and
crying over.

—My father could not help blushing.

'Twould be a pity, Trim, quoth my uncle Toby, thou
shouldst ever feel sorrow of thy own ;—thou feelest it
so tenderly for others.—Alack-a-day, replied the corporal,
brightening up his face,—your Honour knows I have
neither wife nor child ;—I can have no sorrows in this
world.——My father could not help smiling.——As few as
any man, Trim, replied my uncle Toby ; nor can I see how
a fellow of thy light heart can suffer, but from the distress
of poverty in thy old age, when thou art past all services,
Trim,—and hast outlived thy friends.——An' please your
Honour, never fear, replied Trim cheerly.——But I would
have thee never fear, Trim, replied my uncle Toby ; and
therefore, continued my uncle Toby, throwing down his
crutch and getting up upon his legs as he uttered the word
therefore,— in recompence, Trim, of thy long fidelity to me
and that goodness of thy heart I have had such proofs of,—
whilst thy master is worth a shilling,—thou shalt never ask
elsewhere, Trim, for a penny.——Trim attempted to thank
my uncle Toby,—but had not power ;—tears trickled down
his cheeks faster than he could wipe them off.—He laid his
hands upon his breast,—made a bow to the ground, and
shut the door.

——I have left Trim my bowling-green, cried my uncle
Toby.—My father smiled.——I have left him, moreover, a
pension, continued my uncle Toby.——My father looked
grave.

——————

CHAPTER V.

Is this a fit time, said my father to himself, to talk of
pensions and grenadiers ?

CHAPTER VI.

WHEN my uncle Toby first mentioned the grenadier, my father, I said, fell down with his nose flat to the quilt, and as suddenly as if my uncle Toby had shot him; but it was not added that every other limb and member of my father instantly relapsed, with his nose, into the same precise attitude in which he lay first described; so that when Corporal Trim left the room, and my father found himself disposed to rise off the bed,—he had all the little preparatory movements to run over again, before he could do it. Attitudes are nothing, Madam,—'tis the transition from one attitude to another,—like the preparation and resolution of the discord into harmony, which is all in all.

For which reason, my father played the same jig over again with his toe upon the floor,—pushed the chamber pot still a little farther within the valance,—gave a hem,—raised himself upon his elbow,—and was just beginning to address himself to my uncle Toby,—when recollecting the unsuccessfulness of his first effort in that attitude,—he got upon his legs, and in making the third turn across the room he stopped short before my uncle Toby; and laying the three first fingers of his right hand in the palm of his left, and stooping a little, he addressed himself to my uncle Toby as follows :—

―――

CHAPTER VII.

WHEN I reflect, brother Toby, upon MAN; and take a view of that dark side of him which represents his life as open to so many causes of trouble ;—when I consider, brother Toby, how oft we eat the bread of affliction, and that we are born to it, as to the portion of our inheritance,——I was born to nothing, quoth my uncle Toby, interrupting my father,—but my commission.——Zooks I said my father, did not my uncle leave you a hundred and twenty pounds a year ?——

What could I have done without it? replied my uncle
Toby.——That's another concern, said my father testily;
—but I say, Toby, when one runs over the catalogue of all
the cross-reckonings and sorrowful *items* with which the
heart of man is overcharged, 'tis wonderful by what hidden
resources the mind is enabled to stand it out, and bear itself
up, as it does, against the impositions laid upon our nature.
——'Tis by the assistance of Almighty God! cried my uncle
Toby, looking up, and pressing the palms of his hands close
together,—'tis not from our own strength, brother Shandy;
a sentinel in a wooden sentry-box might as well pretend to
stand it out against a detachment of fifty men.—We are
upheld by the grace and assistance of the best of Beings.

——That is cutting the knot, said my father, instead of
untying it. But give me leave to lead you, brother Toby,
a little deeper into the mystery.

With all my heart, replied my uncle Toby.

My father instantly exchanged the attitude he was in, for
that in which Socrates is so finely painted by Raphael, in
his school of Athens; which your connoisseurship knows is
so exquisitely imagined, that even the particular manner of
the reasoning of Socrates is expressed by it,—for he holds
the fore-finger of his left hand between the fore-finger and
the thumb of his right; and seems as if he was saying to
the libertine he is reclaiming,—" *You grant me* this,—and
this: and this, and this, I don't ask of you;—they follow of
themselves in course."

So stood my father, holding fast his fore-finger betwixt
his finger and his thumb, and reasoning with my uncle
Toby as he sat in his old fringed chair, valanced around
with parti-coloured worsted bobs.——O Garrick!—what a
rich scene of this would thy exquisite powers make! and
how gladly would I write such another to avail myself of
thy immortality, and secure my own behind it!

CHAPTER VIII.

Though man is of all others the most curious vehicle, said my father; yet, at the same time, 'tis of so slight a frame, and so totteringly put together, that the sudden jerks and hard jostlings it unavoidably meets with in this rugged journey, would overset and tear it to pieces a dozen times a day,—was it not, brother Toby, that there is a secret spring within us.——Which spring, said my uncle Toby, I take to be religion.——Will that set my child's nose on? cried my father, letting go his finger, and striking one hand against the other.——It makes everything straight for us, answered my uncle Toby.——Figuratively speaking, dear Toby, it may, for aught I know, said my father; but the spring I am speaking of, is that great and elastic power within us of counterbalancing evil; which, like a secret spring in a well-ordered machine, though it can't prevent the shock,—at least, it imposes upon our sense of it.

Now, my dear brother, said my father, replacing his fore-finger, as he was coming closer to the point,—had my child arrived safe into the world, unmartyr'd in that precious part of him,—fanciful and extravagant as I may appear to the world in my opinion of Christian names, and of that magic bias which good or bad names irresistibly impress upon our characters and conducts,—Heaven is witness, that in the warmest transports of my wishes for the prosperity of my child, I never once wished to crown his head with more glory and honour than what George or Edward would have spread around it.

But, alas! continued my father, as the greatest evil has befallen him,—I must counteract and undo it with the greatest good.

He shall be christened Trismegistus, brother.

I wish it may answer,—replied my uncle Toby, rising up.

CHAPTER IX.

WHAT a chapter of chances, said my father, turning himself about upon the first landing, as he and my uncle Toby
were going downstairs!—what a long chapter of chances
do the events of this world lay open to us! Take pen and
ink in hand, brother Toby, and calculate it fairly.——I
know no more of calculation than this balustrade, said my
uncle Toby (striking short of it with his crutch, and
hitting my father a desperate blow souse upon his shin-
bone).—'Twas a hundred to one,—cried my uncle Toby
——I thought, quoth my father (rubbing his shin) you had
known nothing of calculations, brother Toby.——'Twas a
mere chance, said my uncle Toby.——Then it adds one to
the chapter,—replied my father.

The double success of my father's repartees tickled off
the pain of his shin at once:—it was well it so fell out—
(chance! again)—or the world to this day had never
known the subject of my father's calculation;—to guess it,
—there was no chance.—What a lucky chapter of chances
has this turned out! for it has saved me the trouble of
writing one express; and in truth I have enough already
upon my hands without it.—Have not I promised the
world a chapter of knots? two chapters upon the right
and wrong end of woman? a chapter upon whiskers? a
chapter upon wishes? a chapter of noses?—No; I have
done that:—a chapter upon my uncle Toby's modesty? to
say nothing of a chapter upon chapters, which I will finish
before I sleep.—By my great grandfather's whiskers! I
shall never get half of 'em through this year.

Take pen and ink in hand, and calculate it fairly, brother
Toby, said my father; and it will turn out a million to
one, that of all the parts of the body, the edge of the
forceps should have the ill luck just to fall upon and break
down that one part, which should break down the fortunes
of our house with it.

It might have been worse, replied my uncle Toby.——

I don't comprehend, said my father.——Suppose the hip had presented, replied my uncle Toby, as Dr. Slop foreboded?

My father reflected half a minute,—looked down,—touched the middle of his forehead slightly with his finger——

—True, said he.

———

CHAPTER X.

Is it not a shame to make two chapters of what passed in going down one pair of stairs? for we are got no farther yet than the first landing, and there are fifteen more steps down to the bottom; and, for aught I know, as my father and my uncle Toby are in a talking humour, there may be as many chapters as steps. Let that be as it will, Sir, I can no more help it than my destiny.—A sudden impulse comes across me:—drop the curtain, Shandy:—I drop it. —Strike a line here across the paper, Tristram:—I strike it,—and hey for a new chapter.

The deuce of any other rule have I to govern myself in this affair;—and if I had one,—as I do all things out of all rule,—I would twist it and tear it to pieces, and throw it into the fire when I had done.—Am I warm? I am, and the cause demands it:—a pretty story! is a man to follow rules,—or rules to follow him?

Now this, you must know, being my chapter upon chapters, which I promised to write before I went to sleep, I thought it meet to ease my conscience entirely before I laid down, by telling the world all I knew about the matter at once. Is not this ten times better than to set out dogmatically with a sententious parade of wisdom, and telling the world a story of a roasted horse?—that chapters relieve the mind,—that they assist,—or impose upon the imagination,—and that in a work of this dramatic cast they are as necessary as the shifting of scenes,—with fifty other cold

conceits, enough to extinguish the fire which roasted him!
O! but to understand this, which is a puff at the fire of
Diana's temple,—you must read Longinus:—read away:—
if you are not a jot the wiser for reading him the first time
over,—never fear,—read him again.   Avicenna and Licetus
read Aristotle's Metaphysics forty times through apiece, and
never understood a single word!   But mark the consequence.
—Avicenna turned out a desperate writer at all kinds of
writing;—for he wrote books *de omni scribili;* and for
Licetus (Fortunio)——though all the world knows he was
born a *fœtus** of no more than five inches and a half in
length, yet he grew to that astonishing height in literature,
as to write a book with a title as long as himself.   The
learned know I mean his *Gonopsychanthropologia,* upon the
Origin of the Human Soul.

So much for my chapter upon chapters, which I hold to
be the best chapter in my whole work; and, take my word,
whoever reads it, is full as well employed as in picking
straws.

* Ce fœtus n'étoit pas plus grand que le paume de la main; mais son père
l'ayant examiné en qualité de Médecin, & ayant trouvé que c'étoit quelque
chose de plus qu'un Embryon, le fit transporter tout vivant à Rapallo, où il le
fit voir à Jerôme Bardi & à d'autres Médecins du lieu.   On trouva qu'il ne lui
manquoit rien d'essentiel à la vie; & son père pour faire voir un essai de son
expérience, entrepit d'achever l'ouvrage de la Nature, & de travailler à la
formation de l'Enfant avec le même artifice que celui dont on se sert pour faire
éclore les Poulets en Egypte.   Il instruisit une Nourrice de tout ce qu'elle
avoit à faire, et ayant fait mettre son fils dan un four proprement accommodé,
il réussit à l'élever & à lui faire prendre ses accroissemens nécessaires, par
l'uniformité d'une chaleur étrange, mesurée éxactement sur les dégrés d'un
Thermométre, ou d'un autre instrument équivalent.   (Vide Mich. Giustinian,
ne gli Scritt.   Liguri à Cart. 223, 418.)

On auroit toujours été très satisfait de l'industrie d'un père si expérimenté
dans l'Art de la Génération, quand il n'auroit pû prolonger la vie à son fils
que pour quelques mois, ou pour peu d'années.

Mais quand on se représente que l'Enfant a veçu près de quatrevingt ans,
& qu'il a composé quatre-vingt Ouvrages differents tous fruits d'une longue
lecture—il faut convenir que tout ce qui est incroyable n'est pas toujours faux,
& que la "Vraisemblance n'est pas toujours du côté de la Vérité."

Il n'avoit que dix-neuf ans lorsqu'il composa Gonopsychanthropologia De
Origine Animæ Humanæ.

(Les Enfans célèbres, revûs & corrigés par M. de la Monnoye de l'Académie
Française.)

CHAPTER XI.

WE shall bring all things to rights, said my father, setting his foot upon the first step from the landing.—This Trismegistus, continued my father, drawing his leg back, and turning to my uncle Toby,—was the greatest (Toby) of all earthly beings;—he was the greatest king,—the greatest lawgiver,—the greatest philosopher,—and the greatest priest;——and engineer,—said my uncle Toby.——In course, said my father.

CHAPTER XII.

—AND how does your Mistress? cried my father, taking the same step over again from the landing, and calling to Susannah, whom he saw passing by the foot of the stairs with a huge pin-cushion in her hand,—How does your Mistress?——As well, said Susannah, tripping by, but without looking up, as can be expected.——What a fool am I! said my father, drawing his leg back again,—let things be as they will, brother Toby, 'tis ever the precise answer.—And how is the child, pray?——No answer.—And where is Dr. Slop? added my father, raising his voice aloud, and looking over the balustrades.—Susannah was out of hearing.

Of all the riddles of a married life, said my father, crossing the landing, in order to set his back against the wall whilst he propounded it to my uncle Toby,—of all the puzzling riddles, said he, in the marriage-state,—of which you may trust me, brother Toby, there are more asses' loads than all Job's stock of asses could have carried,—there is not one that has more intricacies in it than this:—that from the very moment that the mistress of the house is brought to bed, every female in it, from my lady's gentlewoman down to the cinder-wench, becomes an inch taller for it;

and gives herself more airs upon that single inch, than all her other inches put together.

I think rather, replied my uncle Toby, that 'tis we who sink an inch lower.—If I meet but a woman with child,—I do it.—'Tis a heavy tax upon that half of our fellow-creatures, brother Shandy, said my uncle Toby.—'Tis a piteous burden upon 'em, continued he, shaking his head.

——Yes, yes, 'tis a painful thing,—said my father, shaking his head too:—but certainly since shaking of heads came into fashion, never did two heads shake together in concert from two such different springs.

God bless } 'em all!—said my uncle Toby and my
Deuce take }
father; each to himself.

CHAPTER XIII.

HOLLA!—you, chairman!—here's sixpence:—do step into that bookseller's shop, and call me a *day-tall* critic. I am very willing to give any one of 'em a crown to help me with his tackling, to get my father and my uncle Toby off the stairs, and to put them to bed.

—'Tis even high time; for, except a short nap, which they both got while Trim was boring the jack-boots,—and which, by the bye, did my father no sort of good, upon the score of the bad hinge,—they have not else shut their eyes since nine hours before the time that Doctor Slop was led into the back parlour in that dirty pickle by Obadiah.

Was every day of my life to be as busy a day as this,—and to take up——Truce:

I will not finish that sentence till I have made an observation upon the strange state of affairs between the reader and myself, just as things stand at present:—an observation never applicable before to any one biographical writer since the creation of the world but myself;—and, I believe, will never hold good to any other, until its final destruction;—

and, therefore, for the very novelty of it alone, it must be worth your Worships attending to.

I am this month one whole year older than I was this time twelvemonth; and having got, as you perceive, almost into the middle of my fourth volume,*—and no farther than to my first day's life,—'tis demonstrative that I have 364 days more life to write just now, than when I first set out; so that, instead of advancing as a common writer, in my work with what I have been doing at it;—on the contrary, I am just thrown so many volumes back.—Was every day of my life to be as busy a day as this,—And why not? —and the transactions and opinions of it to take up as much description,—And for what reason should they be cut short? as at this rate I should just live 364 times faster than I should write,—it must follow, an' please your Worships, that the more I write, the more I shall have to write,—and consequently, the more your Worships read, the more your Worships will have to read.

Will this be good for your Worships' eyes?

It will do well for mine; and, was it not that my *Opinions* will be the death of me, I perceive I shall lead a fine life of it out of this self-same *Life* of mine; or in other words, shall lead a couple of fine lives together.

As for the proposal of twelve volumes a year, or a volume a month, it no way alters my prospect:—write as I will, and rush as I may into the middle of things, as Horace advises,—I shall never overtake myself whipp'd and driven to the last pinch. At the worst I shall have one day the start of my pen,—and one day is enough for two volumes; —and two volumes will be enough for one year.—

Heaven prosper the manufacturers of paper under this propitious reign, which is now opened to us!—as I trust its providence will prosper everything else in it that is taken in hand.

As for the propagation of geese,—I give myself no concern, —Nature is all-bountiful;—I shall never want tools to work with.

* According to the original editions.

—So then, friend, you have got my father and my uncle
Toby off the stairs, and seen them to bed ?—And how did
you manage it ?—You dropp'd a curtain at the stair-foot.—
I thought you had no other way for it.—Here's a crown for
your trouble.

CHAPTER XIV.

—Then reach my breeches off the chair, said my father to
Susannah.——There is not a moment's time to dress you,
Sir, cried Susannah,—the child is as black in the face as my
—— As your what ? said my father ; for, like all orators, he
was a dear searcher into comparisons.——Bless me, Sir, said
Susannah, the child's in a fit.——And where's Mr. Yorick ?
——Never where he should be, said Susannah ; but his
curate's in the dressing-room, with the child upon his arm
waiting for the name ;—and my Mistress bid me run as fast
as I could to know, as Captain Shandy is the godfather,
whether it should not be called after him ?

Were one sure, said my father to himself, scratching his
eye-brow, that the child was expiring, one might as well
compliment my brother Toby as not,—and it would be a
pity, in such a case, to throw away so great a name as
Trismegistus upon him :—but he may recover.

No, no,—said my father to Susannah, I'll get up.——
There is no time, cried Susannah, the child's as black as
my shoe.——Trismegistus, said my father.—But stay,—
thou art a leaky vessel, Susannah, added my father ; canst
thou carry Trismegistus in thy head the length of the
gallery without scattering?——Can I ? cried Susannah,
shutting the door in a huff.——If she can, I'll be shot !
said my father, bouncing out of bed in the dark, and
groping for his breeches.

Susannah ran with all speed along the gallery.

My father made all possible speed to find his breeches.

Susannah got the start and kept it.—'Tis Tris—something, cried Susannah.——There is no christian name in the

world, said the curate, beginning with Tris—, but Tristram.
——Then 'tis Tristram-gistus, quoth Susannah.

——There is no gistus to it, noodle!—'tis my own name,
replied the curate, dipping his hand, as he spoke, into the
bason; Tristram! said he, &c., &c., &c., &c.:—so Tristram
was I called, and Tristram shall I be to the day of my
death.

My father followed Susannah, with his night-gown across
his arm with nothing more than his breeches on; fastened,
through haste, with but a single button; and that button,
through haste, thrust only half into the button-hole.

——She has not forgot the name? cried my father, half-
opening the door.——No, no, said the curate, with a tone
of intelligence.——And the child is better, cried Susannah.
——And how does your Mistress?—— As well, said
Susannah, as can be expected.——Pish! said my father,
the button of his breeches slipping out of the button-hole;
—so that whether the interjection was levelled at Susannah,
or the button-hole;—whether Pish was an interjection of
contempt, or an interjection of modesty, is a doubt; and
must be a doubt till I shall have time to write the three
following favourite chapters; that is, My chapter of
chamber maids, my chapter of pishes, and my chapter of
button-holes.

All the light I am able to give the reader at the present
is this, That the moment my father cried Pish! he whisk'd
himself about,—and with his breeches held up by one hand,
and his night-gown thrown across the arm of the other, he
returned along the gallery to bed, something slower than
he came.

CHAPTER XV.

I wish I could write a chapter on sleep.

A fitter occasion could never have presented itself than
what this moment offers, when all the curtains of the family
are drawn,—the candles put out,—and no creature's eyes

are open but a single one; for the other has been shut these twenty years, of my mother's nurse.

It is a fine subject.

And yet, as fine as it is, I would undertake to write a dozen chapters upon button-holes, both quicker and with more fame, than a single chapter upon this.

Button-holes! there is something lively in the very idea of 'em ;—and trust me, when I get amongst 'em—you gentry with great beards,—look as grave as you will,—I'll make merry work with my button-holes,—I shall have 'em all to myself,—'tis a maiden subject,—I shall run foul of no man's wisdom or fine sayings in it.

But for sleep,—I know I shall make nothing of it before I begin :—I am no dab at your fine sayings, in the first place ;—and in the next, I cannot for my soul set a grave face upon a bad matter,—and tell the world, 'tis the refuge of the unfortunate,—the enfranchisement of the prisoner,— the downy lap of the hopeless, the weary, and the broken-hearted; nor could I set out with a lie in my mouth, by affirming, that of all the soft and delicious functions of our nature, by which the great Author of it, in his bounty, has been pleased to recompense the sufferings wherewith his justice and his good pleasure has wearied us,—that this is the chiefest (I know pleasures worth ten of it) ;—or what a happiness it is to man, when the anxieties and passions of the day are over, and he lies down upon his back, that his soul shall be so seated within him, that whichever way she turns her eyes, the heavens shall look calm and sweet above her,—no desire,—or fear,—or doubt that troubles the air ; nor any difficulty past, present, or to come, that the imagination may not pass over without offence, in that sweet secession.

" God's blessing," said Sancho Pança, " be upon the man who first invented this self-same thing called Sleep !—it covers a man all over like a cloke."—Now there is more to me in this, and it speaks warmer to my heart and affections, than all the dissertations squeez'd out of the heads of the learned together upon the subject.

—Not that I altogether disapprove of what Montaigne advances upon it ;—'tis admirable in its way :—(I quote by memory.)

The world enjoys other pleasures, says he, as they do that of sleep, without tasting or feeling it as it slips and passes by. We should study and ruminate upon it, in order to render proper thanks to Him who grants it to us.——For this end, I cause myself to be disturbed in my sleep, that I may the better and more sensibly relish it :——and yet I see few, says he again, who live with less sleep, when need requires : my body is capable of a firm, but not of a violent and sudden agitation,—I evade of late all violent exercises, —I am never weary with walking ;—but from my youth, I never liked to ride upon pavements. I love to lie hard and alone, and even without my wife.——This last word may stagger the faith of the world ;—but remember, " La Vrais- emblance " (as Bayle says in the affair of Liceti) " n'est pas toujours du Coté de la Verité."——And so much for sleep.

CHAPTER XVI.

If my wife will but venture him,—brother Toby, Trisme- gistus shall be dress'd and brought down to us whilst you and I are getting our breakfasts together.

Go, tell Susannah, Obadiah, to step here.

She is run upstairs, answered Obadiah, this very instant, sobbing and crying and wringing her hands as if her heart would break.——

We shall have a rare month of it, said my father, turning his head from Obadiah, and looking wistfully in my uncle Toby's face for some time,—we shall have a devilish month of it, brother Toby, said my father, setting his arms a-kimbo, and shaking his head : fire, water, women, wind, brother Toby !——'Tis some misfortune, quoth my uncle Toby.—— That it is, cried my father,—to have so many jarring elements breaking loose, and riding triumph in every corner of a gentleman's house.—Little boots it to the peace of a family, brother Toby, that you and I possess ourselves, and sit here silent and unmov'd—whilst such a storm is whistling over our heads.—

And what's the matter, Susannah?——They have called the child Tristram;—and my mistress is just got out of a hysteric fit about it.——No!—'tis not my fault, said Susannah,—I told him it was Tristramgistus.

——Make tea for yourself, brother Toby, said my father, taking down his hat;—but how different from the sallies and agitations of voice and. members which a common reader would imagine!

·——For he spake in the sweetest modulation,—and took down his hat with the genteelest movement of limbs that ever affliction harmonised and attuned together.

——Go to the bowling-green for Corporal Trim, said my uncle Toby, speaking to Obadiah, as soon as my father left the room.

CHAPTER XVII.

WHEN the misfortune of my NOSE fell so heavily upon my father's head,—the reader remembers that he walked instantly upstairs, and cast himself down upon his bed; and from hence, unless he has a great insight into human nature, he will be apt to expect a rotation of the same ascending and descending movements from him upon this misfortune of my NAME.—No.

The different weight, dear Sir,—nay, even the different package of two vexations of the same weight,—makes a very wide difference in our manners of bearing and getting through with them.—It is not half an hour ago, when (in the great hurry and precipitation of a poor Devil's writing for daily bread) I threw a fair sheet, which I had just finished, and carefully wrote out, slap into the fire, instead of the foul one.

Instantly I snatched off my wig, and threw it perpendicularly, with all imaginable violence, up to the top of the room :—indeed I caught it as it fell;—but there was an end of the matter; nor do I think anything else in Nature would have given such immediate ease. She, dear goddess, by an instantaneous impulse, in all *provoking cases*, determines us to a sally of this or that member,—or else she thrusts us into this or that place, or posture of body, we know not why:—but mark, Madam, we live amongst riddles and mysteries :—the most obvious things which come in our way have dark sides, which the quickest sight cannot penetrate into; and even the clearest and most exalted understandings amongst us find ourselves puzzled and at a loss in almost every cranny of Nature's works: so that this, like a thousand other things, falls out for us in a way, which tho' we cannot reason upon it, yet we find the good of it, may it please your Reverences and your Worships,—and that's enough for us.

Now, my father could not lie down with this affliction for his life,—nor could he carry it upstairs like the other; —he walked composedly out with it to the fish-pond.

Had my father leaned his head upon his hand, and reasoned an hour which way to have gone,—Reason, with all her force, could not have directed him to anything like it: there is something, Sir, in fish-ponds;—but what it is, I leave to system-builders and fish-pond diggers betwixt 'em to find out;—but there is something, under the first disorderly transport of the humours, so unaccountably becalming in an orderly and sober walk towards one of them, that I have often wondered that neither Pythagoras, nor Plato, nor Solon, nor Lycurgus, nor Mahomet, nor any one of your noted law-givers, ever gave order about them.

———

CHAPTER XVIII.

YOUR Honour, said Trim, shutting the parlour-door before
he began to speak, has heard, I imagine, of this unlucky
accident.——Oh yes, Trim, said my uncle Toby, and it gives
me great concern.——I am heartily concerned too ; but I
hope your Honour, replied Trim, will do me the justice to
believe, that it was not in the least owing to me.——To
thee,—Trim?—cried my uncle Toby, looking kindly in his
face,—'twas Susannah's and the curate's folly, betwixt
them.——What business could they have together, an'
please your Honour, in the garden?——In the gallery thou
meanest, replied my uncle Toby.

Trim found he was upon a wrong scent, and stopped
short with a low bow.——Two misfortunes, quoth the Corporal to himself, are twice as many at least as are needful
to be talked over at one time ; the mischief the cow has done
in breaking into the fortifications may be told his Honour
hereafter.——Trim's casuistry and address, under the cover
of his low bow, prevented all suspicion in my uncle Toby ;
so he went on with what he had to say to Trim as follows :

——For my own part, Trim, though I can see little or
no difference betwixt my nephew's being called Tristram or
Trismegistus ;—yet as the thing sits so near my brother's
heart, Trim,—I would freely have given a hundred pounds
rather than it should have happened.——A hundred pounds,
an' please your Honour! replied Trim,—I would not give
a cherrystone to boot.——Nor would I, Trim, upon my
own account, quoth my uncle Toby ;—but my brother,
whom there is no arguing with in this case,—maintains that
a great deal more depends, Trim, upon christian-names than
what ignorant people imagine ;—for he says there never was
a great or heroic action performed since the world began,
by one called Tristram. Nay, he will have it, Trim, that
a man can neither be learned, nor wise, nor brave.——'Tis
all fancy, an' please your Honour :—I fought just as well,
replied the Corporal, when the regiment called me Trim, as

Tristram Shandy. Ch.18.

when they called me James Butler.——And for my own part, said my uncle Toby, tho' I should blush to boast of myself, Trim ;—yet, had my name been Alexander, I could have done no more at Namur than my duty.——Bless you Honour! cried Trim, advancing three steps as he spoke, does a man think of his christian-name when he goes upon the attack ?——Or when he stands in the trench, Trim? cried my uncle Toby, looking firm.——Or, when he enters a breach? said Trim, pushing in between two chairs.——Or forces the lines? cried my uncle, rising up, and pushing his crutch like a pike.——Or facing a platoon? cried Trim, presenting his stick like a firelock.——Or when he marches up the glacis? cried my uncle Toby, looking warm, and setting his foot upon his stool.——

CHAPTER XIX.

My father was returned from his walk to the fish-pond,—and opened the parlour-door in the very height of the attack, just as my uncle Toby was marching up the glacis.—Trim recovered his arms. Never was my uncle Toby caught riding at such a desperate rate in his life! Alas! my uncle Toby! had not a weightier matter called forth all the ready eloquence of my father,—how hadst thou then, and thy poor *hobby-horse* too, been insulted!

My father hung up his hat with the same air he took it down ; and, after giving a slight look at the disorder of the room, he took hold of one of the chairs which had formed the corporal's breach, and placing it over against my uncle Toby, he sat down in it ; and as soon as the tea-things were taken away, and the door shut, he broke out into a lamentation as follows :

MY FATHER'S LAMENTATION.

It is in vain longer, said my father, addressing himself as much to Ernulphus's curse, which was laid upon the corner of the chimney-piece,—as to my uncle Toby, who sat under it ;—it is in vain longer, said my father, in the most querulous monotony imaginable, to struggle as I have done against this most uncomfortable of human persuasions.—I see it plainly, that either for my own sins, brother Toby, or the sins and follies of the Shandy family, Heaven has thought fit to draw forth the heaviest of its artillery against me ; and that the prosperity of my child is the point upon which the whole force of it is directed to play.—Such a thing would batter the whole universe about our ears, brother Shandy, said my uncle Toby, if it was so.——Unhappy Tristram ! child of wrath ! child of decrepitude ! interruption ! mistake ! and discontent !   What one misfortune or disaster in the book of embryotic evils, that could unmechanise thy frame, or entangle thy filaments, which has not fallen upon thy head, ere ever thou camest into the world !—what evils in thy passage into it :—what evils since !—produced into being, in the decline of thy father's days, when the powers of his imagination and of his body were waxing feeble,— when radical heat and radical moisture, the elements which should have temper'd thine, were drying up ; and nothing left to found thy stamina in, but negations !—'Tis pitiful,— brother Toby, at the best, and called out for all the little helps that care and attention on both sides could give it. But how were we defeated !   You know the event, brother Toby !—'tis too melancholy a one to be repeated now,— when the few animal spirits I was worth in the world, and with which memory, fancy, and quick parts should have been conveyed,—were all dispersed, confused, confounded, and sent to the devil.

Here then was the time to have put a stop to this persecution against him,—and tried an experiment at least,— whether calmness and serenity of mind in your sister, with a due attention, brother Toby, to her evacuation and repletions,—and the rest of her non-naturals, might not, in the course of nine months' gestation, have set all things to rights. —My child was bereft of these !—What a teasing life did she lead herself, and, consequently, her foetus too, with that nonsensical anxiety of hers about lying-in in town:——I thought my sister submitted with the greatest patience, replied my uncle Toby ;—I never heard her utter one fretful word about it.——She fumed inwardly, cried my father, and that, let me tell you, brother, was ten times worse for the child,—and then, what battles did she fight with me! and what perpetual storms about the midwife!——There she gave vent, said my uncle Toby.——Vent! cried my father, looking up.

But what was all this, my dear Toby, to the injuries done us by my child's coming head foremost into the world, when all I wished, in this general wreck of his frame, was to have saved this little casket unbroke, unrifled!—

With all my precautions, how was my system turned topsy-turvy in the womb with my child! his head exposed to the hand of violence, and a pressure of 470 pounds avoir-dupois weight acting so perpendicularly upon its apex,—that, at this hour, 'tis ninety *per cent.* insurance, that the fine net-work of the intellectual web be not rent and torn into a thousand tatters.

——Still we could have done!—Fool, Coxcomb, Puppy, —give him but a *Nose;*—Cripple, Dwarf, Driveller, Goose-cap,—(shape him as you will) the door of fortune stands open,—O Licetus! Licetus! had I been blest with a fœtus five inches long and a half, like thee,—Fate might have done her worst.

Still, brother Toby, there was one cast of the die left for our child, after all:—O Tristram! Tristram! Tristram!

We will send for Mr. Yorick, said my uncle Toby.

——You may send for whom you will, replied my father.

CHAPTER XX.

WHAT a rate have I gone on at, curvetting and frisking it away, two up and two down, for three volumes,* together,

* According to the original editions.

without looking once behind, or even on one side of me, to
see whom I trod upon!—I'll tread upon no one,———quoth
I to myself, when I mounted;—I'll take a good rattling
gallop; but I'll not hurt the poorest jack-ass upon the road.
—So off I set,—up one lane,—down another,—through this
turnpike,—over that, as if the arch-jockey of jockeys had
got behind me.

Now, ride at this rate with what good intention and
resolution you may,—'tis a million to one you'll do some
one a mischief, if not yourself.—He's flung,—he's off,—he's
lost his seat,—he's down,—he'll break his neck!—see! if he
has not galloped full among the scaffolding of the undertaking critics!—he'll knock his brains out against some of
their posts!—he's bounced out!—look,—he's now riding like
a mad-cap full tilt through a whole crowd of painters,
fiddlers, poets, biographers, physicians, lawyers, logicians,
players, schoolmen, churchmen, statesmen, soldiers, casuists,
connoisseurs, prelates, popes, and engineers.—Don't fear,
said I,—I'll not hurt the poorest jack-ass upon the king's
highway.———But your horse throws dirt: see, you've splashed
a bishop!—I hope in God 'twas only Ernulphus! said I.—
But you have squirted full in the faces of Messrs. Le Moyne,
De Romigny, and De Marcilly, doctors of the Sorbonne.—
That was last year, replied I.—But you have trod this
moment upon a king.—King's have had times on't, said I,
to be trod upon by such people as me.

You have done it, replied my accuser.

I deny it, quoth I, and so have got off, and here am I
standing with my bridle in one hand, and with my cap in
the other, to tell my story.———And what is it?———You
shall hear in the next chapter.

———

CHAPTER XXI.

As Francis the First, of France, was one winterly night warming himself over the embers of a wood fire, and talking with his first minister of sundry things for the good of the state,*—It would not be amiss, said the king, stirring up the embers with his cane, if this good understanding betwixt ourselves and Switzerland was a little strengthened.——There is no end, Sire, replied the minister, in giving money to these people,—they would swallow up the treasury of France.——Poo! poo! answered the king,—there are more ways, Mons. le Premier, of bribing states, besides that of giving money;—I'll pay Switzerland the honour of standing god-father for my next child.——Your majesty, said the minister, in so doing, would have all the grammarians in Europe upon your back;—Switzerland, as a republic, being a female, can in no construction be godfather.——She may be godmother, replied Francis hastily;—so, announce my intentions by a courier to-morrow morning.

I am astonished, said Francis the First (that day fortnight), speaking to his minister as he entered the closet, that we have had no answer from Switzerland.——Sire, I wait upon you this moment, said Mons. le Premier, to lay before you my despatches upon that business.——They take it kindly, said the king.——They do, Sire, replied the minister, and have the highest sense of the honour your majesty has done them;—but the republic, as godmother, claims her right, in this case, of naming the child.

In all reason, quoth the king;—she will christen him Francis, or Henry, or Lewis, or some other name that she knows will be agreeable to us.——Your majesty is deceived, replied the minister.—I have this hour received a despatch from our Resident, with the determination of the republic on that point also.——And what name has the republic fixed upon for the Dauphin?——Shadrach, Meshech, Abednego, replied the minister.——By Saint Peter's girdle, I will

* Vide Menagiana, Vol. I.

have nothing to do with the Swiss! cried Francis the First, pulling up his breeches, and walking hastily across the floor.

Your majesty, replied the minister calmly, cannot bring yourself off.

We'll pay them in money,—said the king.

Sire, there are not sixty thousand crowns in the treasury, answered the minister. —— I'll pawn the best jewel in my crown, quoth Francis the First.

Your honour stands pawn'd already in this matter, answered Monsieur le Premier.

Then, Mons. le Premier, said the king, by——we'll go to war with 'em.

CHAPTER XXII.

ALBEIT, gentle reader, I have lusted earnestly and endeavoured carefully (according to the measure of such a slender skill as God has vouchsafed me, and as convenient leisure from other occasions of needful profit, and healthful pastime have permitted) that these little books, which I here put into thy hands, might stand instead of many bigger books,—yet have I carried myself towards thee in such fanciful guise of careless disport, that right sore am I ashamed now to intreat thy lenity seriously,—in beseeching thee to believe it of me, that, in the story of my father and his christian names,—I have no thoughts of treading upon Francis the First,—nor, in the affair of the nose,—upon Francis the Ninth,—nor, in the character of my uncle Toby,—of characterising the militiating spirits of my country;—the wound upon his groin is a wound to every comparison of that kind;—nor by Trim,—that I mean the Duke of Ormond,—or that my book is wrote against predestination, or free-will, or taxes;—if 'tis wrote against anything,—'tis wrote, an' please your Worships, against the spleen! in order, by a more frequent and a more convulsive elevation and depression of the diaphragm, and the succussations of the intercostal and abdominal muscles in laughter, to drive the *gall* and other *bitter juices* from the gall-bladder, liver, and sweet-bread of his majesty's subjects, with all the inimicitious passions which belong to them, down into their duodenums.

CHAPTER XXIII.

—But can the thing be undone, Yorick? said my father; —for in my opinion, continued he, it cannot. I am a vile canonist, replied Yorick;—but of all evils, holding suspense to be the most tormenting, we shall at least know the worst of this matter. I hate these great dinners, said my father. ——The size of the dinner is not the point, answered Yorick,—we want, Mr. Shandy, to dive into the bottom of this doubt, whether the name can be changed or not;— and as the beards of so many commissaries, officials, advocates, proctors, registrars, and of the most eminent of our school-divines, and others, are all to meet in the middle of one table, and Didius has so pressingly invited you,—who, in your distress, would miss such an occasion? All that is requisite, continued Yorick, is to apprise Didius, and let him manage a conversation after dinner so as to introduce the subject.—Then my brother Toby, cried my father, clapping his two hands together, shall go with us.

—— Let my old tie-wig, quoth my uncle Toby, and my laced regimentals, be hung to the fire all night, Trim.

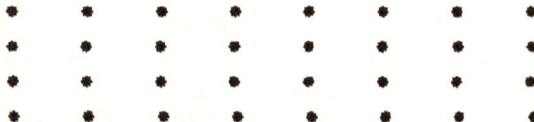

CHAPTER XXV.

——No doubt, Sir,—There is a whole chapter wanting
here,—and a chasm of ten pages made in the book by it;—
but the bookbinder is neither a fool, nor a knave, nor a
puppy,—nor is the book a jot more imperfect (at least upon
that score);—but, on the contrary, the book is more perfect
and complete by wanting the chapter, than having it, as I
shall demonstrate to your Reverences in this manner.—I
question first, by the bye, whether the same experiment
might not be made as successfully upon sundry other
chapters;—but there is no end, an' please your Reverences,
in trying experiments upon chapters,—we have had enough
of it;—so there's an end of that matter.

But before I begin my demonstration, let me only tell
you, that the chapter which I have torn out, and which
otherwise you would all have been reading just now, instead
of this,—was the description of my father's, my uncle
Toby's, Trim's, and Obadiah's setting out and journeying
to the Visitation at * * * *.

We'll go in the coach, said my father.—Prithee, have the
arms been altered, Obadiah?—It would have made my
story much better to have begun with telling you, that at
the time my mother's arms were added to the Shandy's,
when the coach was repainted upon my father's marriage,
it had so fallen out, that the coach-painter, whether by performing all his works with the left-hand, like Turpilius the
Roman, or Hans Holbein of Basil,—or whether it was more
from the blunder of his head than hand,—or whether, lastly,
it was from the sinister turn which everything relating to
our family was apt to take,—it so fell out, however, to our
reproach, that instead of the *bend-dexter*, which, since
Henry the Eighth's reign, was honestly our due,—a *bend-
sinister*, by some of these fatalities, had been drawn quite
across the field of the Shandy arms. 'Tis scarce credible
that the mind of so wise a man as my father was, could be

so much incommoded with so small a matter. The word
Coach,—let it be whose it would,—or coach-man, or coach-
horse, or coach-hire, could never be named in the family,
but he constantly complained of carrying this vile mark of
illegitimacy upon the door of his own : he never once was
able to step into the coach, or out of it, without turning
round to take a view of the arms, and making a vow at the
same time, that it was the last time he would ever set his
foot in it again, till the *bend-sinister* was taken out ;—but,
like the affair of the hinge, it was one of the many things
which the Destinies had set down in their books ever to be
grumbled at (and in wiser families than ours)—but never to
be mended.

—Has the *bend-sinister* been brush'd out, I say? said
my father.——There has been nothing brush'd out, Sir,
answered Obadiah, but the lining.——We'll go o'horseback,
said my father, turning to Yorick.——Of all things in the
world, except politics, the clergy know the least of heraldry,
said Yorick.——No matter for that, cried my father; I
should be sorry to appear with a blot in my escutcheon
before them.——Never mind the *bend-sinister*, said my
uncle Toby, putting on his tie-wig.——No, indeed, said
my father: you may go with my aunt Dinah to a Visitation with a *bend-sinister*, if you think fit.——My poor
uncle Toby blush'd. My father was vexed at himself.——
No,—my dear brother Toby, said my father, changing his
tone; but the damp of the coach-lining about my loins
may give me the sciatica again, as it did December,
January, and February, last winter; so, if you please, you
shall ride my wife's pad:—and, as you are to preach,
Yorick, you had better make the best of your way before,
and leave me to take care of my brother Toby, and to
follow at our own rates.

Now, the chapter I was obliged to tear out, was a
description of this cavalcade, in which Corporal Trim and
Obadiah, upon two coach-horses abreast, led the way as
slow as a patrol,—whilst my uncle Toby, in his lace regimentals and tie-wig, kept his rank with my father, in deep

roads and dissertations alternately, upon the advantage of learning and arms, as each could get the start.

——But the painting of this journey, upon reviewing it, appears to be so much above the style and manner of anything else I could have been able to paint in this book, that it could not have remained in it, without depreciating every other scene, and destroying, at the same time, that necessary equipoise and balance (whether of good or bad) betwixt chapter and chapter, from whence the just proportions and harmony of the whole work results. For my own part, I am but just set up in the business, so knew little about it;—but, in my opinion, to write a book, is for all the world like humming a song;—be but in tune with yourself, Madam, 'tis no matter how high or low you take it.

—This is the reason, may it please your Reverences, that some of the lowest and flattest compositions pass off very well—(as Yorick told my uncle Toby one night) by siege.

——My uncle Toby looked brisk at the sound of the word *siege;* but could make neither head nor tail of it.

I'm to preach at court next Sunday, said Homenas;—run over my notes:——so I humm'd over Doctor Homenas's notes;—the modulation's very well;—'twill do, Homenas, if it holds on at this rate ;—so on I humm'd,—and a tolerable tune I thought it was ; and to this hour, may it please your Reverences, had never found out how low, how flat, how spiritless and jejune it was, but that, all of a sudden, up started an air in the middle of it, so fine, so rich, so heavenly,—it carried my soul up with it into the other world: now had I (as Montaigne complained in a parallel accident)—had I found the declivity easy, or the ascent accessible,—certes I had been outwitted.—Your notes, Homenas, I should have said, are good notes;—but it was so perpendicular a precipice,—so wholly cut off from the rest of the work, that, by the first note I humm'd, I found myself flying into the other world, and from thence discovered the vale from whence I came, so deep, so low, and dismal, that I shall never have the heart to descend into it again.

☞ A dwarf who brings a standard along with him to measure his own size,—take my word, is a dwarf in more articles than one.—And so much for tearing out of chapters.

CHAPTER XXVI.

—SEE, if he is not cutting it all into slips, and giving them about him to light their pipes!——'Tis abominable! answered Didius.——It should not go unnoticed, said Doctor. Kysarcius:——☞ he was of the Kysarcii of the Low Countries.

Methinks, said Didius, half rising from his chair, in order to remove a bottle and a tall decanter, which stood in a direct line betwixt him and Yorick,—you might have spared this sarcastic stroke, and have hit upon a more proper place, Mr. Yorick;—or at least upon a more proper occasion to have shewn your contempt of what we have been about. If the sermon is of no better worth than to light pipes with,— 'twas certainly, Sir, not good enough to be preached before so learned a body; and if 'twas good enough to be preached before so learned a body,—'twas certainly, Sir, too good to light their pipes with afterwards.

——I have got him fast hung up, quoth Didius to himself, upon one of the two horns of my dilemma;—let him get off as he can.

I have undergone such unspeakable torments, in bringing forth this sermon, quoth Yorick, upon this occasion,—that I declare, Didius, I would suffer martyrdom,—and, if it was possible, my horse with me, a thousand times over, before I would sit down and make such another: I was delivered of it at the wrong end of me;—it came from my head instead of my heart;—and it is for the pain it gave me, both in the writing and preaching of it, that I revenge myself of it in this manner.—To preach, to shew the extent of our reading, or the subtleties of our wit,—to parade it in the eyes of the vulgar with the beggarly accounts of a little learning, tin-

sell'd over with a few words which glitter, but convey little
light and less warmth—is a dishonest use of the poor single
half hour in a week which is put into our hands:—'tis not
preaching the Gospel,—but ourselves.—For my own part,
continued Yorick, I had rather direct five words point-
blank to the heart.

As Yorick pronounced the word *point-blank*, my uncle
Toby rose up to say something upon projectiles,—when a
single word, and no more, uttered from the opposite side of
the table, drew every one's ears towards it;—a word of all
others in the dictionary the last in that place to be expected;
—a word I am ashamed to write,—yet must be written,—
must be read;—illegal,—uncanonical,—guess ten thousand
guesses, multiplied into themselves,—rack—torture your
invention for ever, you're where you was.—In short, I'll
tell it in the next chapter.

CHAPTER XXVII.

Zounds! ——————————————————————————————

———————————————————————————Z——ds! cried Phutatorius,
partly to himself,—and yet high enough to be heard;—and
what seemed odd, 'twas uttered in a construction of look,
and in a tone of voice, somewhat between that of a man in
amazement, and one in bodily pain.

One or two who had very nice ears, and could distinguish
the expression and mixture of the two tones as plainly as a
third or a *fifth*, or any other chord in music,—were the
most puzzled and perplexed with it.—The concord was good
itself;—but then 'twas quite out of the key, and no way
applicable to the subject started;—so that, with all their
knowledge, they could not tell what in the world to make
of it.

Others, who knew nothing of musical expression, and
merely lent their ears to the plain import of the word,
imagined that Phutatorius, who was somewhat of a choleric

spirit, was just going to snatch the cudgels out of Didius's hands, in order to bemaul Yorick to some purpose;—and that the desperate monosyllable, Z——ds, was the exordium to an oration, which, as they judged from the sample, presaged but a rough kind of handling of him; so that my uncle Toby's good-nature felt a pang for what Yorick was about to undergo. But seeing Phutatorius stop short, without any attempt or desire to go on,—a third party began to suppose that it was no more than an involuntary respiration, casually forming itself into the shape of a twelvepenny oath,—without the sin or substance of one.

Others, and especially one or two who sat next him, looked upon it, on the contrary, as a real and substantial oath, propensely formed against Yorick, to whom he was known to bear no good liking;—which said oath, as my father philosophised upon it, actually lay fretting and fuming at that very time in the upper regions of Phutatorius's purtenance; and so was naturally, and according to the due course of things, first squeezed out by the sudden influx of blood which was driven into the right ventricle of Phutatorius's heart, by the stroke of surprise which so strange a theory of preaching had excited.

How finely we argue upon mistaken facts!

There was not a soul busied in all these various reasonings upon the monosyllable which Phutatorius uttered,—who did not take this for granted, proceeding upon it as from an axiom, namely, that Phutatorius's mind was intent upon the subject of debate which was arising between Didius and Yorick; and indeed, as he looked first towards the one and then towards the other, with the air of a man listening to what was going forwards,—who would not have thought the same? But the truth was, that Phutatorius knew not one word or one syllable of what was passing;—but his whole thoughts and attention were taken up with a transaction which was going forwards at that very instant within the precincts of his own Galligaskins, and in a part of them where of all others he stood most interested to watch accidents: so that, notwithstanding he looked with all the attention in the world, and had gradually screwed up every nerve and muscle in his face to the utmost pitch the instrument would bear, in order, as it was thought, to give a sharp reply to Yorick, who sat over-against him,—yet, I say, was Yorick never once in any one domicile of Phutatorius's brain; but the true cause of his exclamation lay at least a yard below.

This I will endeavour to explain to you with all imaginable decency.

You must be informed then, that Gastripheres, who had taken a turn into the kitchen a little before dinner, to see how things went on,—observing a wicker-basket of fine chestnuts standing upon the dresser, had ordered that a hundred or two of them might be roasted and sent in as soon as dinner was over;—Gastripheres enforcing his orders about them, that Didius, but Phutatorius especially, were particularly fond of 'em.

About two minutes before the time that my uncle Toby interrupted Yorick's harangue,—Gastripheres's chestnuts were brought in;—and as Phutatorius's fondness for 'em was uppermost in the waiter's head, he laid them directly before Phutatorius, wrapt up hot in a clean damask napkin.

Now, whether it was physically impossible, with half a dozen hands all thrust into the napkin at one time,—but that some one chestnut, of more life and rotundity than the rest, must be put in motion,—it so fell out, however, that one was actually sent rolling off the table: and as Phutatorius sat straddling under,—it fell perpendicularly into that particular aperture of Phutatorius's breeches, for which, to the shame and indelicacy of our language be it spoke, there is no chaste word throughout all Johnson's Dictionary: —let it suffice to say,—it was that particular aperture which, in all good societies, the laws of decorum do strictly require, like the temple of Janus (in peace at least), to be universally shut up.

The neglect of this punctilio in Phutatorius (which by the bye should be a warning to all mankind) had opened a door to this accident.—

Accident I call it, in compliance to a received mode of speaking;—but in no opposition to the opinion either of Acrites or Mythogeras in this matter; I know they were both prepossessed and fully persuaded of it,—and are so to this hour, That there was nothing of accident in the whole event,—but that the chestnut's taking that particular course, and in a manner of its own accord,—and then falling with all its heat directly into that one particular place, and no other,—was a real judgment upon Phutatorius for that filthy and obscene treatise *de Concubinis retinendis*, which Phutatorius had published about twenty years ago,—and was that identical week going to give the world a second edition of.

It is not my business to dip my pen in this controversy : —much, undoubtedly, may be wrote on both sides of the question :—all that concerns me as an historian, is to represent the matter of fact, and render it credible to the reader, that the hiatus in Phutatorius's breeches was sufficiently wide to receive the chestnut :—and that the chestnut, somehow or other, did fall perpendicularly, and piping hot, into it, without Phutatorius's perceiving it, or any one else at that time.

The genial warmth which the chestnut imparted, was not undelectable for the first twenty or five-and-twenty seconds; —and did no more than gently solicit Phutatorius's attention towards the part :—but the heat gradually increasing, and in a few seconds more getting beyond the point of all sober pleasure, and then advancing with all speed into the regions of pain, the soul of Phutatorius, together with all his ideas, his thoughts, his attention, his imagination, judgment, resolution, deliberation, and ratiocination, memory, fancy, with ten battalions of animal spirits, all tumultuously crowded down, through different defiles and circuits, to the place in danger, leaving all his upper regions, as you may imagine, as empty as my purse.

With the best intelligence which all these messengers could bring him back, Phutatorius was not able to dive into the secret of what was going forward below; nor could he make any kind of conjecture what the devil was the matter with it. However, as he knew not what the true cause might turn out, he deemed it most prudent, in the situation he was in at present,—to bear it, if possible, like a Stoic; which, with the help of some wry faces and compursions of the mouth, he had certainly accomplished, had his imagination continued neuter:—but the sallies of the imagination are ungovernable in all things of this kind;—a thought instantly darted into his mind, that tho' the anguish had the sensation of glowing heat,—it might, notwithstanding that, be a bite as well as a burn; and if so, that possibly a Newt or an Asker, or some such detested reptile, had crept up, and was fastening his teeth;—the horrid idea of which, with a fresh glow of pain arising that instant from the chestnut, seized Phutatorius with a sudden panic,—and in the first terrifying disorder of the passion, it threw him, as it has done the best generals upon earth, quite off his guard:—the effect of which was this, that he leap'd incontinently up, uttering as he rose that interjection of surprise so much descanted upon, with the aposiopestic break after it marked thus, Z——ds! —which, though not strictly canonical, was still as little as any man could have said upon the occasion;—and which, by the bye, whether canonical or not, Phutatorius could no more help than he could the cause of it.

Though this has taken up some time in the narrative, it took up little more time in the transaction than just to allow time for Phutatorius to draw forth the chestnut, and throw it down with violence upon the floor,—and for Yorick to rise from his chair, and pick the chestnut up.

It is curious to observe the triumph of slight incidents over the mind.—What incredible weight they have in forming and governing our opinions, both of men and things!— that trifles, light as air, shall waft a belief into the soul, and plant it so immovably within it,—that Euclid's demonstrations, could they be brought to batter it in breach, should not all have power to overthrow it!

Yorick, I said, picked up the chestnut which Phutatorius's wrath had flung down:—the action was trifling;—I am ashamed to account for it:—he did it,—for no reason, but that he thought the chestnut not a jot worse for the adven-

ture;—and that he held a good chestnut worth stooping for.
—But this incident, trifling as it was, wrought differently
in Phutatorius's head: he considered this act of Yorick's, in
getting off his chair and picking up the chestnut, as a plain
acknowledgment in him, that the chestnut was originally
his;—and, in course, that it must have been the owner of
the chestnut, and no one else, who could have played him
such a prank with it. What greatly confirmed him in this
opinion, was this, That the table being parallelogramical,
and very narrow, it afforded a fair opportunity for Yorick,
who sat directly over against Phutatorius, of slipping the
chestnut in;—and consequently that he did it. The look
of something more than suspicion, which Phutatorius cast
full upon Yorick as these thoughts arose, too evidently spoke
his opinion;—and as Phutatorius was naturally supposed to
know more of the matter than any person besides, his
opinion at once became the general one; and for a reason
very different from any which have been yet given, in a little
time it was put out of all manner of dispute.

When great or unexpected events fall out upon the stage
of this sublunary world,—the mind of man, which is an
inquisitive kind of a substance, naturally takes a flight behind
the scenes, to see what is the cause and first spring of them.
—The search was not long in this instance.

It was well known that Yorick had never a good opinion
of the Treatise which Phutatorius had wrote *de Concubinis
retinendis*, as a thing which he feared had done hurt in the
world:—and 'twas easily found out, that there was a
mystical meaning in Yorick's prank,—and that his chuck-
ing the chestnut hot into Phutatorius's ***—*****, was a
sarcastical fling at his book;—the doctrines of which, they
said, had enflamed many an honest man in the same place.

This conceit awakened Somnolentius; made Agelastes
smile;—and, if you can recollect the precise look and air
of a man's face intent in finding out a riddle,—it threw
Gastripheres's into that form;—and, in short, was thought
by many to be a masterstroke of arch wit.

This, as the reader has seen from one end to the other,

was as groundless as the dreams of philosophy. Yorick, no doubt, as Shakspeare said of his ancestor,—"was a man of jest," but it was temper'd with something which withheld him from that, and many other ungracious pranks, of which he as undeservedly bore the blame ;—but it was his misfortune, all his life long, to bear the imputation of saying and doing a thousand things, of which (unless my esteem blinds me) his nature was incapable. All I blame him for,—or rather, all I blame and alternately like him for, was that singularity of his temper, which would never suffer him to take pains to set a story right with the world, however in his power. In every ill-usage of that sort, he acted precisely as in the affair of his lean horse.—He could have explained it to his honour, but his spirit was above it ; and besides, he ever looked upon the inventor, the propagator, and believer of an illiberal report, alike so injurious to him,—he could not stoop to tell his story to them ;—and so trusted to time and truth to do it for him.

This heroic cast produced him inconveniences in many respects ;—in the present, it was followed by the fixed resentment of Phutatorius, who, as Yorick had just made an end of his chestnut, rose up from his chair a second time, to let him know it ;—which indeed he did with a smile ; saying only —That he would endeavour not to forget the obligation.

But you must mark and carefully separate and distinguish these two things in your mind :—

—The smile was for the company ;

—The threat was for Yorick.

CHAPTER XXVIII.

—Can you tell me, quoth Phutatorius, speaking to Gastripheres, who sat next to him,—for one would not apply to a surgeon in so foolish an affair,—Can you tell me, Gastripheres, what is best to take out the fire ?——Ask Eugenius, said Gastripheres.——That greatly depends, said Eugenius,

pretending ignorance of the adventure, upon the nature of
the part.—If it is a tender part, and a part which can con-
veniently be wrapt up,——It is both the one and the other,
replied Phutatorius, laying his hand as he spoke, with an
emphatical nod of his head, upon the part in question, and
lifting up his right leg at the same time, to ease and venti-
late it.——If that is the case, said Eugenius, I would advise
you, Phutatorius, not to tamper with it by any means; but
if you will send to the next printer, and trust your cure to
such a simple thing as a soft sheet of paper just come off the
press,—you need do nothing more than twist it round.——
The damp paper, quoth Yorick (who sat next to his friend
Eugenius), though I know it has a refreshing coolness in it,
—yet, I presume, is no more than the vehicle;—and that
the oil and lamp-black, with which the paper is so strongly
impregnated, does the business.——Right, said Eugenius;
and is, of any outward application I would venture to
recommend, the most anodyne and safe.

Was it my case, said Gastripheres, as the main thing is
the oil and lamp-black, I should spread them thick upon a
rag, and clap it on directly.——That would make a very
devil of it, replied Yorick.——And besides, added Eugenius,
it would not answer the intention, which is the extreme
neatness and elegance of the prescription; which the faculty
hold to be half in half:—for consider, if the type is a very
small one (which it should be), the sanative particles, which
come into contact in this form, have the advantage of being
spread so infinitely thin, and with such a mathematical
equality (fresh paragraphs and large capitals excepted), as
no art or management of the spatula can come up to.——
It falls out very luckily, replied Phutatorius, that the second
edition of my Treatise, *De Concubinis retinendis*, is at this
instant in the press.——You may take any leaf out of it,
said Eugenius;—no matter which.——Provided, quoth
Yorick, there is no bawdry in it.——

They are just now, replied Phutatorius, printing off the
ninth chapter;—which is the last chapter but one in the
book.——Pray, what is the title of that chapter? said

Yorick; making a respectful bow to Phutatorius as he spoke.——I think, answered Phutatorius, 'tis that *de Re Concubinariâ*.

For Heaven's sake, keep out of that chapter! quoth Yorick.

——By all means—added Eugenius.

———

CHAPTER XXIX.

—Now, quoth Didius, rising up, and laying his right hand, with his fingers spread, upon his breast,—had such a blunder about a Christian-name happened before the Refor-mation,——[It happened the day before yesterday, quoth my uncle Toby to himself]—and when baptism was administer'd in Latin,—['Twas all in English, said my uncle]—many things might have coincided with it; and upon the authority of sundry decreed cases, to have pro-nounced the baptism null, with a power of giving the child a new name.—Had a priest, for instance, which was no uncommon thing, through ignorance of the Latin tongue, baptised a child of Tom-o'Stiles, *id nomine patriæ & filea & spiritum sanctos*,—the baptism was held null.——I beg your pardon, replied Kysarcius;—in that case, as the mis-take was only the terminations, the baptism was valid ;— and to have rendered it null, the blunder of the priest should have fallen upon the first syllable of each noun ;— and not, as in your case, upon the last.

My father delighted in subtleties of this kind, and listen'd with infinite attention.

Gastripheres, for example, continued Kysarcius, baptizes a child of John Stradling's *in gomine Gatris, &c. &c.*, instead of *in nomine Patris, &c.*——Is this a baptism ?— No,—say the ablest canonists; inasmuch as the radix of each word is hereby torn up, and the sense and meaning of them removed and changed quite to another object; for *gomine* does not signify a name, nor *Gatris* a father.

——What do they signify? said my uncle Toby.—— Nothing at all,—quoth Yorick.——Ergo, such a baptism is null, said Kysarcius.——

In course! answered Yorick,——in a tone two parts jest and one part earnest.

But in the case cited, continued Kysarcius, where *patriæ* is put for *patris, filia* for *filii*, and so on;—as it is a fault only in the declension, and the roots of the word continue untouch'd, the inflections of their branches, either this way or that, does not in any sort hinder the baptism, inasmuch as the same sense continues in the words as before.——But then, said Didius, the intention of the priest's pronouncing them grammatically must have been proved to have gone along with it.——Right, answered Kysarcius; and of this, brother Didius, we have an instance in a decree of the decretals of Pope Leo the Third.——But my brother's child, cried my uncle Toby, has nothing to do with the Pope;—'tis the plain child of a Protestant gentleman christen'd Tristram against the wills and wishes both of his father and mother, and all who are akin to it.——

If the wills and wishes, said Kysarcius, interrupting my uncle Toby, of those only who stand related to Mr. Shandy's child, were to have weight in this matter, Mrs. Shandy, of all people, has the least to do in it.——My uncle Toby laid down his pipe, and my father drew his chair still closer to the table, to hear the conclusion of so strange an introduction.

——It has not only been a question, Captain Shandy, amongst the best lawyers * and civilians in this land, con- tinued Kysarcius, "Whether the mother be of kin to her child;"—but, after much dispassionate inquiry and jactita- tion of the arguments on all sides,—it has been adjudged for the negative;—namely, "That the mother is not of kin to her child." † My father instantly clapp'd his hand upon my uncle Toby's mouth, under colour of whispering in his ear;—the truth was, he was alarmed for *Lillibullero*,—and

* *Vide* Swinburne on Testaments, Part 7, § 8.
† *Vide* Brooke's Abridg. Tit. Administr. N. 47.

having a great desire to hear more of so curious an argument,—he begg'd my uncle Toby, for Heaven's sake, not to disappoint him in it.——My uncle Toby gave a nod,—resumed his pipe, and contenting himself with whistling *Lillibullero* inwardly,—Kysarcius, Didius, and Triptolemus went on with the discourse as follows :—

This determination, continued Kysarcius, how contrary soever it may seem to run to the stream of vulgar ideas, yet had reason strongly on its side, and has been put out of all manner of dispute from the famous case, known commonly by the name of the Duke of Suffolk's Case.——It is cited in Brooke, said Triptolemus.——And taken notice of by Lord Coke, added Didius.——And you may find it in Swinburne on Testaments, said Kysarcius.

The case, Mr. Shandy, was this :—

In the reign of Edward the Sixth, Charles Duke of Suffolk having issue a son by one venter, and a daughter by another venter, made his last will, wherein he devised goods to his son, and died; after whose death the son died also ;—but without will, without wife, and without child,—his mother and his sister by the father's side (for she was born of the former venter) then living. The mother took the administration of her son's goods, according to the statute of the 21st of Harry the Eighth; whereby it is enacted, That in case any person die intestate, the administration of his goods shall be committed to the next of kin.

The administration being thus (surreptitiously) granted to the mother,—the sister, by the father's side, commenced a suit before the Ecclesiastical Judge, alleging, 1st, That she herself was next of kin ; and, 2ndly, That the mother was not of kin at all to the party deceased ; and therefore prayed the Court, that the administration granted to the mother might be revoked, and be committed unto her, as next of kin to the deceased, by force of the said statute.

Hereupon, as it was a great cause, and much depending upon its issue,—and many causes of great property likely to be decided, in times to come, by the precedent to be then made,—the most learned, as well in the laws of this realm as in the civil law, were consulted together, Whether the mother was of kin to her son, or no?—Whereunto not only the temporal lawyers,—but the Church lawyers,—the juris-consulti,—the juris-prudentes,—the civilians,—the advo-cates,—the commissaries,—the judges of the consistory and prerogative courts of Canterbury and York, with the master of the faculties, were all unanimously of opinion, That the mother was not of kin * to her child.——

And what said the Duchess of Suffolk to it? said my uncle Toby.

The unexpectedness of my uncle Toby's question con-founded Kysarcius more than the ablest advocate.—He stopp'd a full minute, looking in my uncle Toby's face without replying;—and in that single minute Triptolemus put by him, and took the lead as follows :—

'Tis a ground and principle in the law, said Triptolemus, that things do not ascend, but descend in it; and I make no doubt 'tis for this cause, that however true it is that the child may be of the blood and seed of its parents,—that the parents, nevertheless, are not of the blood and seed of it; inasmuch as the parents are not begot by the child, but the child by the parents;—for so they write, *Lilera sunt de sanguine patris & matris, sed pater & mater non sunt de sanguine liberorum.*

——But this, Triptolemus, cried Didius, proves too much; —for, from this authority cited, it would follow, not only what indeed is granted on all sides, that the mother is not of kin to her child,—but the father likewise.——It is held, said Triptolemus, the better opinion; because the father, the mother, and the child, though they be three persons, yet are they but (*una caro* †) one flesh; and consequently no degree of kindred,—or any method of acquiring one *in nature.*——There you push the argument again too far, cried Didius,—for there is no prohibition *in nature*, though there is in the Levitical law,—but that a man may beget a child

* Mater non numeratur inter consanguineos, Bald. in ult. C. de Verb. signific.

† *Vide* Brooke's Abridg. Tit. Administr. N. 47.

upon his grandmother ;—in which case, supposing the issue a daughter, she would stand in relation both of——But who ever thought, cried Kysarcius, of lying with his grandmother? ——The young gentleman, replied Yorick, whom Selden speaks of,—who not only thought of it, but justified his intention to his father by the argument drawn from the law of retaliation :—"You lay, Sir, with my mother," said the lad ; "why may I not lie with yours?"——'Tis the *argumentum commune*, added Yorick.——'Tis as good, replied Eugenius, taking down his hat, as they deserve.

The company broke up.

CHAPTER XXX.

——AND pray, said my uncle Toby, leaning upon Yorick, as he and my father were helping him leisurely down the stairs,—don't be terrified, Madam; this staircase conversation is not so long as the last.——And pray, Yorick, said my uncle Toby, which way is this said affair of Tristram at length settled by these learned men?——Very satisfactorily, replied Yorick: no mortal, Sir, has any concern with it ;— for Mrs. Shandy, the mother, is nothing at all akin to him ; —and as the mother's is the surest side,—Mr. Shandy, in course, is still less than nothing.—In short, he is not as much akin to him, Sir, as I am.——

——That may well be, said my father, shaking his head.

——Let the learned say what they will, there must certainly, quoth my uncle Toby, have been some sort of consanguinity betwixt the Duchess of Suffolk and her son.

The vulgar are of the same opinion, quoth Yorick, to this hour.

CHAPTER XXXI.

Though my father was hugely tickled with the subtleties of these learned discourses, 'twas still but like the anointing of a broken bone.—The moment he got home, the weight of his afflictions returned upon him but so much the heavier, as is ever the case when the staff we lean on slips from under us.—He became pensive,—walked frequently forth to the fish-pond,—let down one loop of his hat,—sigh'd often,—forbore to snap;—and, as the hasty sparks of temper, which occasion snapping, so much assist perspiration and digestion, as Hippocrates tells us,—he had certainly fallen ill with the extinction of them, had not his thoughts been critically drawn off, and his health rescued by a fresh train of disquietudes left him, with a legacy of a thousand pounds, by my aunt Dinah.

My father had scarce read the letter, when, taking the thing by the right end, he instantly began to plague and puzzle his head how to lay it out mostly to the honour of his family.—A hundred and fifty odd projects took possession of his brains by turns;—he would do this, and that, and t'other.—He would go to Rome;—he would go to law;—he would buy stock;—he would buy John Hobson's farm;—he would new fore-front his house, and add a new wing to make it even.—There was a fine water-mill on this side; and he would build a windmill on the other side of the river, in full view, to answer it.——But, above all things in the world, he would enclose the great Oxmoor, and send out my brother Bobby immediately upon his travels.

But as the sum was *finite*, and consequently could not do everything;—and, in truth, very few of these 'to any purpose,—of all the projects which offered themselves upon this occasion, the two last seemed to make the deepest impression; and he would infallibly have determined upon both at once, but for the small inconvenience hinted at above, which absolutely put him under a necessity of deciding in favour either of the one or the other.

This was not altogether so easy to be done: for though 'tis certain my father had long before set his heart upon this necessary part of my brother's education, and, like a prudent man, had actually determined to carry it into execution, with the first money that returned from the second creation of actions in the Mississippi-scheme, in which he was an adventurer; yet the Ox-moor, which was a fine, large, whinny, undrained, unimproved common, belonging to the Shandy estate, had almost as old a claim upon him; he had long and affectionately set his heart upon turning it likewise to some account.

But having never hitherto been pressed with such a conjecture of things as made it necessary to settle either the priority or justice of their claims,—like a wise man he had refrained entering into any nice or critical examination about them: so that upon the dismission of every other project at this crisis,—the two old projects, the Ox-moor and my brother, divided him again; and so equal a match were they for each other, as to become the occasion of no small contest in the old gentleman's mind,—which of the two should be set a-going first.

——People may laugh as they will;—but the case was this:—

It had never been the custom of the family, and by length of time had almost become a matter of common right, that the eldest son of it should have free ingress, egress, and regress into foreign parts before marriage,—not only for the sake of bettering his own private parts, by the benefit of exercise and change of so much air,—but simply for the mere delectation of his fancy, by the feather put into his cap of having been abroad.—*Tantum valet*, my father would say, *quantum sonat*.

Now as this was a reasonable, and in course a most Christian indulgence,—to deprive him of it, without why or wherefore,—and thereby make an example of him, as the first Shandy unwhirl'd about Europe in a post-chaise, and only because he was a heavy lad,—would be using him ten times worse than a Turk.

On the other hand, the case of the Ox-moor was full as hard.

Exclusive of the original purchase-money, which was eight hundred pounds,—it had cost the family eight hundred pounds more in a lawsuit about fifteen years before,—besides, the Lord knows what trouble and vexation.

It had been moreover in possession of the Shandy family ever since the middle of the last century; and though it lay full in view before the house, bounded on one extremity by the water-mill; and on the other by the projected windmill spoken of above;—and for all these reasons seemed to have the fairest title of any part of the estate to the care and protection of the family,—yet, by an unaccountable fatality common to men, as well as the ground they tread on,—it had all along most shamefully been overlook'd; and to speak the truth of it, had suffered so much by it, that it would have made any man's heart have bled (Obadiah said) who understood the value of land, to have rode over it, and only seen the condition it was in.

However, as neither the purchasing this track of ground, —nor indeed the placing of it where it lay, were either of them, properly speaking, of my father's doing,—he had never thought himself any way concerned in the affair—till the fifteen years before, when the breaking out of that cursed lawsuit mentioned above (and which had arose about its boundaries)—which being altogether my father's own act and deed, it naturally awakened every other argument in its favour; and upon summing them all up together, he saw, not merely in interest, but in honour, he was bound to do something for it;—and that now or never was the time.

I think there must certainly have been a mixture of ill-luck in it, that the reasons on both sides should happen to be so equally balanced by each other; for though my father weigh'd them in all humours and conditions, spent many an anxious hour in the most profound and abstracted meditation

upon what was best to be done;—reading books of farming
one day,—books of travels another,—laying aside all passion
whatever,—viewing the arguments on both sides in all their
lights and circumstances,—communing every day with my
uncle Toby,—arguing with Yorick, and talking over the
whole affair of the Ox-moor with Obadiah,—yet nothing in
all that time appeared so strongly in behalf of the one, which
was not either strictly applicable to the other, or at least so
far counterbalanced by some consideration of equal weight,
as to keep the scales even.

For to be sure, with proper helps, and in the hands of
some people, though the Ox-moor would undoubtedly have
made a different appearance in the world from what it did,
or ever could do in the condition it lay,—yet every tittle of
this was true with regard to my brother Bobby,—let Obadiah
say what he would.——

In point of interest,—the contest, I own, at first sight, did
not appear so undecisive betwixt them; for whenever my
father took pen and ink in hand, and set about calculating
the simple expense of paring and burning, and fencing in
the Ox-moor, &c. &c.—with the certain profit it would
bring him in return,—the latter turned out so prodigiously
in his way of working the account, that you would have
sworn the Ox-moor would have carried all before it; for it
was plain he should reap a hundred lasts of rape, at twenty
pounds a last, the very first year,—besides an excellent crop
of wheat the year following;—and the year after that, to
speak within bounds, a hundred,—but in all likelihood, a
hundred and fifty,—if not two hundred quarters of pease
and beans,—besides potatoes without end.—But then, to
think he was all this while breeding up my brother like a
hog to eat them, knocked all on the head again, and generally left the old gentleman in such a state of suspense,—
that, as he often declared to my uncle Toby,—he knew no
more than his heels what to do.

Nobody but he who has felt it, can conceive what a
plaguing thing it is to have a man's mind torn asunder by
two projects of equal strength, both obstinately pulling in a

contrary direction at the same time; for, to say nothing of the havoc, which by a certain consequence is unavoidably made by it all over the finer system of the nerves, which you know convey the animal spirits and more subtle juices from the heart to the head, and so on,—it is not to be told in what degree such a wayward kind of friction works upon the more gross and solid parts, wasting the fat and impairing the strength of a man every time it goes backwards and forwards.

My father had certainly sunk under this evil, as certainly as he had done under that of my CHRISTIAN NAME, had he not been rescued out of it, as he was out of that, by a fresh evil:—the misfortune of my brother Bobby's death.

What is the life of man? is it not to shift from side to side?—from sorrow to sorrow?—to button up one cause of vexation,—and unbutton another?

CHAPTER XXXII.

FROM this moment I am to be considered as heir-apparent to the Shandy family;—and it is from this point properly, that the story of my LIFE and OPINIONS sets out. With all my hurry and precipitation, I have been but clearing the ground to raise the building;—and such a building do I foresee it will turn out, as never was planned, and as never was executed since Adam. In less than five minutes I shall have thrown my pen into the fire, and the little drop of thick ink which is left remaining at the bottom of my ink-horn, after it:—I have but half a score things to do in the time;—I have a thing to name,—a thing to lament,—a thing to hope,—a thing to promise,—and a thing to threaten. —I have a thing to suppose,—a thing to declare,—a thing to conceal,—a thing to choose,—and a thing to pray for.— This chapter, therefore, I *name* the chapter of THINGS,—and my next chapter to it, that is, the first chapter of my next volume, if I live, shall be my chapter upon WHISKERS, in order to keep up some sort of connection in my works.

The thing I lament is, that things have crowded in so thick upon me, that I have not been able to get into that part of my work, towards which I have all the way looked forwards with so much earnest desire; and that is the campaigns, but especially the amours of my uncle Toby, the events of which are of so singular a nature, and so Cervantic a cast, that if I can so manage it, as to convey but the same impressions to every other brain which the occurrences themselves excite in my own,—I will answer for it, the book shall make its way in the world much better than its master has done before it.—O Tristram! Tristram! can this but be once brought about,—the credit which will attend thee as an author, shall counterbalance the many evils which have befallen thee as a man;—thou wilt feast upon the one,—when thou hast lost all sense and remembrance of the other!——-

No wonder I itch so much as I do to get at these amours:—they are the choicest morsel of my whole story! and when I do get at 'em,—assure yourselves, good folks— (nor do I value whose squeamish stomach takes offence at it) I shall not be at all nice in the choice of my words!— and that's the thing I have to *declare.*—I shall never get all through in five minutes, that I *fear:*—and the thing I *hope* is, that your Worships and Reverences are not offended:—if you are, depend upon't I'll give you something, my good gentry, next year to be offended at;—that's my dear Jenny's way;—but who my Jenny is,—and which is the right and which is the wrong end of a woman,—is the thing to be *concealed:*—it shall be told you in the next chapter but one to my chapter of Buttonholes;—and not one chapter before.

And now that you have just got to the end of these four volumes,*—the thing I have to *ask* is, how you feel your heads? my own aches dismally.—As for your healths, I know they are much better.—True Shandeism, think what you will against it, opens the heart and lungs; and, like all those affections which partake of its nature, it forces

---

* According to the original editions.

the blood and other vital fluids of the body to run freely through their channels, and makes the wheel of life run long and cheerfully round.

Was I left, like Sancho Pança, to choose my kingdom, it should not be maritime,—or a kingdom of blacks, to make a penny of;—no, it should be a kingdom of hearty laughing subjects: and as the bilious and more saturnine passions, by creating disorders in the blood and humours, have as bad an influence, I see, upon the body politic as body natural;—and as nothing but a habit of virtue can fully govern those passions, and subject them to reason,— I should add to my prayer,—that God would give my subjects grace to be WISE as they were MERRY; and then should I be the happiest monarch, and they the happiest people under Heaven.

And so with this moral for the present, may it please your Worships and your Reverences, I take my leave of you till this time twelvemonth, when (unless this vile cough kills me in the meantime) I'll have another pluck at your beards, and lay open a story to the world you little dream of.